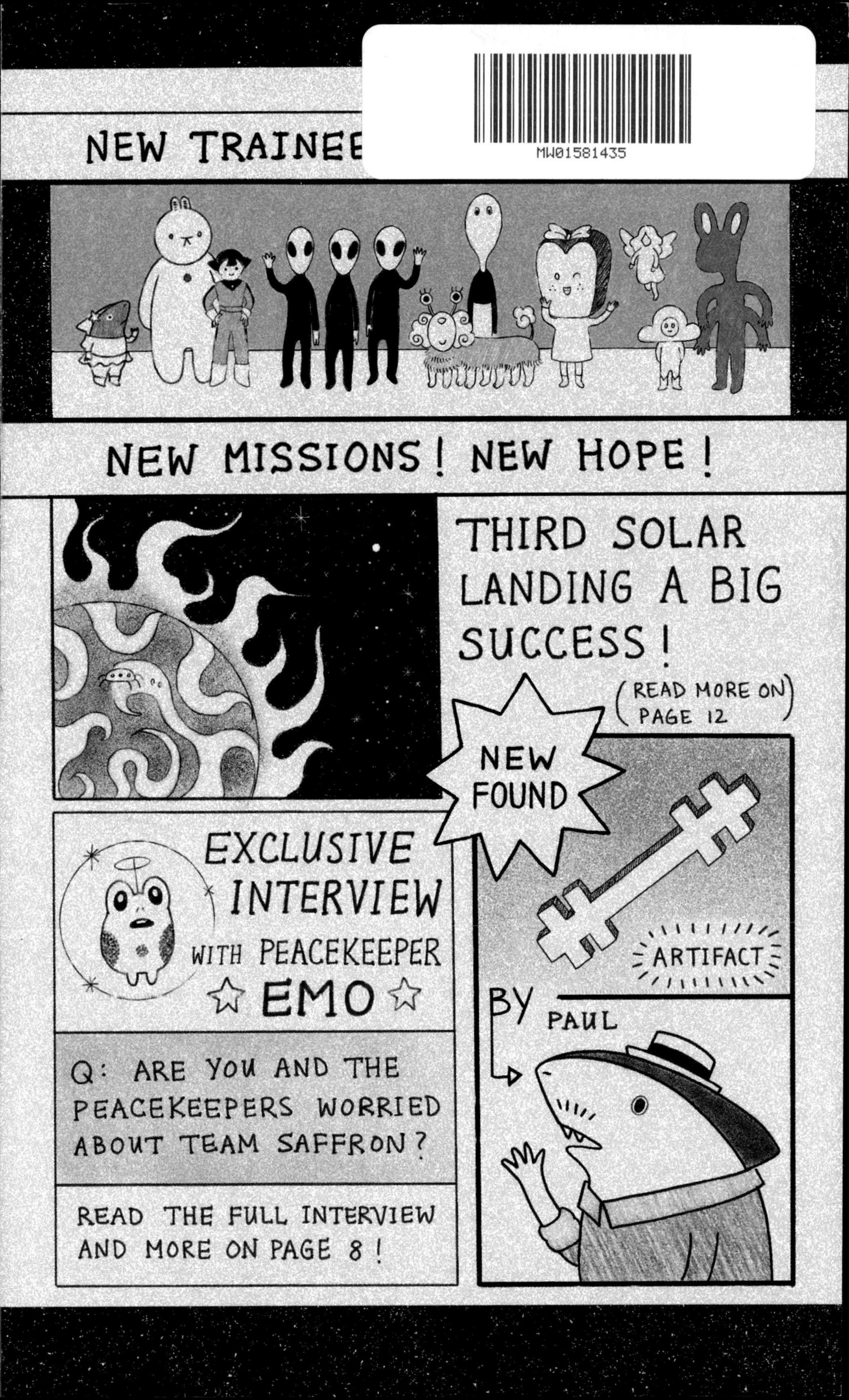
NEW TRAINEE
NEW MISSIONS! NEW HOPE!
THIRD SOLAR LANDING A BIG SUCCESS!
(READ MORE ON PAGE 12)
NEW FOUND
ARTIFACT
BY PAUL
EXCLUSIVE INTERVIEW WITH PEACEKEEPER ☆ EMO ☆
Q: ARE YOU AND THE PEACEKEEPERS WORRIED ABOUT TEAM SAFFRON?
READ THE FULL INTERVIEW AND MORE ON PAGE 8!

FOR MY WILD FAMILY :)

THIS IS AN ARTHUR A. LEVINE BOOK
PUBLISHED BY LEVINE QUERIDO

LQ
LEVINE QUERIDO

WWW.LEVINEQUERIDO.COM • INFO@LEVINEQUERIDO.COM
LEVINE QUERIDO IS DISTRIBUTED BY CHRONICLE BOOKS, LLC
TEXT AND ART COPYRIGHT © 2026 BY FRANCES LEE
ALL RIGHTS RESERVED
LIBRARY OF CONGRESS CONTROL NUMBER: 2024950979

HARDCOVER ISBN 978-1-64614-578-2
PAPERBACK ISBN 978-1-64614-579-9

PRINTED AND BOUND IN CHINA

PUBLISHED FEBRUARY 2026
FIRST PRINTING

BOOK DESIGN BY FRANCES LEE AND ANDREA MILLER

FRANCES LEE CREATED THIS BOOK ON HER IPAD USING THE PROCREATE APP WHILE LISTENING TO A STEADY STREAM OF SPACE PODCASTS, STAR TREK NEXT GENERATION AND WATCHING STAR WARS ON REPEAT WITH HER SON.

SHE HAND-LETTERED THE TYPE.

AMi MOON
& the GALACTIC PEACEKEEPERS

BY FRANCES LEE

LQ

LEVINE QUERIDO

MONTCLAIR · AMSTERDAM · HOBOKEN

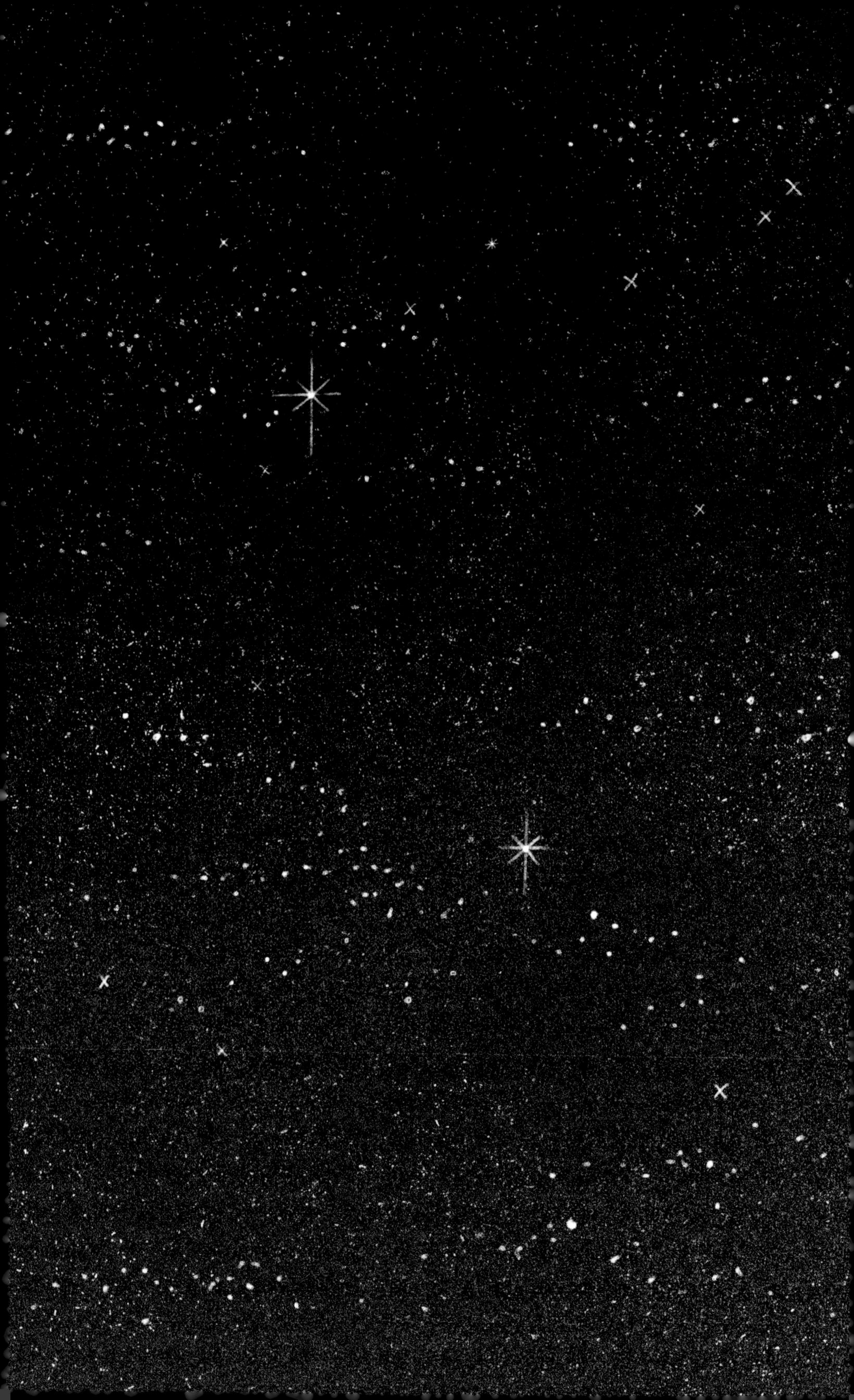

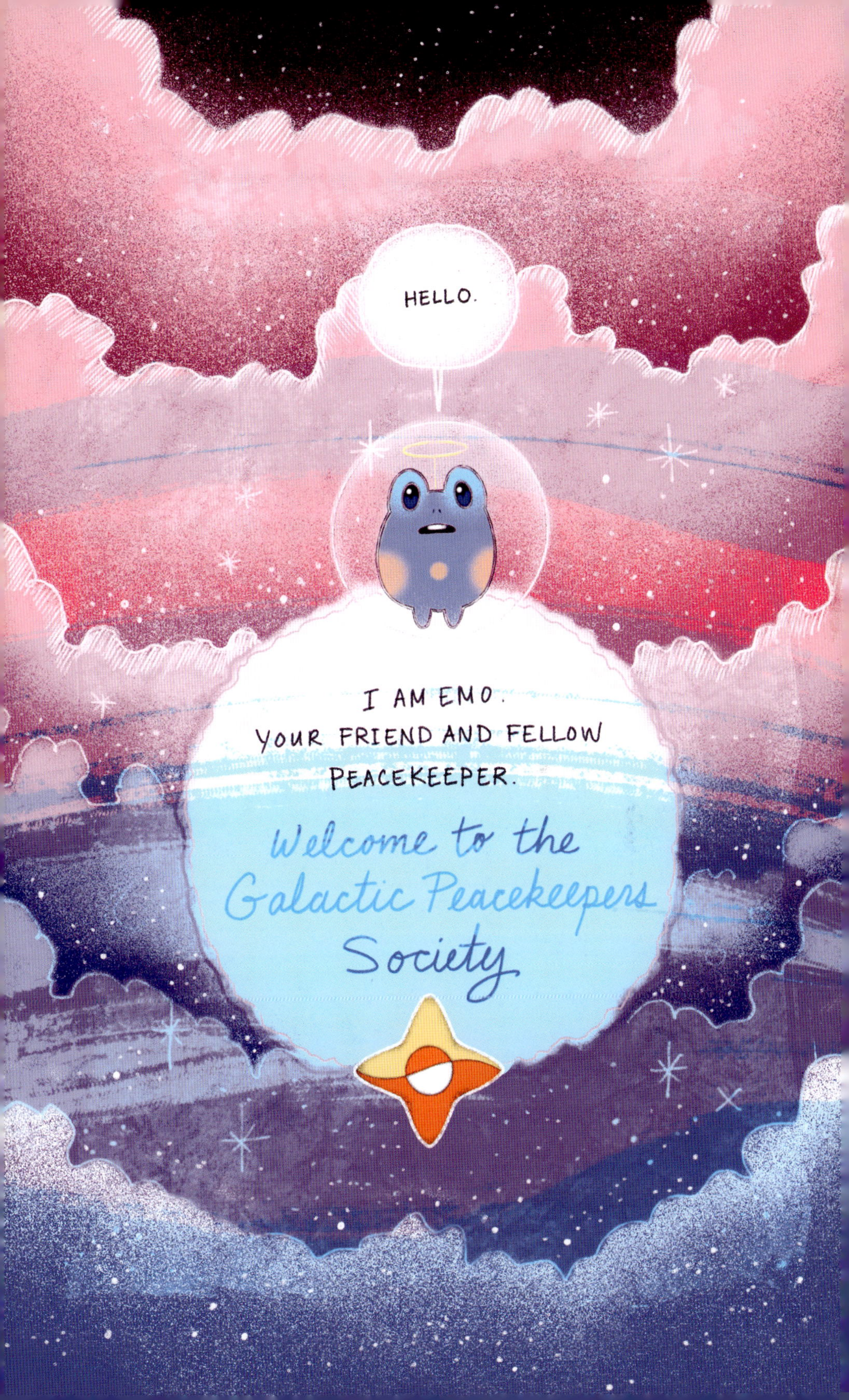
HELLO.
I AM EMO. YOUR FRIEND AND FELLOW PEACEKEEPER.
Welcome to the Galactic Peacekeepers Society

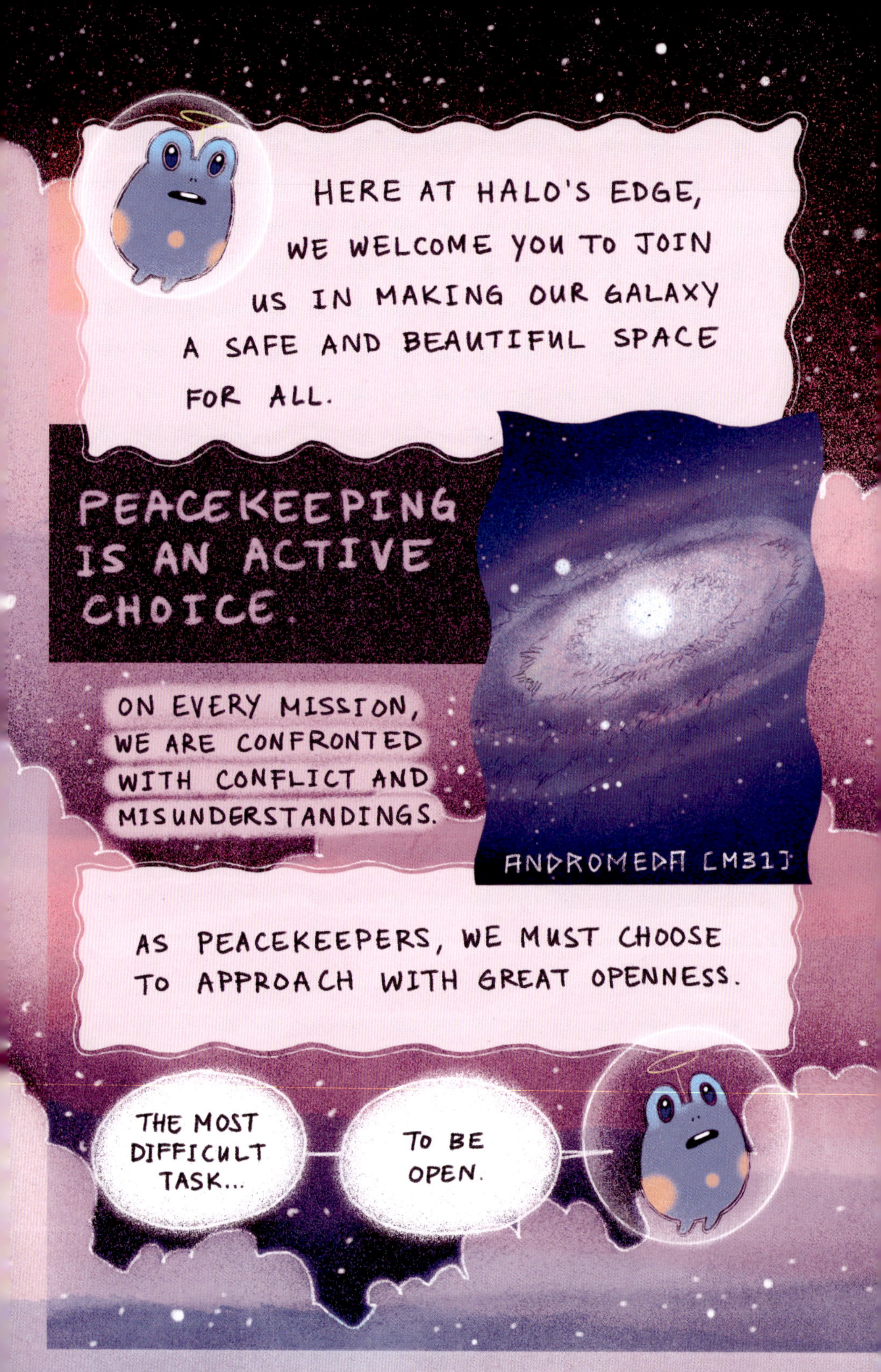
HERE AT HALO'S EDGE, WE WELCOME YOU TO JOIN US IN MAKING OUR GALAXY A SAFE AND BEAUTIFUL SPACE FOR ALL.
PEACEKEEPING IS AN ACTIVE CHOICE.
ON EVERY MISSION, WE ARE CONFRONTED WITH CONFLICT AND MISUNDERSTANDINGS.
ANDROMEDA [M31]
AS PEACEKEEPERS, WE MUST CHOOSE TO APPROACH WITH GREAT OPENNESS.
THE MOST DIFFICULT TASK...
TO BE OPEN.

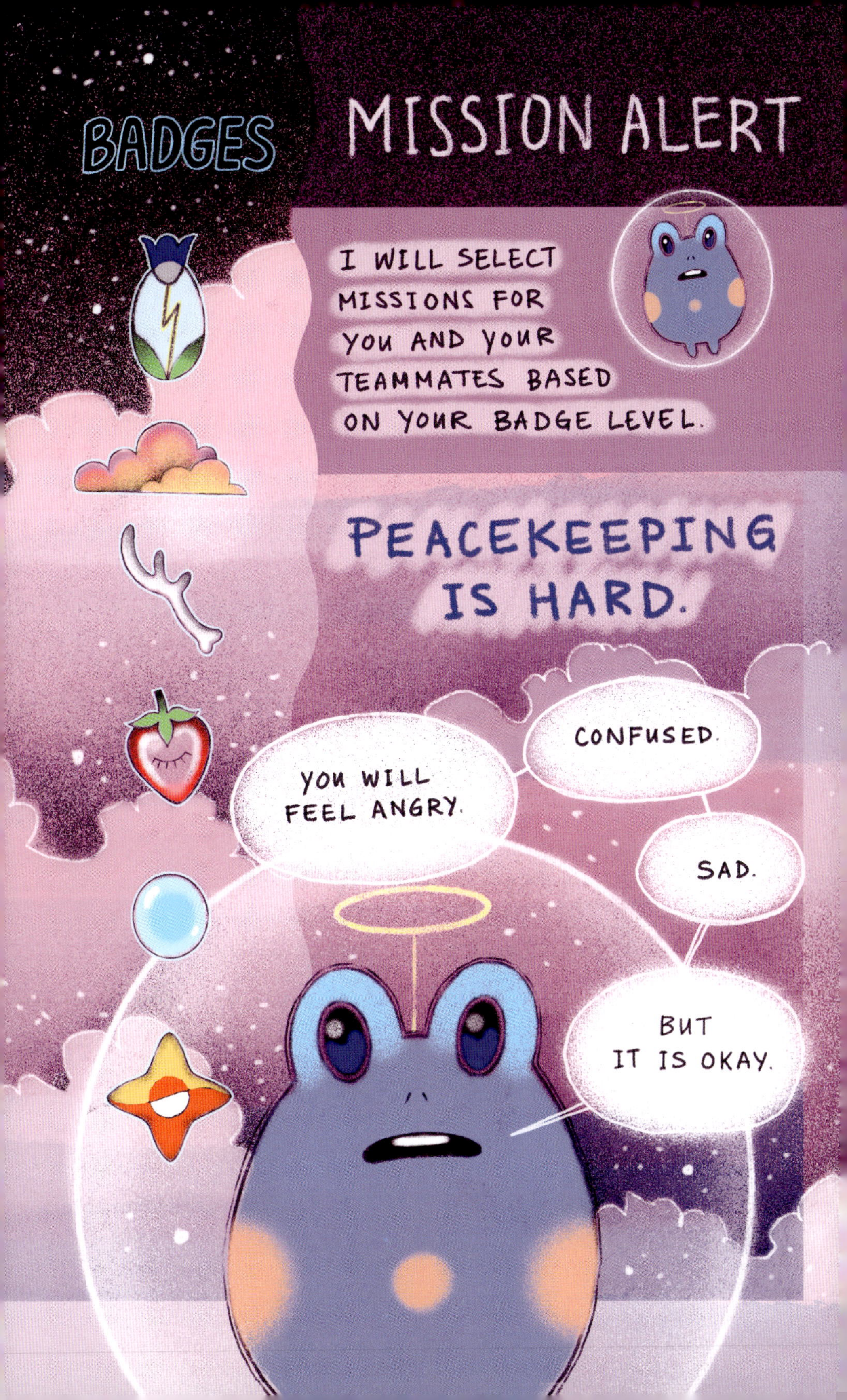
BADGES
MISSION ALERT
I WILL SELECT MISSIONS FOR YOU AND YOUR TEAMMATES BASED ON YOUR BADGE LEVEL.
PEACEKEEPING IS HARD.
YOU WILL FEEL ANGRY.
CONFUSED.
SAD.
BUT IT IS OKAY.

ANDROMEDA

AKA MESSIER 31 [M31]

- IS A BARRED SPIRAL GALAXY.
- THERE ARE ABOUT 10.3 BILLION PLANETS, CLOSE TO A TRILLION STARS, AND AN UNKNOWN NUMBER OF MOONS.

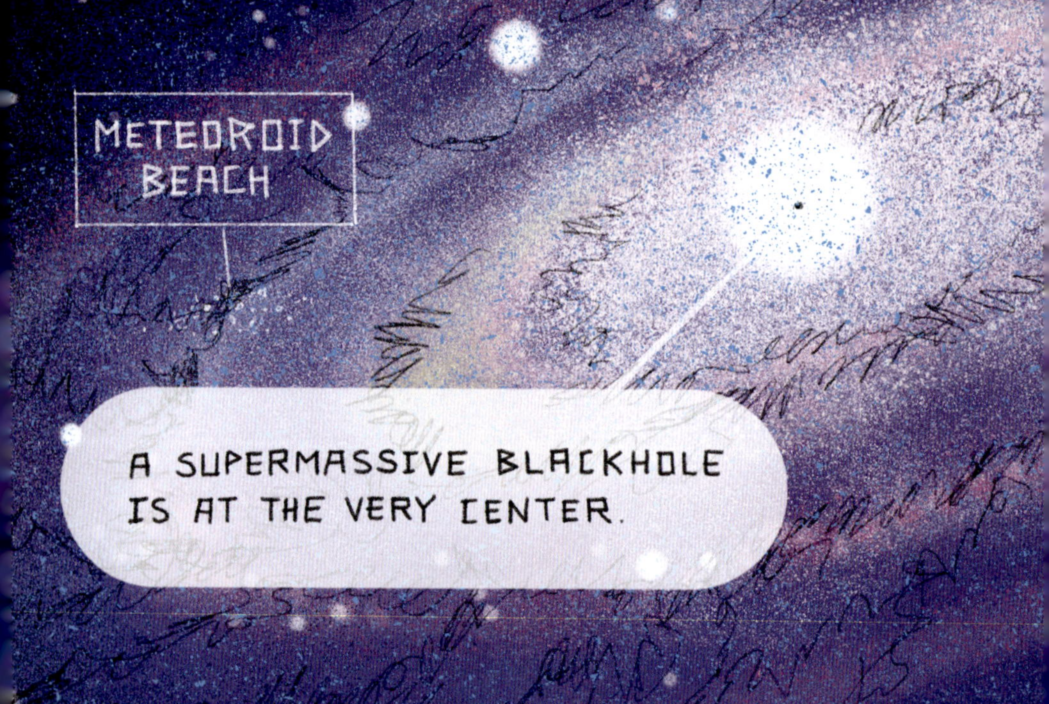
METEOROID BEACH
A SUPERMASSIVE BLACKHOLE IS AT THE VERY CENTER.

- THERE ARE STILL A GREAT NUMBER OF CLUSTERS TO EXPLORE.
  - CIVILIZATIONS TO VISIT.

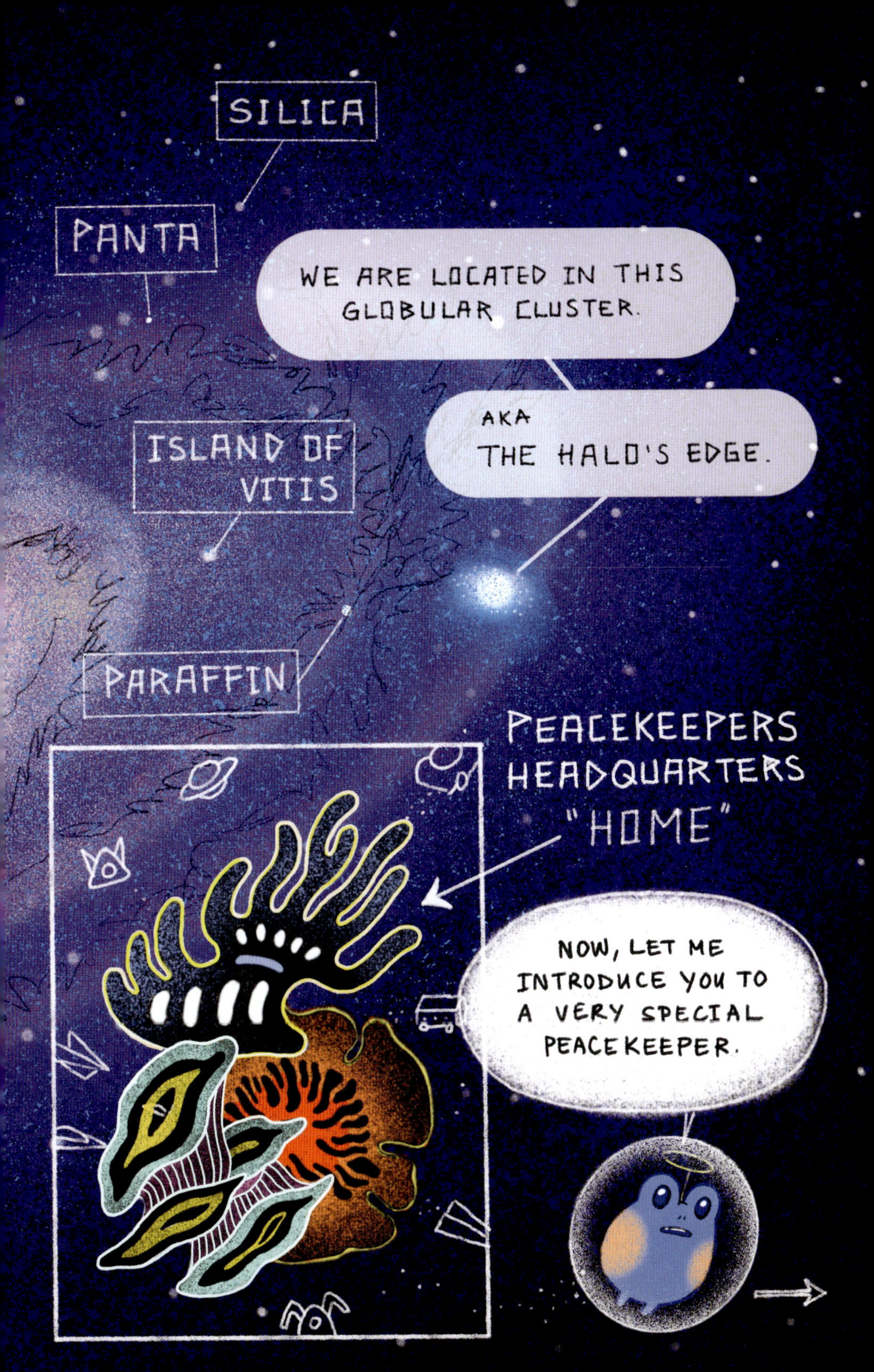
SILICA
PANTA
WE ARE LOCATED IN THIS GLOBULAR CLUSTER.
AKA THE HALO'S EDGE.
ISLAND OF VITIS
PARAFFIN
PEACEKEEPERS HEADQUARTERS "HOME"
NOW, LET ME INTRODUCE YOU TO A VERY SPECIAL PEACEKEEPER.

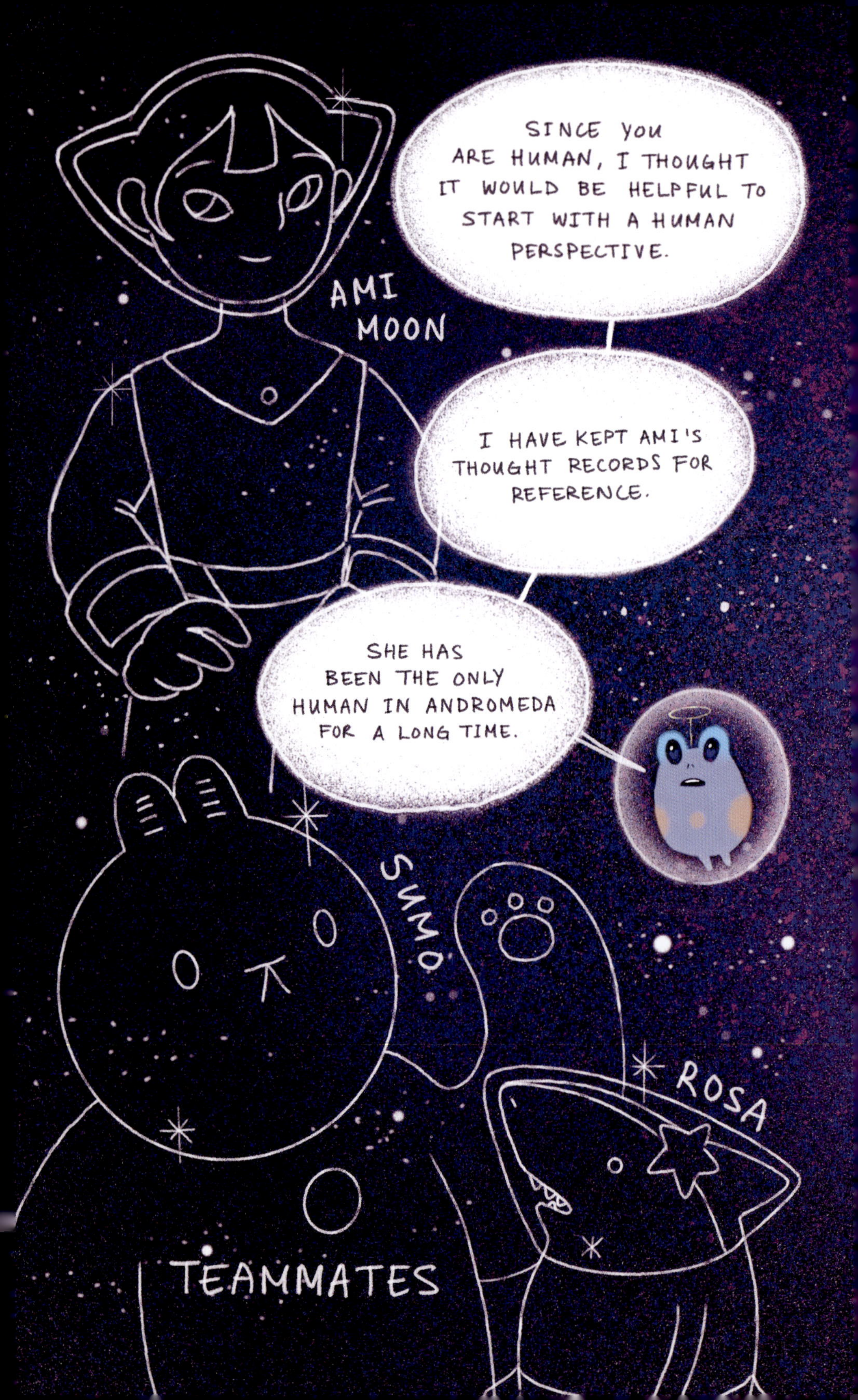
SINCE YOU ARE HUMAN, I THOUGHT IT WOULD BE HELPFUL TO START WITH A HUMAN PERSPECTIVE.
AMI MOON
I HAVE KEPT AMI'S THOUGHT RECORDS FOR REFERENCE.
SHE HAS BEEN THE ONLY HUMAN IN ANDROMEDA FOR A LONG TIME.
SUMO
ROSA
TEAMMATES

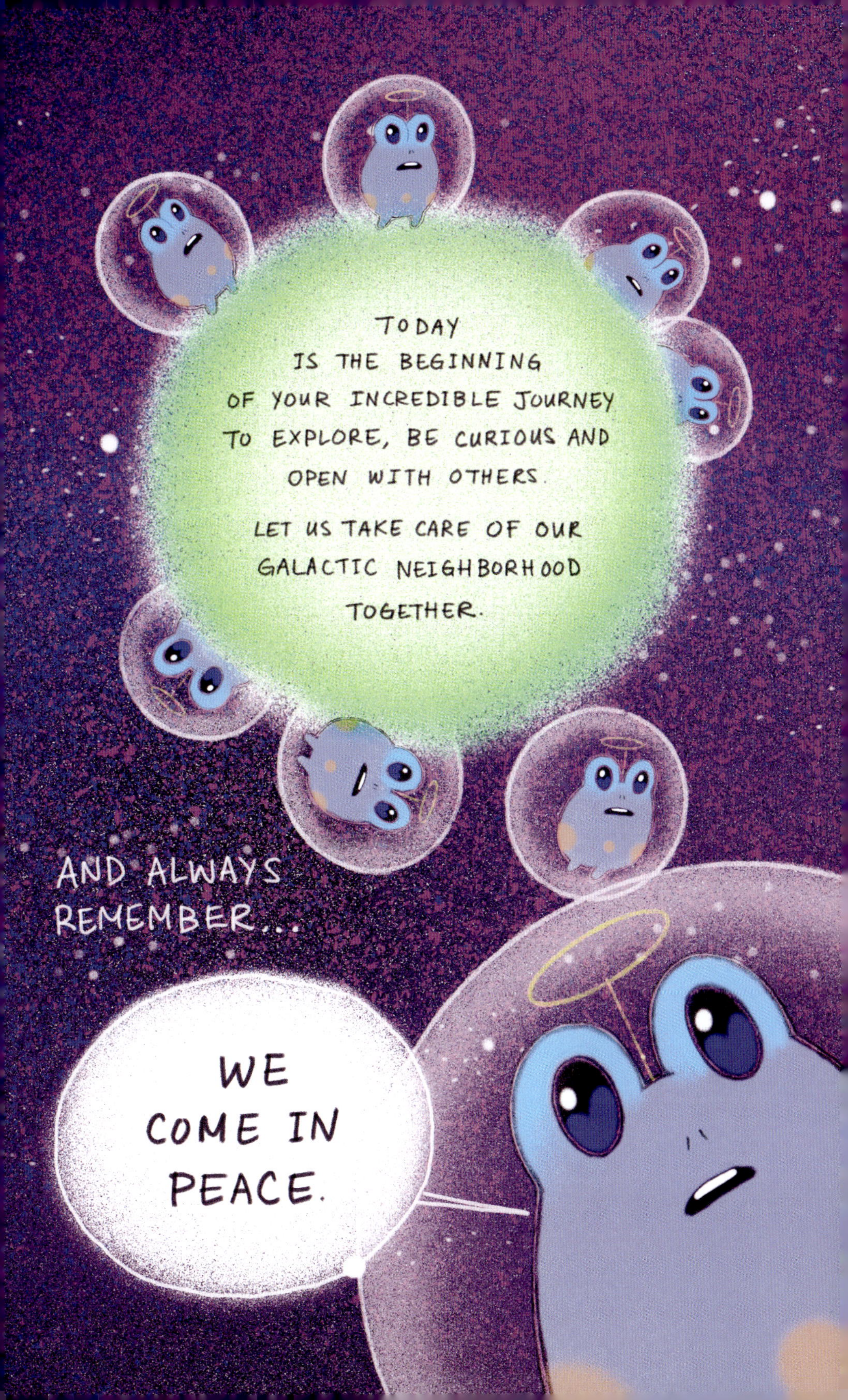
TODAY IS THE BEGINNING OF YOUR INCREDIBLE JOURNEY TO EXPLORE, BE CURIOUS AND OPEN WITH OTHERS.
LET US TAKE CARE OF OUR GALACTIC NEIGHBORHOOD TOGETHER.
AND ALWAYS REMEMBER...
WE COME IN PEACE.

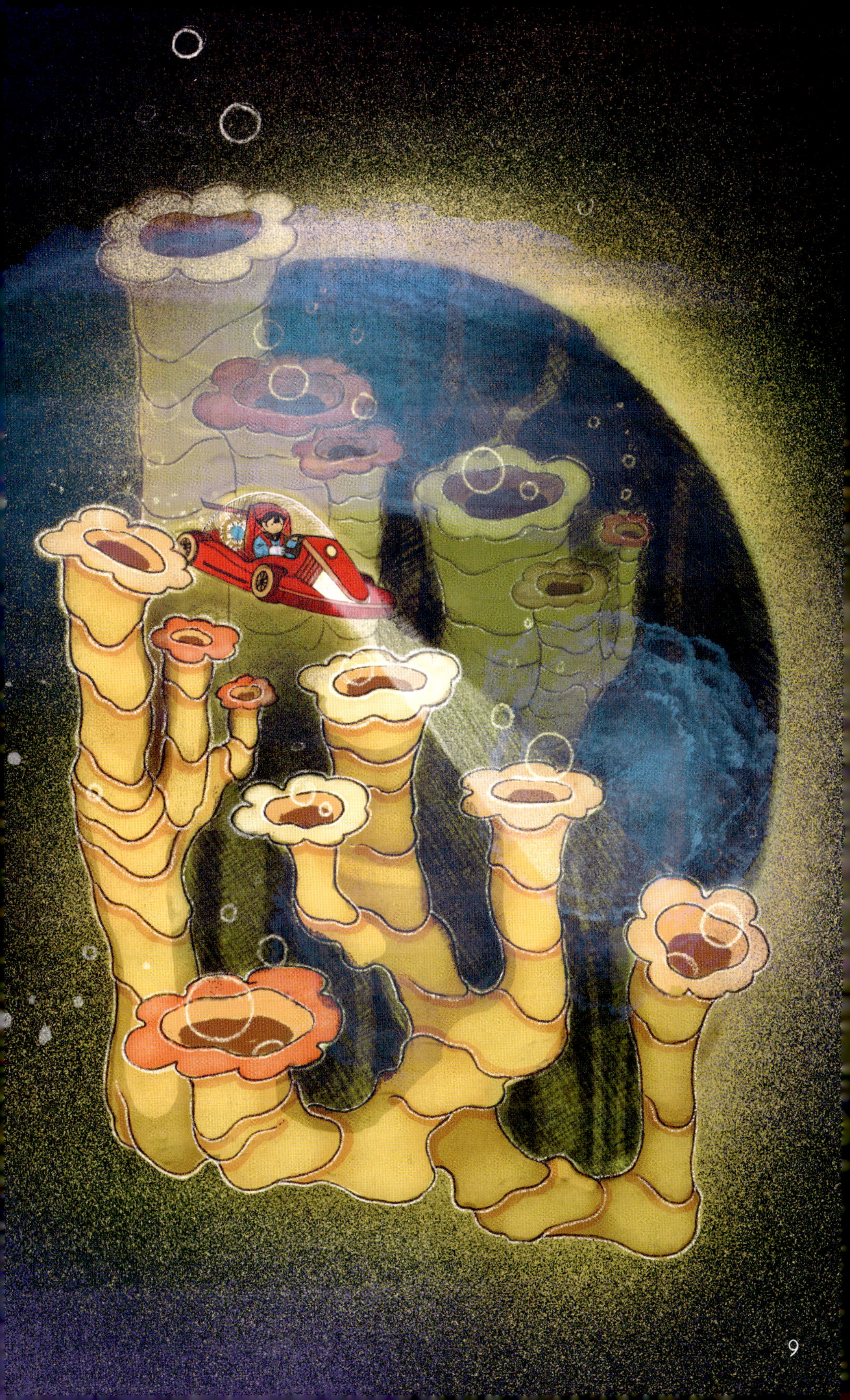

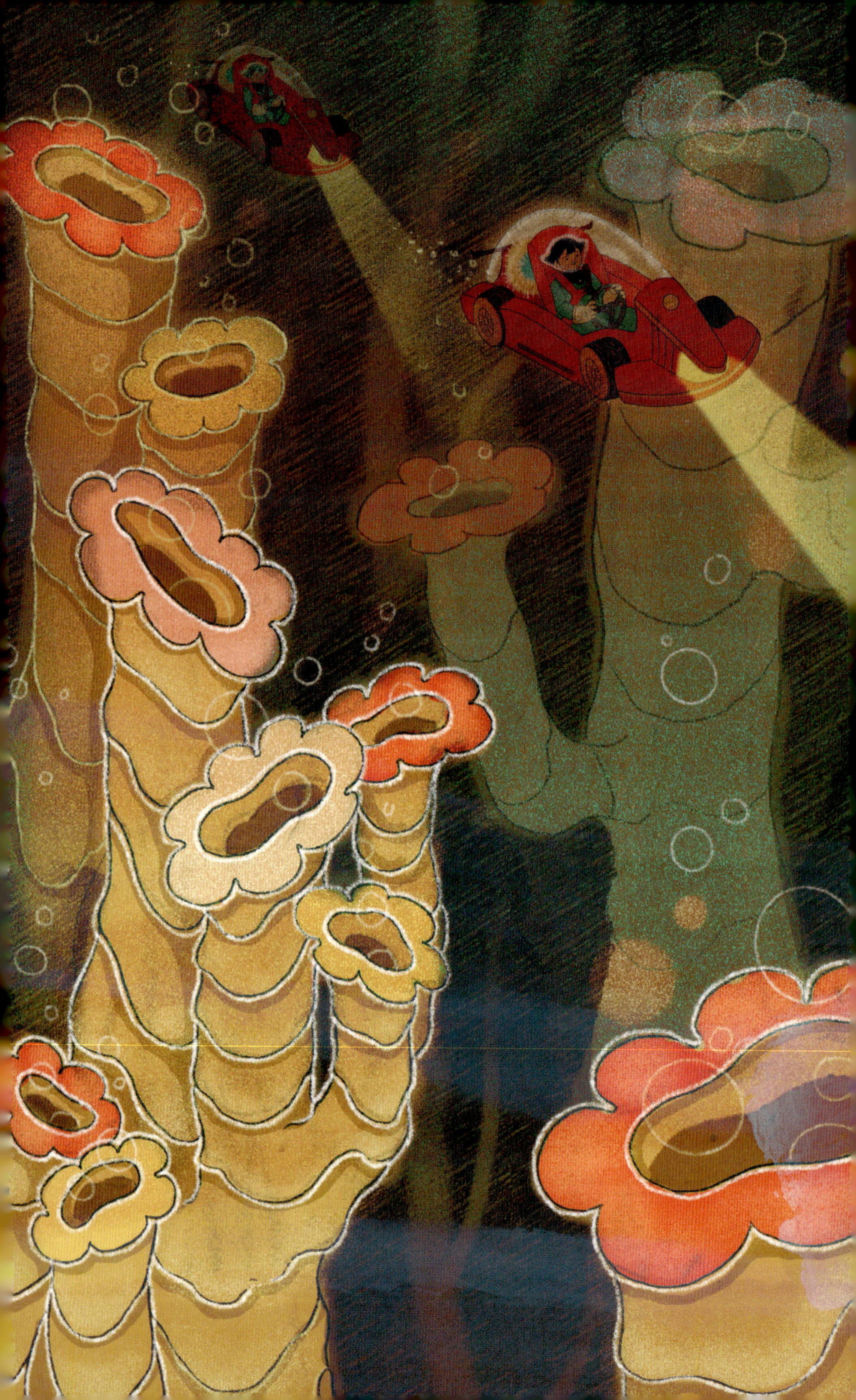

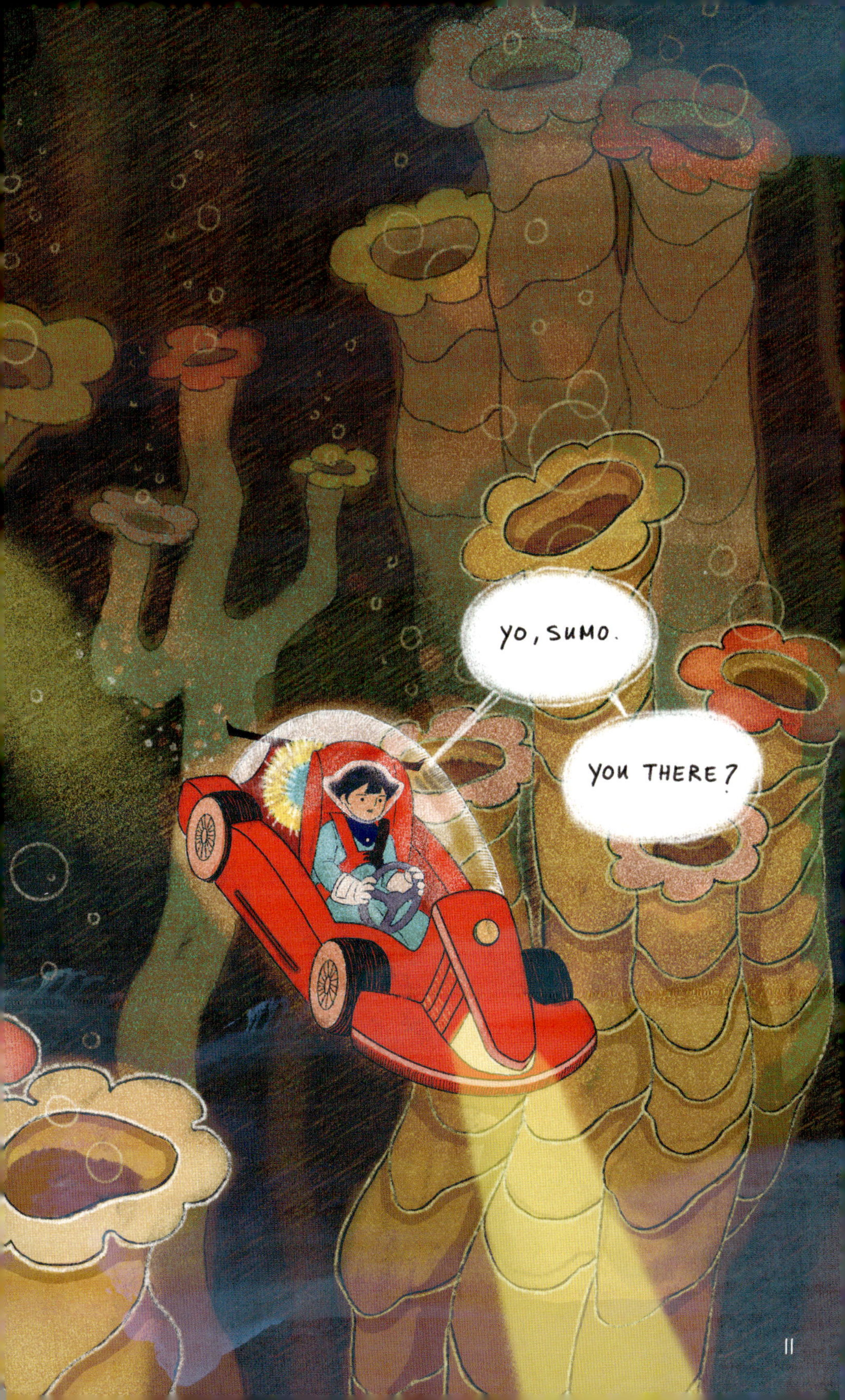
YO, SUMO.
YOU THERE?

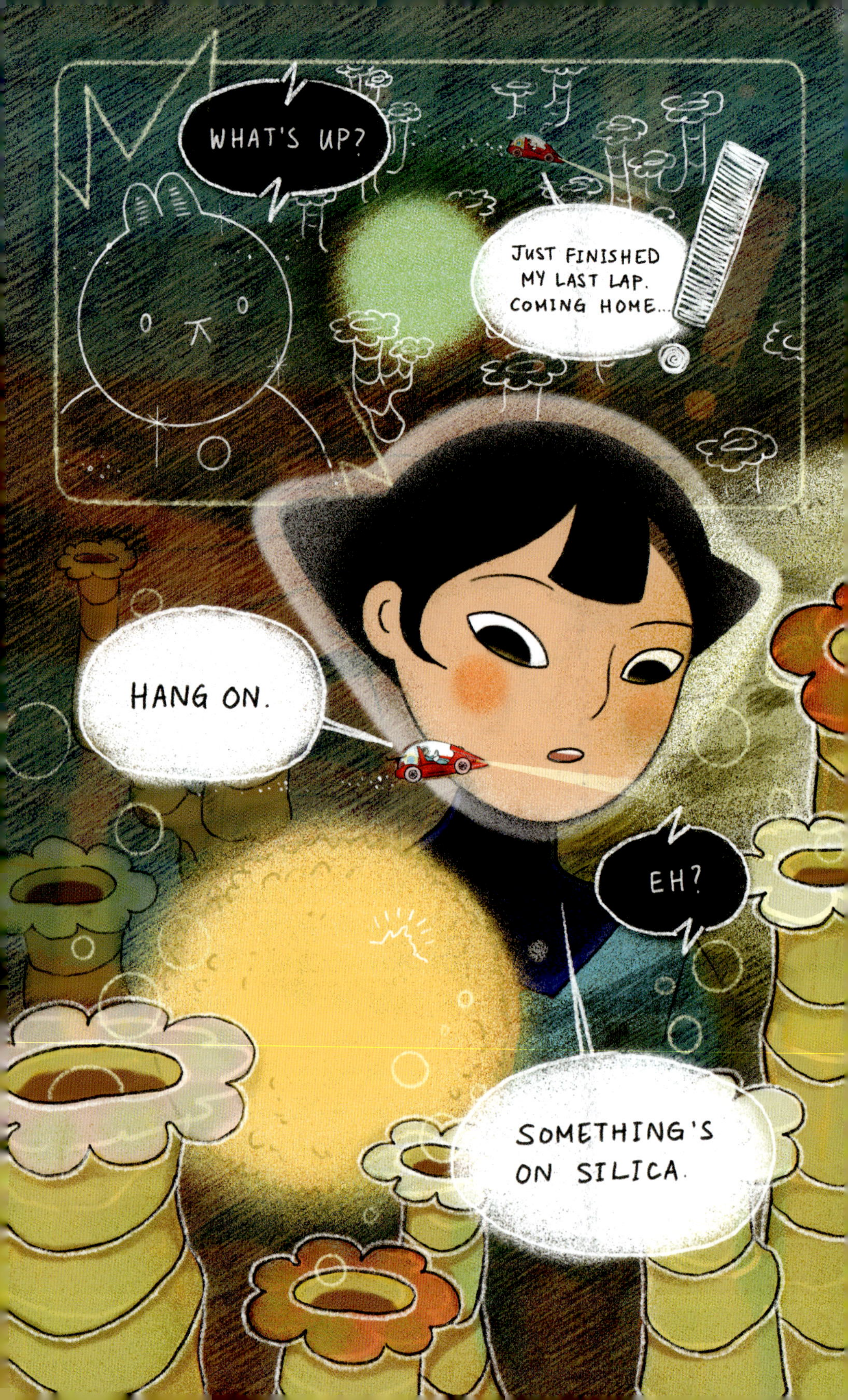
WHAT'S UP?
JUST FINISHED MY LAST LAP. COMING HOME...
HANG ON.
EH?
SOMETHING'S ON SILICA.

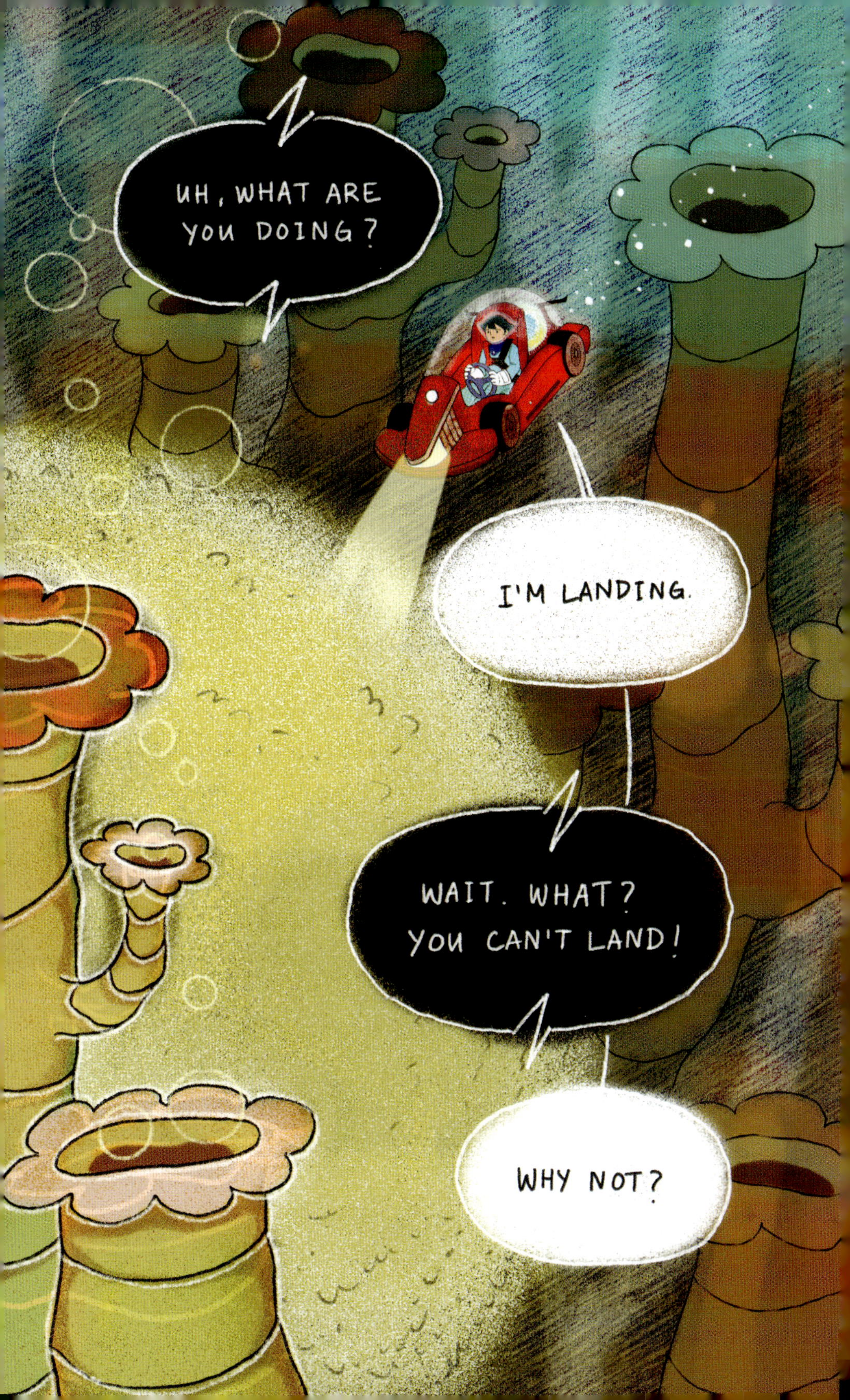
UH, WHAT ARE YOU DOING?
I'M LANDING.
WAIT. WHAT? YOU CAN'T LAND!
WHY NOT?

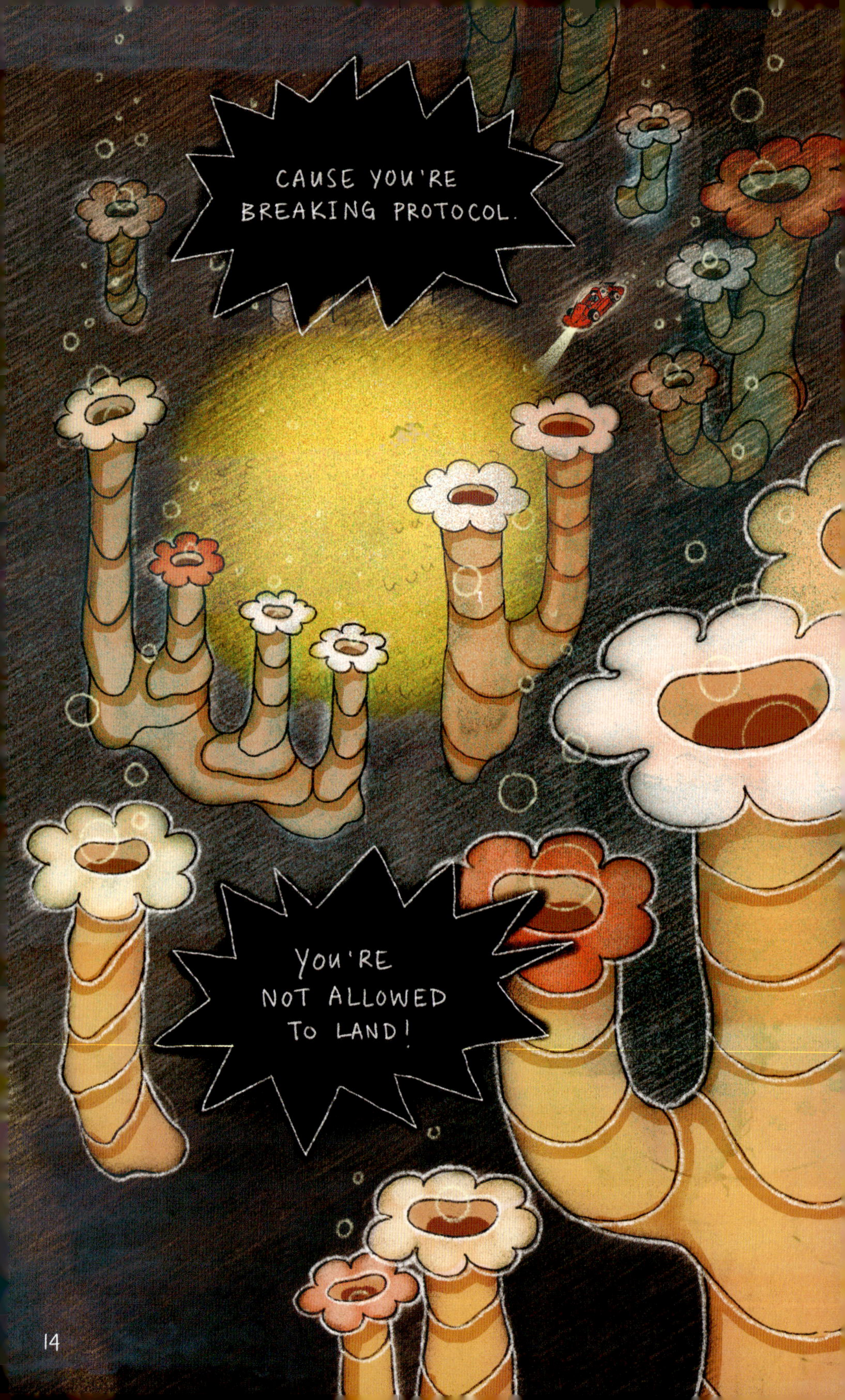
CAUSE YOU'RE BREAKING PROTOCOL.
YOU'RE NOT ALLOWED TO LAND!

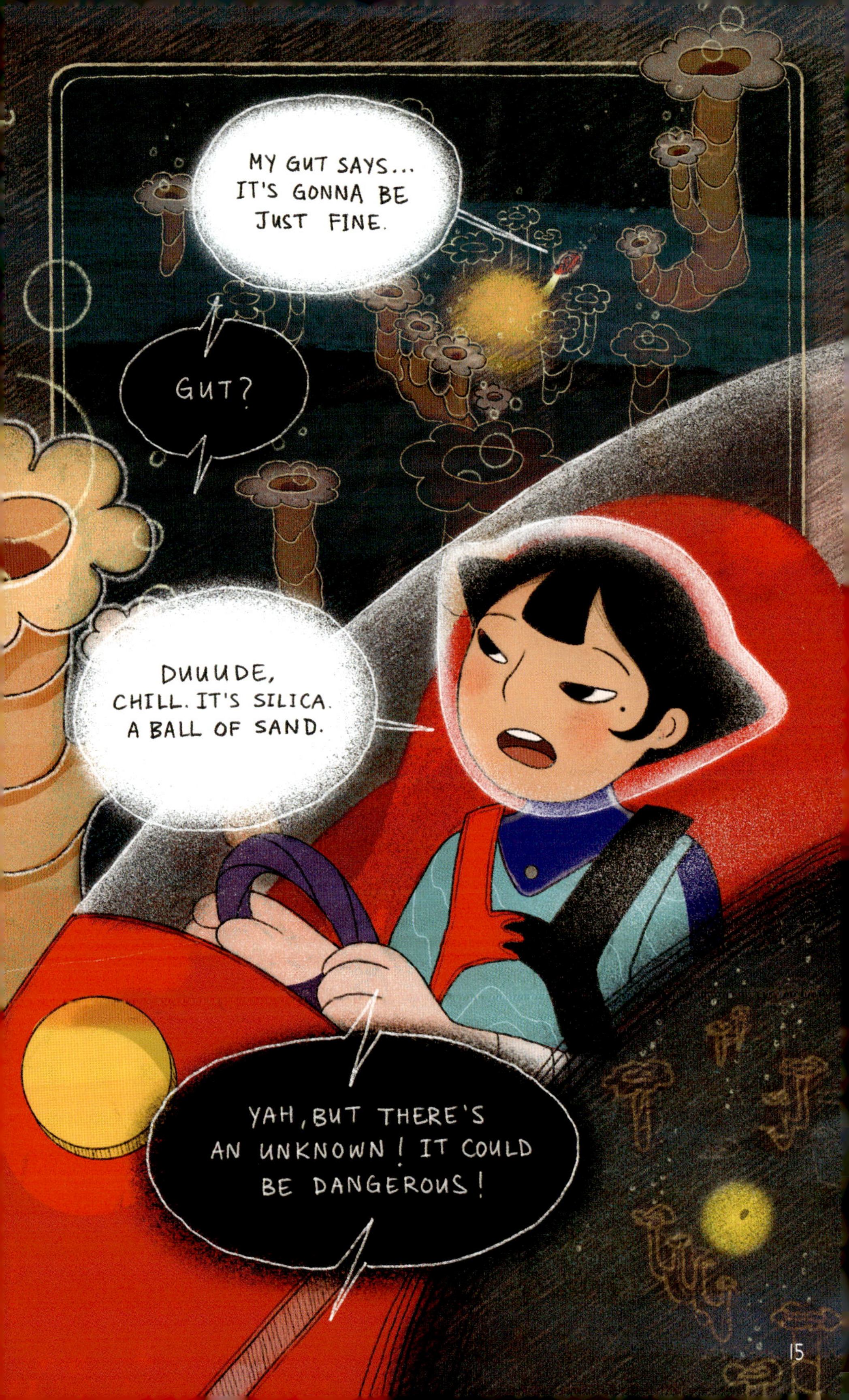
MY GUT SAYS... IT'S GONNA BE JUST FINE.
GUT?
DUUUDE, CHILL. IT'S SILICA. A BALL OF SAND.
YAH, BUT THERE'S AN UNKNOWN! IT COULD BE DANGEROUS!

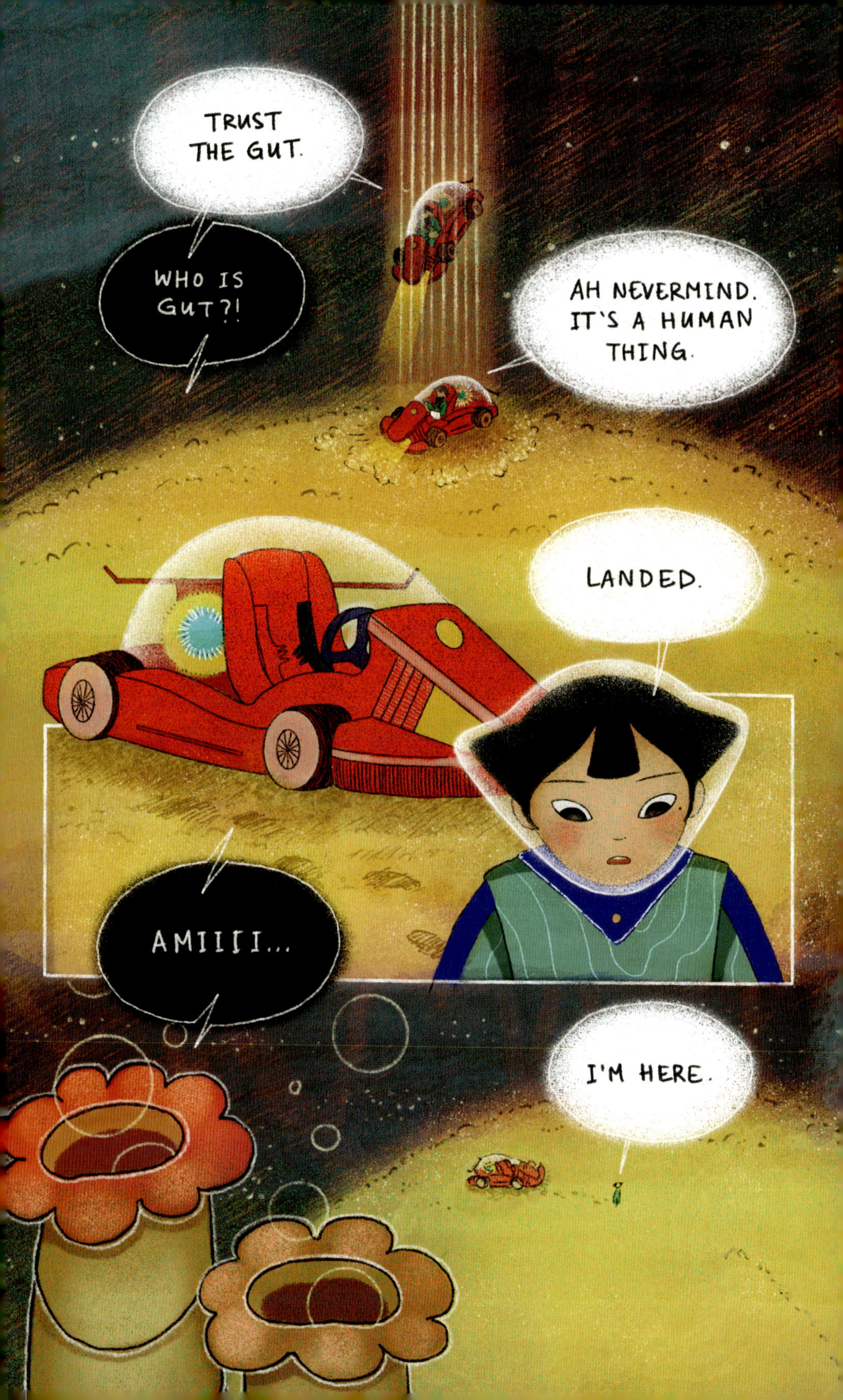
TRUST THE GUT.
WHO IS GUT?!
AH NEVERMIND. IT'S A HUMAN THING.
LANDED.
AMIIII...
I'M HERE.

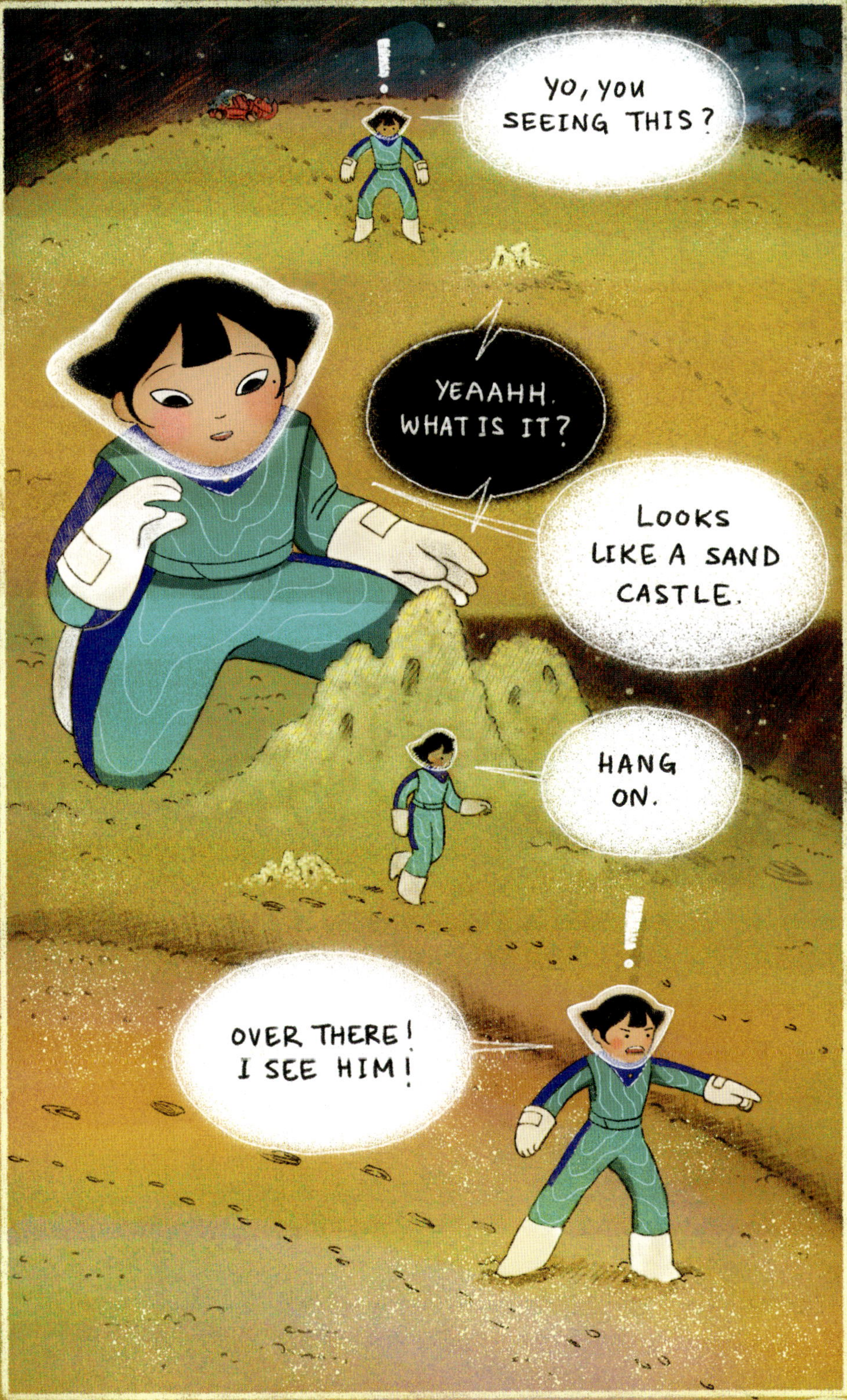

YO, YOU SEEING THIS?
YEAAHH. WHAT IS IT?
LOOKS LIKE A SAND CASTLE.
HANG ON.
OVER THERE! I SEE HIM!

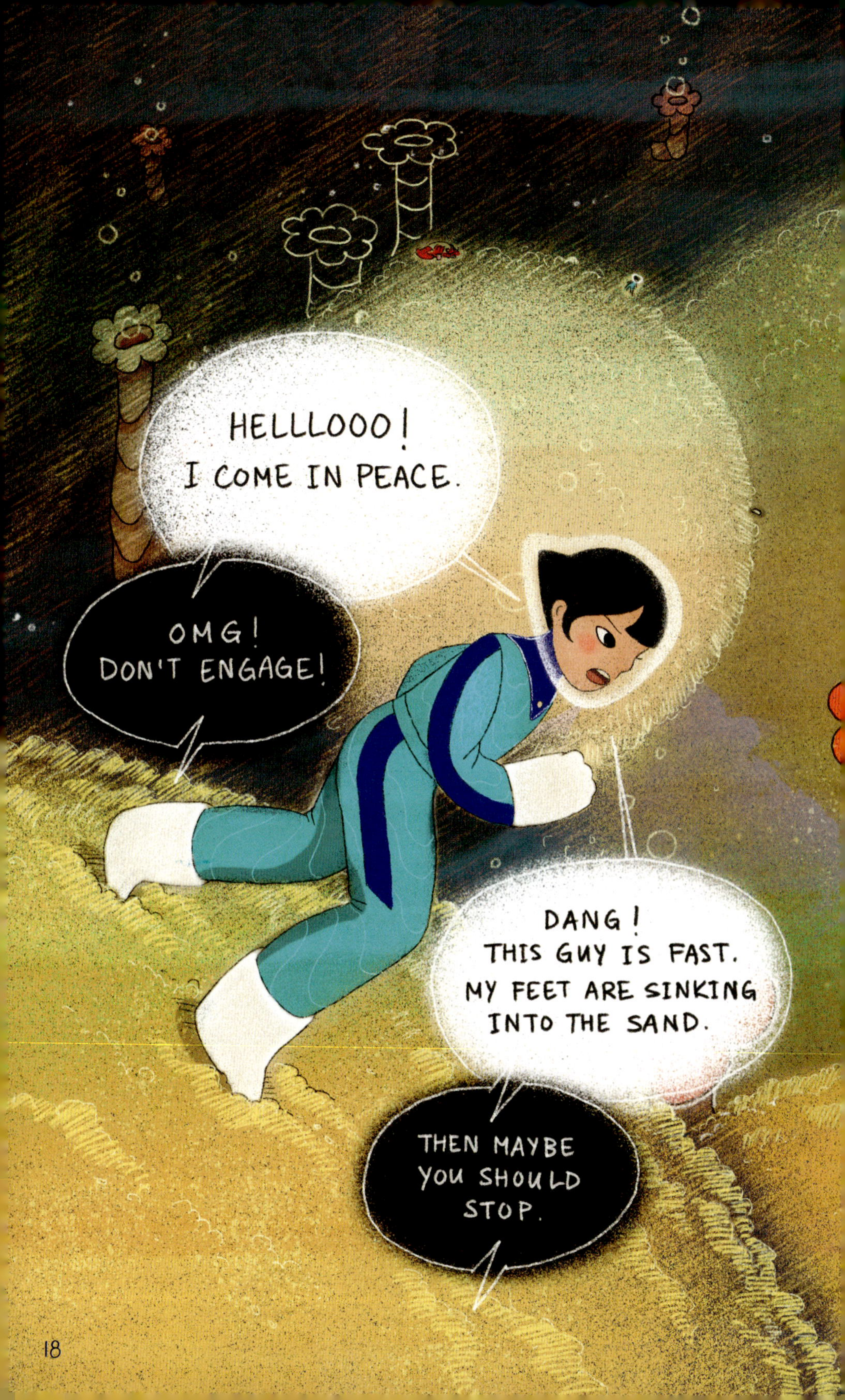
HELLLOOO! I COME IN PEACE.
OMG! DON'T ENGAGE!
DANG! THIS GUY IS FAST. MY FEET ARE SINKING INTO THE SAND.
THEN MAYBE YOU SHOULD STOP.

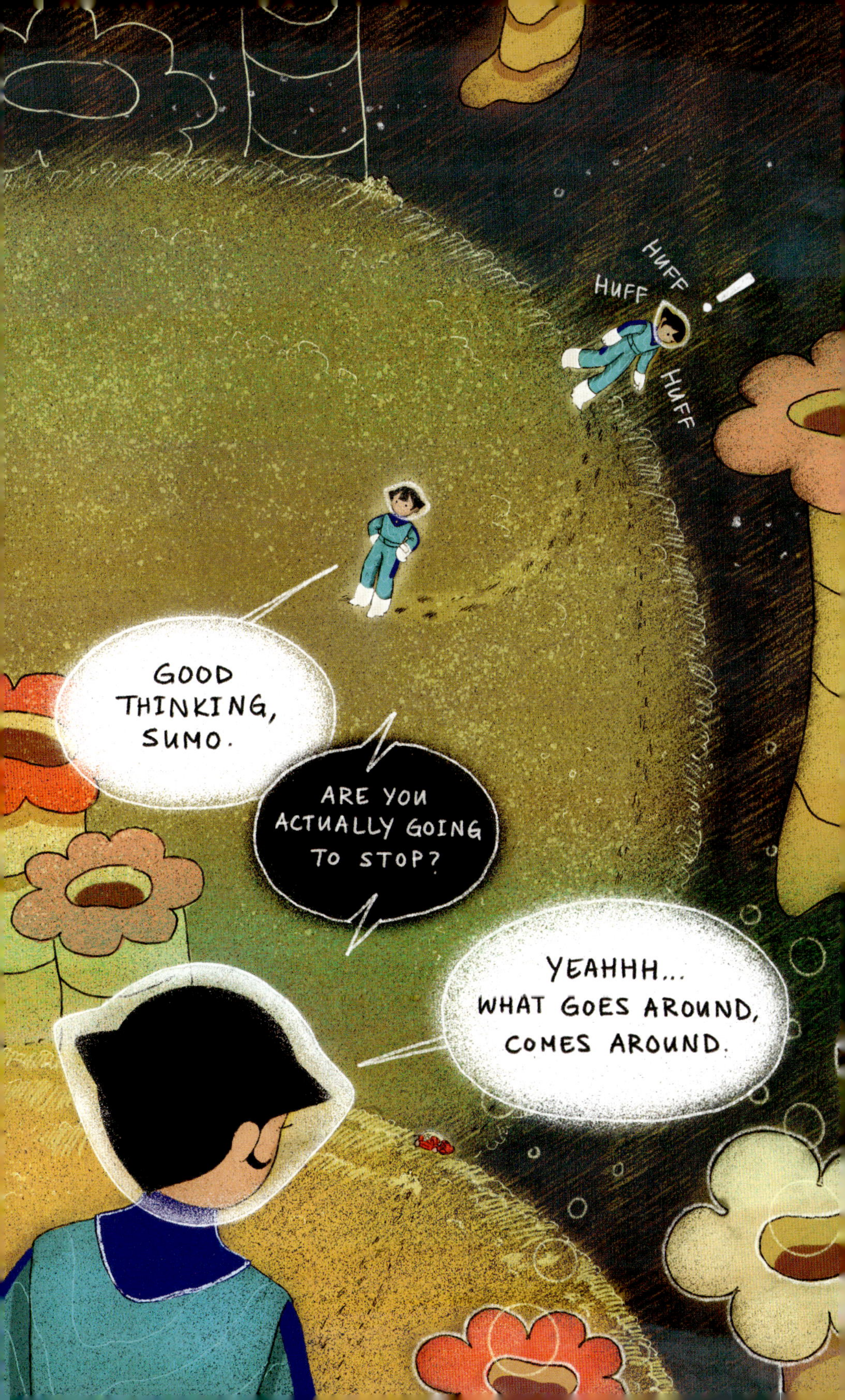
HUFF
HUFF
!
HUFF
GOOD THINKING, SUMO.
ARE YOU ACTUALLY GOING TO STOP?
YEAHHH... WHAT GOES AROUND, COMES AROUND.

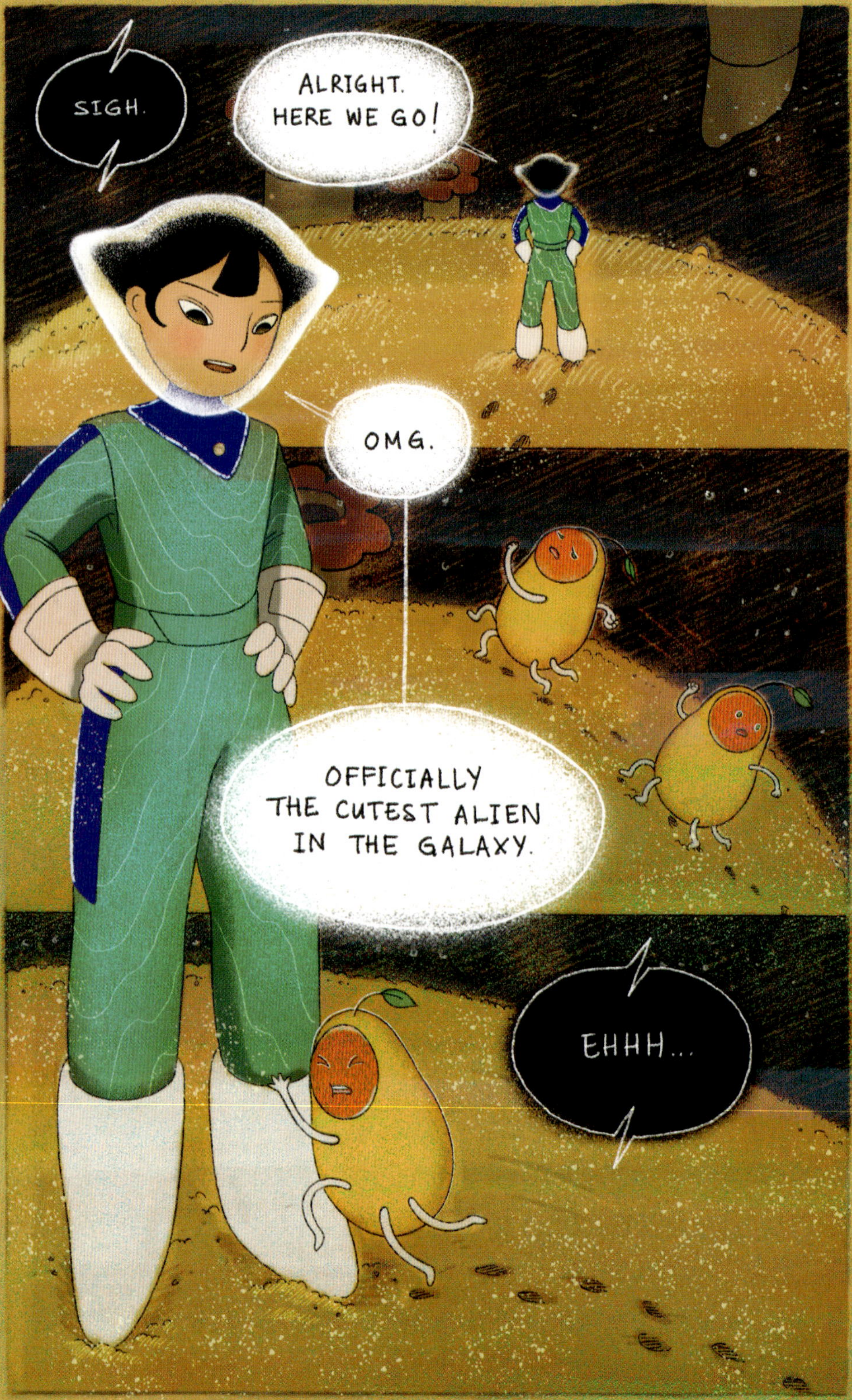
SIGH.
ALRIGHT. HERE WE GO!
OMG.
OFFICIALLY THE CUTEST ALIEN IN THE GALAXY.
EHHH...

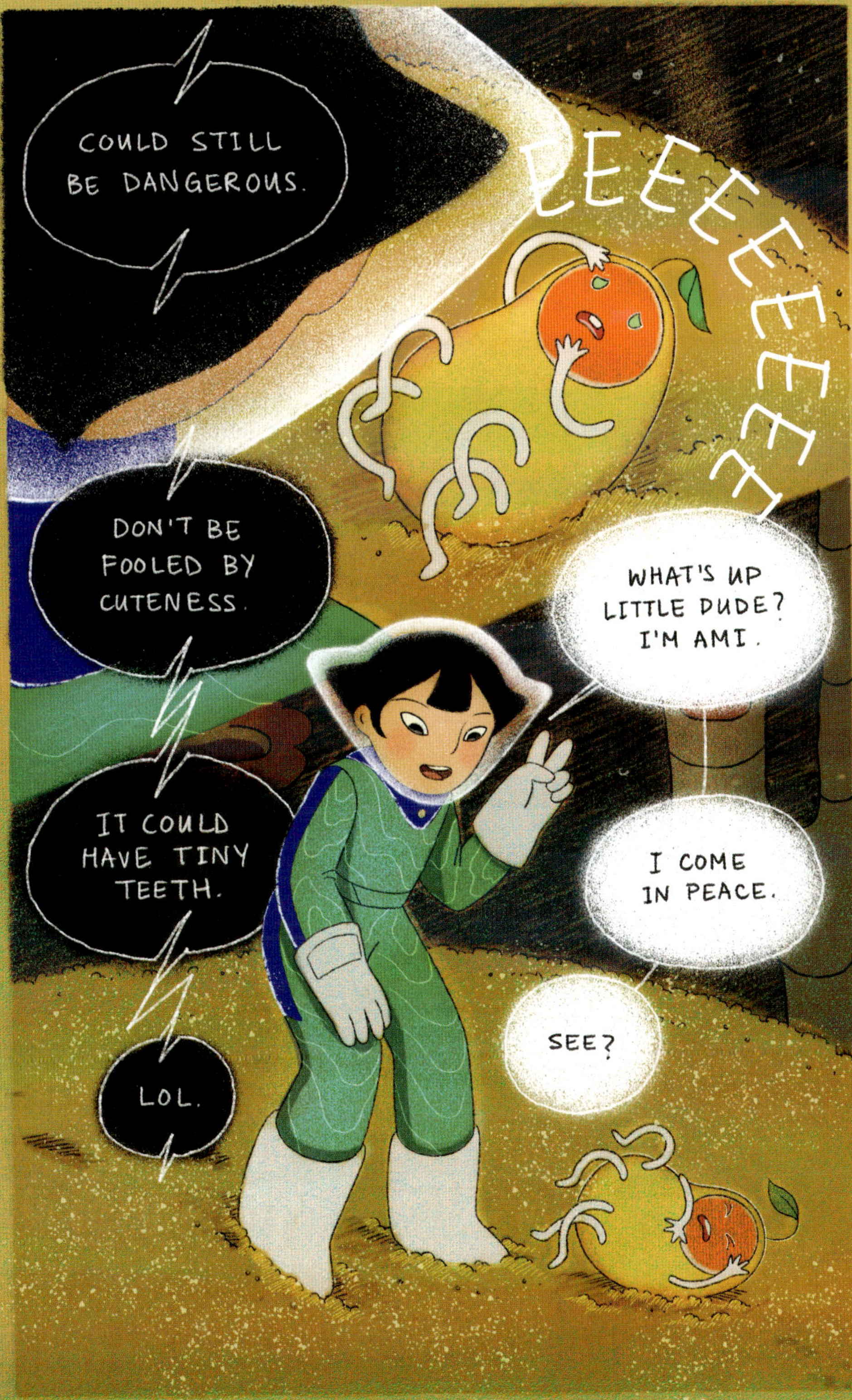
COULD STILL BE DANGEROUS.
EEEEEEEEEEEE
DON'T BE FOOLED BY CUTENESS.
WHAT'S UP LITTLE DUDE? I'M AMI.
IT COULD HAVE TINY TEETH.
I COME IN PEACE.
SEE?
LOL.

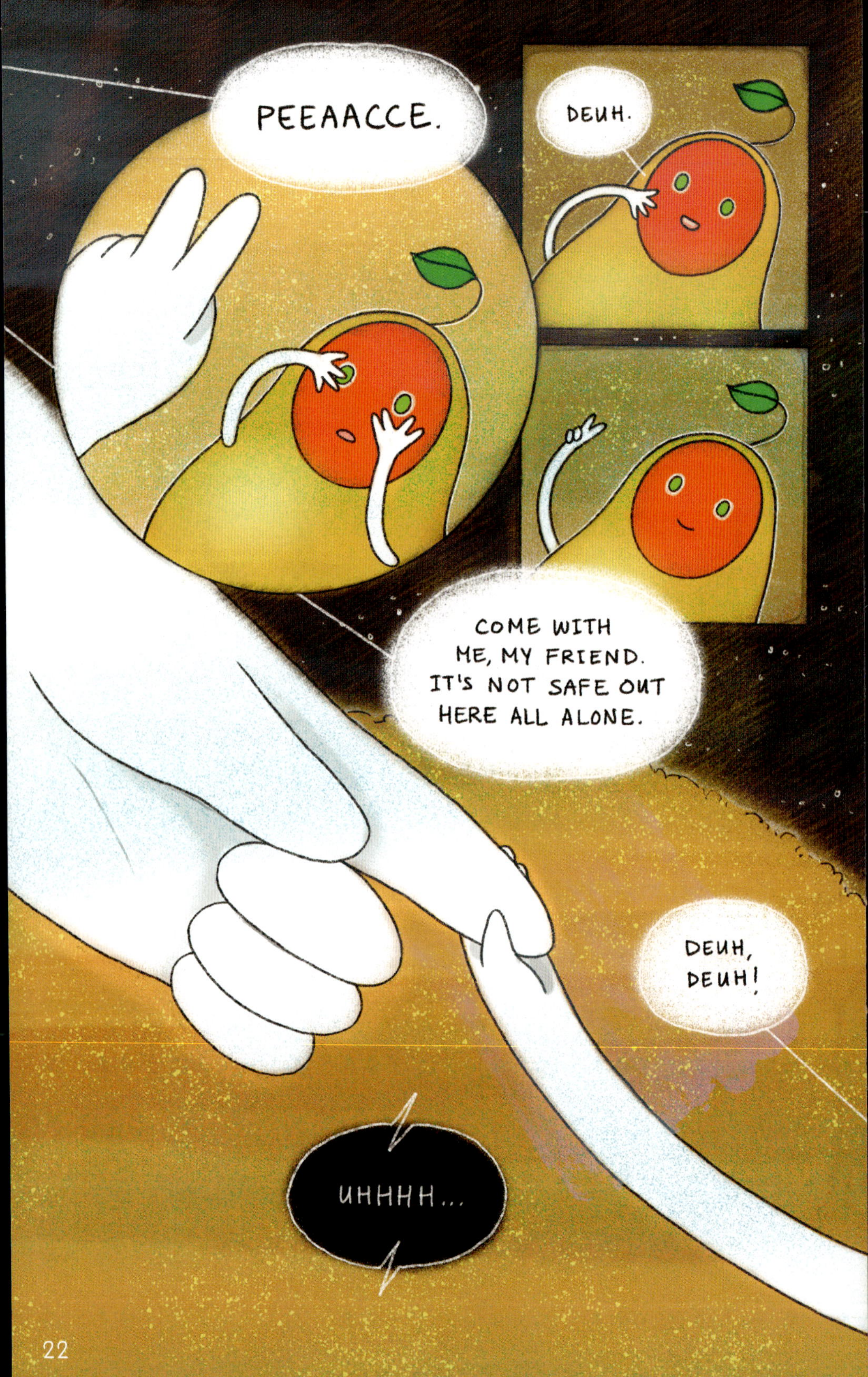
PEEAACCE.
DEUH.
COME WITH ME, MY FRIEND. IT'S NOT SAFE OUT HERE ALL ALONE.
DEUH, DEUH!
UHHHH...

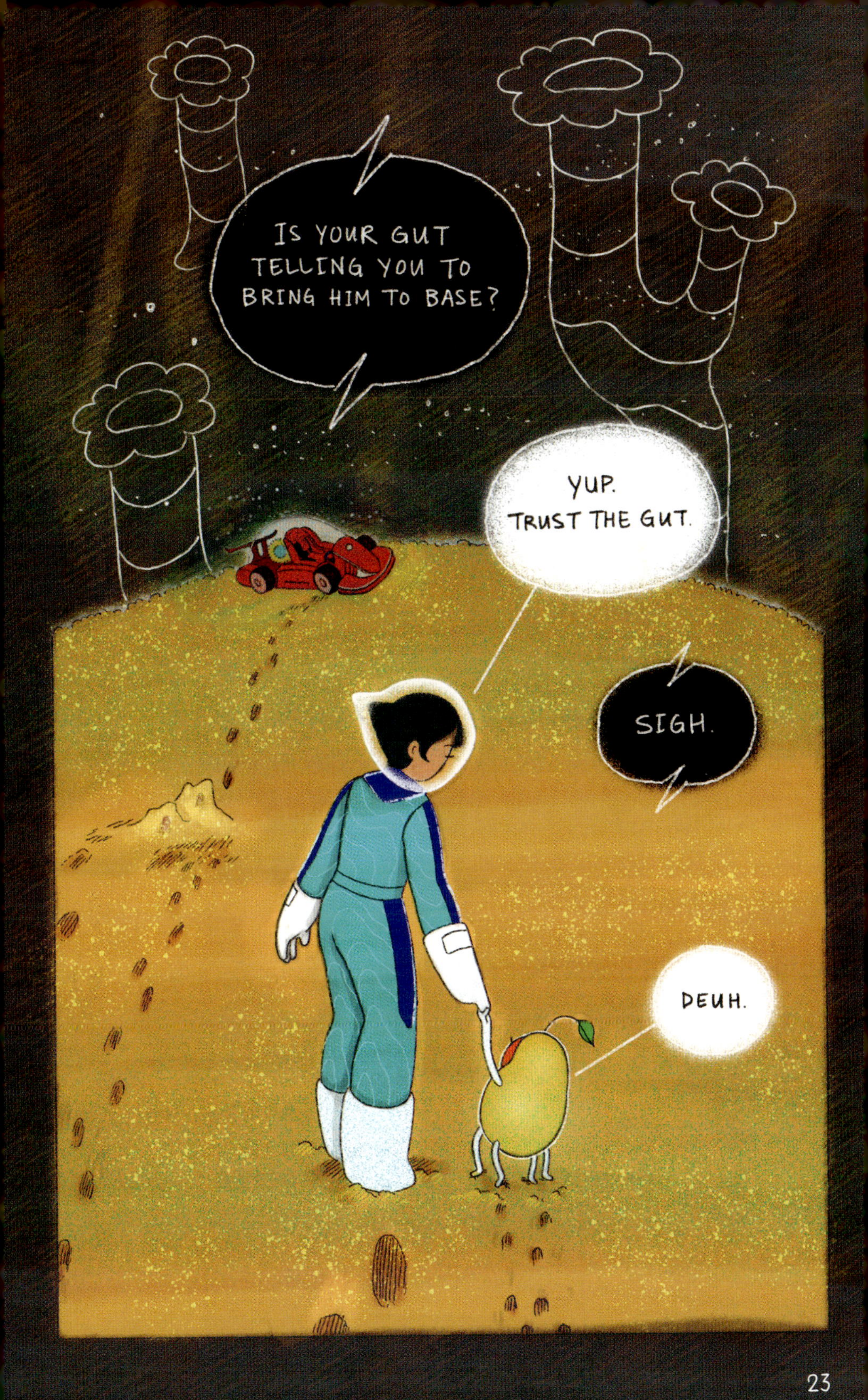
IS YOUR GUT TELLING YOU TO BRING HIM TO BASE?
YUP. TRUST THE GUT.
SIGH.
DEUH.

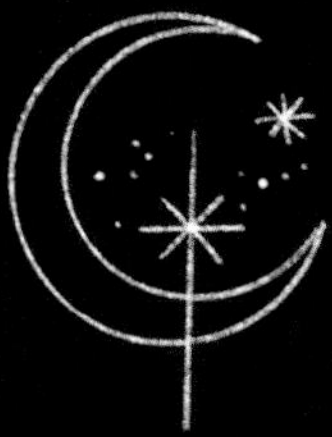

Dear Friend,

Last night I had a dream about my dog Sadie.

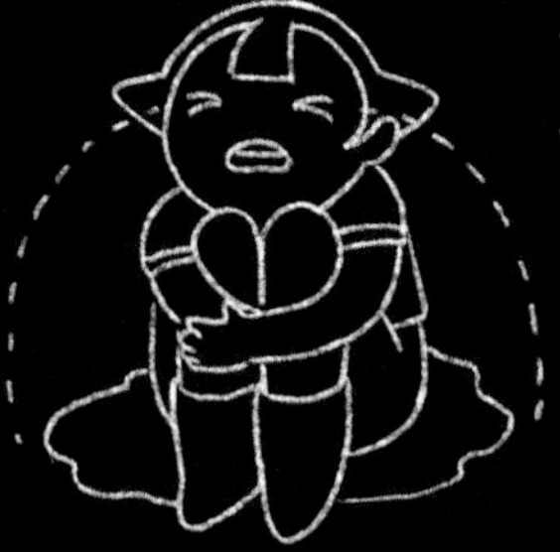

I was lost in a shopping mall with no windows or doors. I had no idea how I got there, why I was there, who I came with or how to get out. I sat on a bench and started to cry.

"Why do you cry, Hooman?"

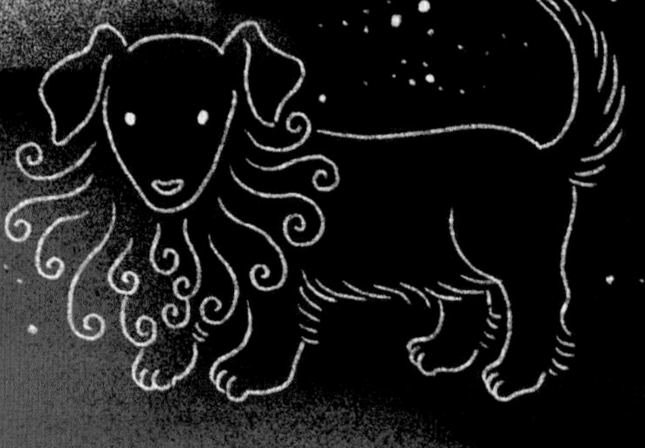

I looked up and it was Sadie! When did she learn how to talk?

"Follow me, little one."

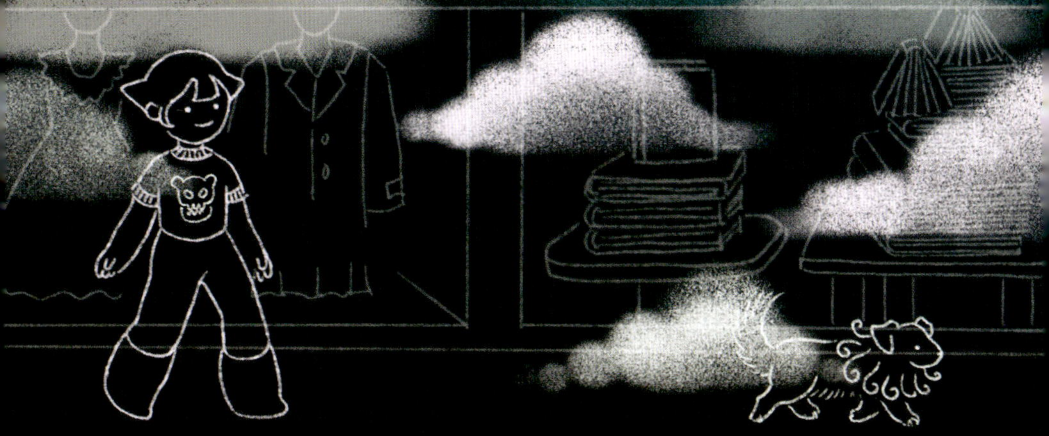

She led me to a toy store and pointed. I climbed the shelf and got her the rubber ostrich. She led me to the food court and pointed again.

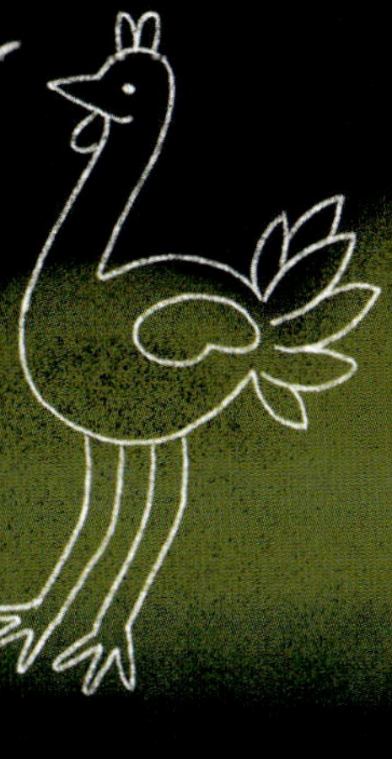

I jumped the counter
and got us some ice cream.
Then she took me to a hat shop
and we got hats!
We looked super cool :)

We went store to store until I
heard a loud whistle and a voice
calling her name.
" SADIE! GO PEE AND
COME INSIDE!"

MOM?! I looked around wildly, but she wasn't there...

What was going on? Suddenly Sadie let out a howl and a portal opened in front of us.

"I must go now. I am glad you are doing well. Keep being a good Hooman."

She jumped into the portal and I woke up. It was the only dream I've ever had since arriving in Andromeda.

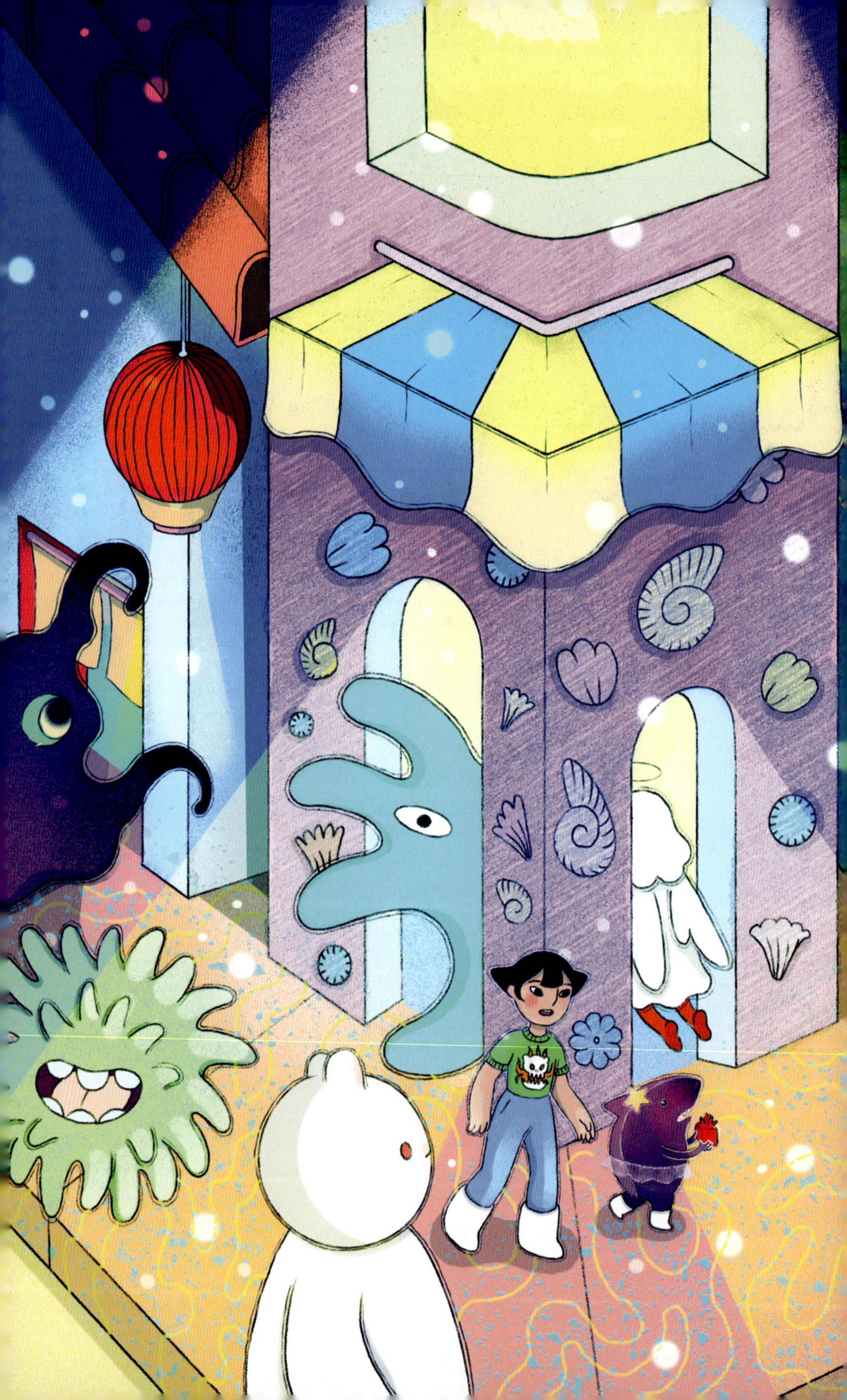

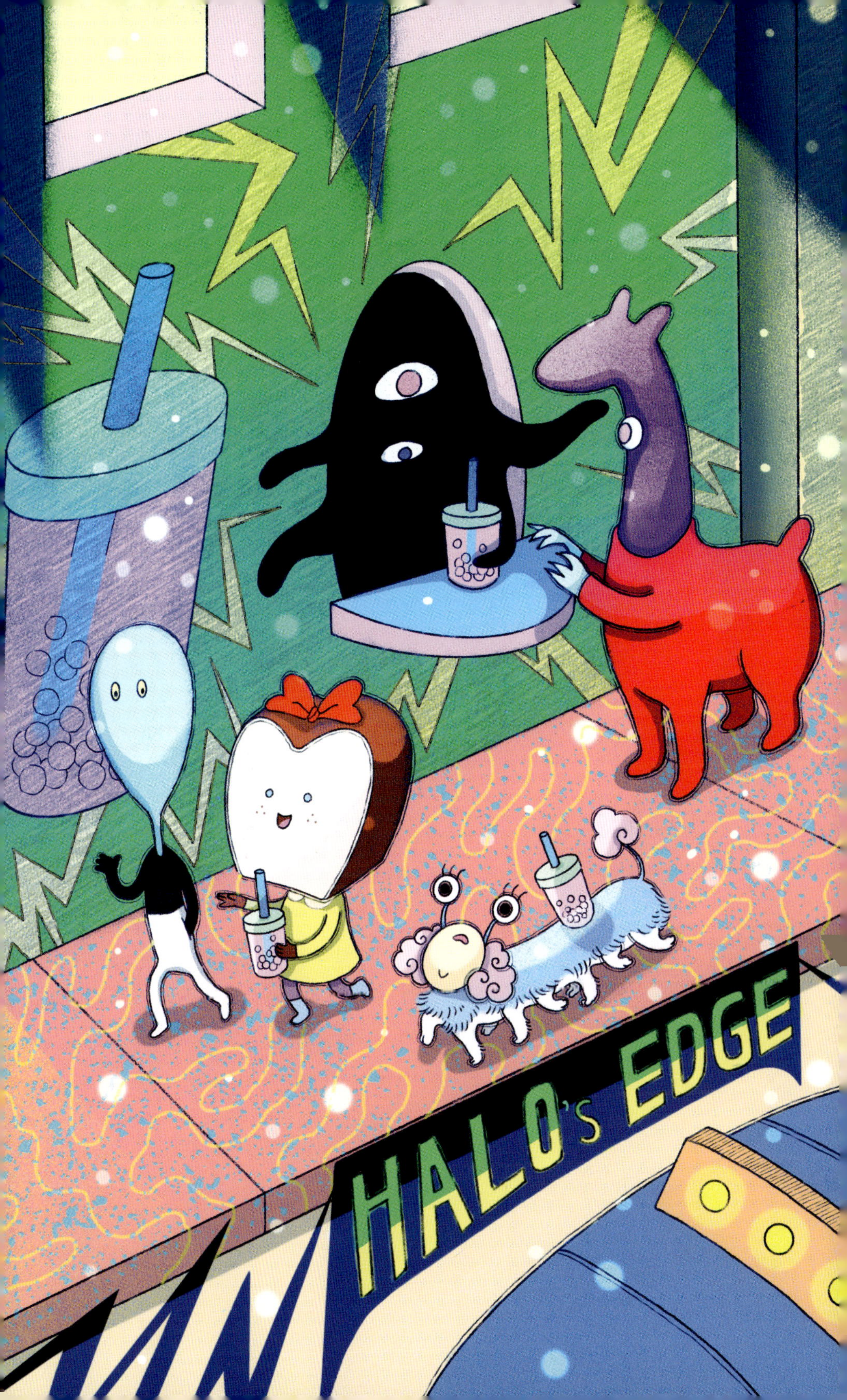
HALO's EDGE

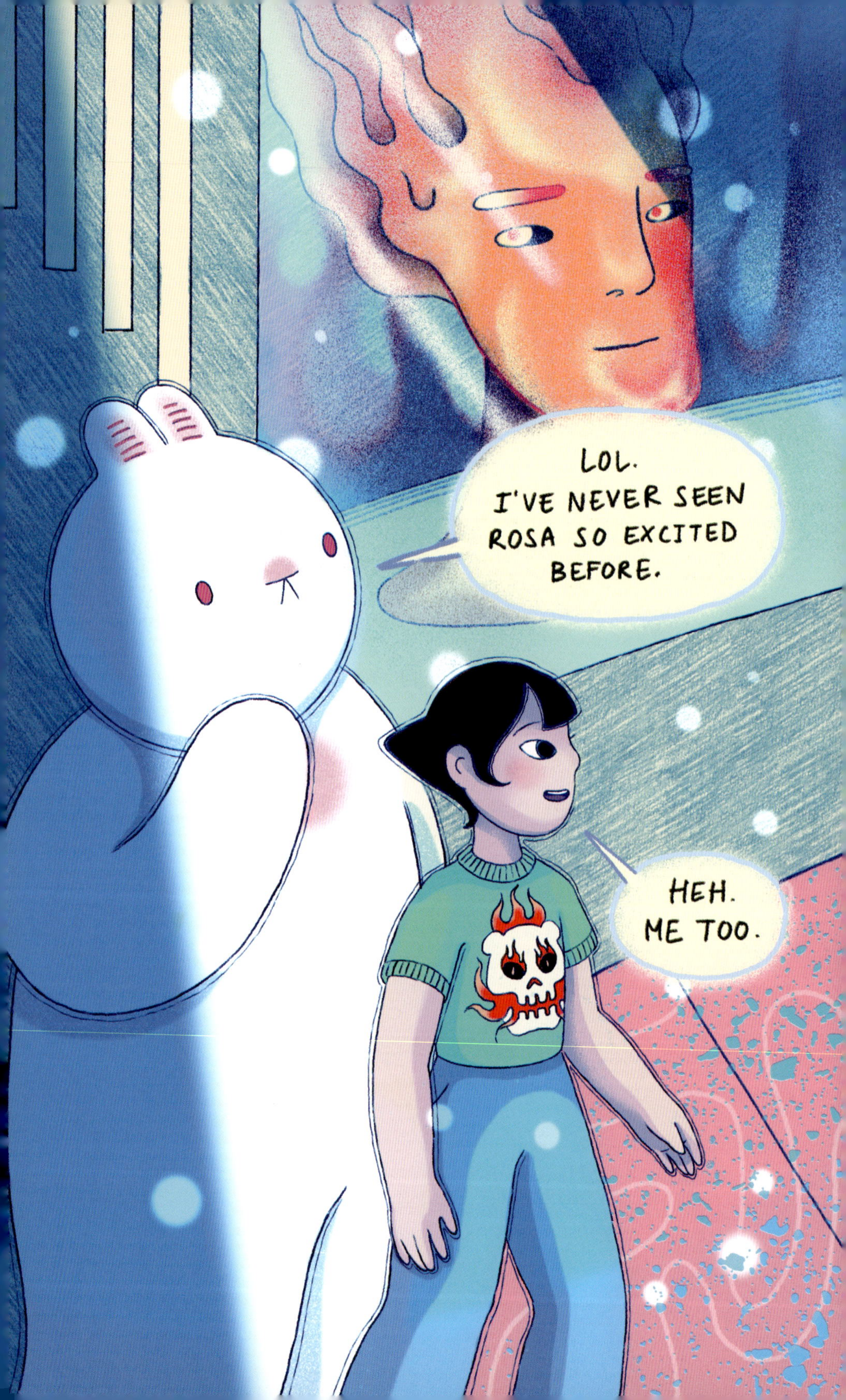
LOL.
I'VE NEVER SEEN ROSA SO EXCITED BEFORE.
HEH. ME TOO.

Have you ever seen an alien? Like a real alien...

I don't mean the kind in movies or shows. The kind that everyone talks about: big black eyes, huge heads, green skin.

"OMG! HURRY UP! YOU GUYS ARE WALKING SOOO SLOWWW!"

Those kinds exist, but there are others out there. All shapes and sizes, textures, colors, etc.

I think humans are too scared to even imagine...

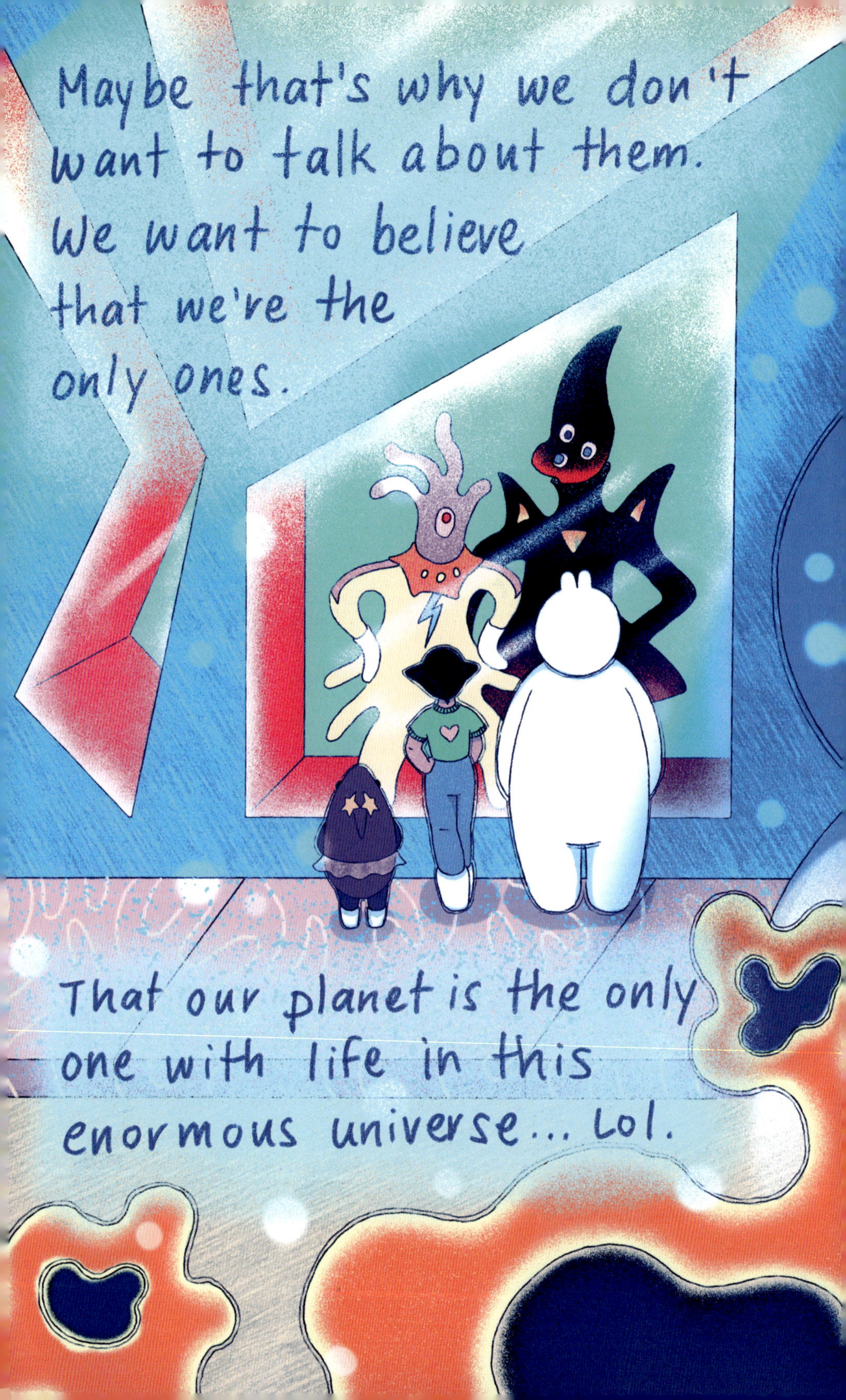
Maybe that's why we don't want to talk about them. We want to believe that we're the only ones.
That our planet is the only one with life in this enormous universe... Lol.

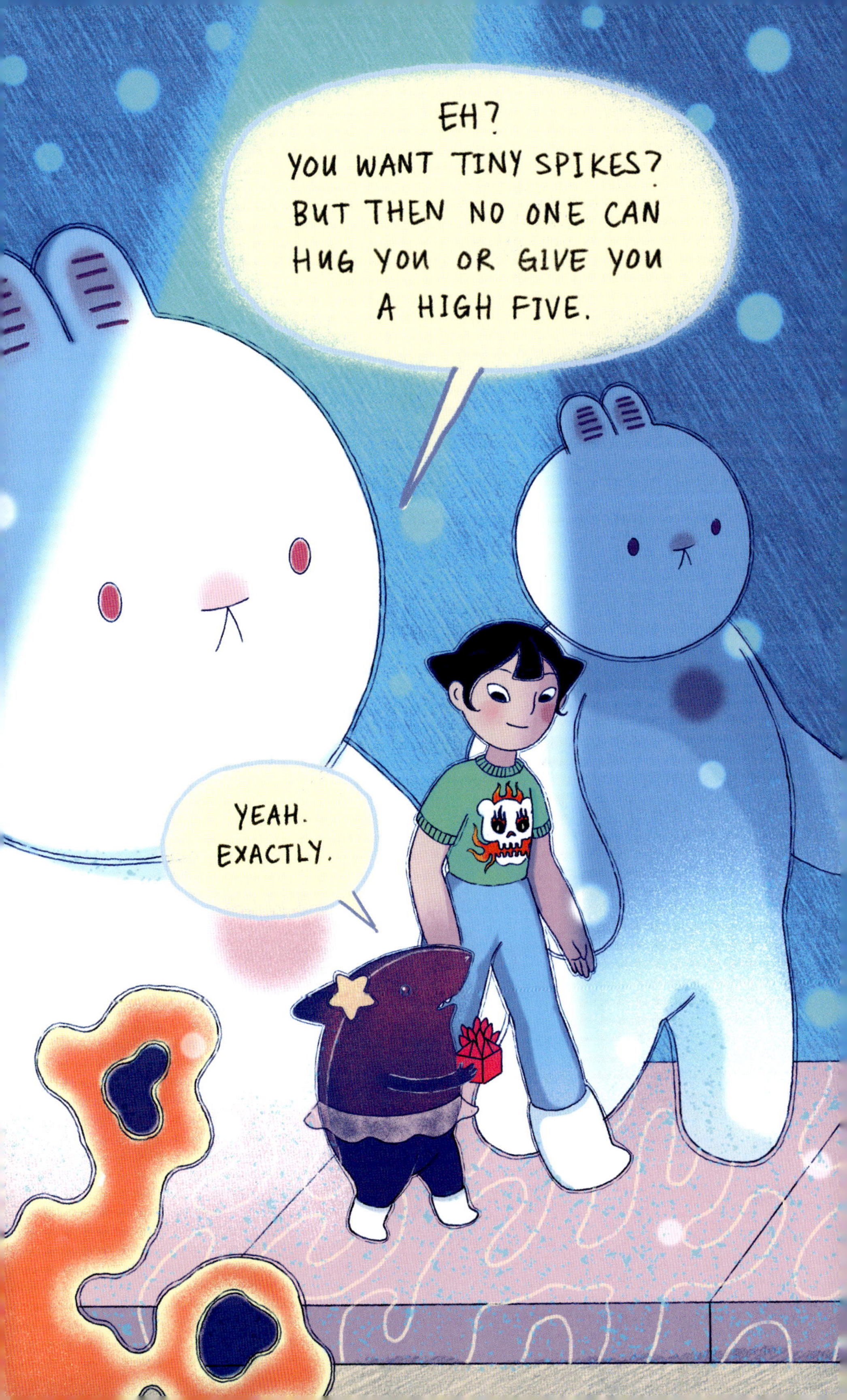
EH? YOU WANT TINY SPIKES? BUT THEN NO ONE CAN HUG YOU OR GIVE YOU A HIGH FIVE.
YEAH. EXACTLY.

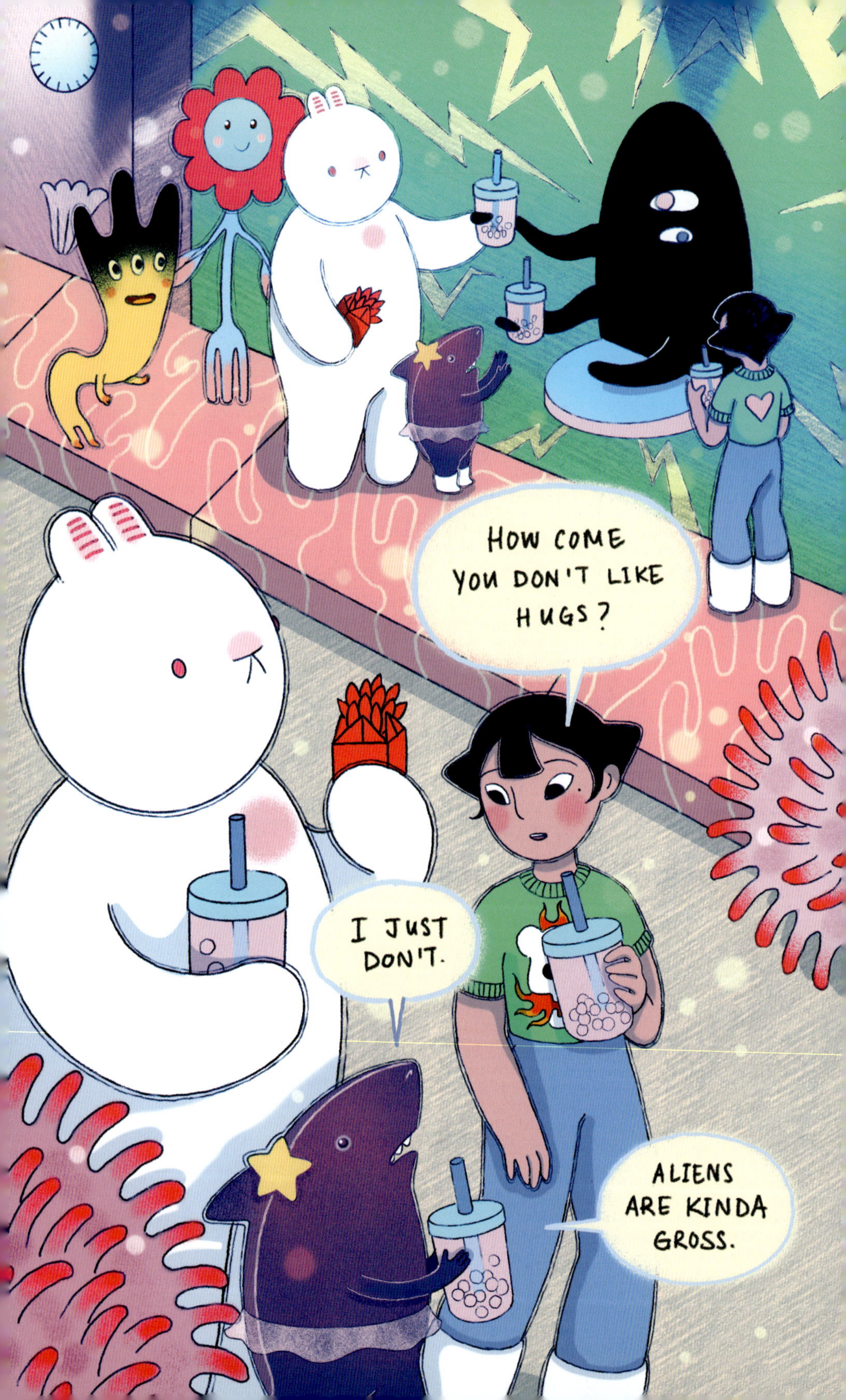
HOW COME YOU DON'T LIKE HUGS?
I JUST DON'T.
ALIENS ARE KINDA GROSS.

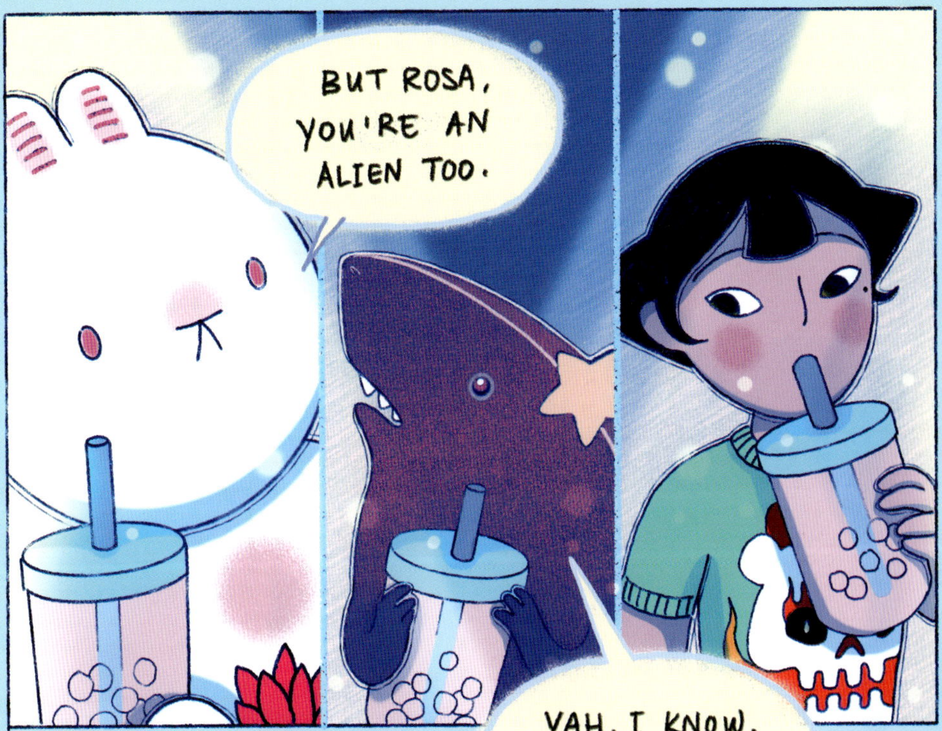
BUT ROSA, YOU'RE AN ALIEN TOO.
YAH, I KNOW. I GROSS MYSELF OUT.

Did you know only humans call Earth, Earth? I've asked everyone here if they know where Earth is and nothing.

NADA. ZIP, ZILCH.

No one's even heard of it.

"WHAT GALAXY ARE YOU FROM?"

I don't even know...

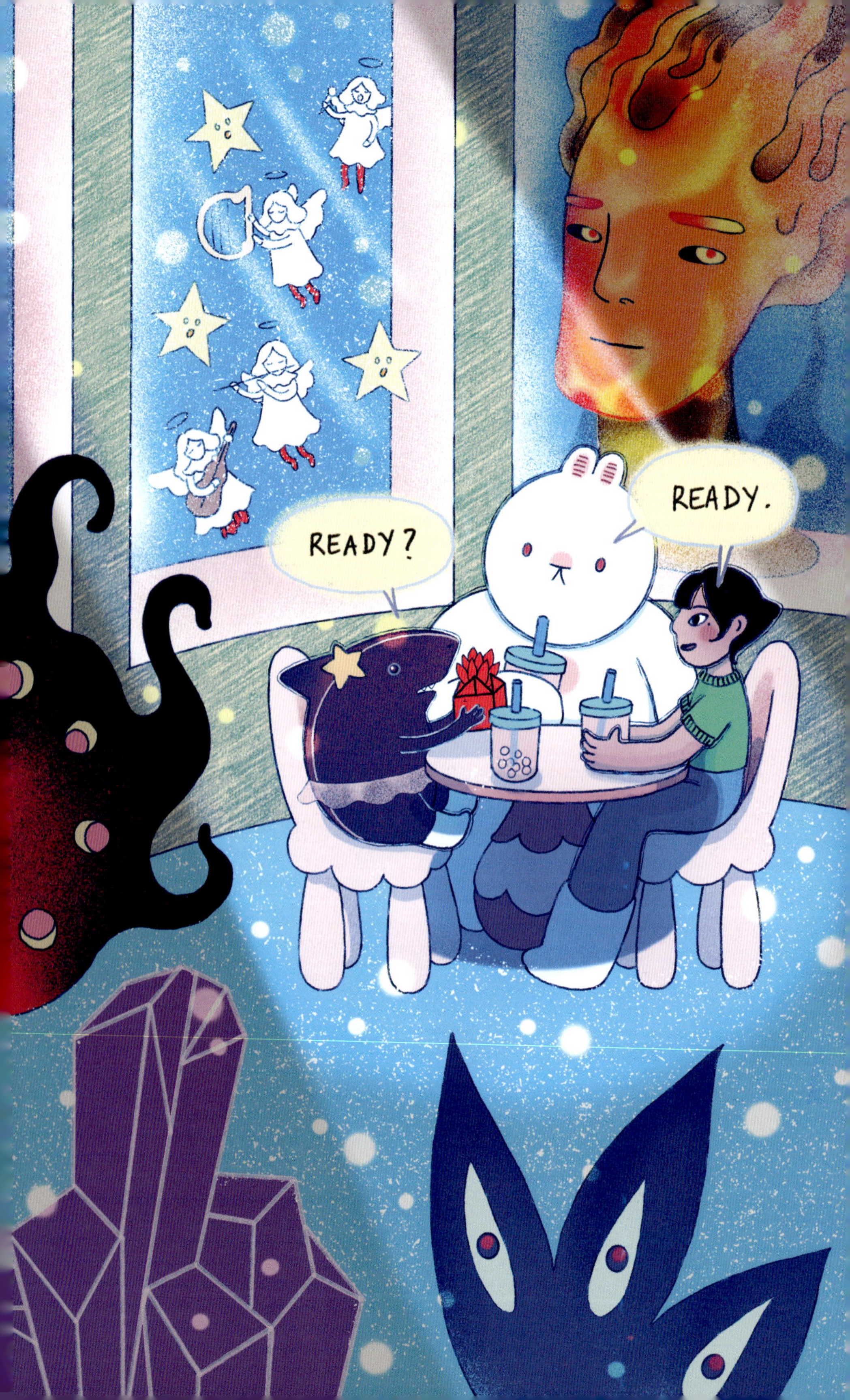
READY?
READY.

If I could just figure out what galaxy humans are from...

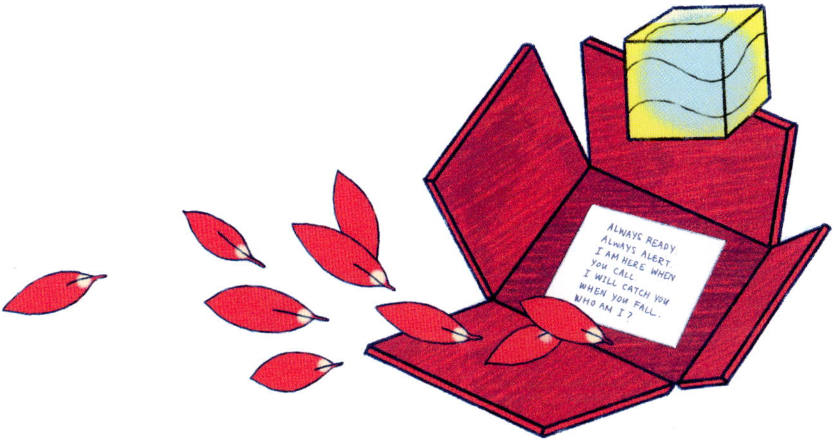
ALWAYS READY.
ALWAYS ALERT.
I AM HERE WHEN
YOU CALL.
I WILL CATCH YOU
WHEN YOU FALL.
WHO AM I?

Then maybe I can find my way back...

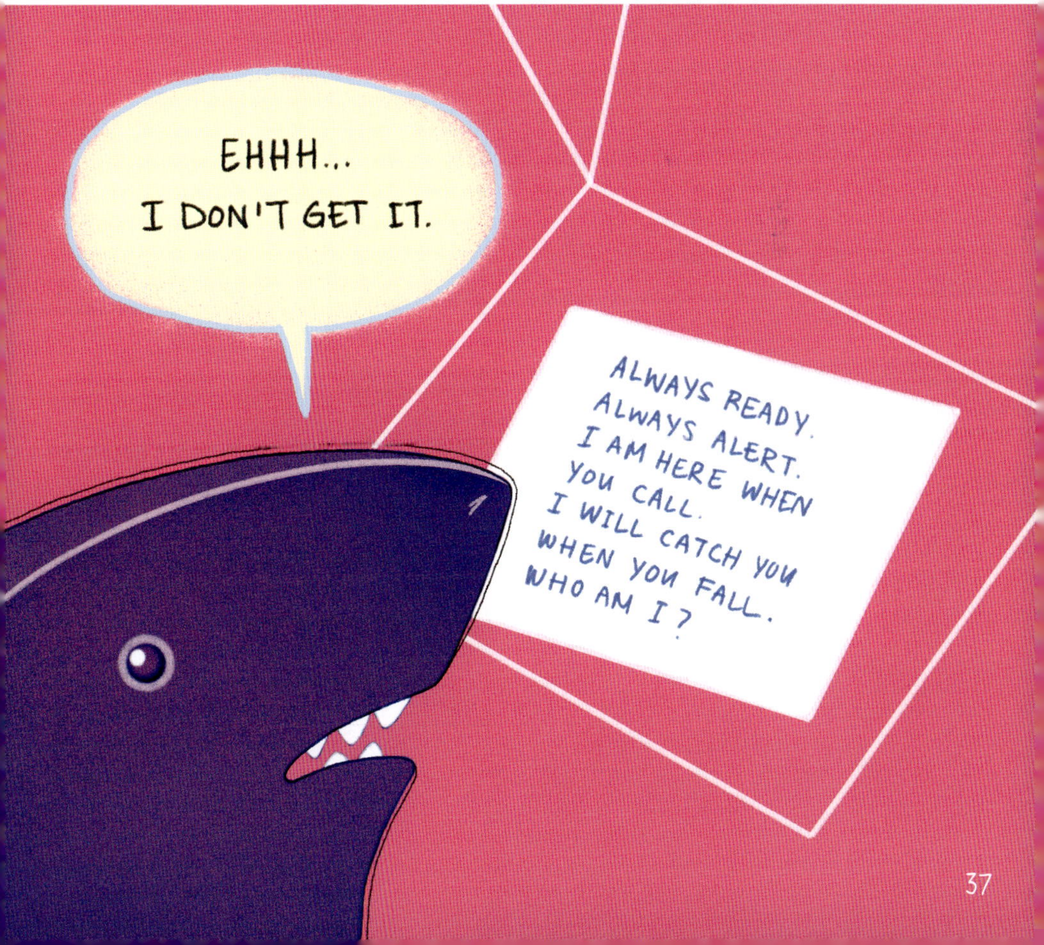
EHHH...
I DON'T GET IT.
ALWAYS READY.
ALWAYS ALERT.
I AM HERE WHEN
YOU CALL.
I WILL CATCH YOU
WHEN YOU FALL.
WHO AM I?

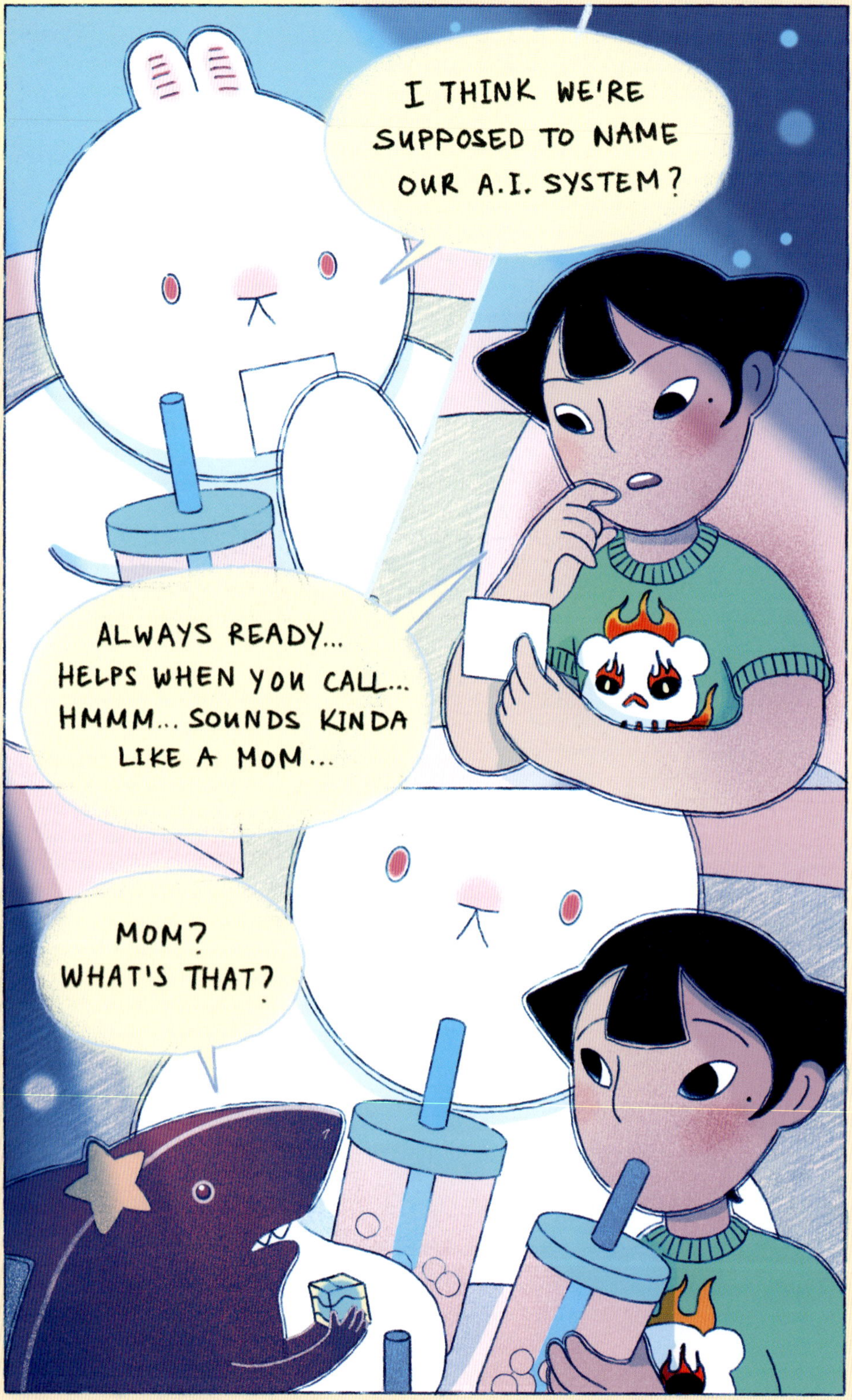
I THINK WE'RE SUPPOSED TO NAME OUR A.I. SYSTEM?
ALWAYS READY... HELPS WHEN YOU CALL... HMMM... SOUNDS KINDA LIKE A MOM...
MOM? WHAT'S THAT?

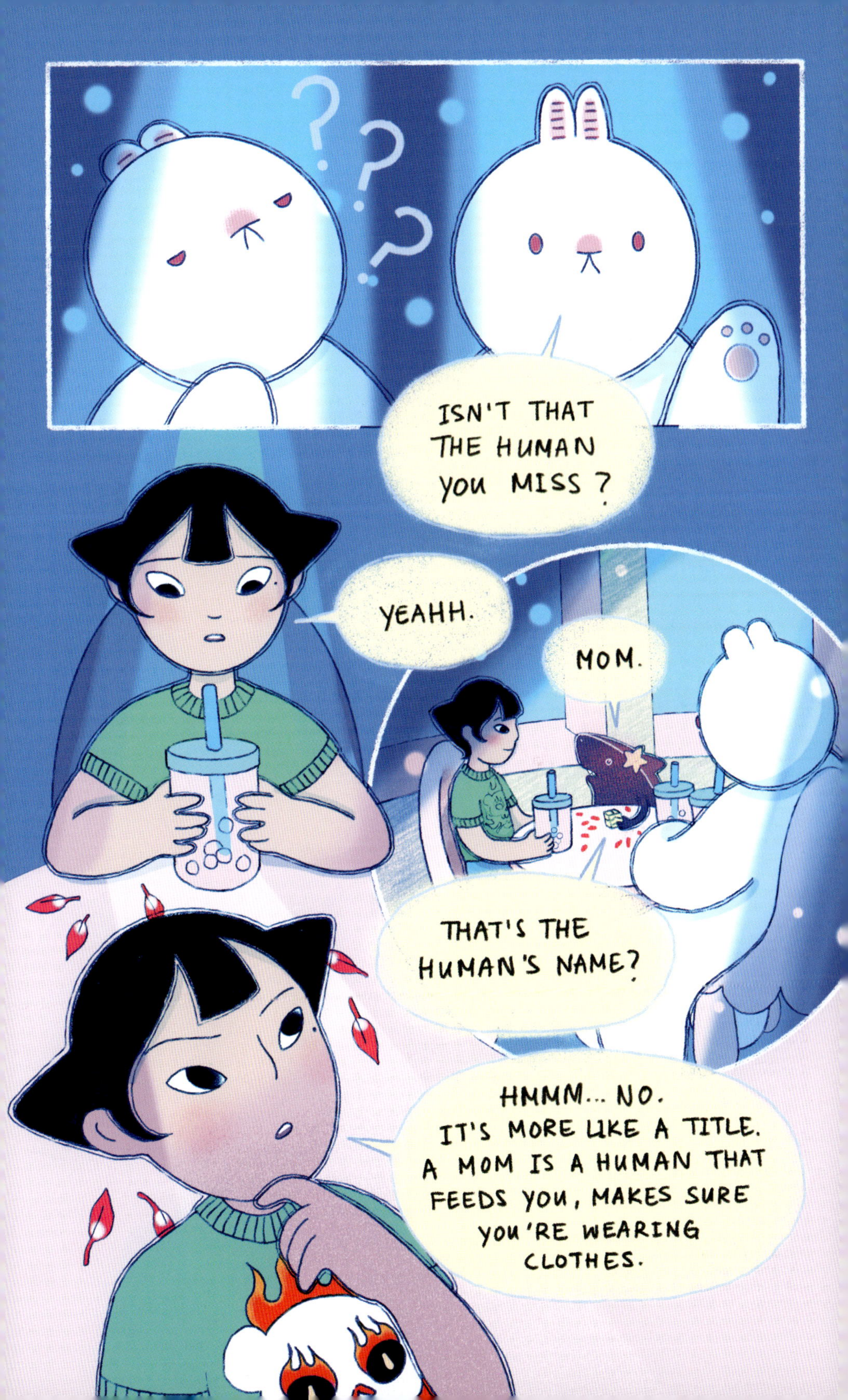

ISN'T THAT THE HUMAN YOU MISS?
YEAHH.
MOM.
THAT'S THE HUMAN'S NAME?
HMMM... NO. IT'S MORE LIKE A TITLE. A MOM IS A HUMAN THAT FEEDS YOU, MAKES SURE YOU'RE WEARING CLOTHES.

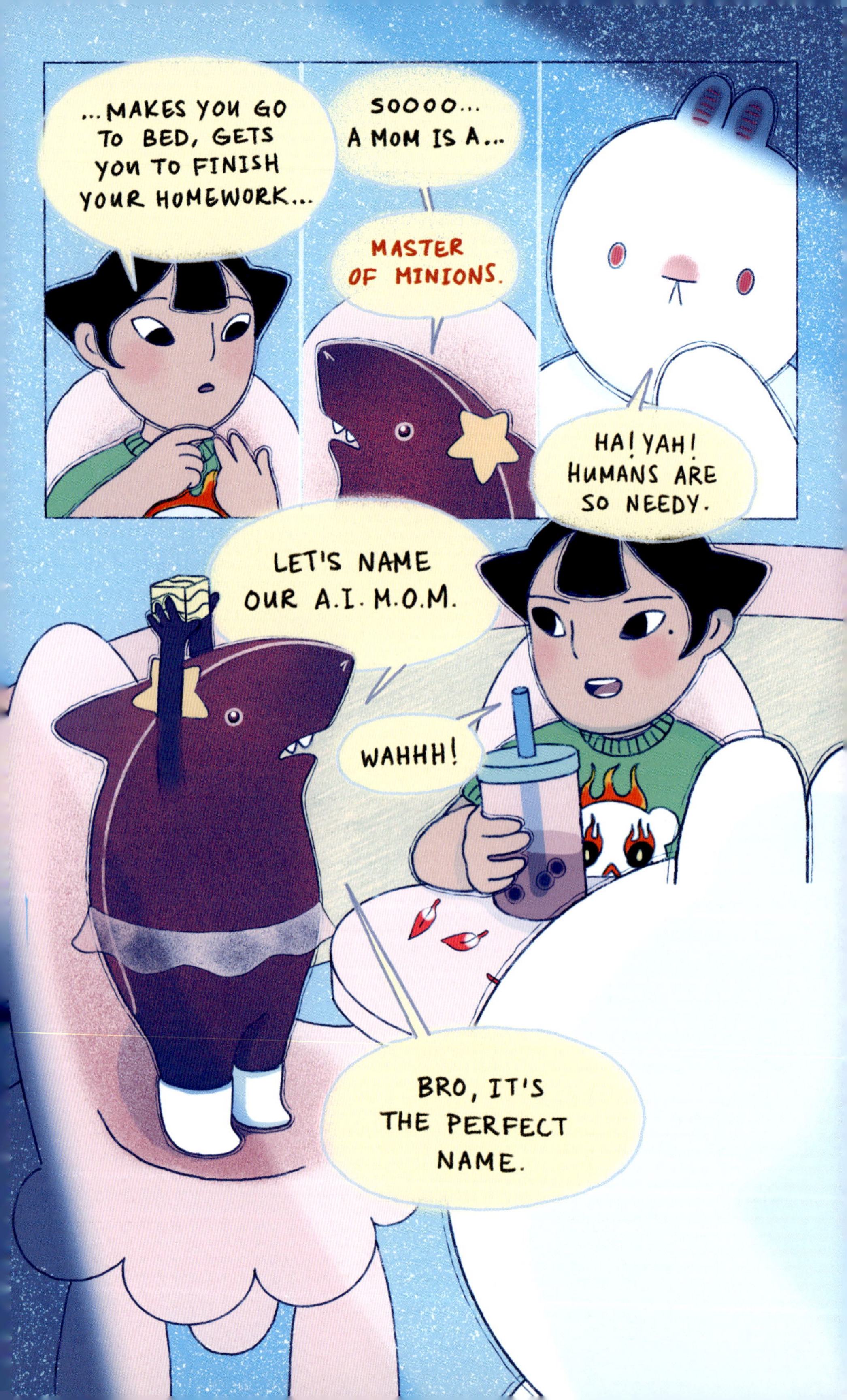
...MAKES YOU GO TO BED, GETS YOU TO FINISH YOUR HOMEWORK...
SOOOO... A MOM IS A...
MASTER OF MINIONS.
HA! YAH! HUMANS ARE SO NEEDY.
LET'S NAME OUR A.I. M.O.M.
WAHHH!
BRO, IT'S THE PERFECT NAME.

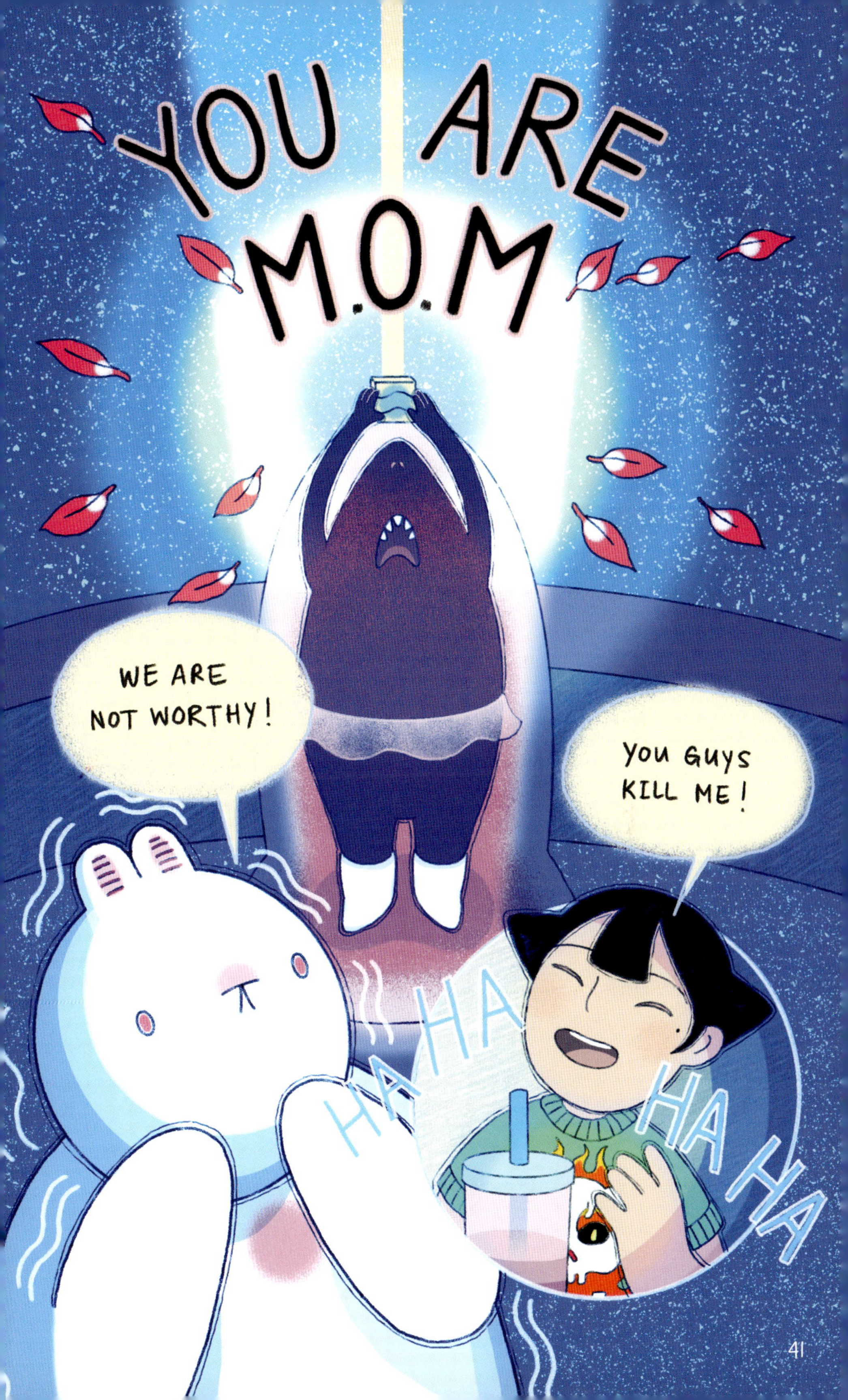
YOU ARE M.O.M
WE ARE NOT WORTHY!
YOU GUYS KILL ME!
HA HA HA HA HA HA

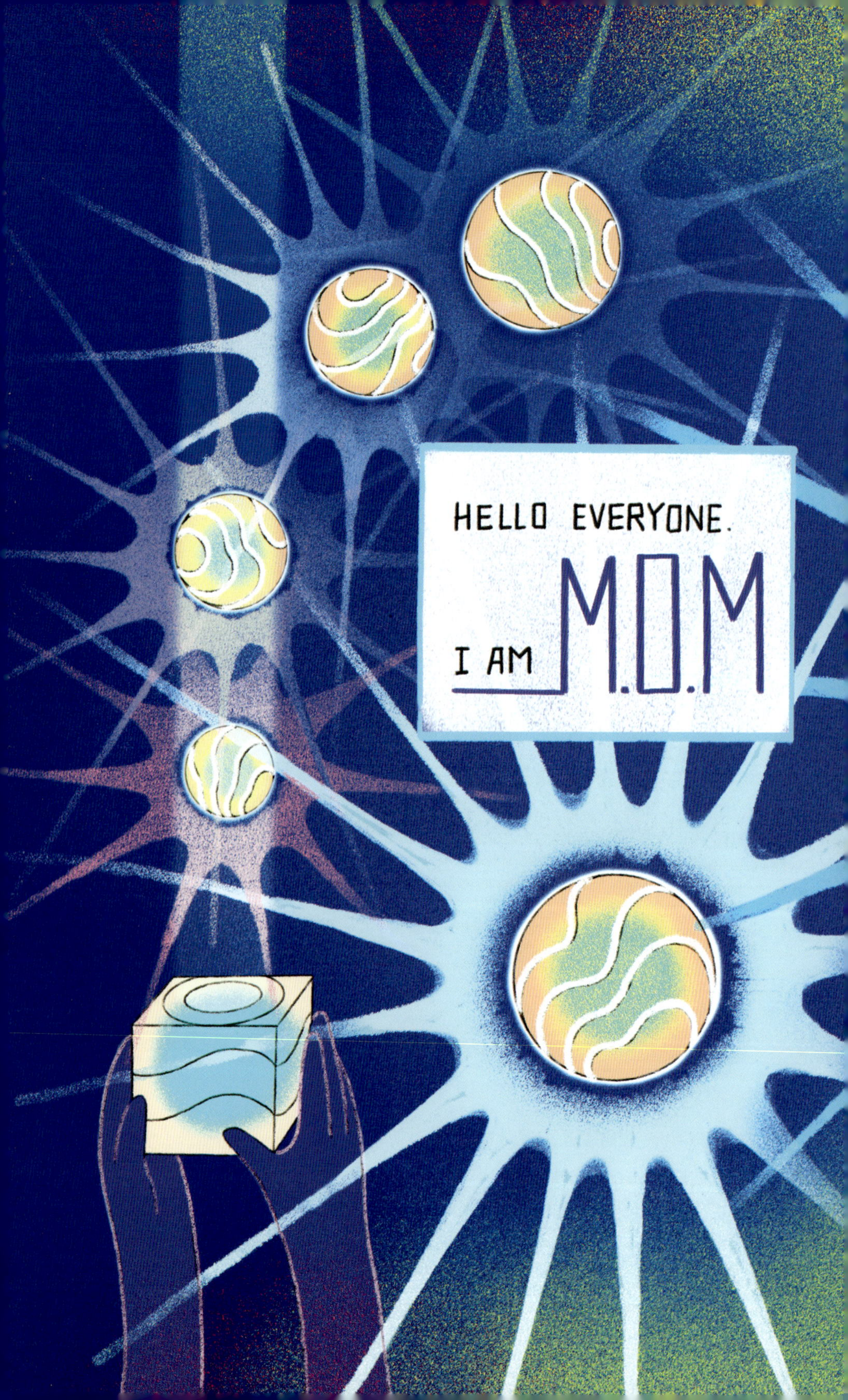
HELLO EVERYONE.
I AM M.O.M

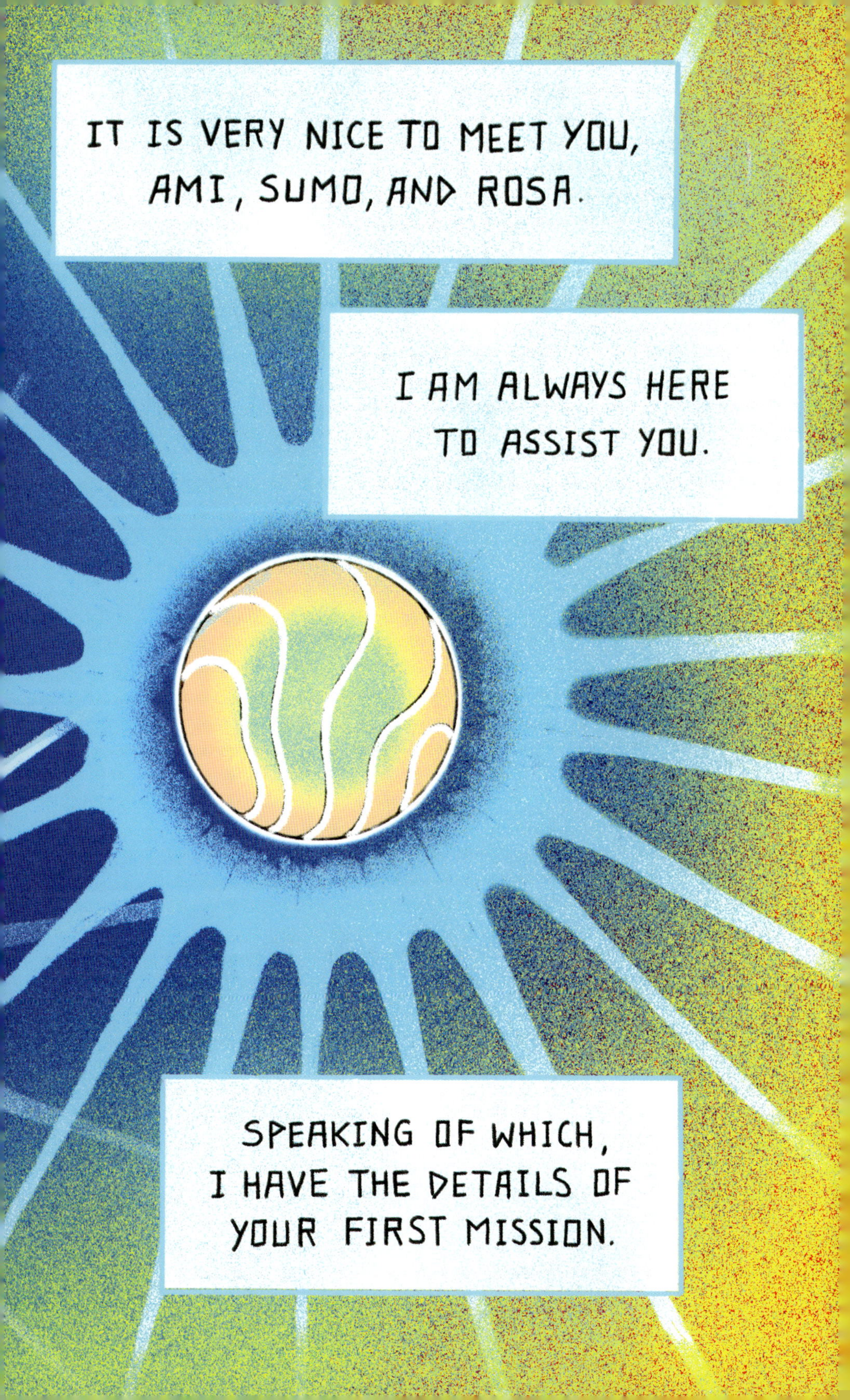
IT IS VERY NICE TO MEET YOU, AMI, SUMO, AND ROSA.
I AM ALWAYS HERE TO ASSIST YOU.
SPEAKING OF WHICH, I HAVE THE DETAILS OF YOUR FIRST MISSION.

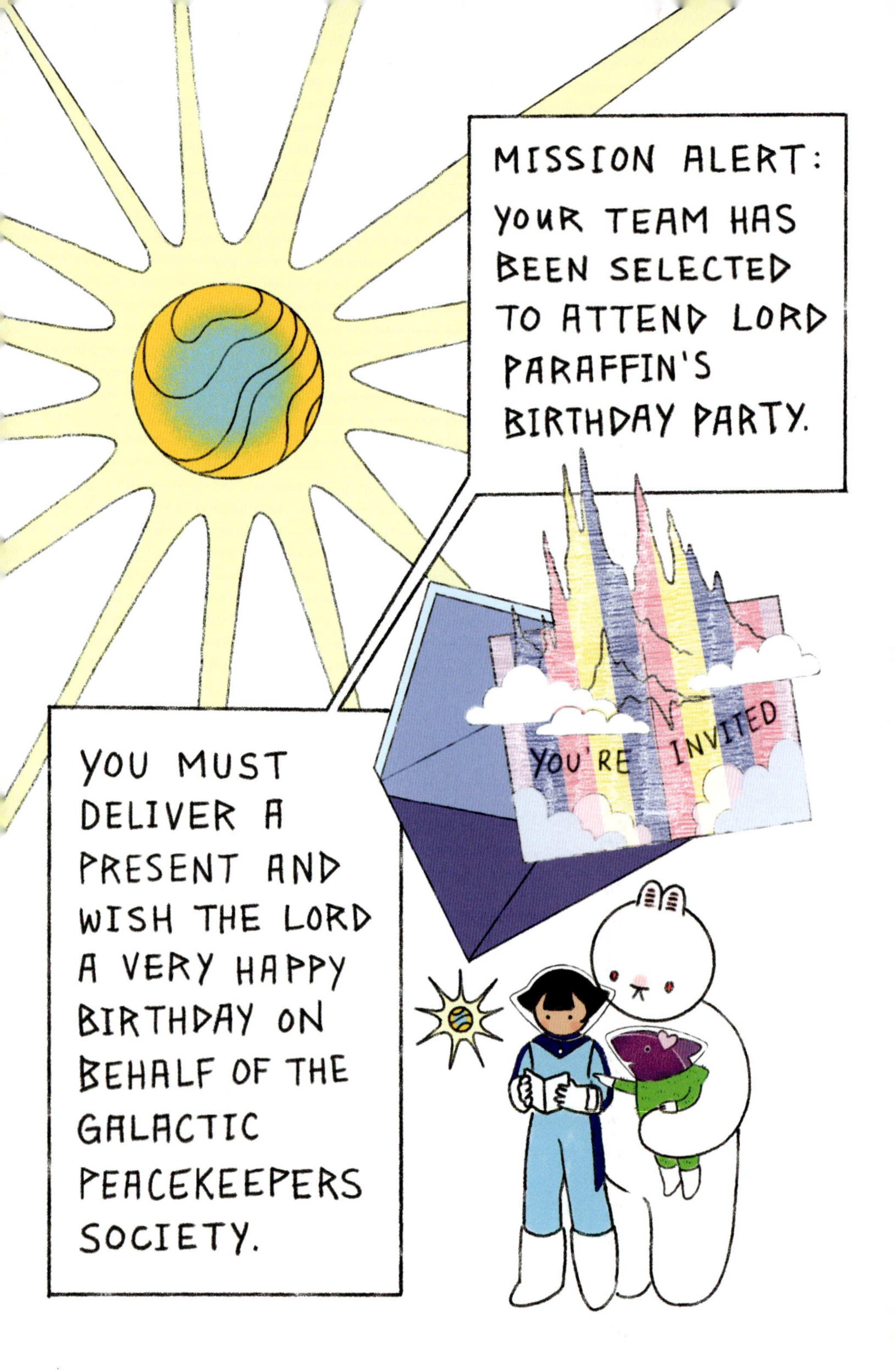
MISSION ALERT: YOUR TEAM HAS BEEN SELECTED TO ATTEND LORD PARAFFIN'S BIRTHDAY PARTY.
YOU'RE INVITED
YOU MUST DELIVER A PRESENT AND WISH THE LORD A VERY HAPPY BIRTHDAY ON BEHALF OF THE GALACTIC PEACEKEEPERS SOCIETY.

DUUUUDDDEEE. This is so unreal. My first mission with the team!

AND LOOK!

I got a new spacesuit from the OUTERSPACE shop!

My helmet fits my giant head perfectly.

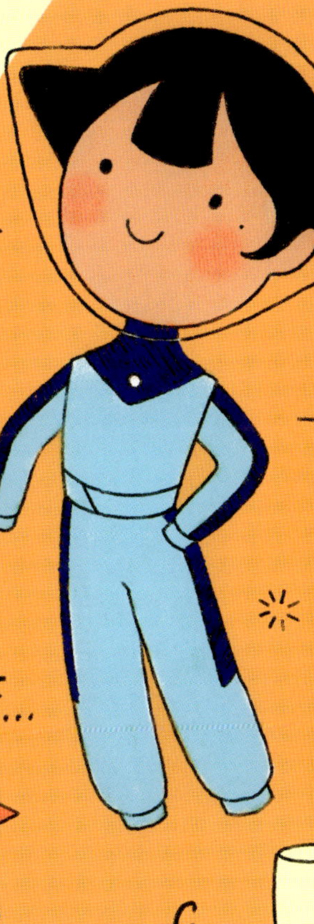

Our suits are WATERPROOF, SLIMEPROOF, TEMPERATURE PROOF...

I think **EVERYTHING** proof.

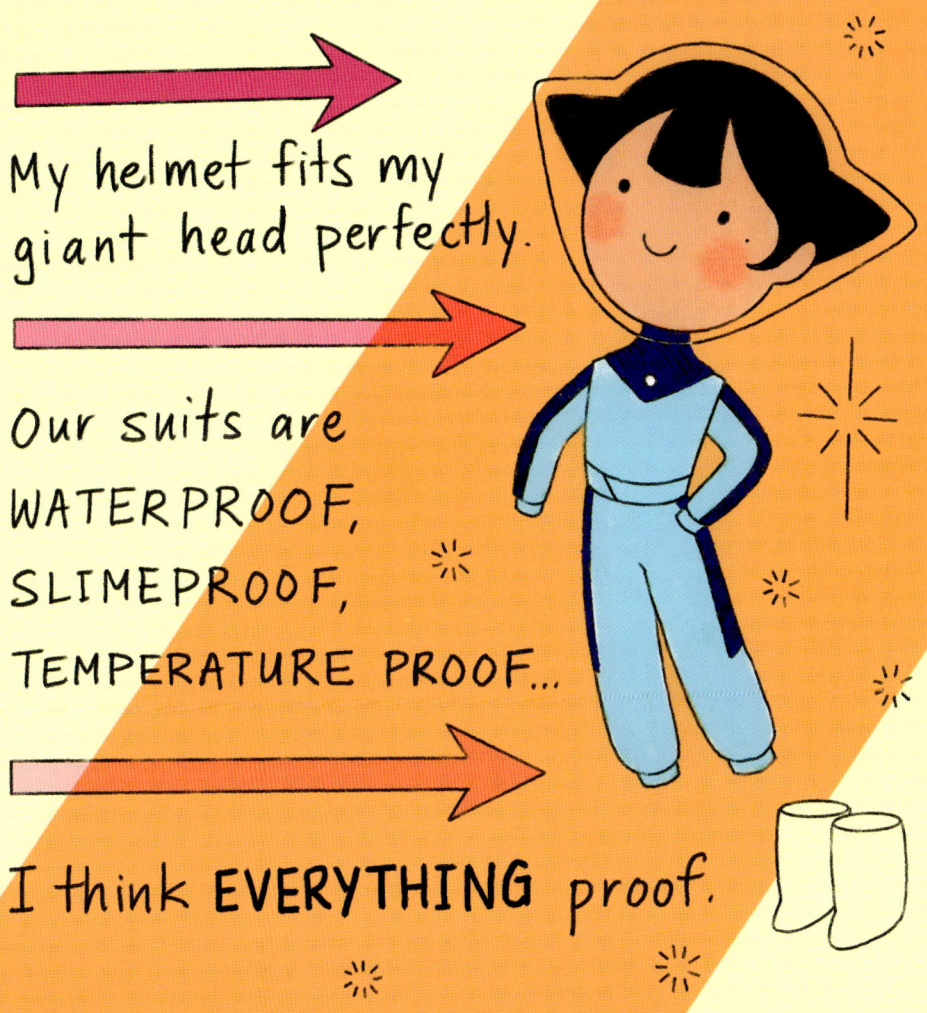

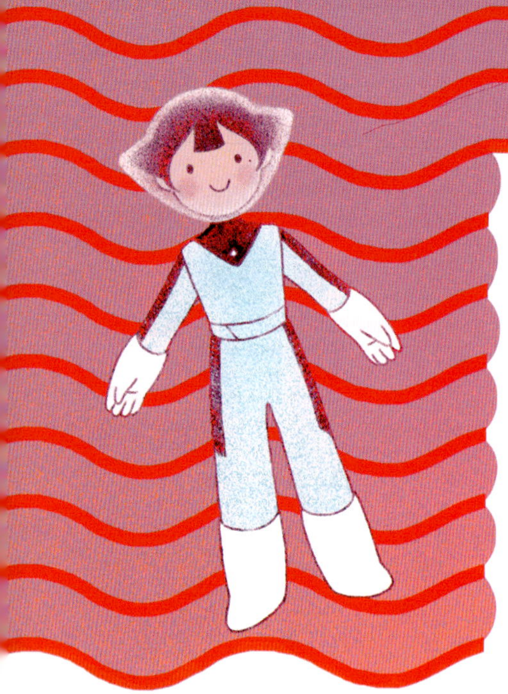

I bet I could even fall into LAVA and swim around without melting into SLIME.

ROSA couldn't get tiny spikes all over her suit, but M.O.M said she could get a fuzzy soft one that gives a little static shock if someone touches it for too long.

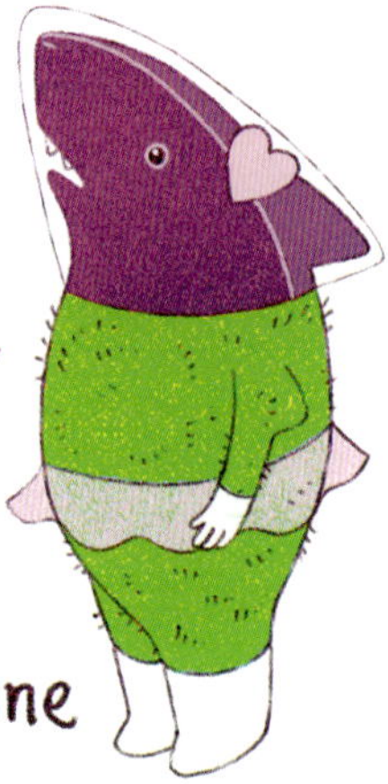

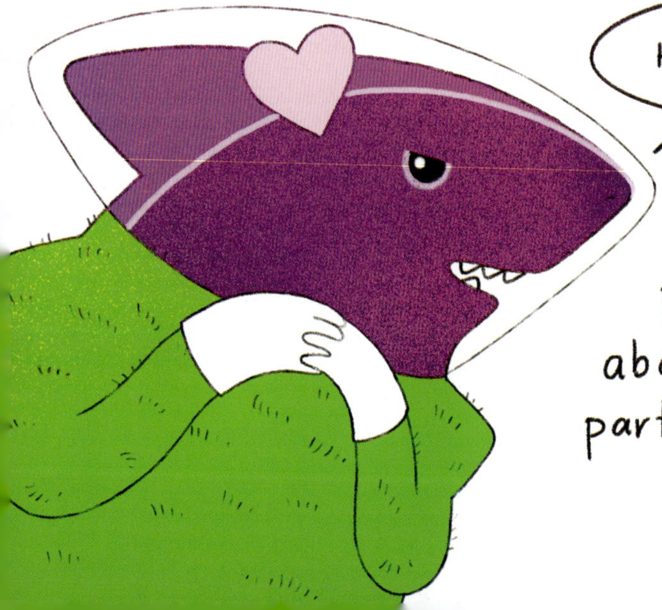
HEH HEH HEH.

She seemed pretty happy about the static part. LOL!

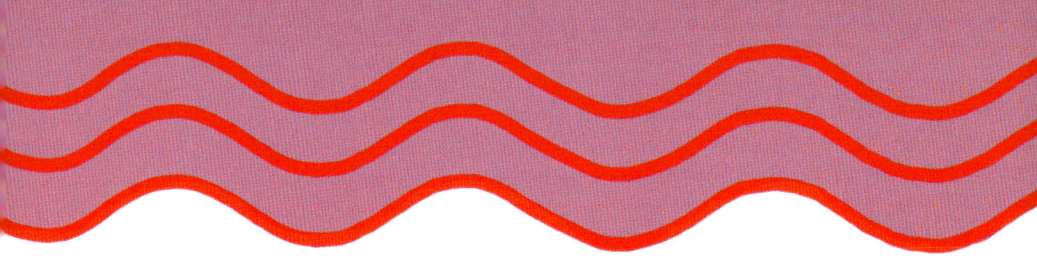

Sumo doesn't need a suit.
Turns out that his skin is
INDESTRUCTIBLE

PAPER PLANES?
REALLY GUYS?
DO YOU FEEL THE POINTY PART?
ARROWS NEXT!
LET'S GOOOO!

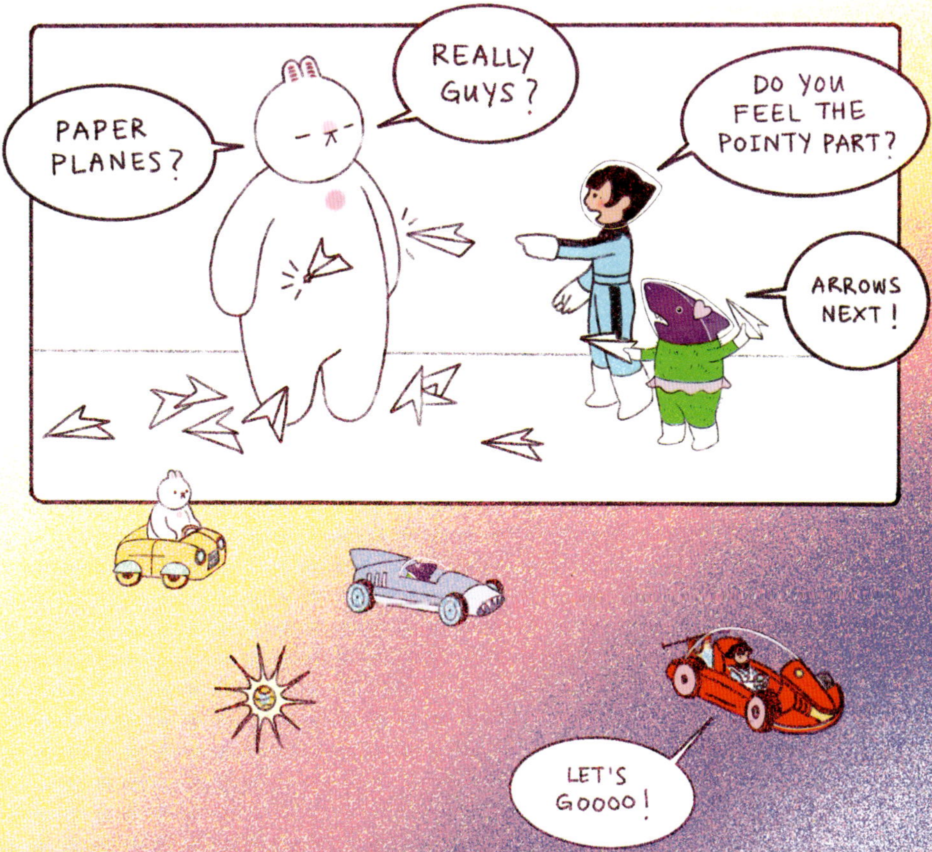

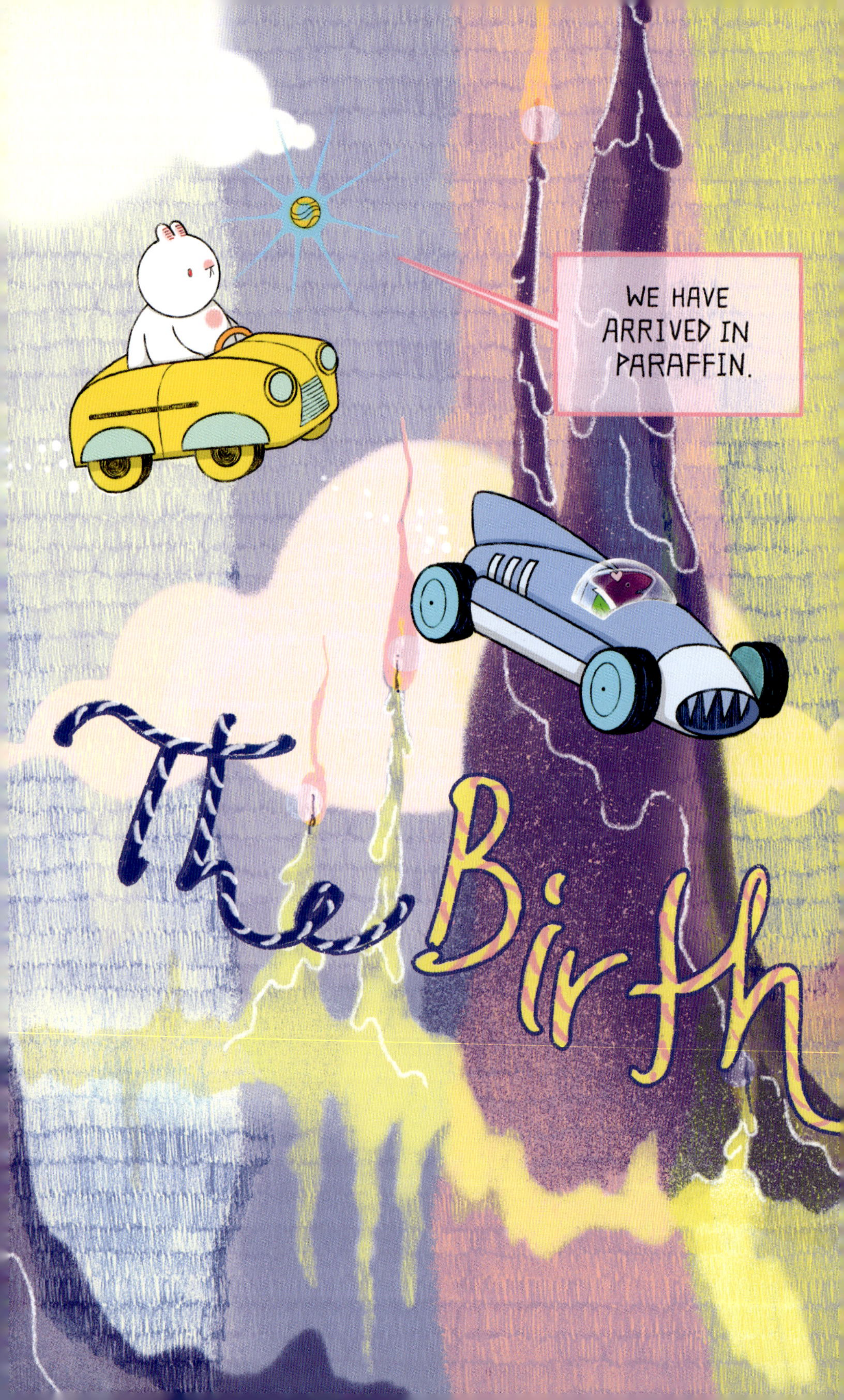
WE HAVE ARRIVED IN PARAFFIN.
The Birth

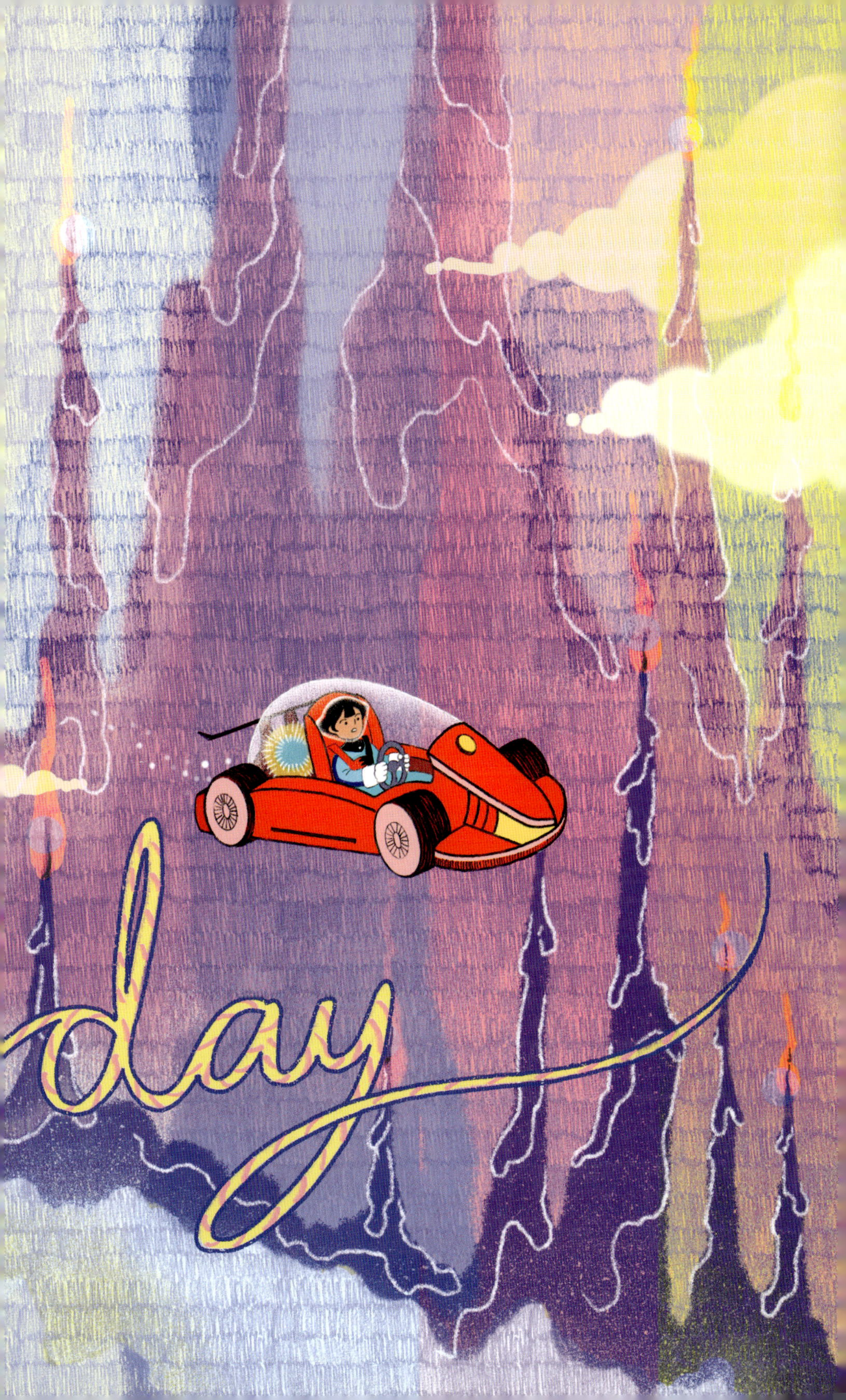
day

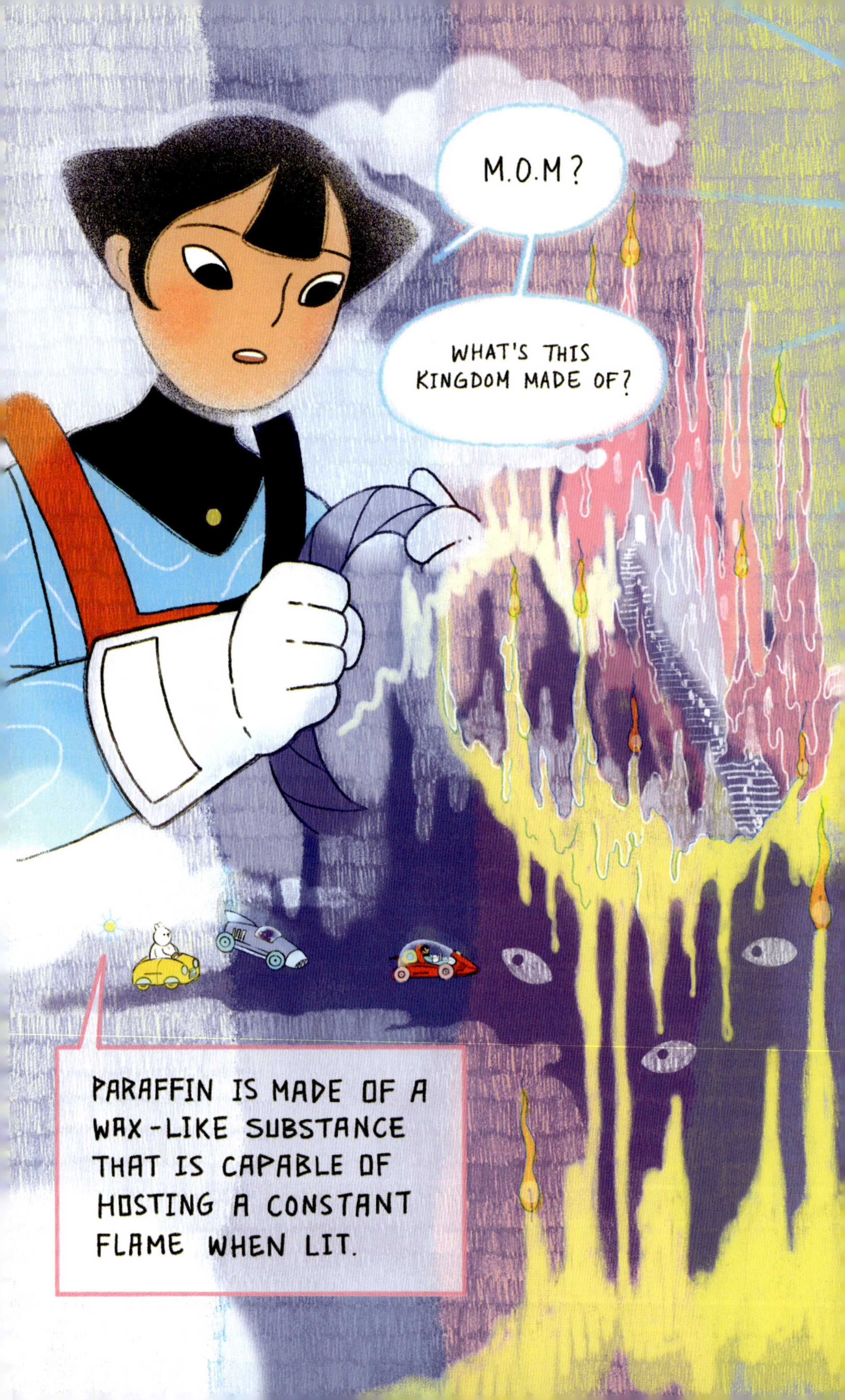
M.O.M?
WHAT'S THIS KINGDOM MADE OF?
PARAFFIN IS MADE OF A WAX-LIKE SUBSTANCE THAT IS CAPABLE OF HOSTING A CONSTANT FLAME WHEN LIT.

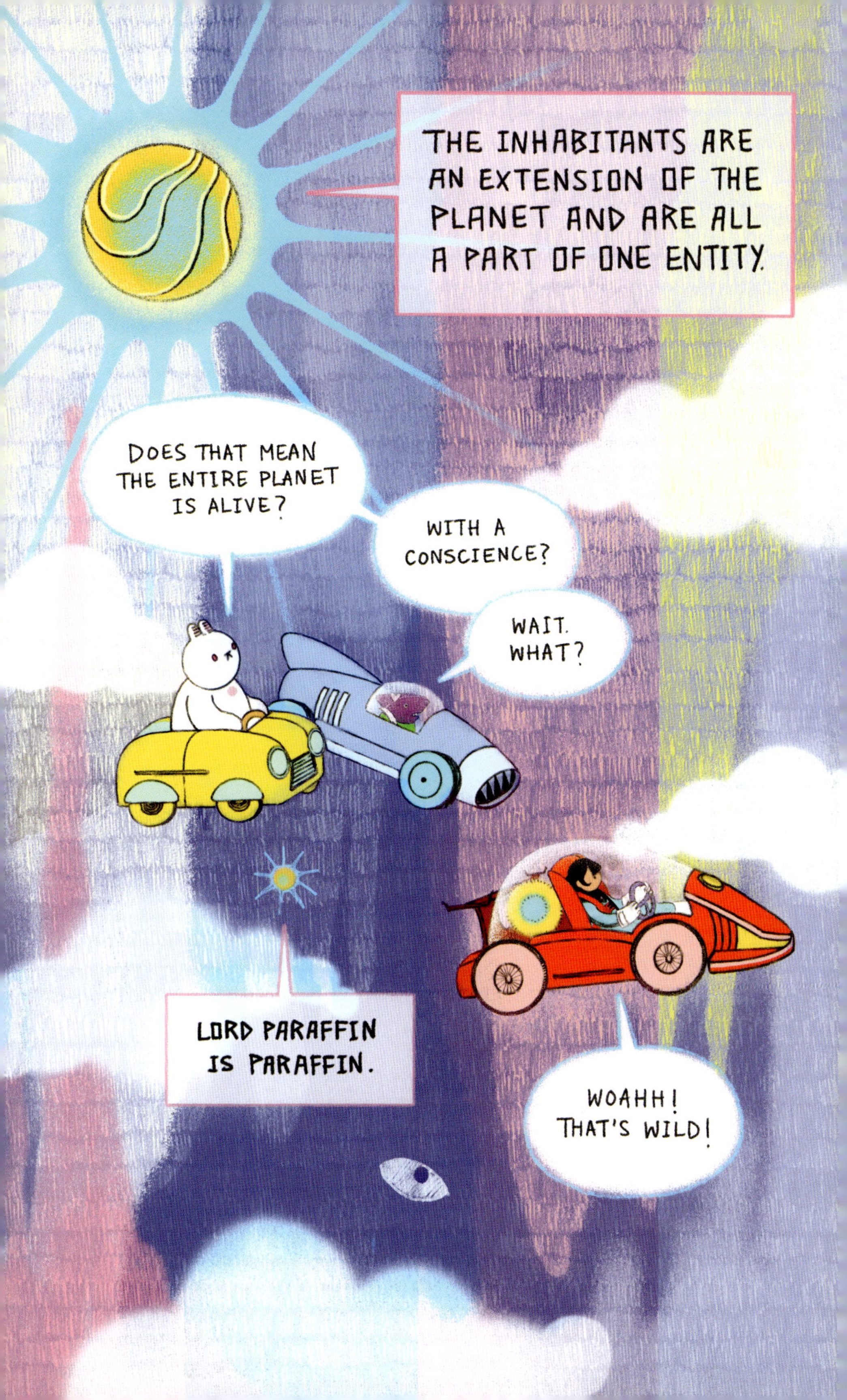
THE INHABITANTS ARE AN EXTENSION OF THE PLANET AND ARE ALL A PART OF ONE ENTITY.
DOES THAT MEAN THE ENTIRE PLANET IS ALIVE?
WITH A CONSCIENCE?
WAIT. WHAT?
LORD PARAFFIN IS PARAFFIN.
WOAHH! THAT'S WILD!

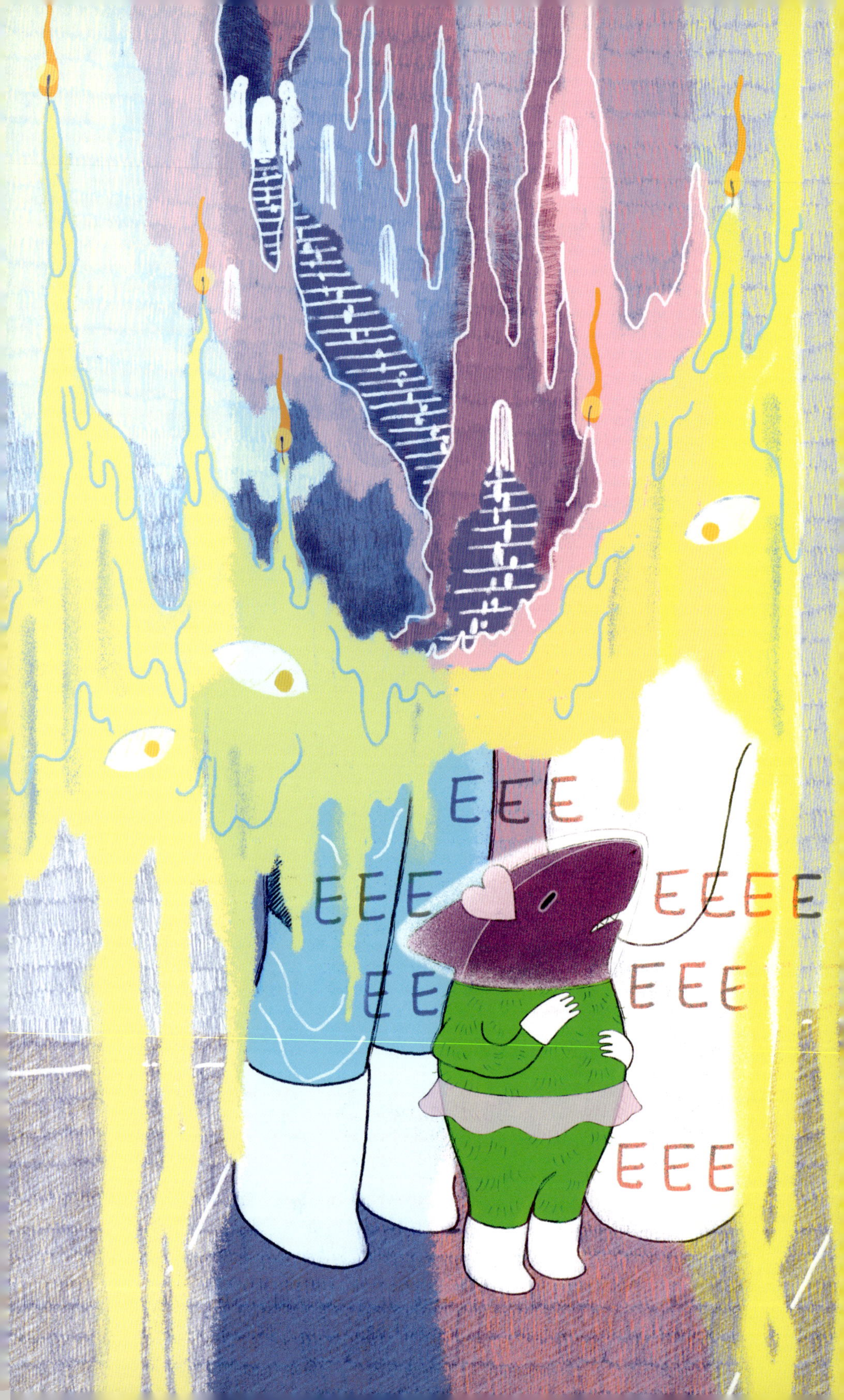
EEE
EEE
EEEEE
EE
EEE
EEE

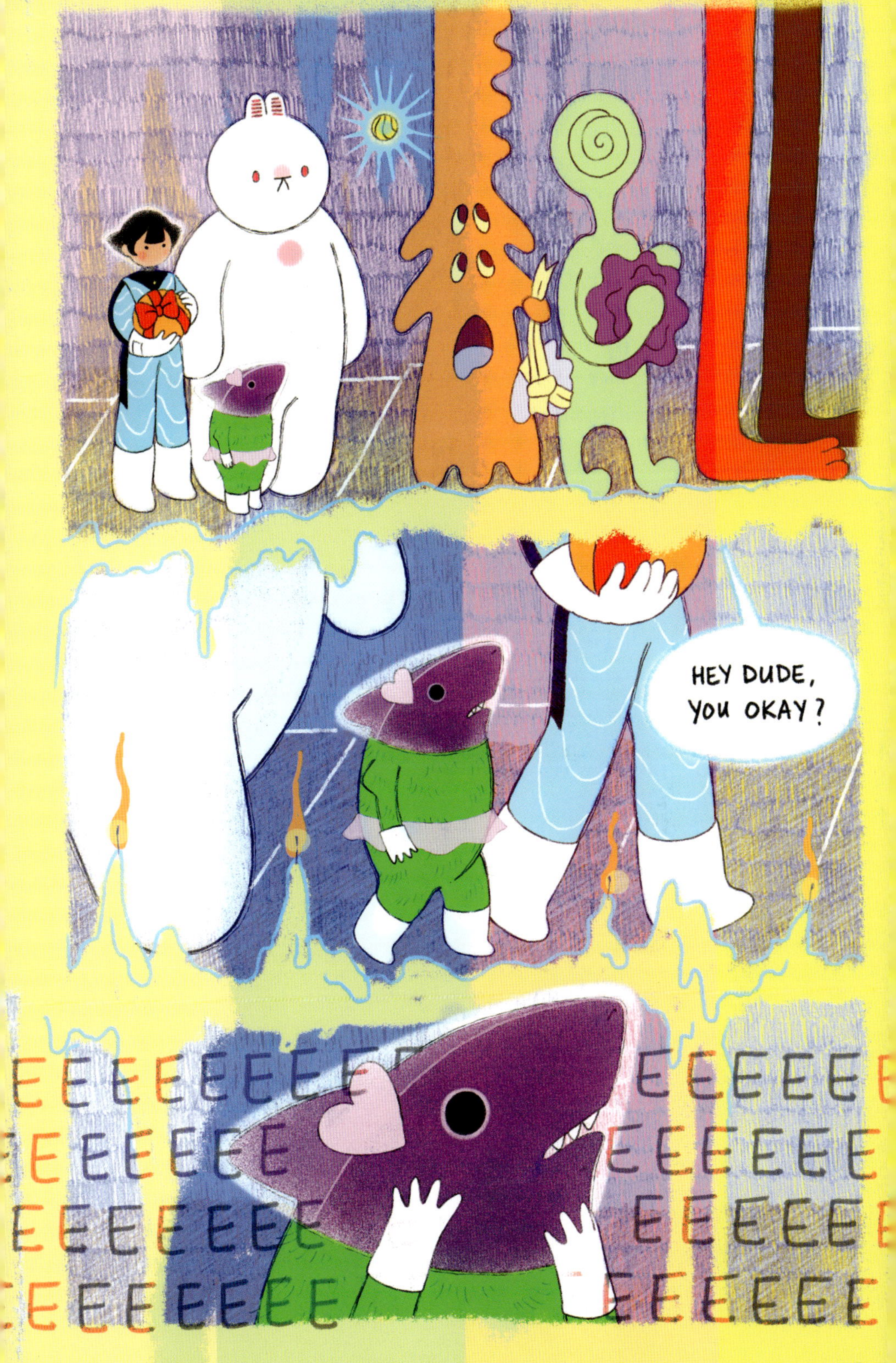
HEY DUDE, YOU OKAY?

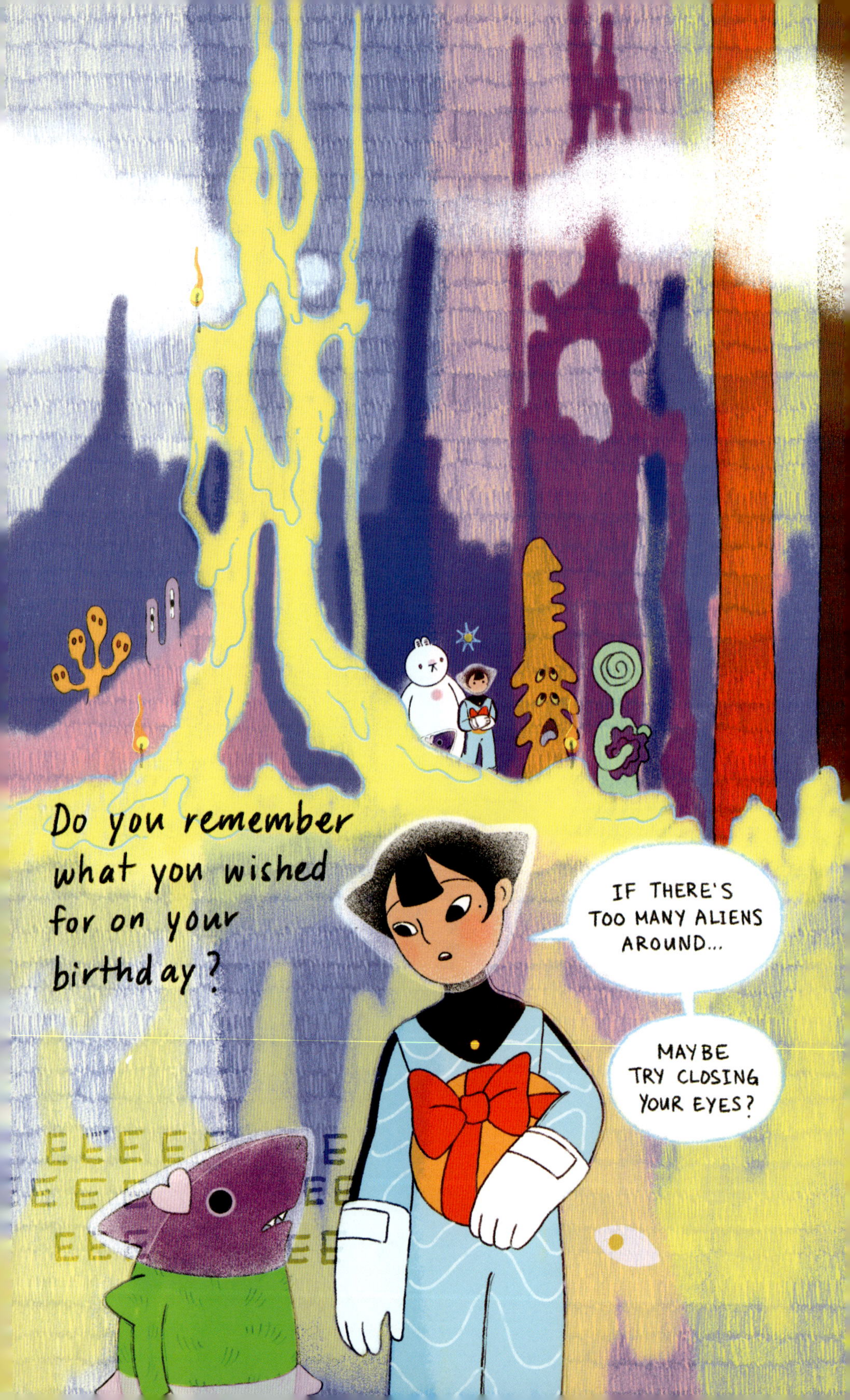
Do you remember what you wished for on your birthday?
IF THERE'S TOO MANY ALIENS AROUND...
MAYBE TRY CLOSING YOUR EYES?

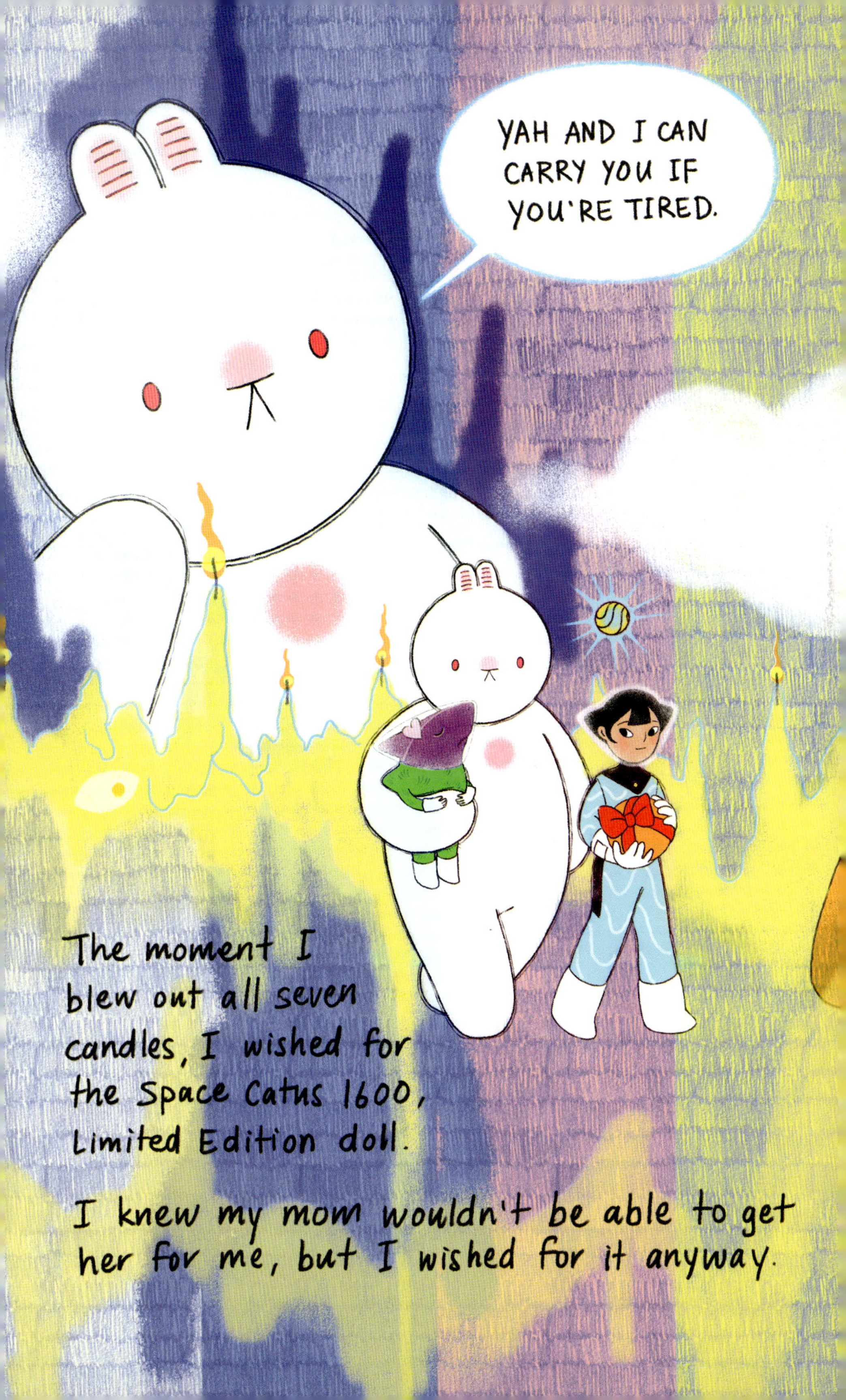
YAH AND I CAN CARRY YOU IF YOU'RE TIRED.
The moment I blew out all seven candles, I wished for the Space Catus 1600, Limited Edition doll.
I knew my mom wouldn't be able to get her for me, but I wished for it anyway.

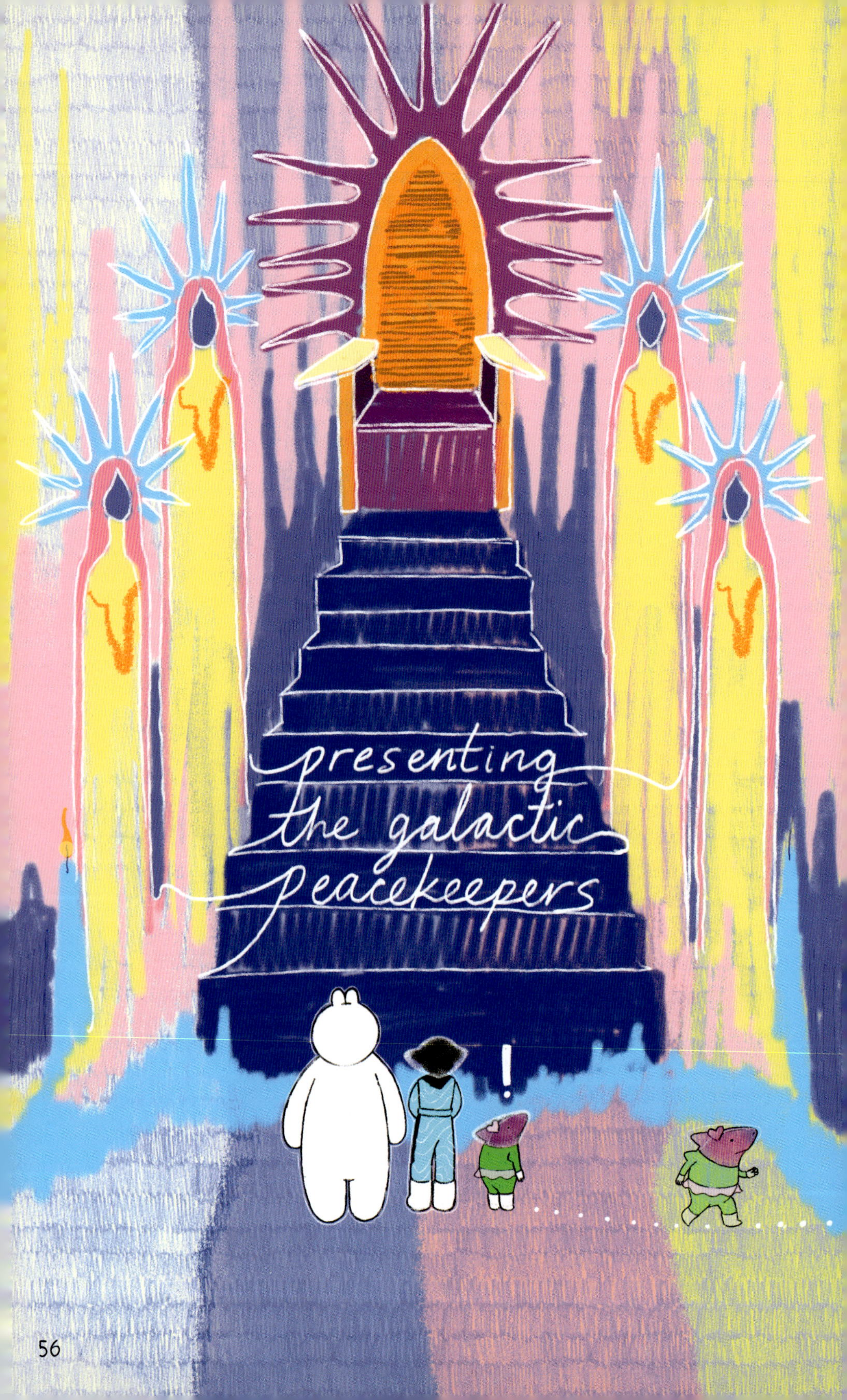
presenting
the galactic
peacekeepers
!

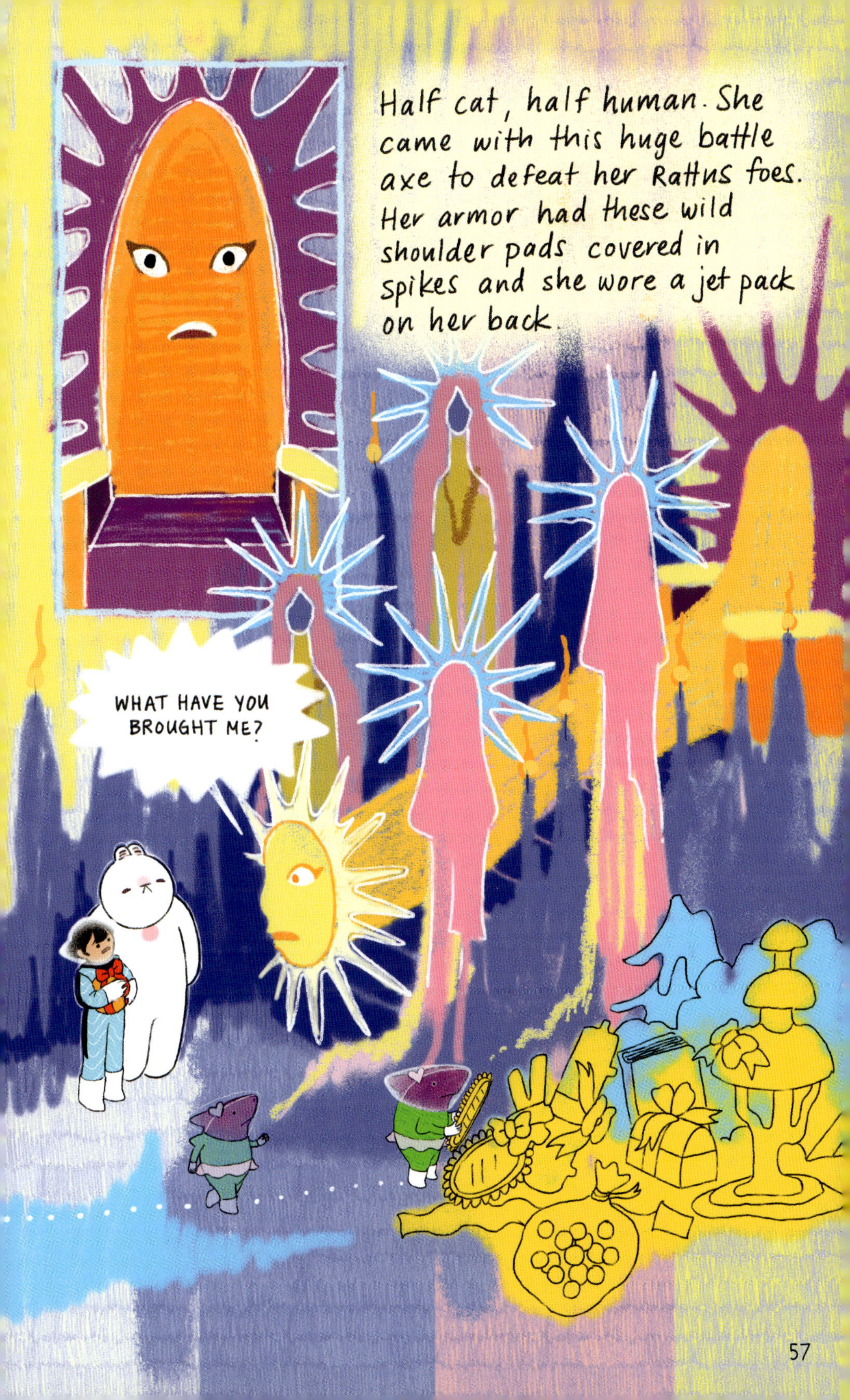
Half cat, half human. She came with this huge battle axe to defeat her Rattus foes. Her armor had these wild shoulder pads covered in spikes and she wore a jet pack on her back.
WHAT HAVE YOU BROUGHT ME?

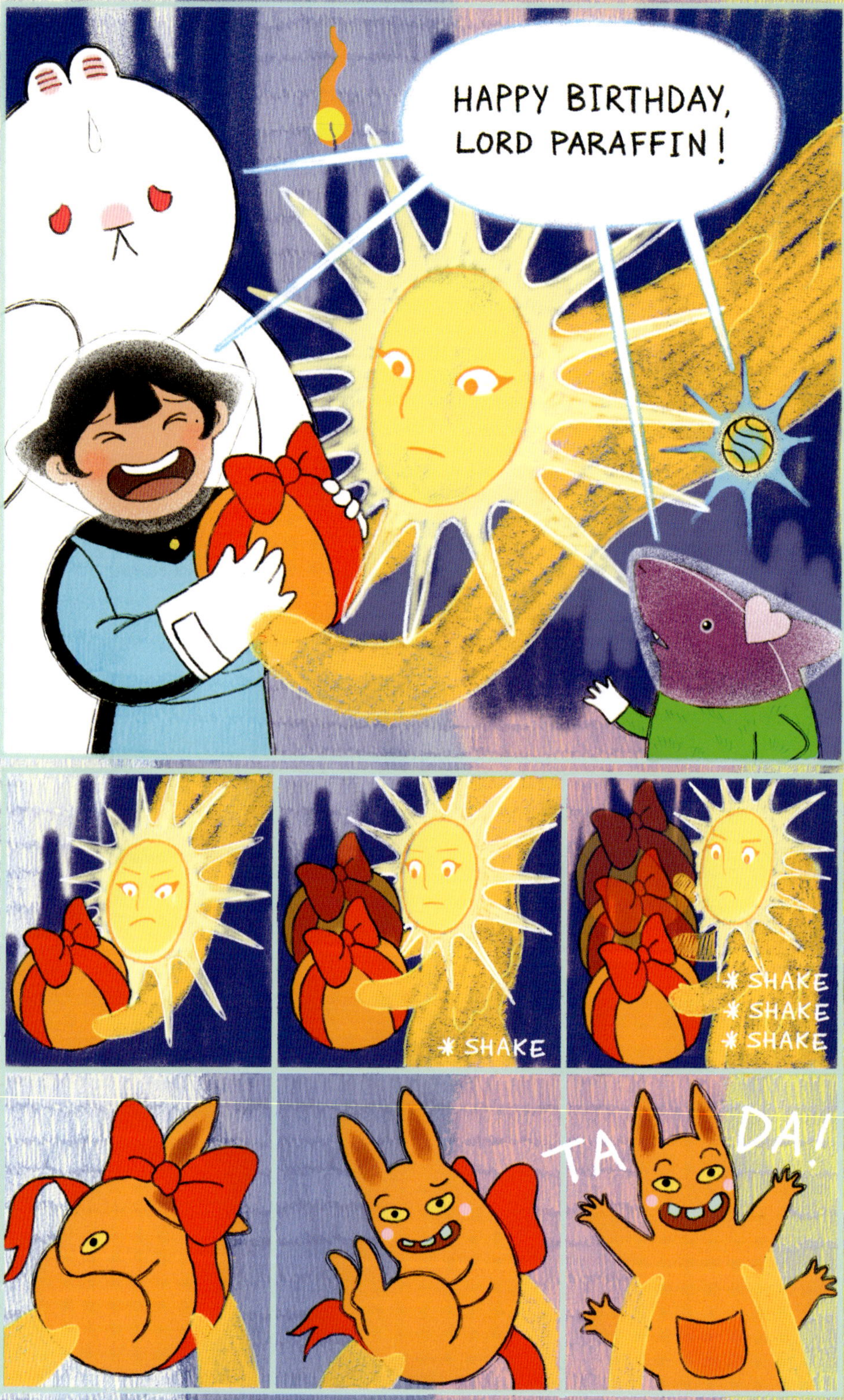

HAPPY BIRTHDAY, LORD PARAFFIN!
* SHAKE
* SHAKE
* SHAKE
* SHAKE
TA DA!

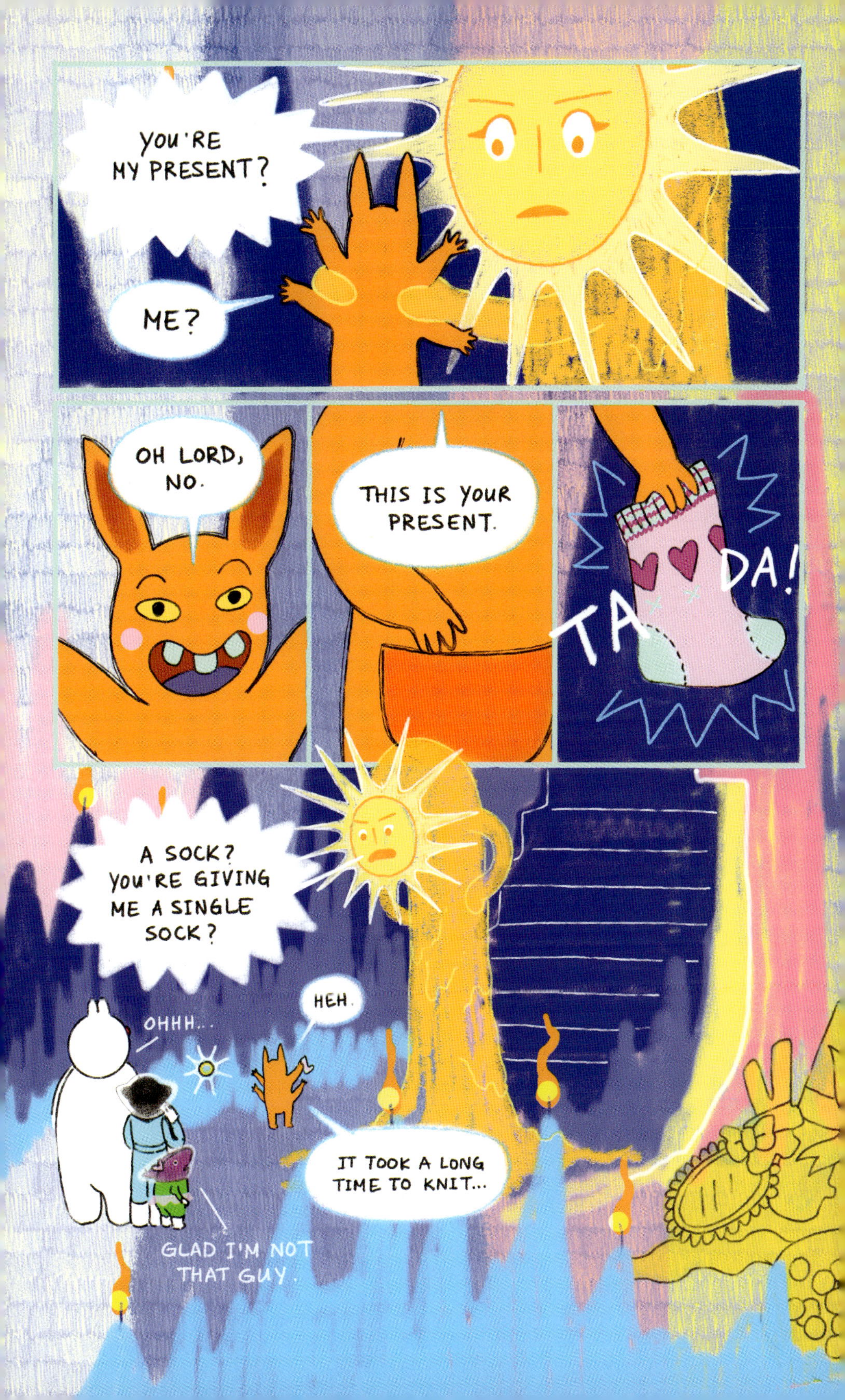
YOU'RE MY PRESENT?
ME?
OH LORD, NO.
THIS IS YOUR PRESENT.
TA DA!
A SOCK? YOU'RE GIVING ME A SINGLE SOCK?
OHHH...
HEH.
IT TOOK A LONG TIME TO KNIT...
GLAD I'M NOT THAT GUY.

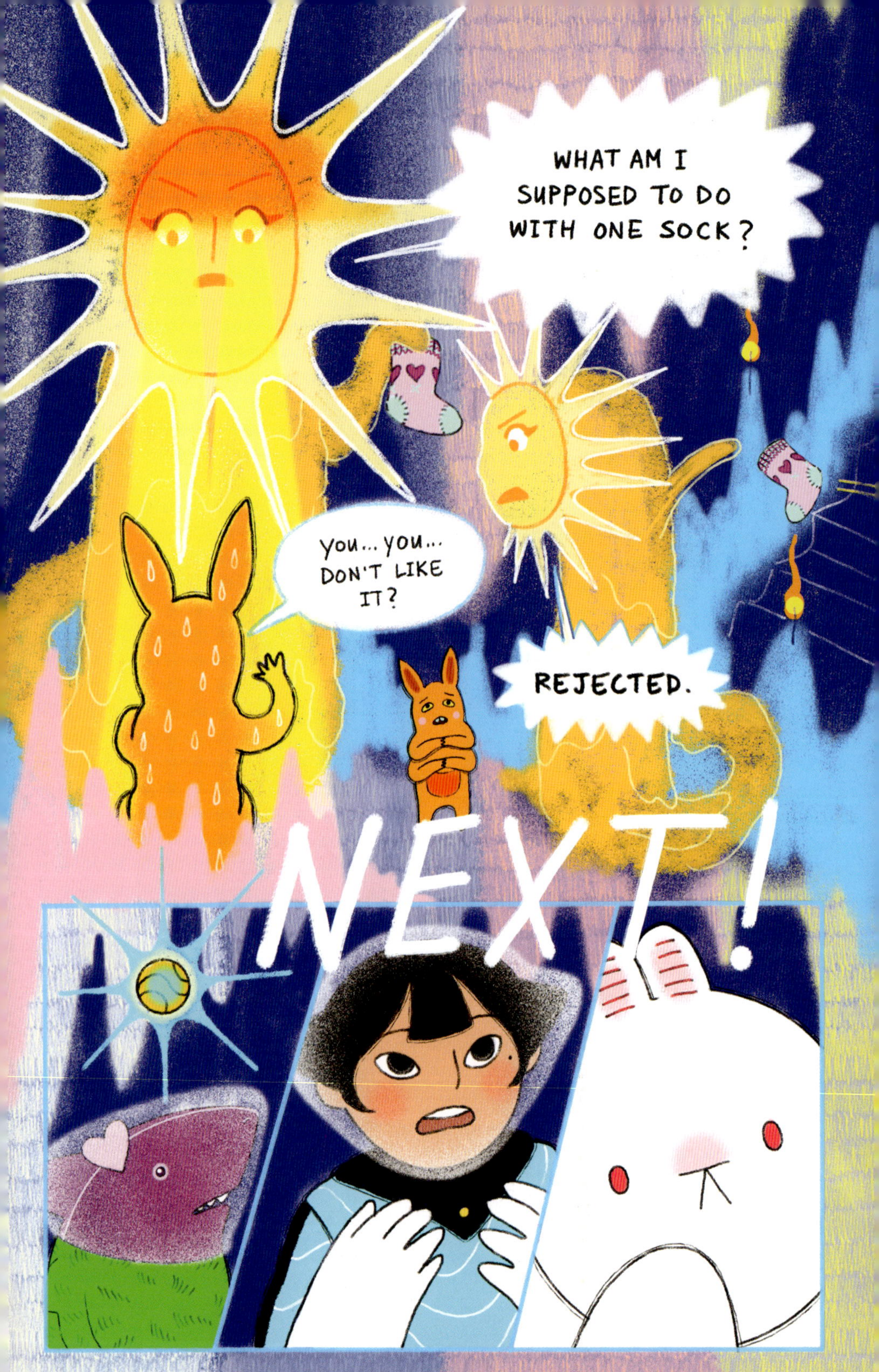
WHAT AM I SUPPOSED TO DO WITH ONE SOCK?
YOU... YOU... DON'T LIKE IT?
REJECTED.
NEXT!

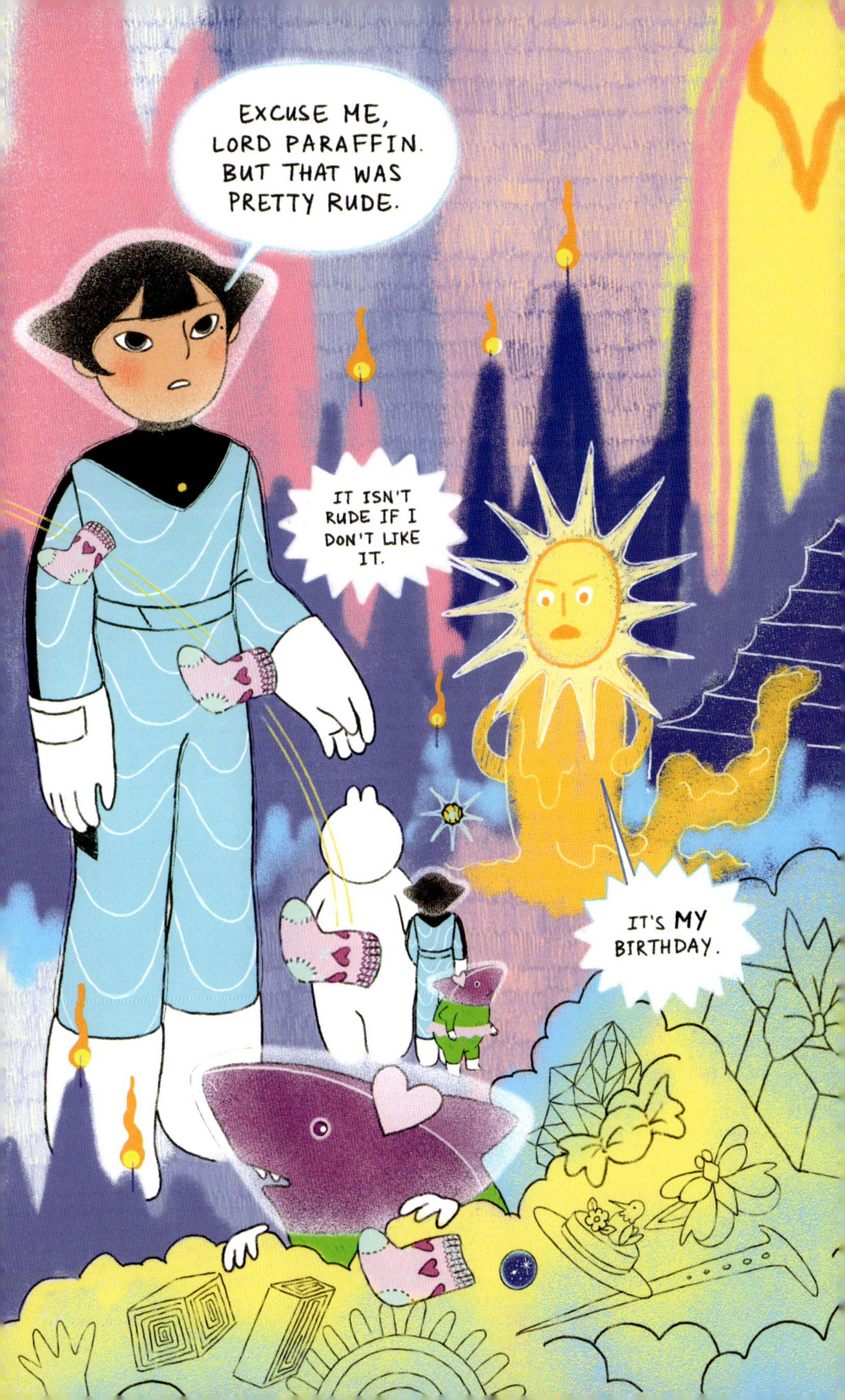
EXCUSE ME, LORD PARAFFIN. BUT THAT WAS PRETTY RUDE.
IT ISN'T RUDE IF I DON'T LIKE IT.
IT'S MY BIRTHDAY.

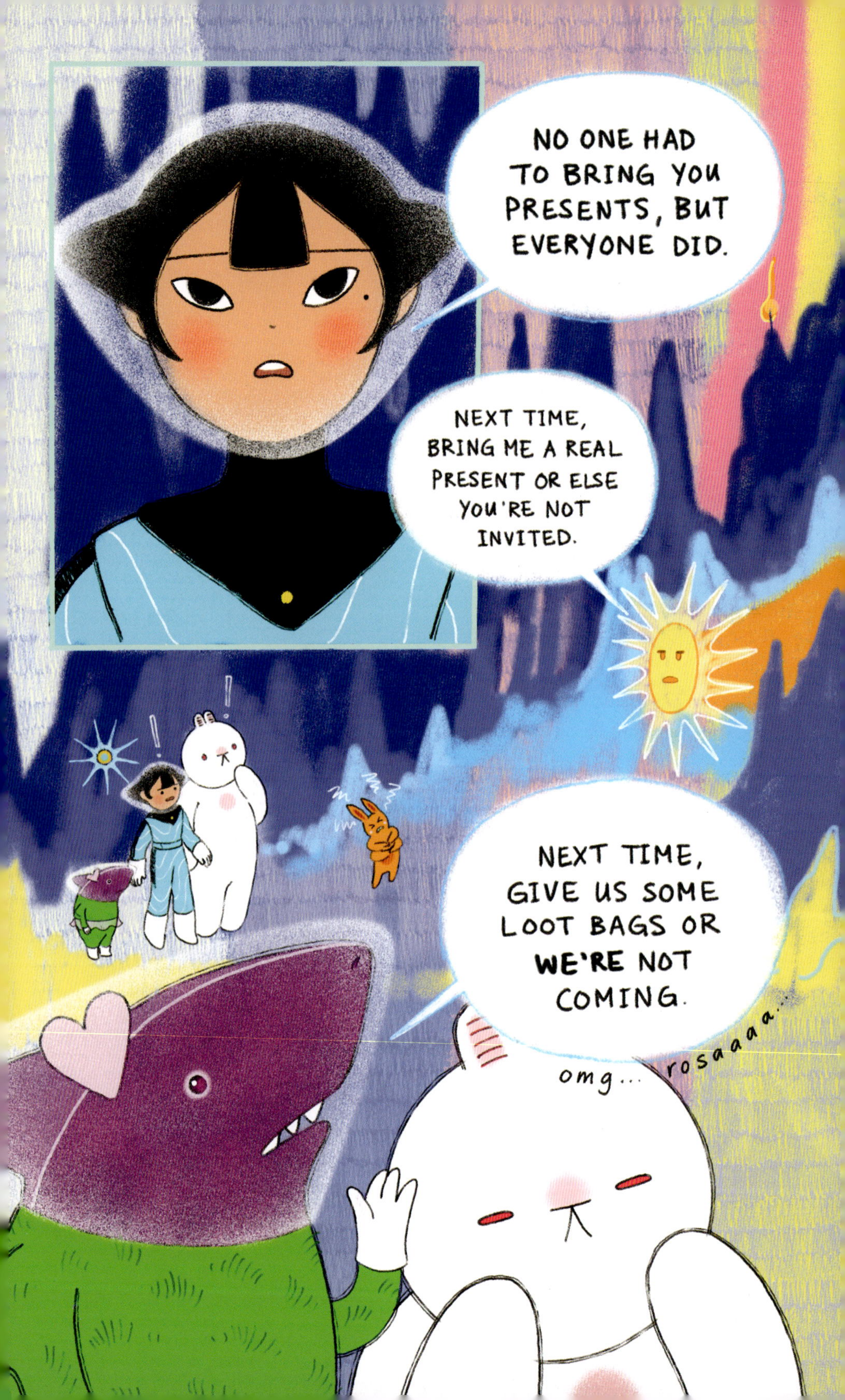
NO ONE HAD TO BRING YOU PRESENTS, BUT EVERYONE DID.
NEXT TIME, BRING ME A REAL PRESENT OR ELSE YOU'RE NOT INVITED.
NEXT TIME, GIVE US SOME LOOT BAGS OR **WE'RE** NOT COMING.
omg...
rosaaaa...

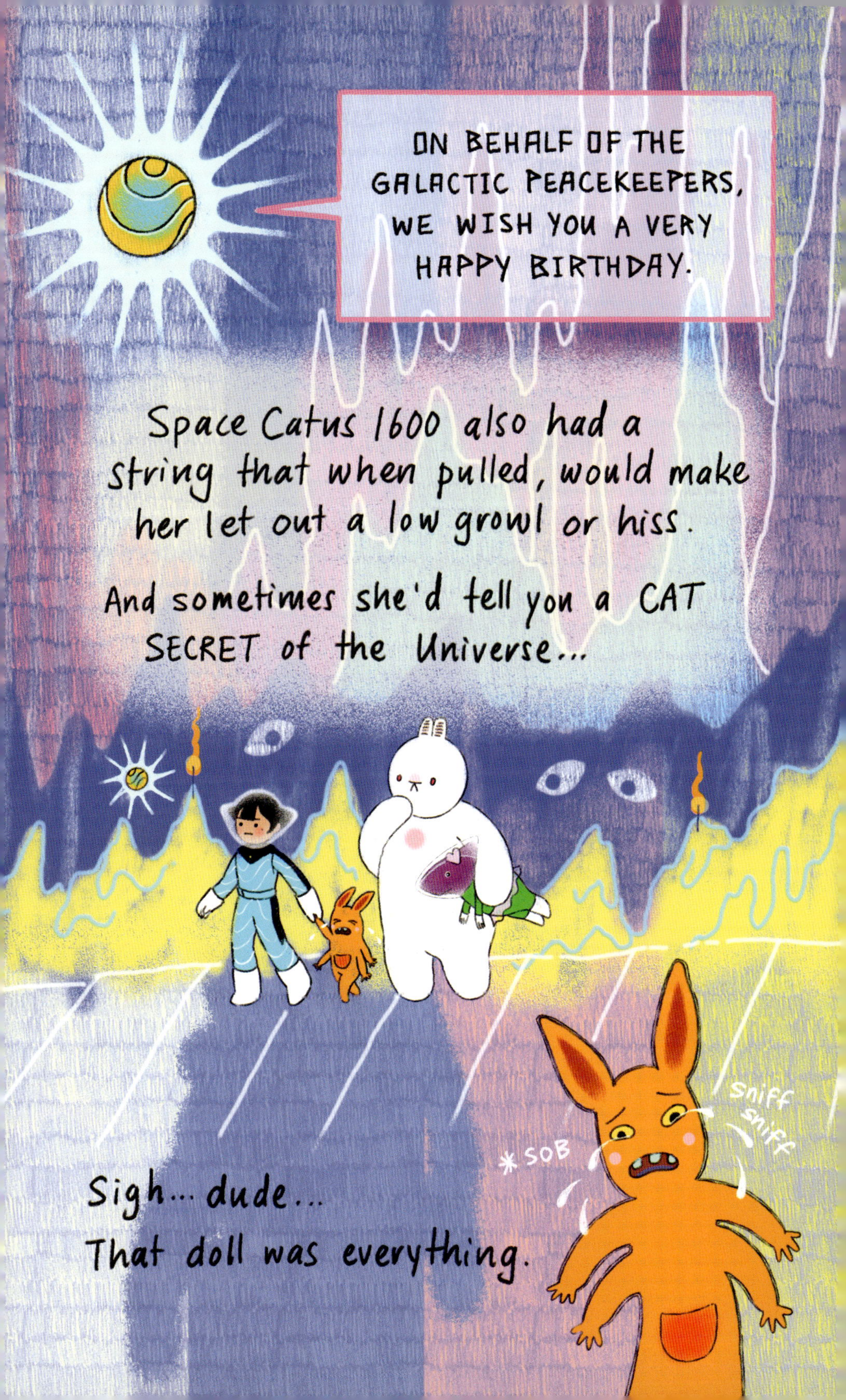
ON BEHALF OF THE GALACTIC PEACEKEEPERS, WE WISH YOU A VERY HAPPY BIRTHDAY.
Space Catus 1600 also had a string that when pulled, would make her let out a low growl or hiss.
And sometimes she'd tell you a CAT SECRET of the Universe...
Sigh... dude...
That doll was everything.
*SOB
sniff sniff

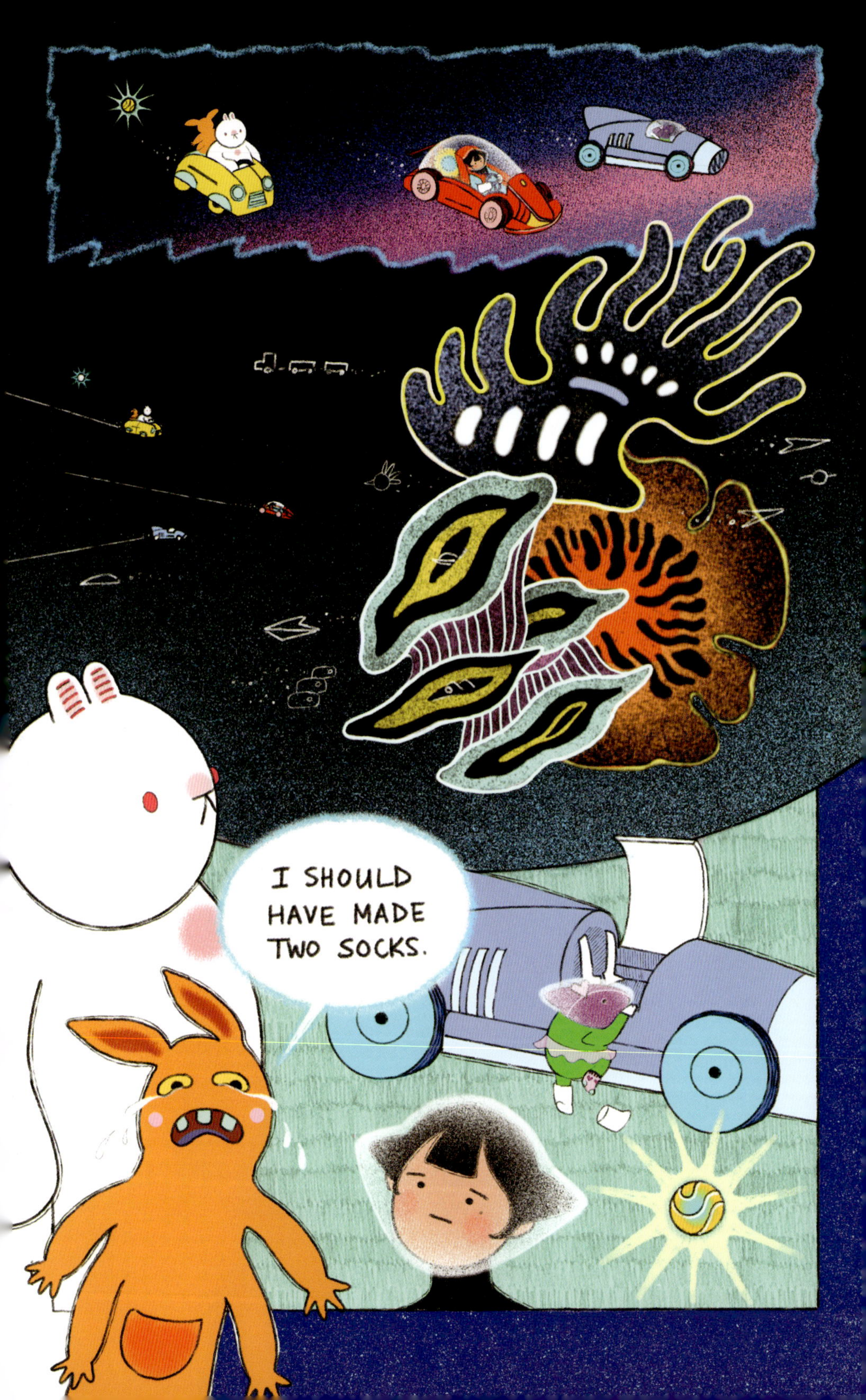
I SHOULD HAVE MADE TWO SOCKS.

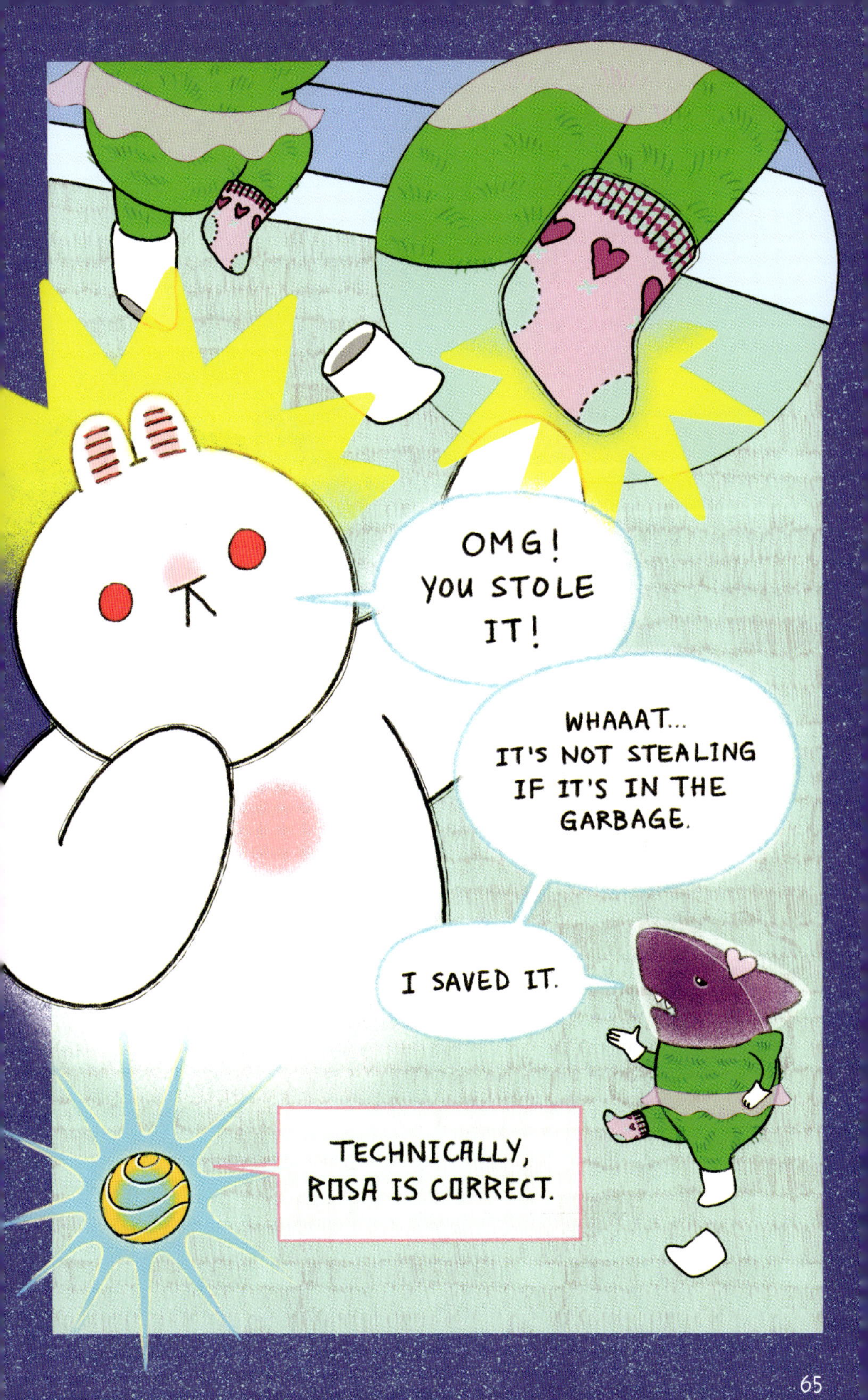
OMG! YOU STOLE IT!
WHAAAT... IT'S NOT STEALING IF IT'S IN THE GARBAGE.
I SAVED IT.
TECHNICALLY, ROSA IS CORRECT.

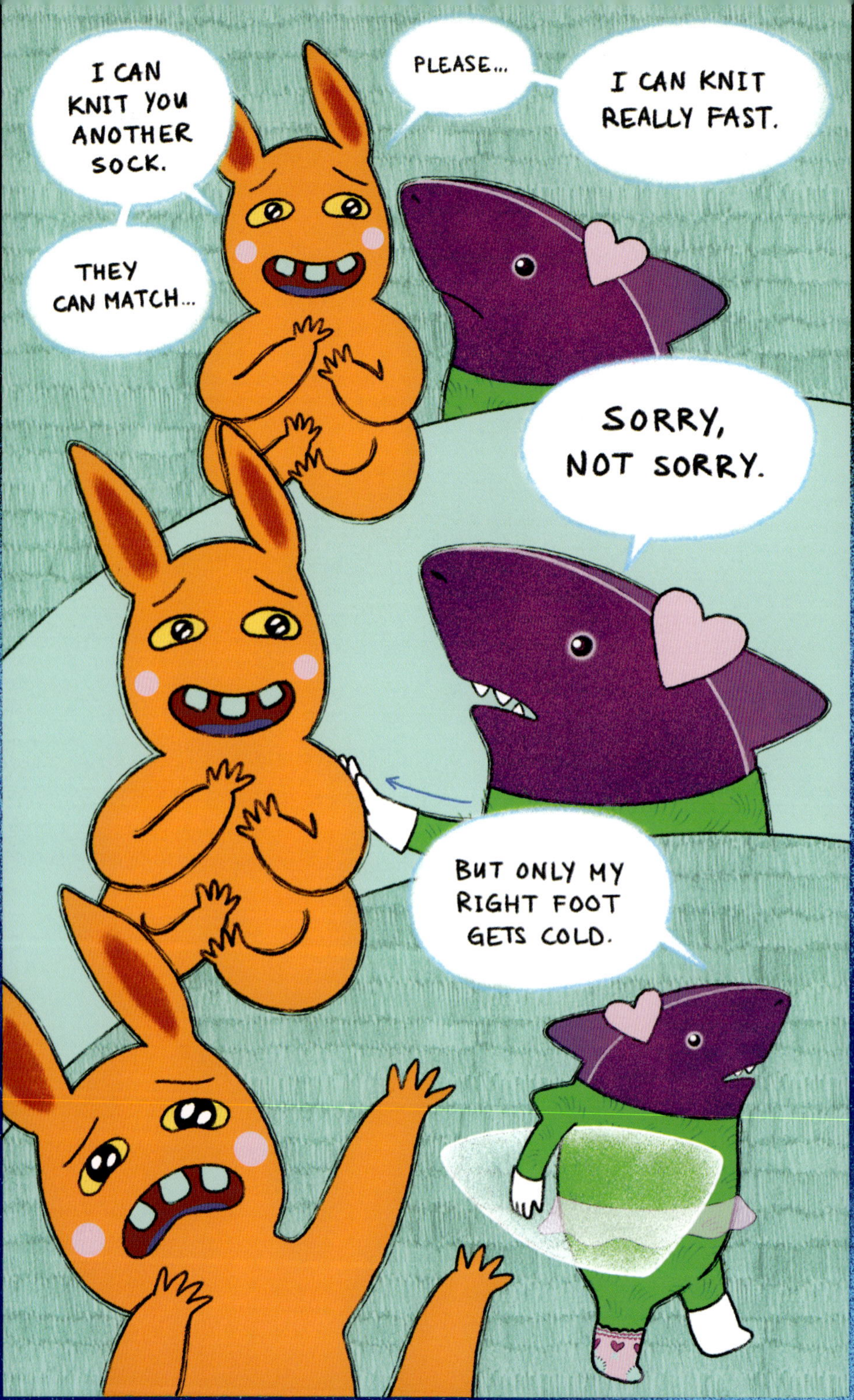
I CAN KNIT YOU ANOTHER SOCK.
THEY CAN MATCH...
PLEASE...
I CAN KNIT REALLY FAST.
SORRY, NOT SORRY.
BUT ONLY MY RIGHT FOOT GETS COLD.

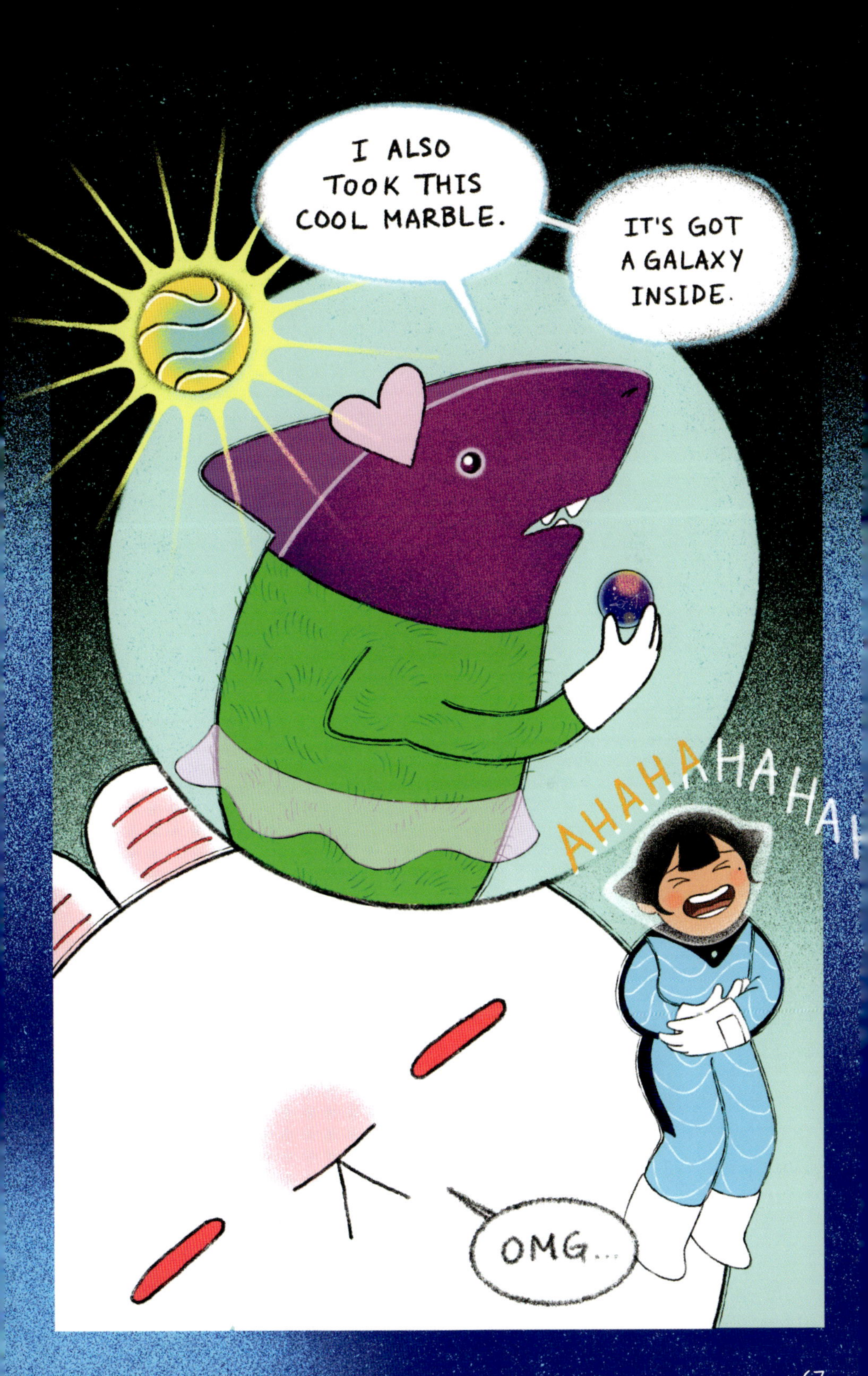
I ALSO TOOK THIS COOL MARBLE.
IT'S GOT A GALAXY INSIDE.
AHAHAHAHAH
OMG...

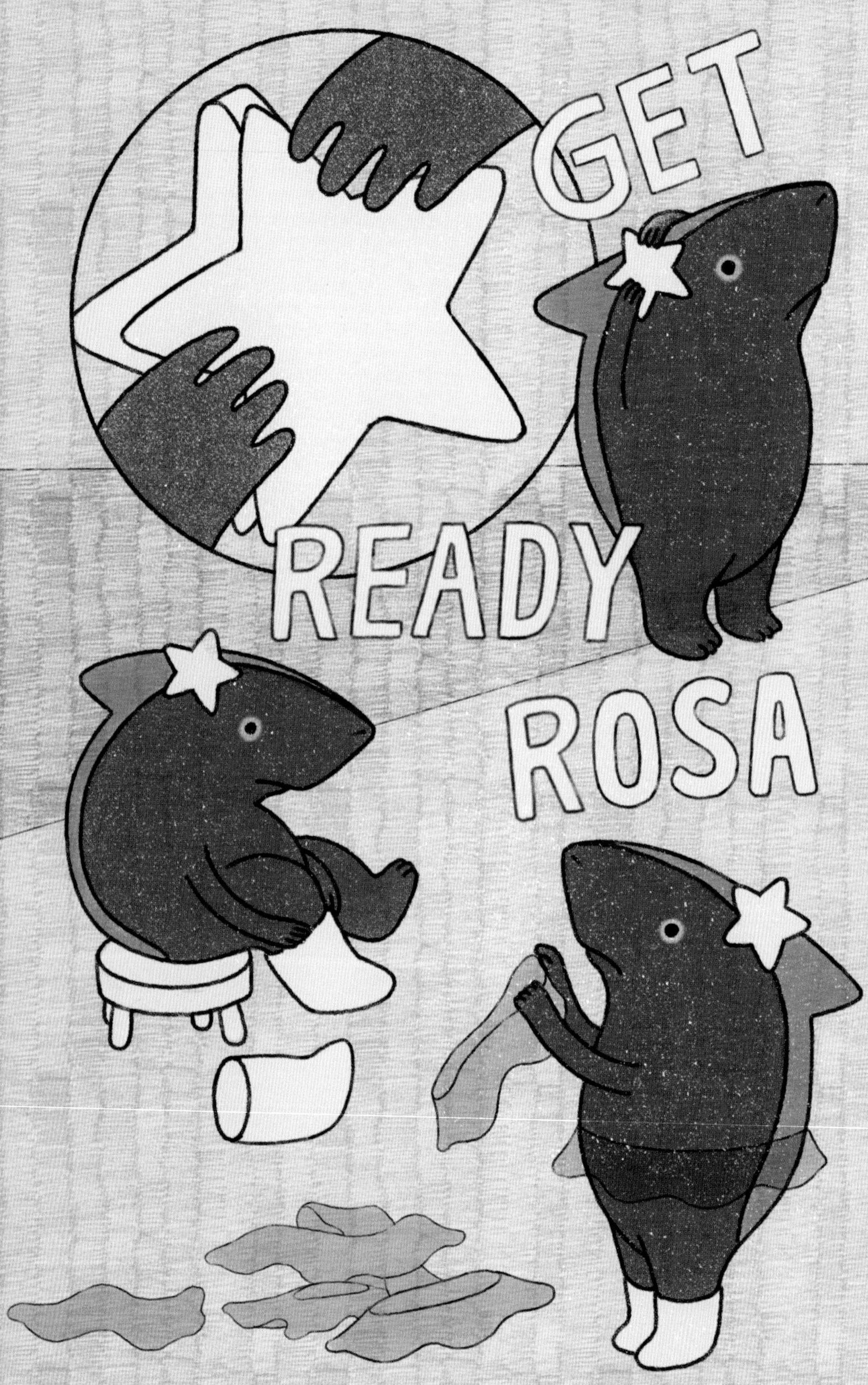
GET
READY
ROSA

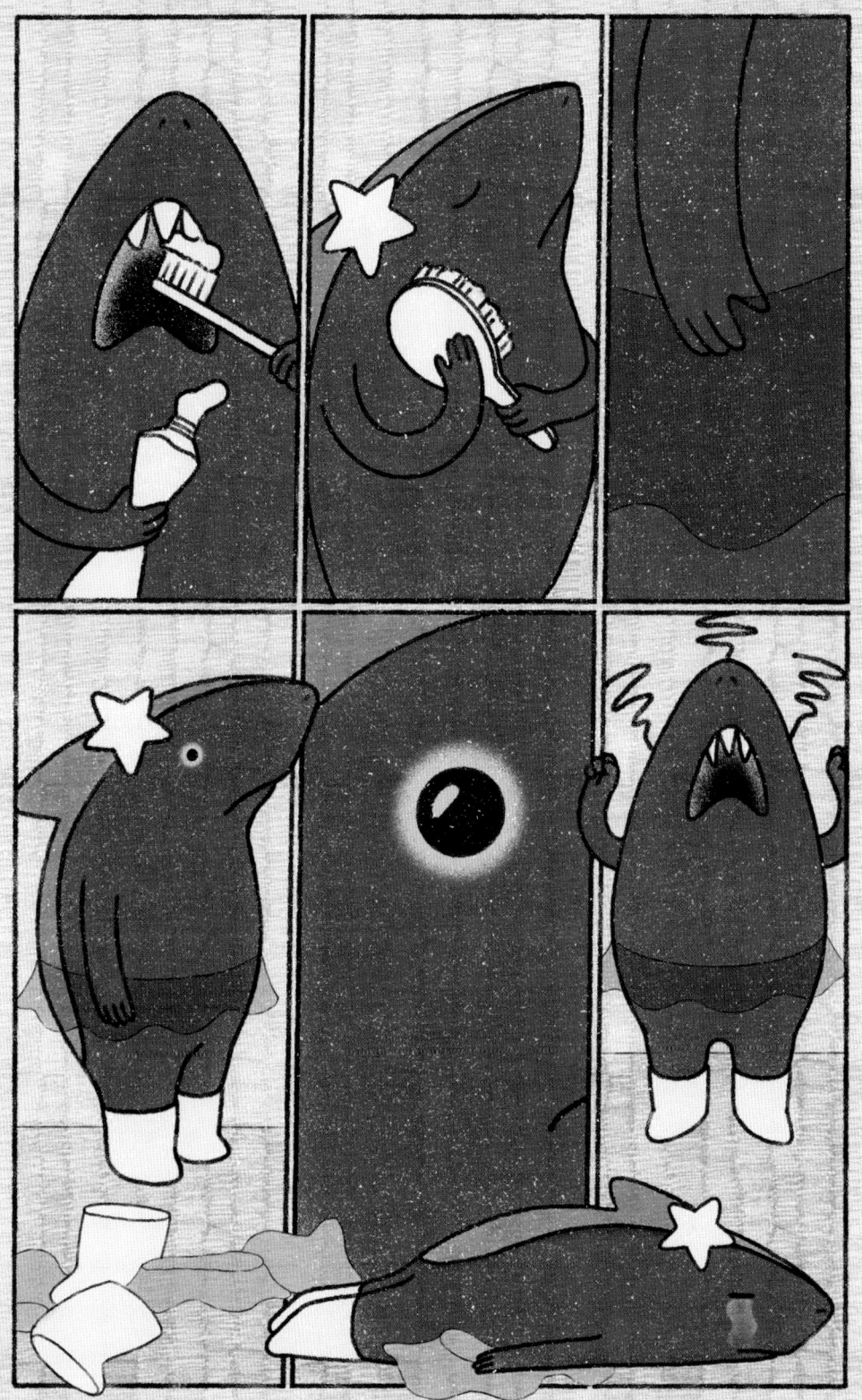

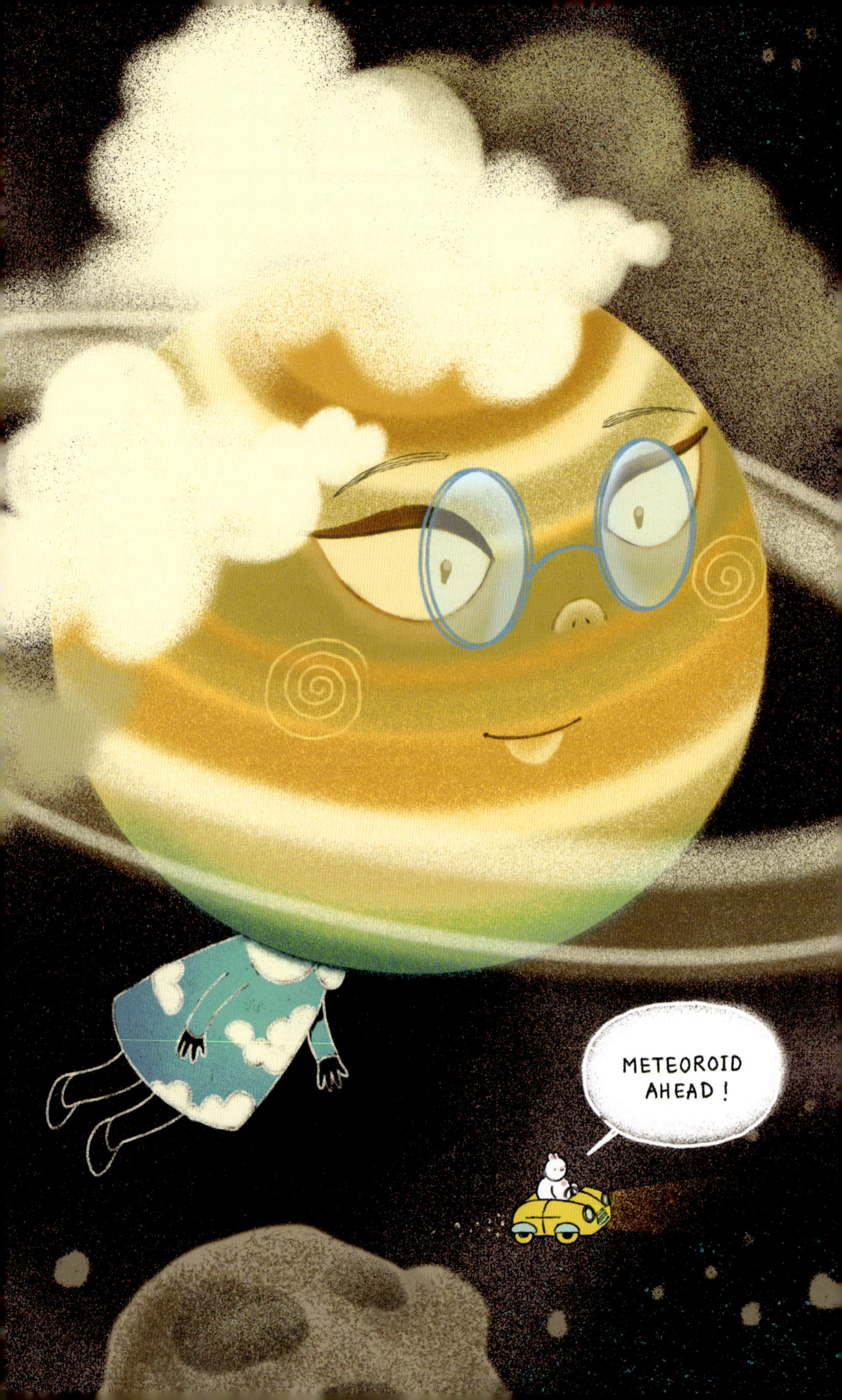
METEOROID AHEAD!

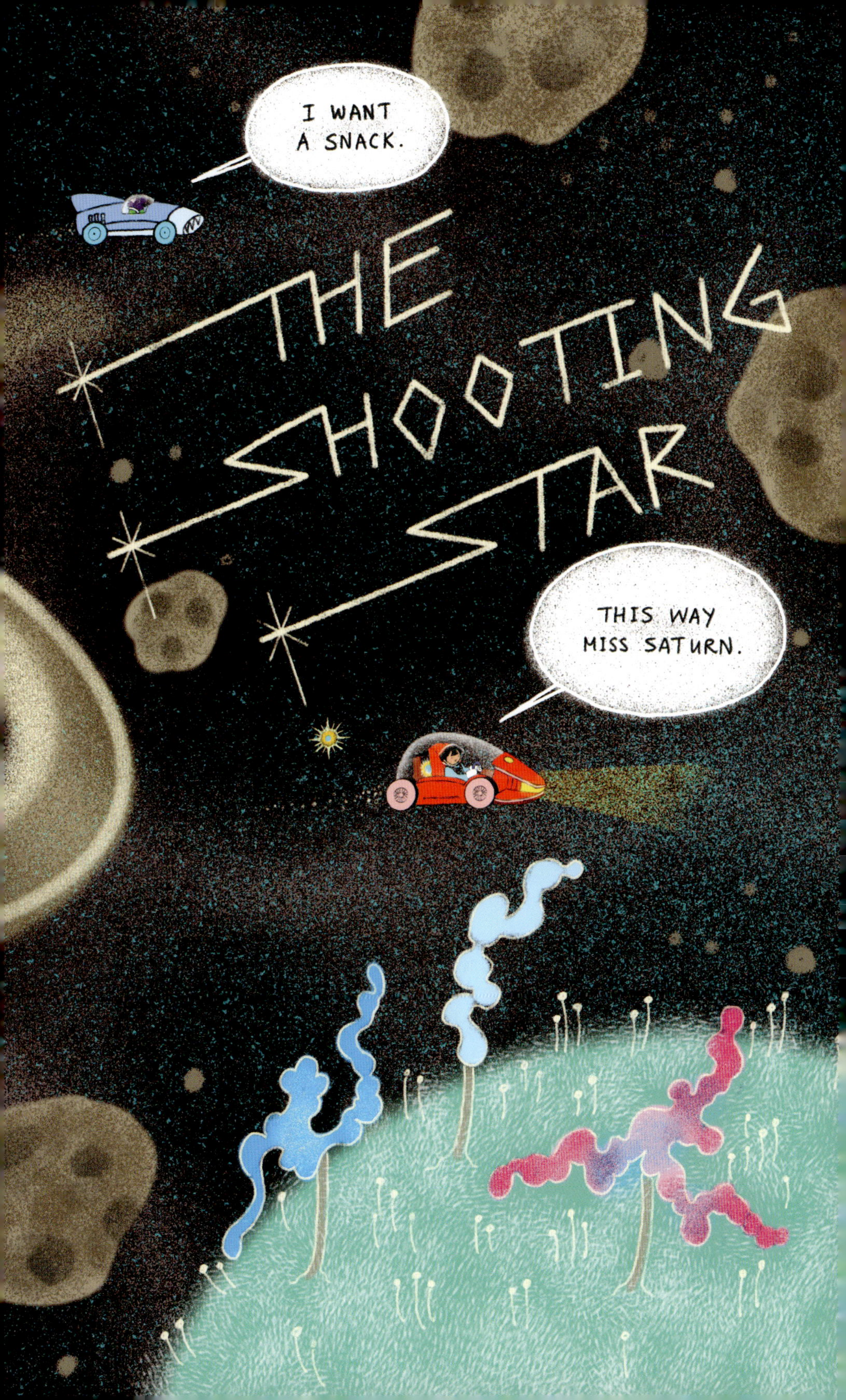
I WANT A SNACK.
THE SHOOTING STAR
THIS WAY MISS SATURN.

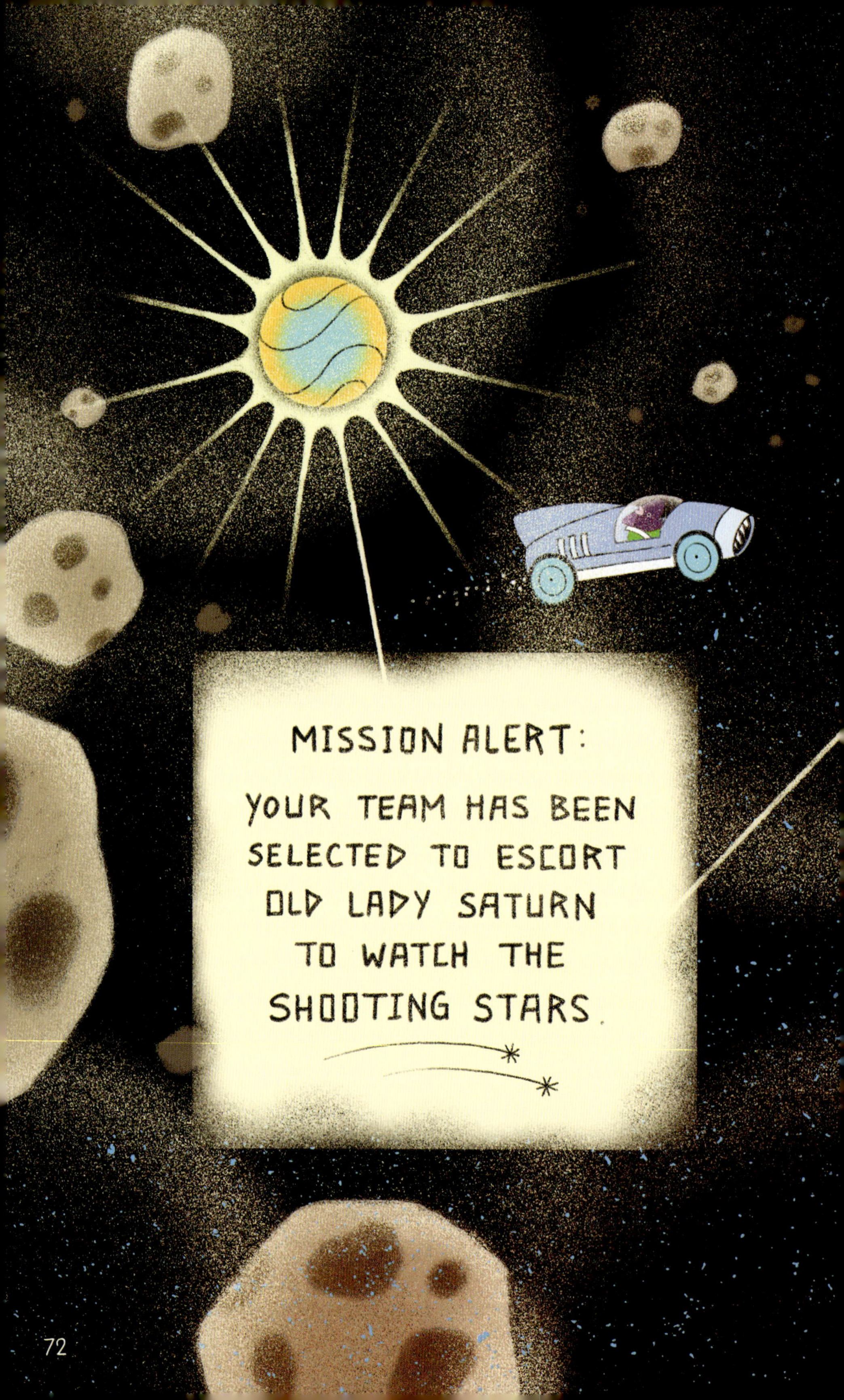
MISSION ALERT:
YOUR TEAM HAS BEEN SELECTED TO ESCORT OLD LADY SATURN TO WATCH THE SHOOTING STARS.

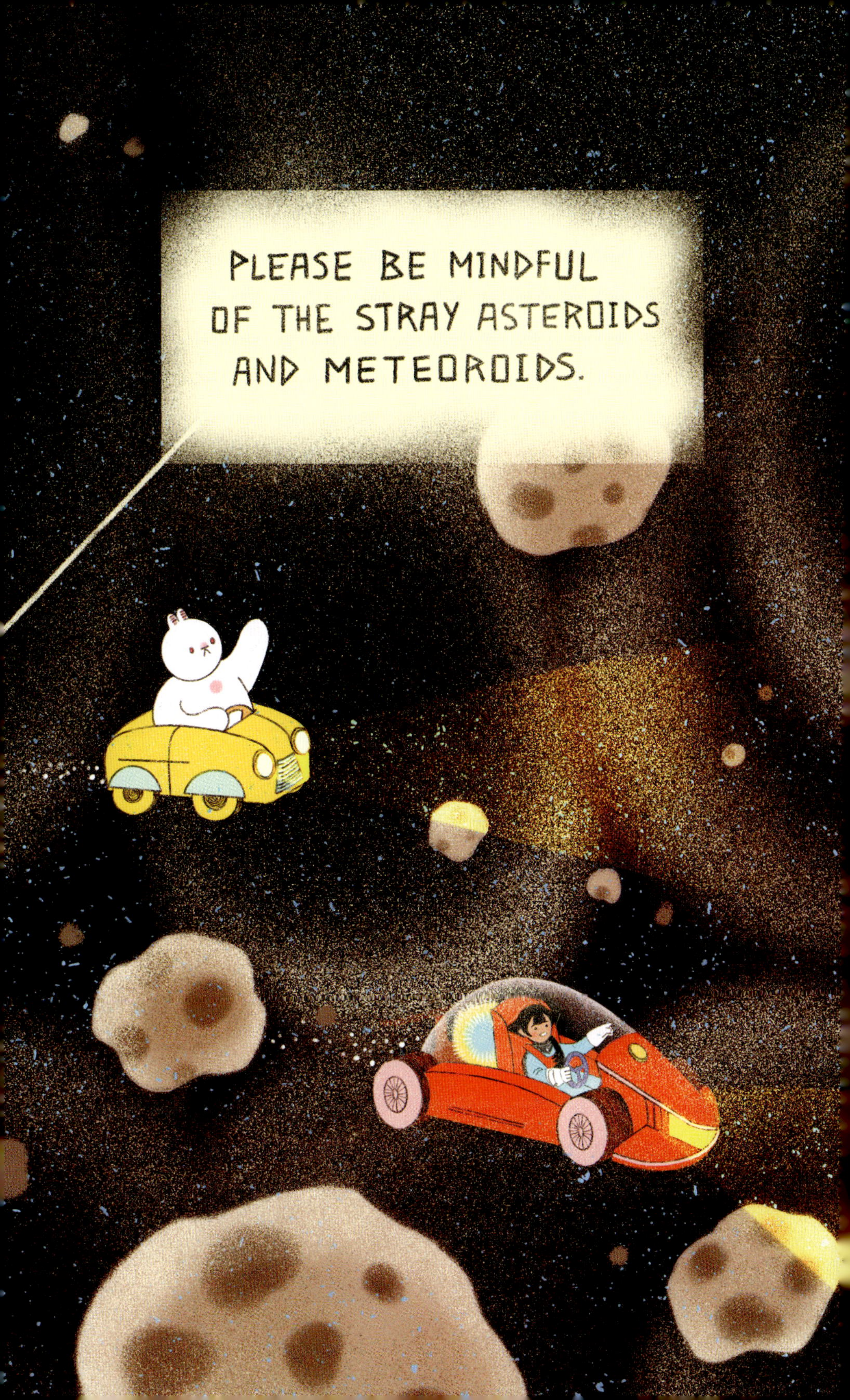
PLEASE BE MINDFUL OF THE STRAY ASTEROIDS AND METEOROIDS.

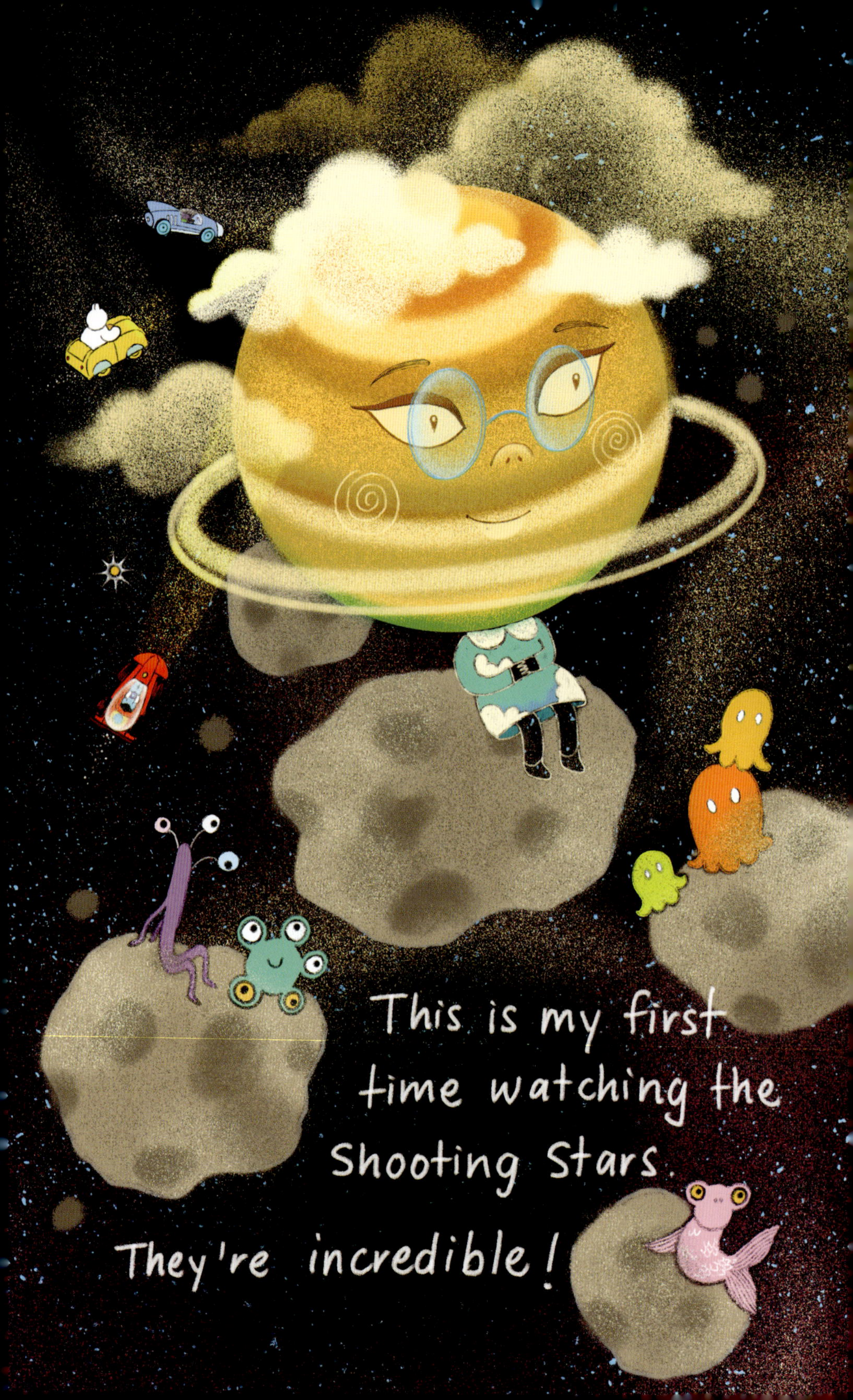

This is my first time watching the Shooting Stars.

They're incredible!

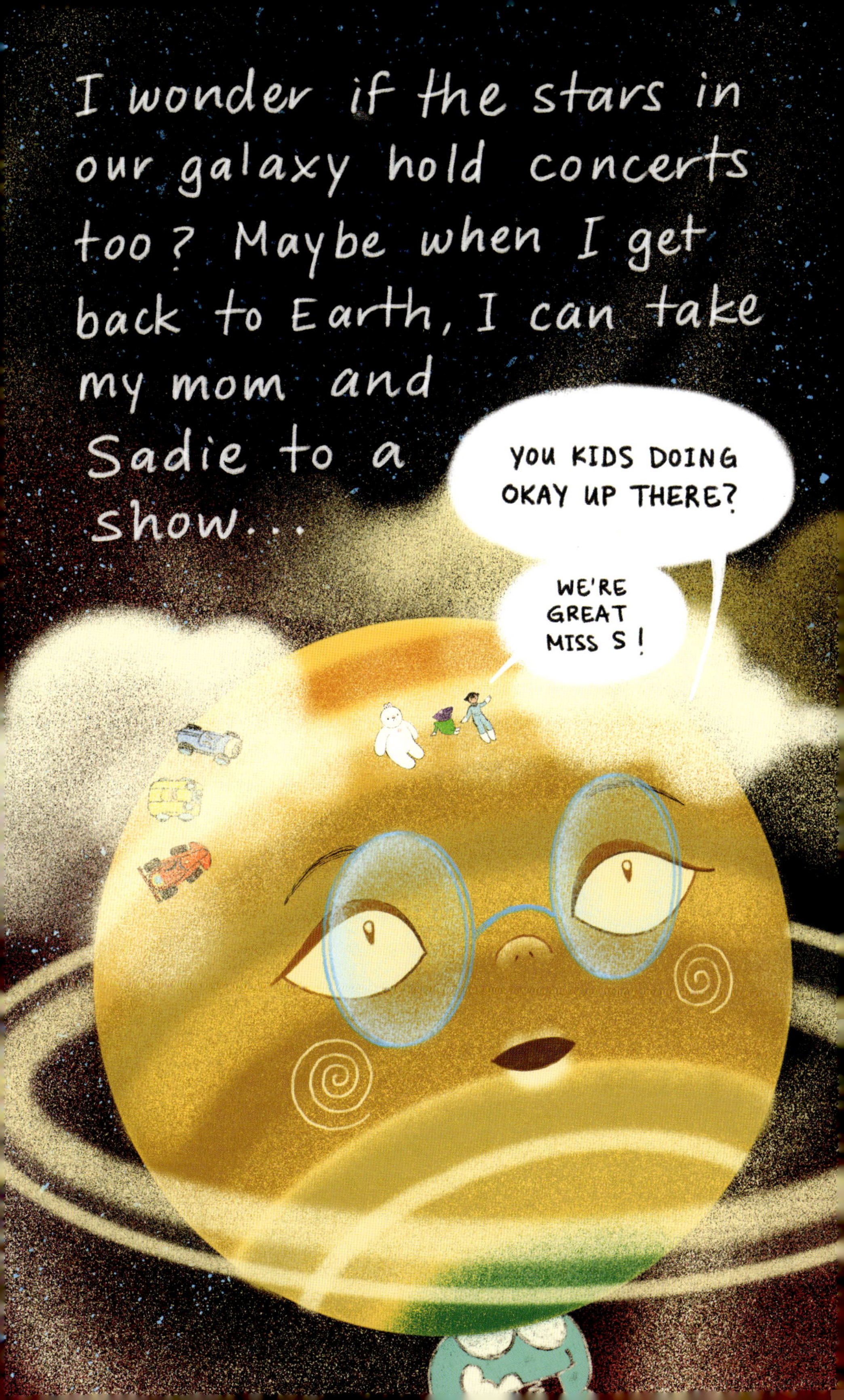
I wonder if the stars in our galaxy hold concerts too? Maybe when I get back to Earth, I can take my mom and Sadie to a show...
YOU KIDS DOING OKAY UP THERE?
WE'RE GREAT MISS S!

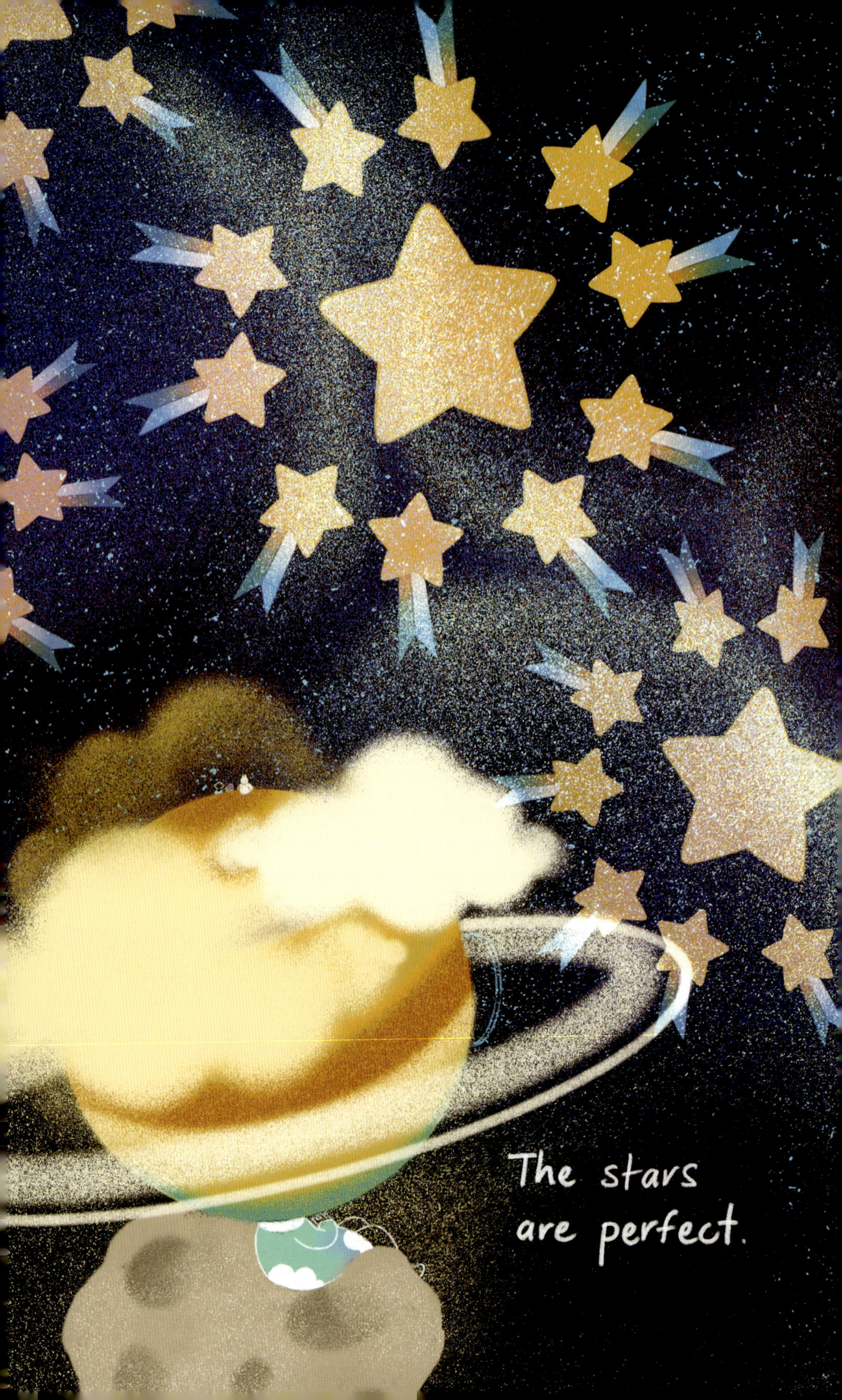

The stars are perfect.

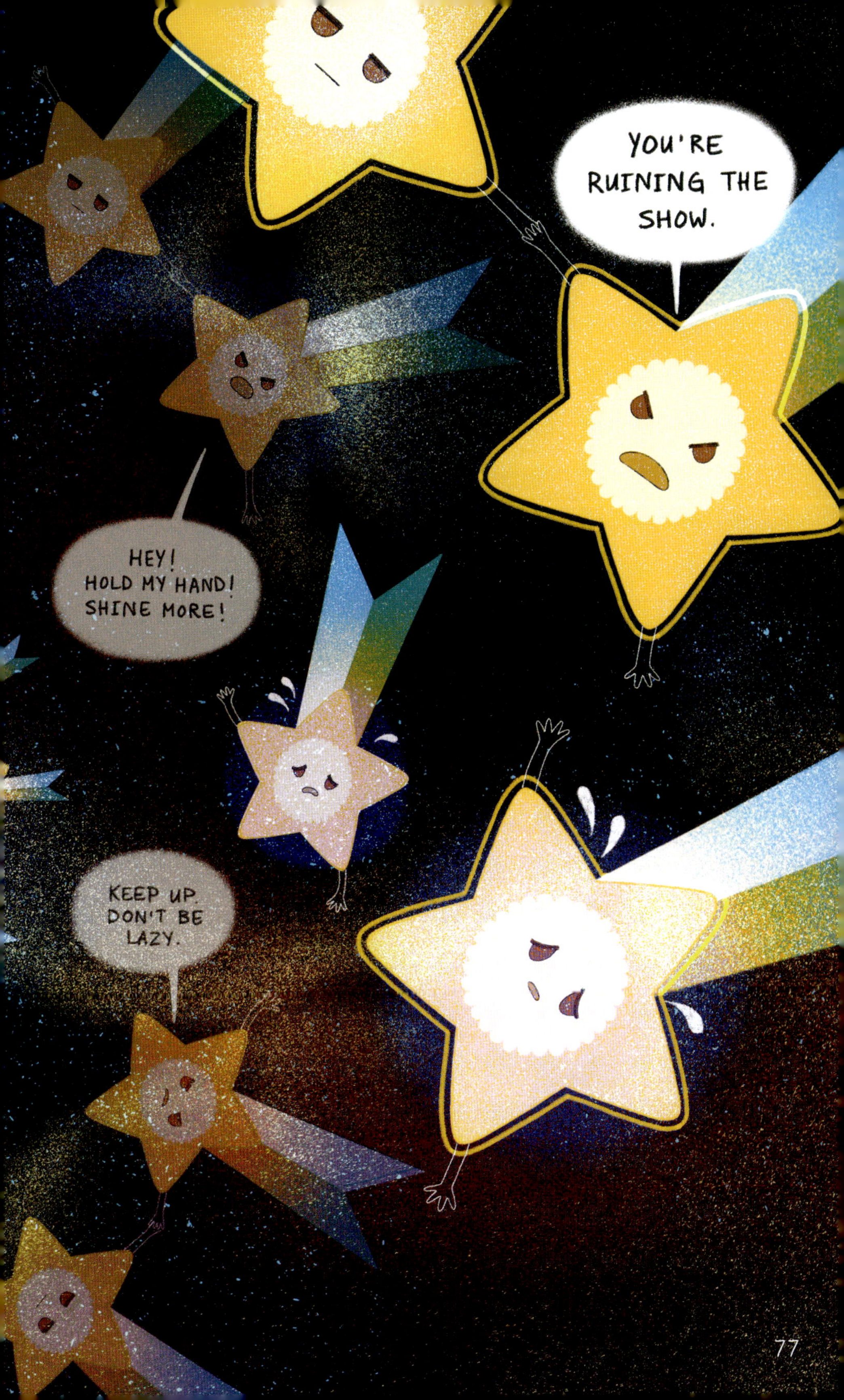
YOU'RE RUINING THE SHOW.
HEY! HOLD MY HAND! SHINE MORE!
KEEP UP. DON'T BE LAZY.

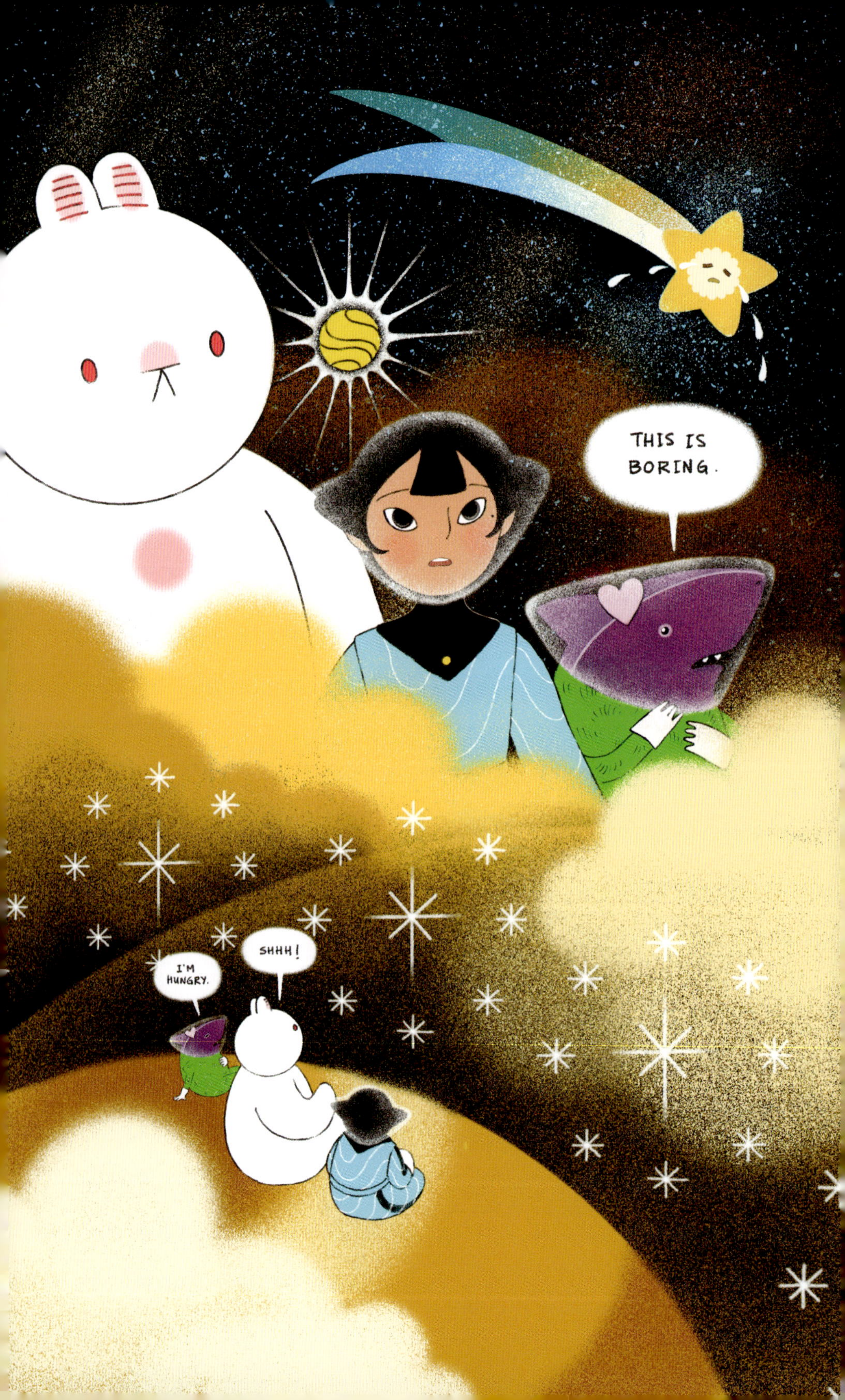
THIS IS BORING.
I'M HUNGRY.
SHHH!

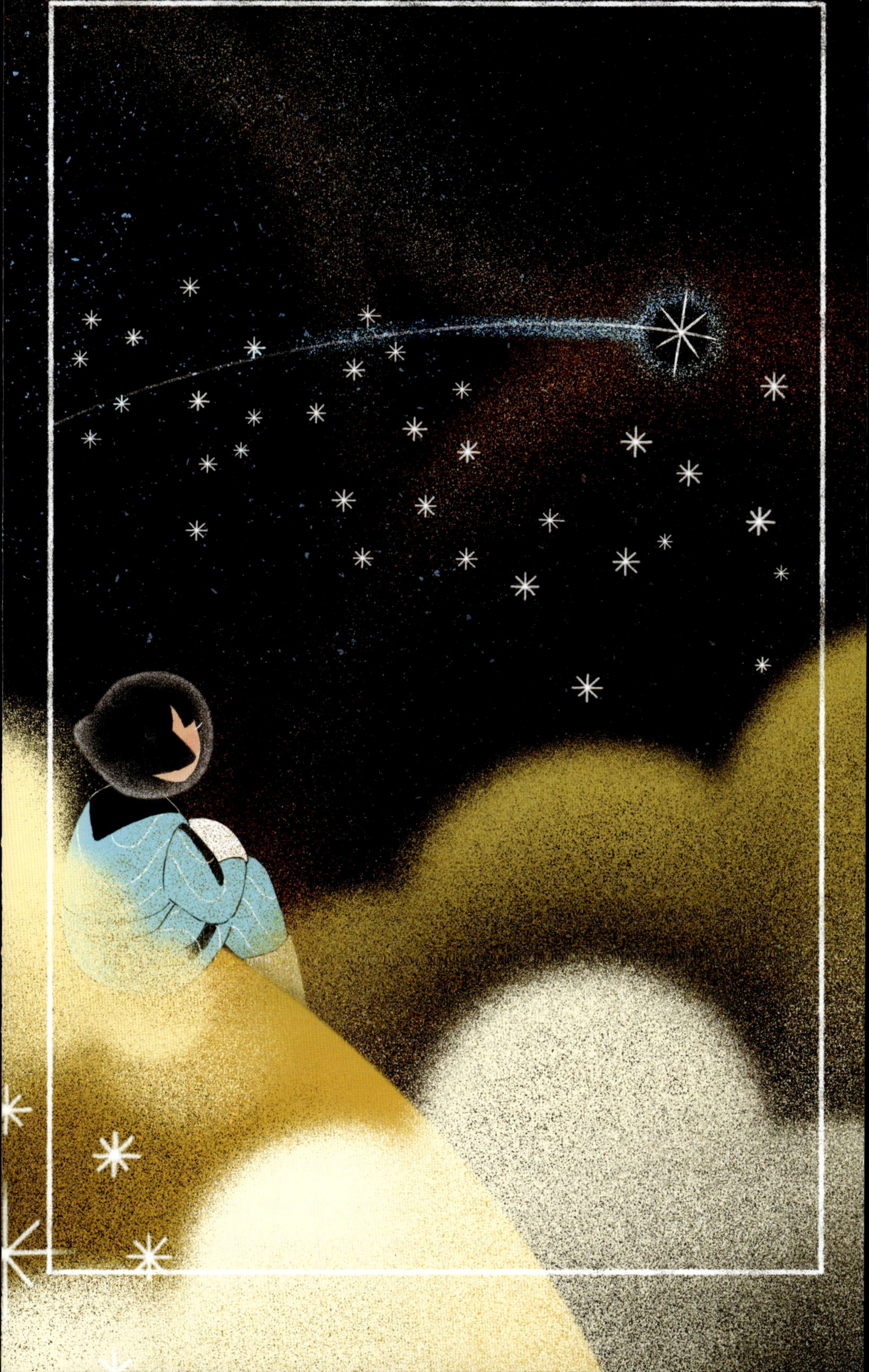

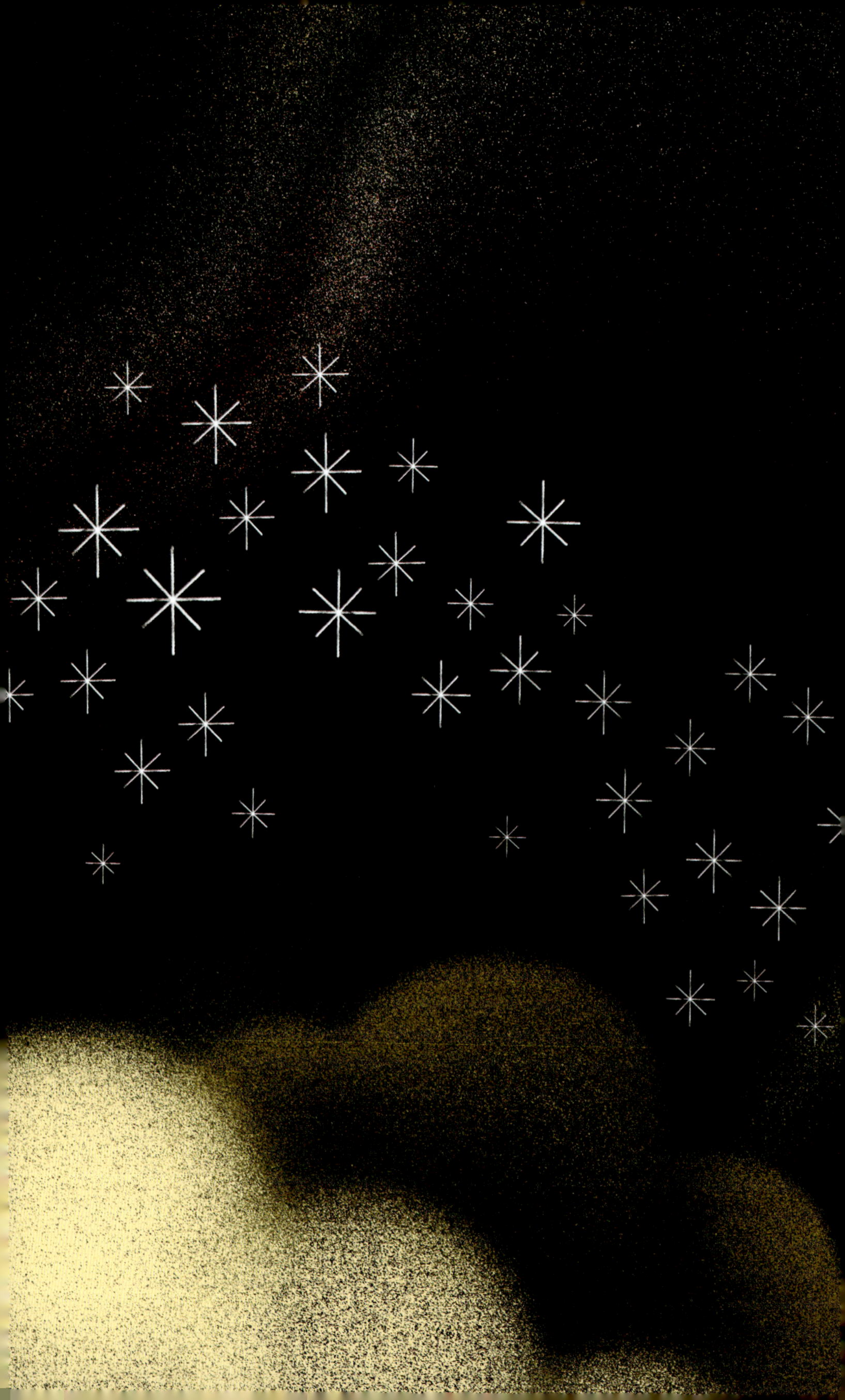

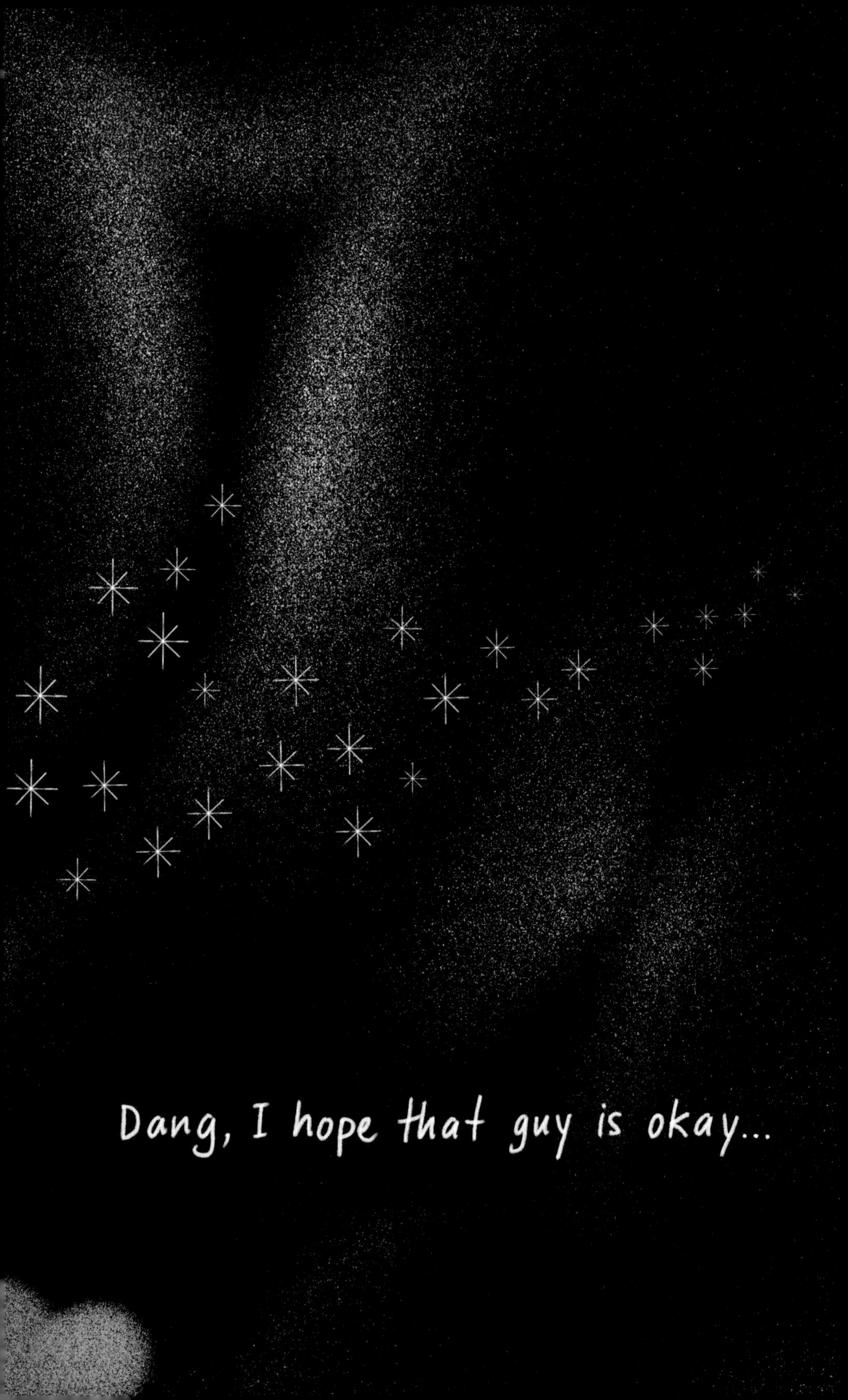
Dang, I hope that guy is okay...

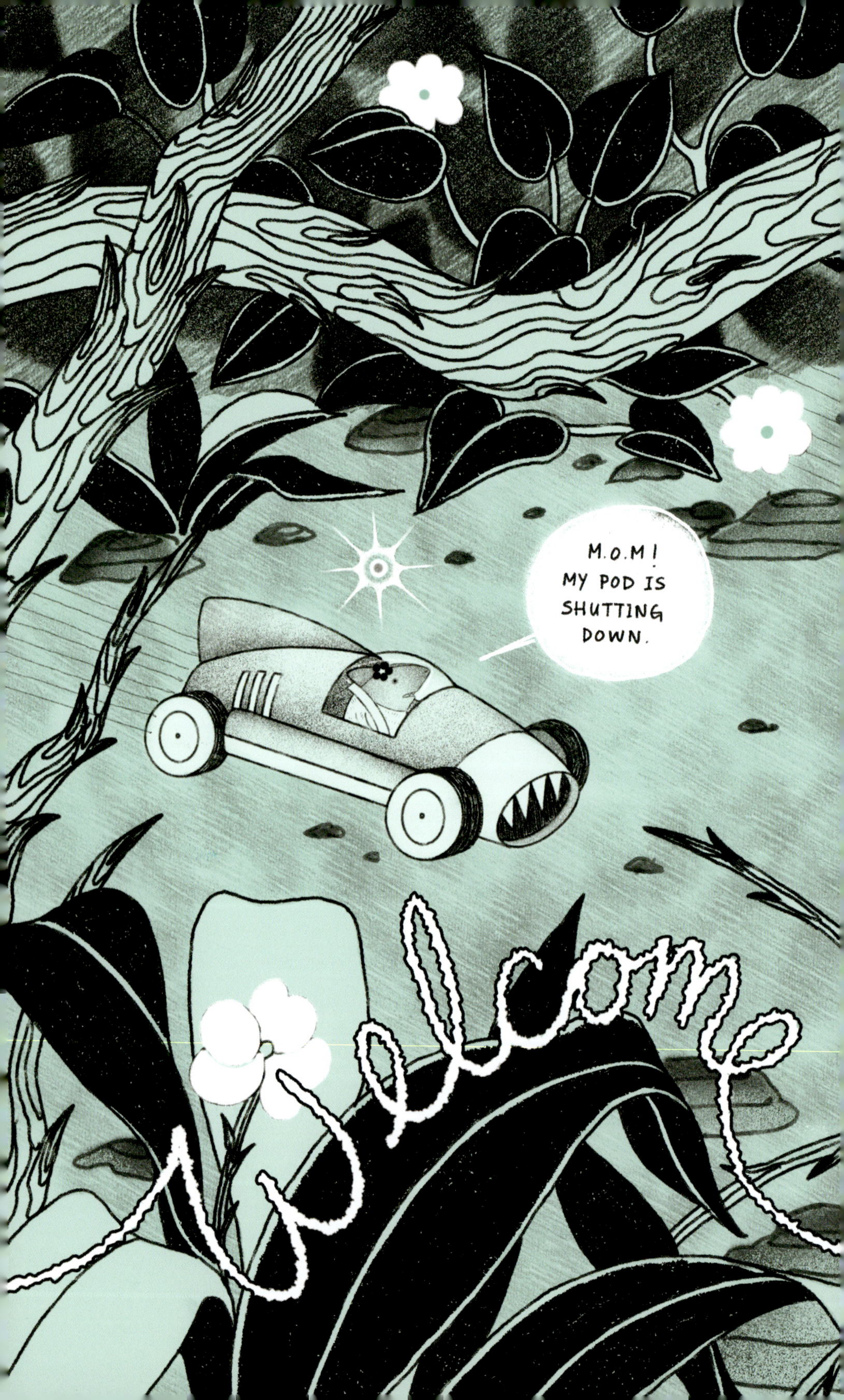
M.O.M!
MY POD IS
SHUTTING
DOWN.
Welcome

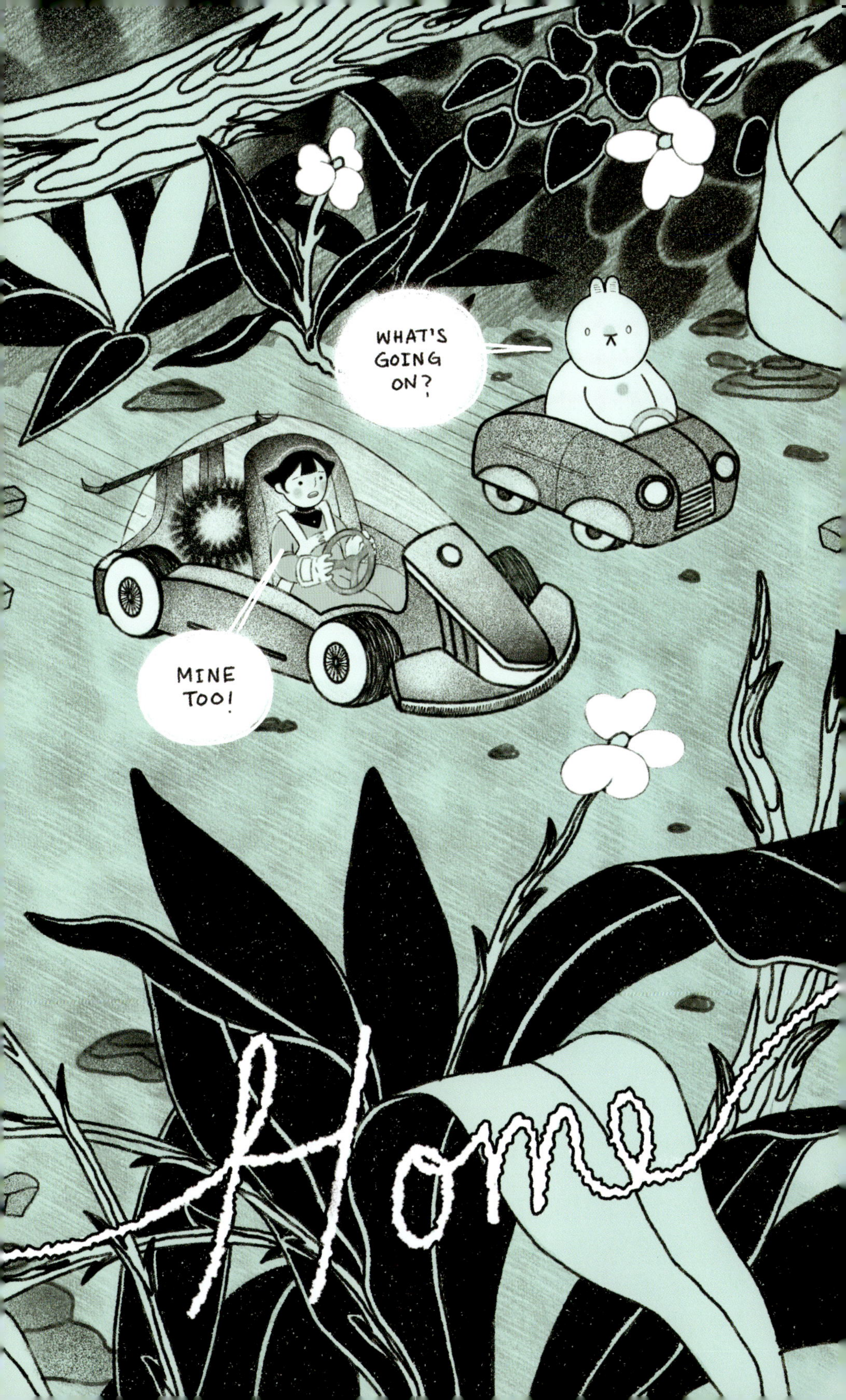
WHAT'S GOING ON?
MINE TOO!
Home

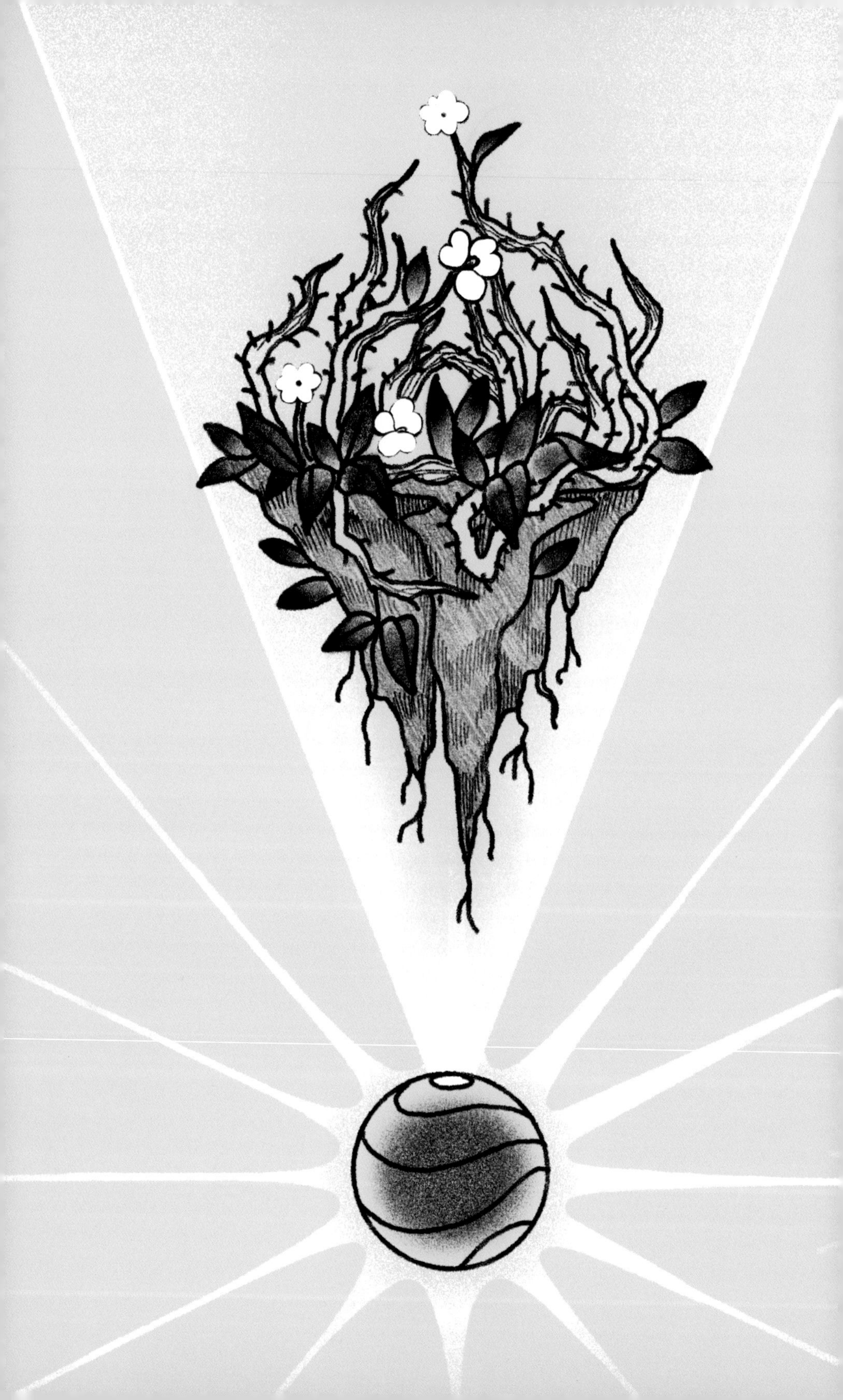

MISSION ALERT:

YOUR TEAM HAS BEEN SELECTED TO ASSIST THE PHASMATOIDS ON THE ISLAND OF VITIS.

DUE TO TERRITORIAL WARFARE, THEIR HOME PLANET HAS BEEN DAMAGED.

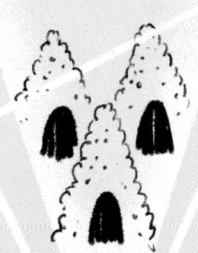

THIS IS A TEMPORARY PLACEMENT UNTIL REPAIRS ARE COMPLETED.

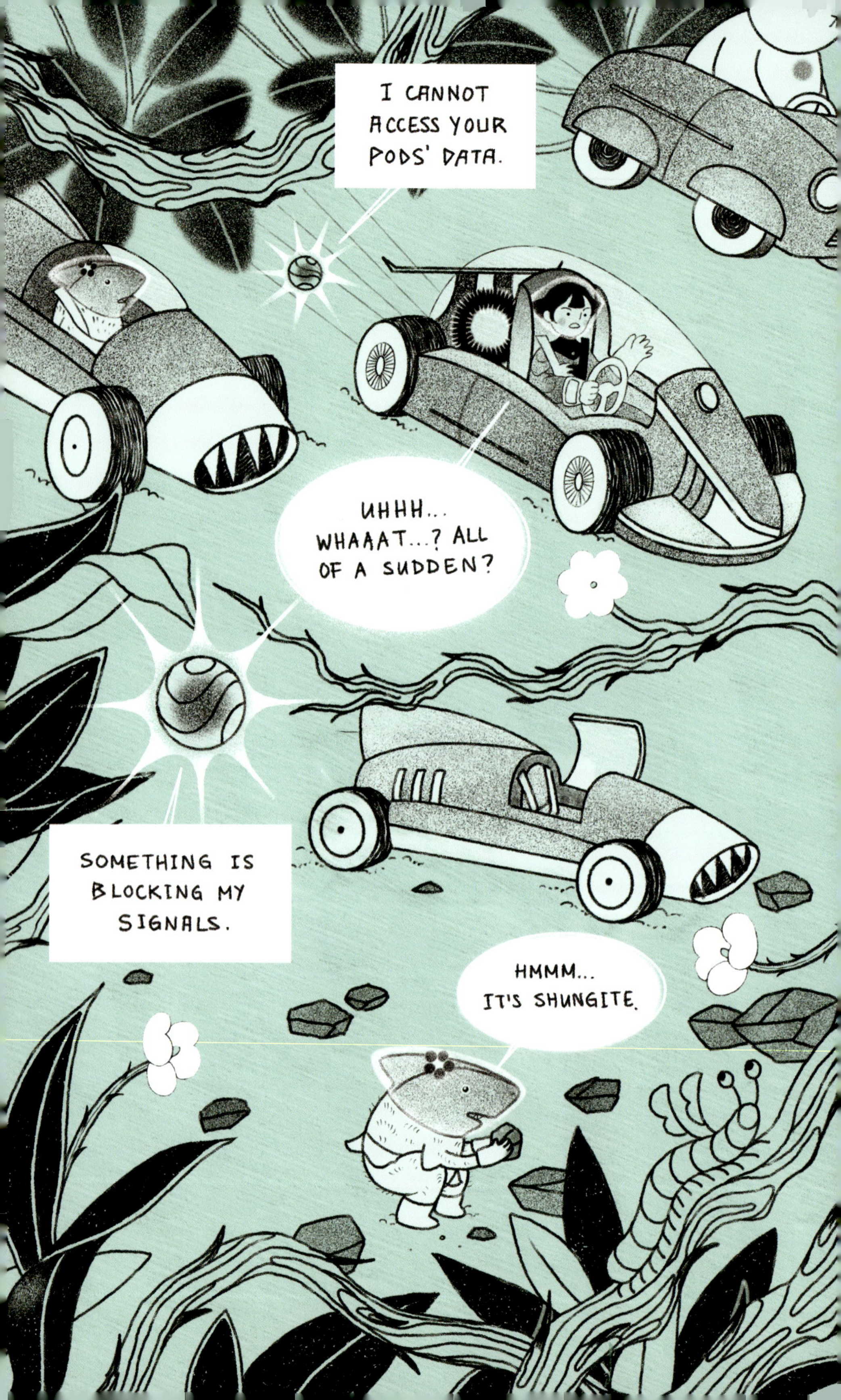
I CANNOT ACCESS YOUR PODS' DATA.
UHHH... WHAAAT...? ALL OF A SUDDEN?
SOMETHING IS BLOCKING MY SIGNALS.
HMMM... IT'S SHUNGITE.

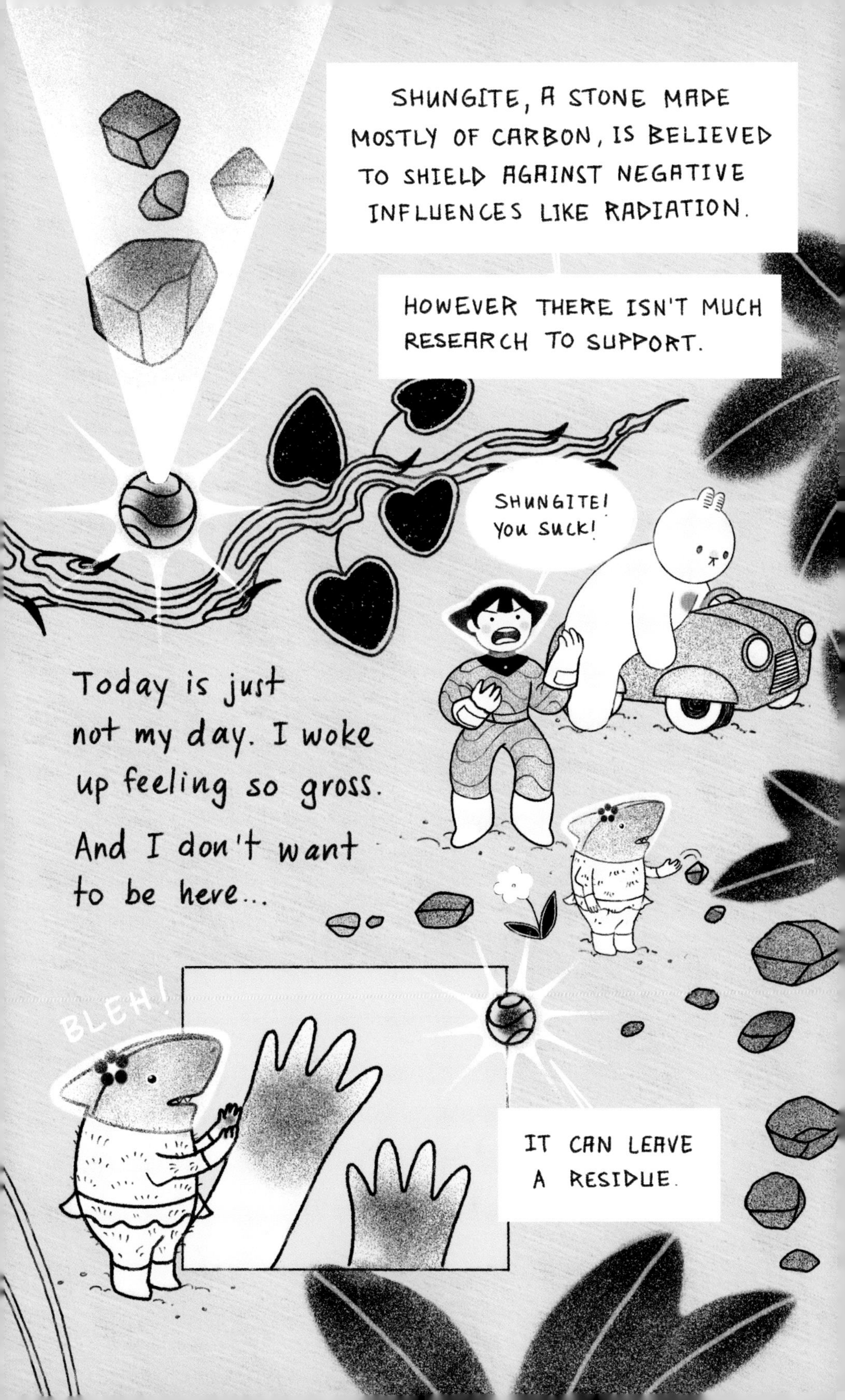
SHUNGITE, A STONE MADE MOSTLY OF CARBON, IS BELIEVED TO SHIELD AGAINST NEGATIVE INFLUENCES LIKE RADIATION.
HOWEVER THERE ISN'T MUCH RESEARCH TO SUPPORT.
SHUNGITE! YOU SUCK!
Today is just not my day. I woke up feeling so gross.
And I don't want to be here...
BLEH!
IT CAN LEAVE A RESIDUE.

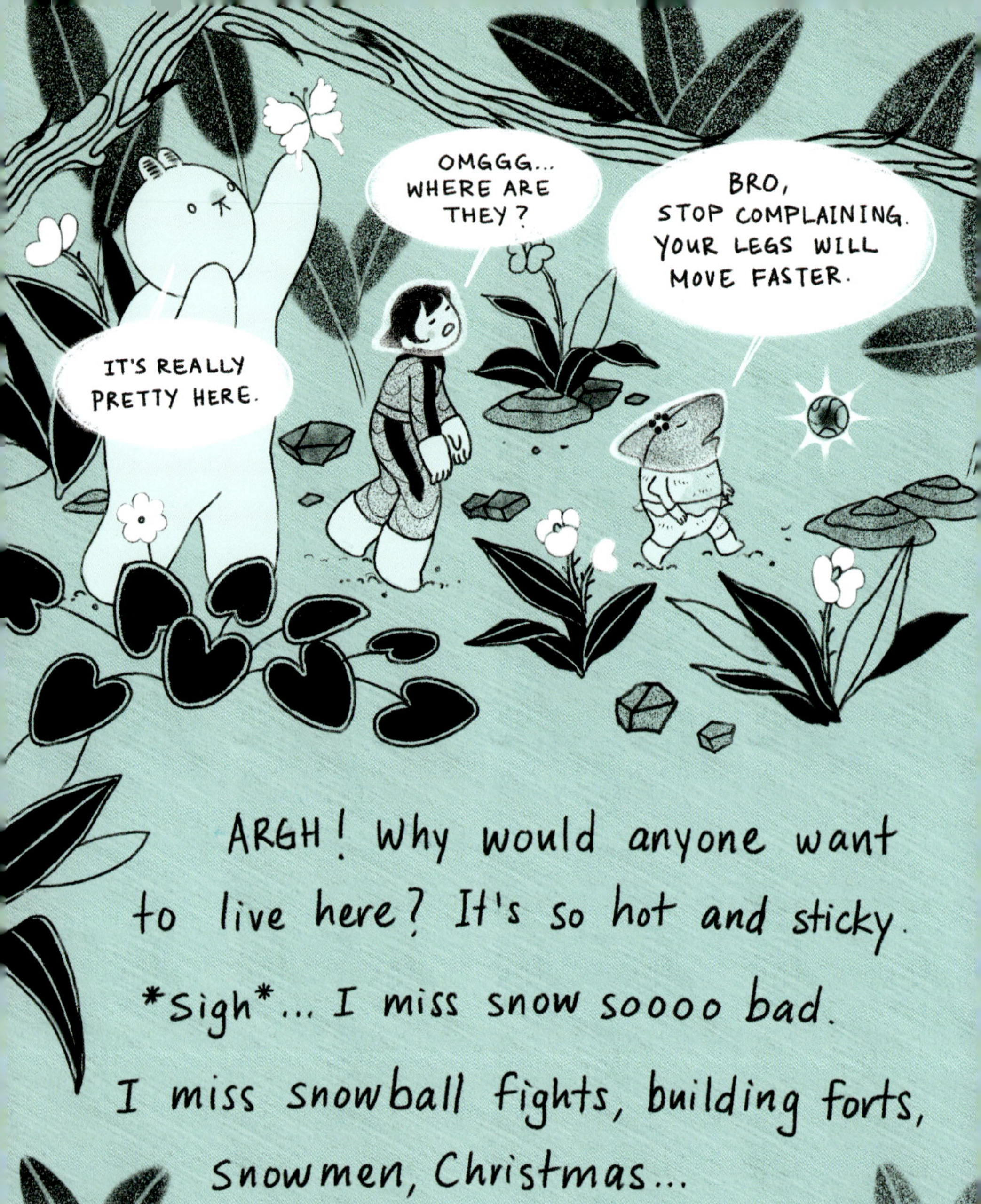
IT'S REALLY PRETTY HERE.
OMGGG... WHERE ARE THEY?
BRO, STOP COMPLAINING. YOUR LEGS WILL MOVE FASTER.

ARGH! Why would anyone want to live here? It's so hot and sticky. *sigh*... I miss snow soooo bad. I miss snowball fights, building forts, snowmen, Christmas...

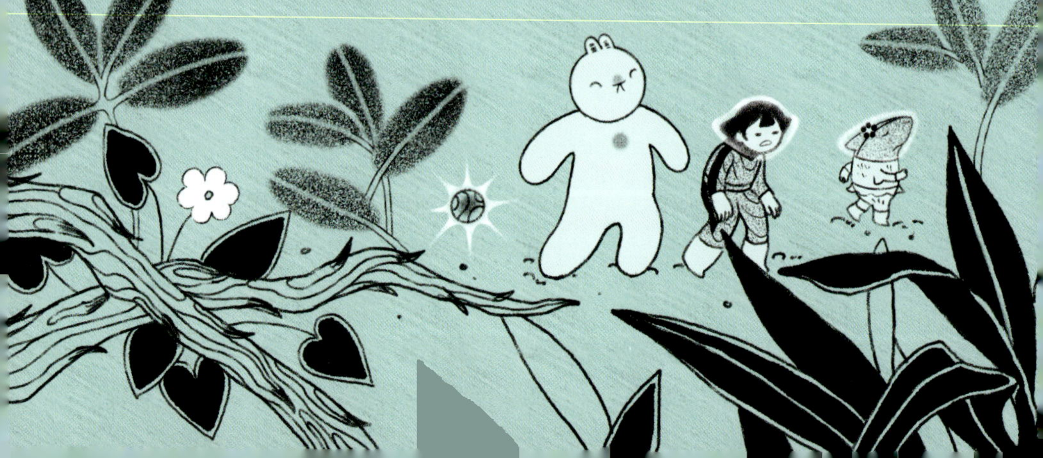

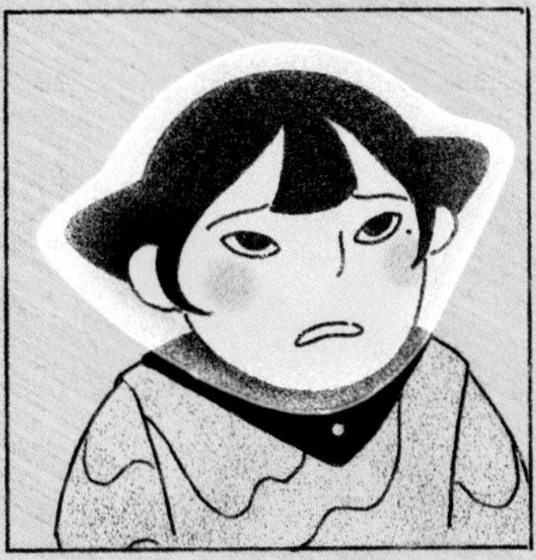

I miss when my mom would make me hot chocolate with milk. The real stuff.

Not with water, cause that's gross.

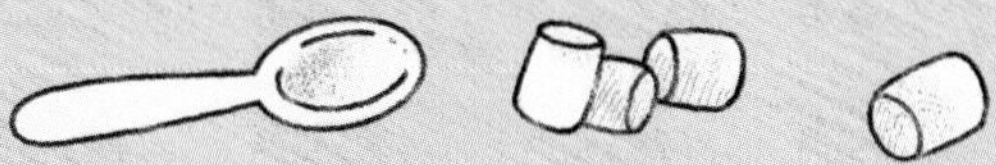

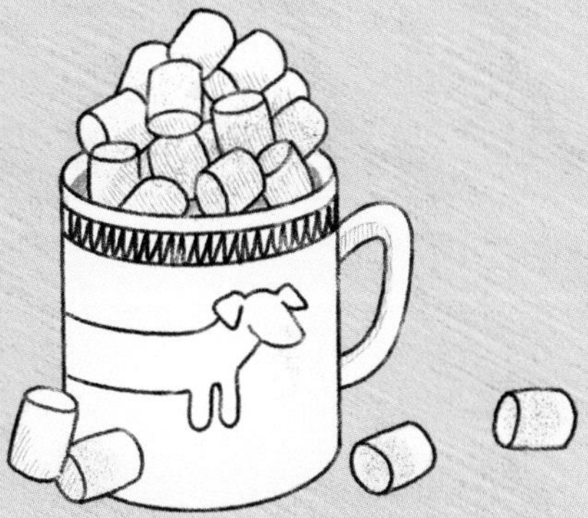

She always let me add my own marshmellows. The tiny ones. I'd pile them as high as possible and eat the ones that fell off first—

WHY IS THE GROUND SHAKING!

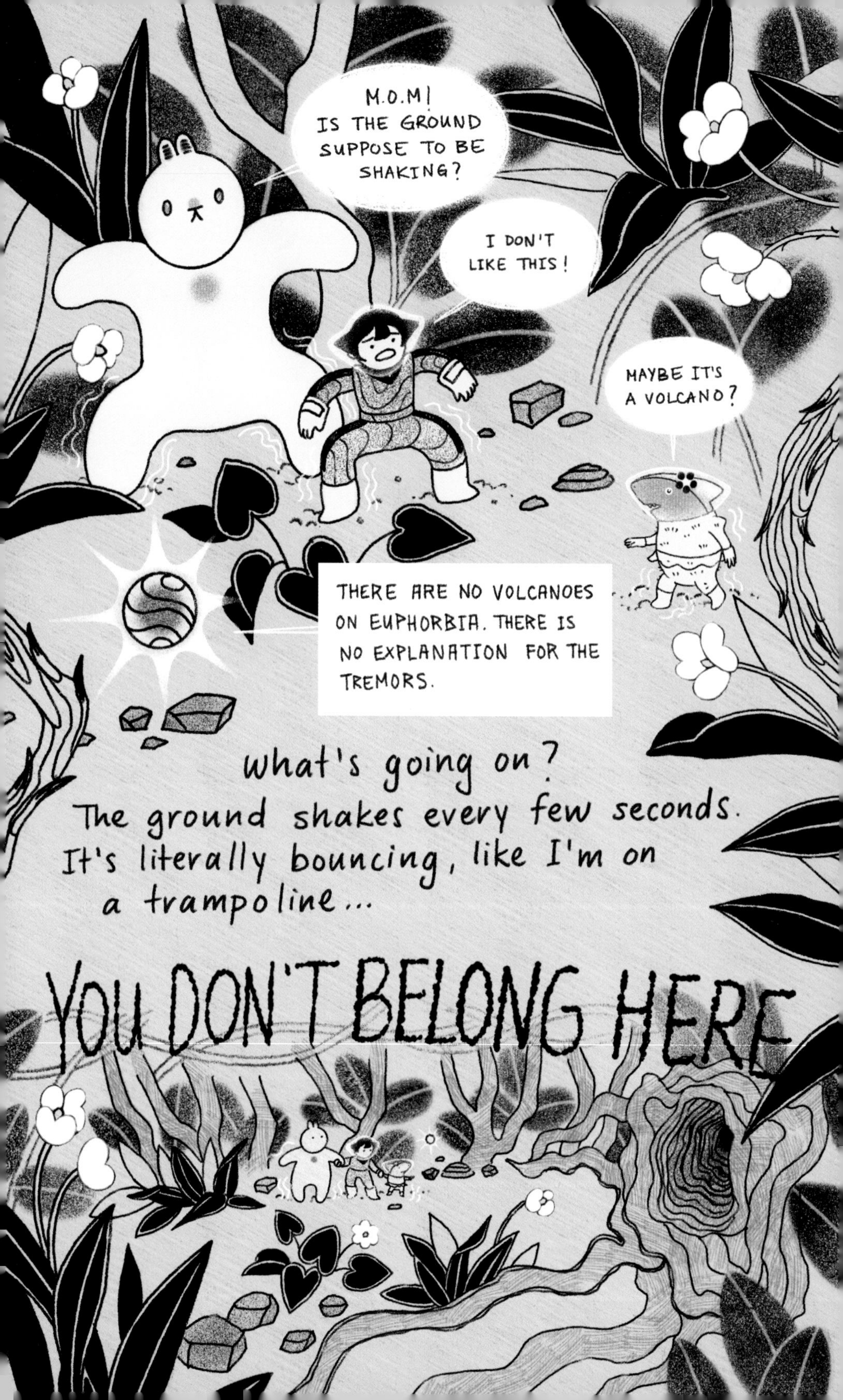
M.O.M!
IS THE GROUND SUPPOSE TO BE SHAKING?
I DON'T LIKE THIS!
MAYBE IT'S A VOLCANO?
THERE ARE NO VOLCANOES ON EUPHORBIA. THERE IS NO EXPLANATION FOR THE TREMORS.
what's going on?
The ground shakes every few seconds. It's literally bouncing, like I'm on a trampoline...
YOU DON'T BELONG HERE

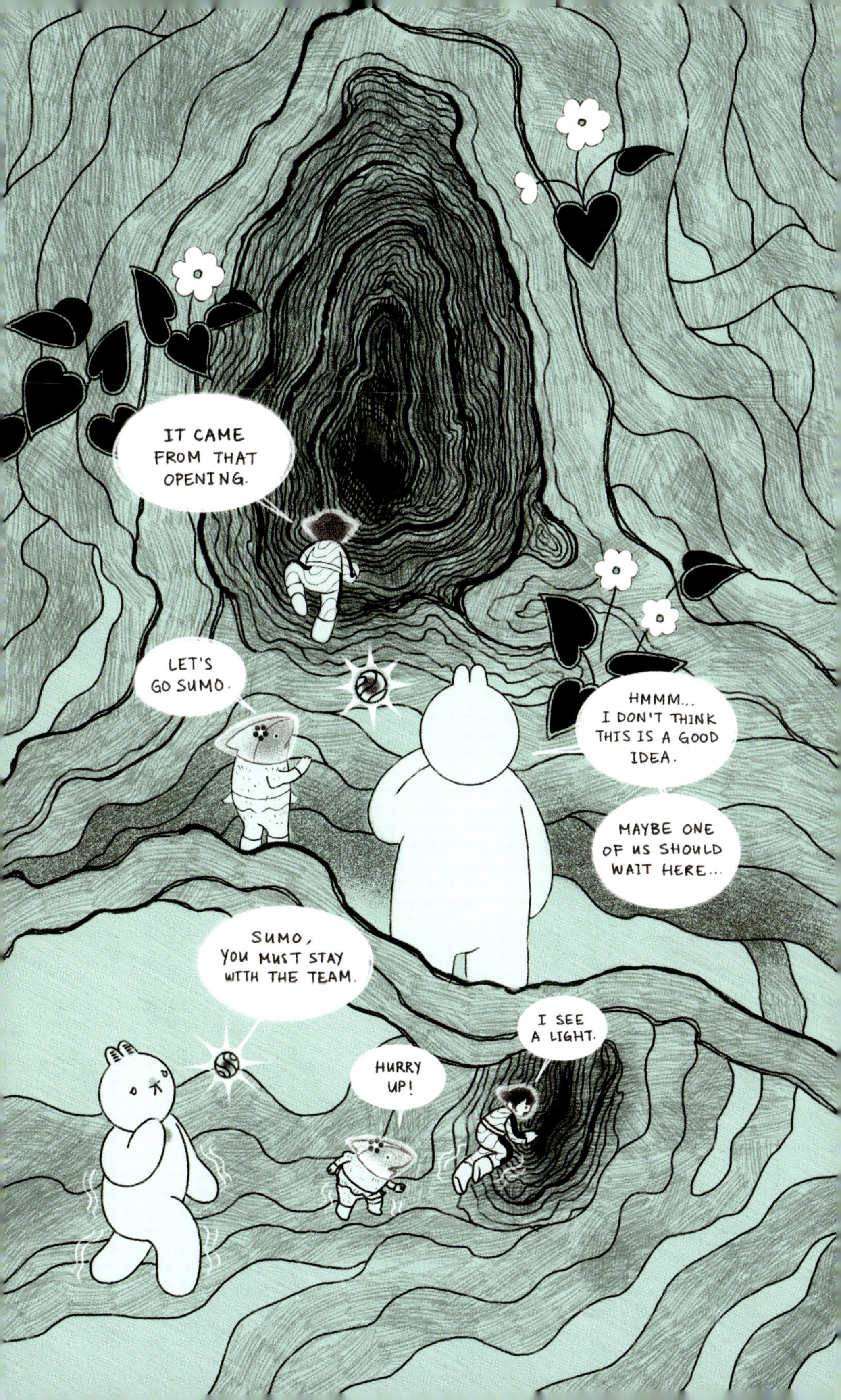
IT CAME FROM THAT OPENING.
LET'S GO SUMO.
HMMM... I DON'T THINK THIS IS A GOOD IDEA.
MAYBE ONE OF US SHOULD WAIT HERE...
SUMO, YOU MUST STAY WITH THE TEAM.
I SEE A LIGHT.
HURRY UP!

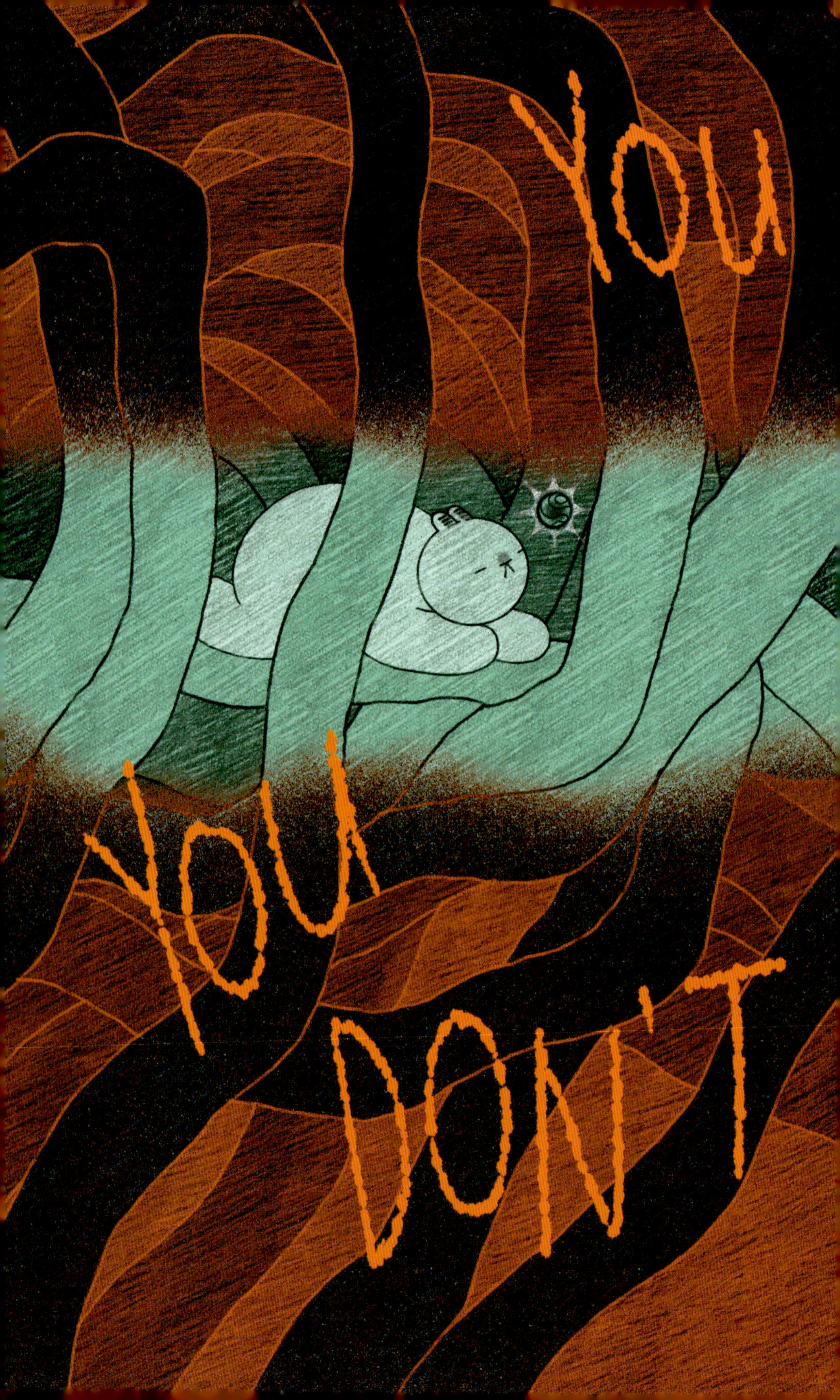
YOU
YOU
DON'T

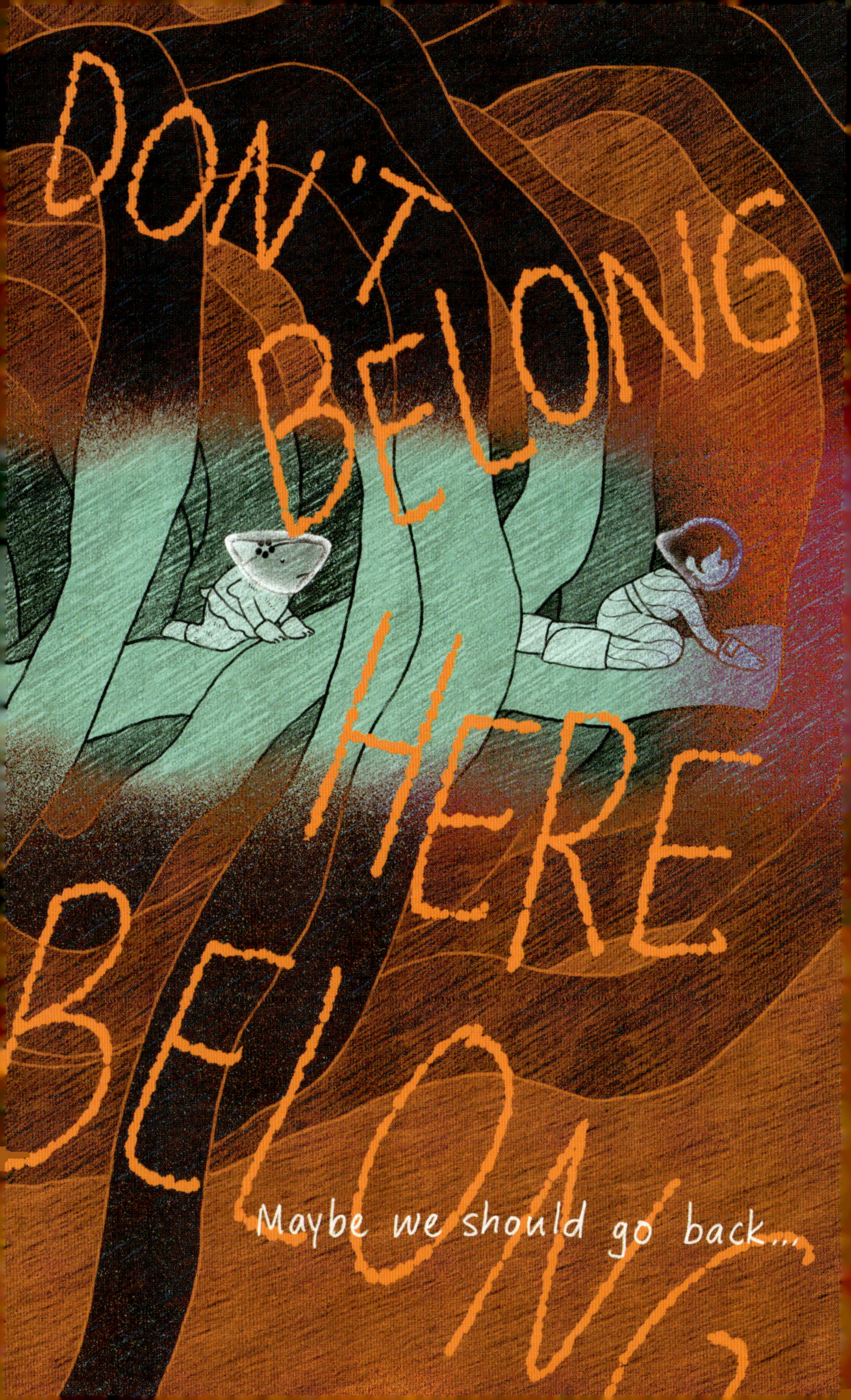
DON'T BELONG
BELONG
HERE
HERE
BELONG
Maybe we should go back...

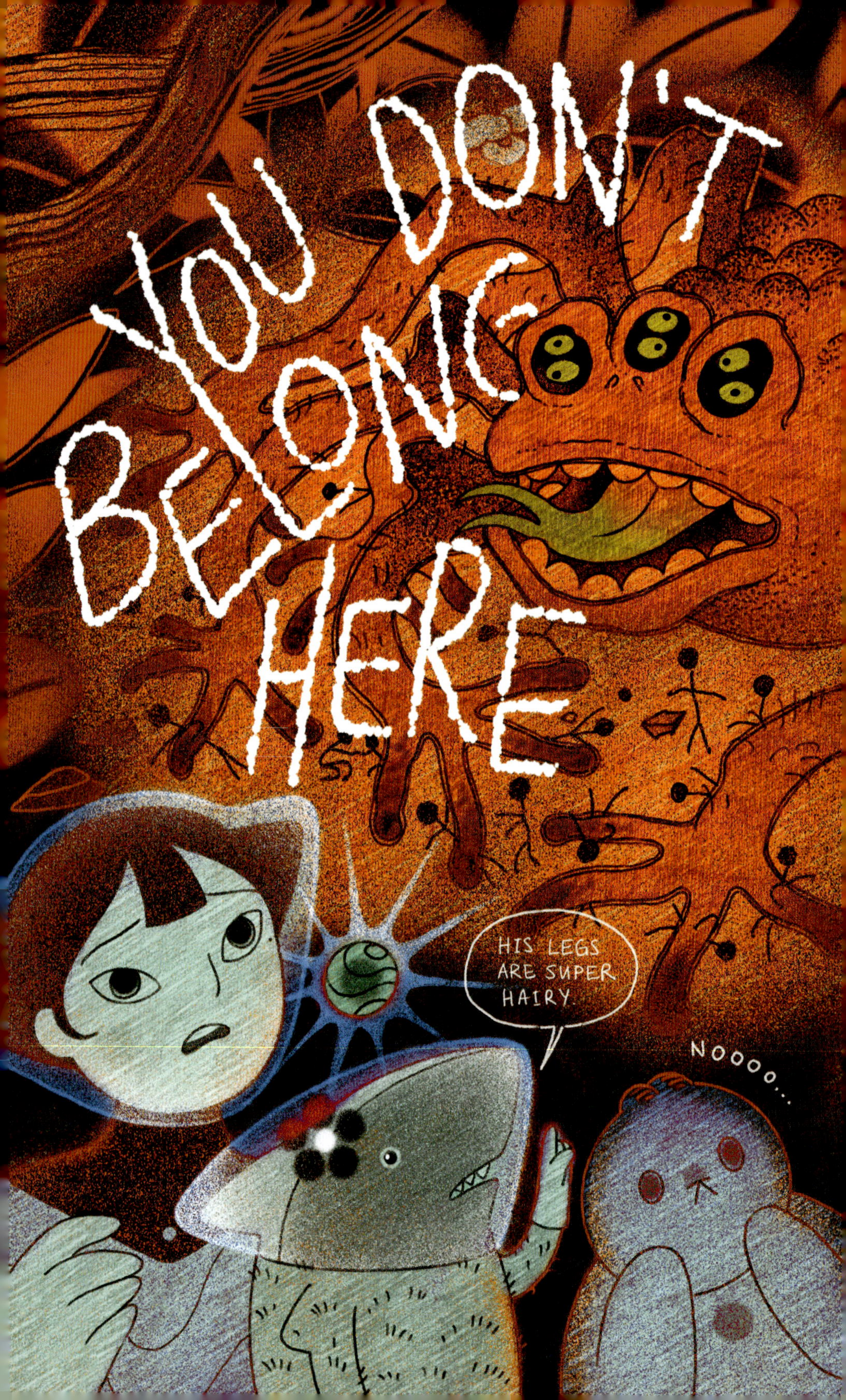
YOU DON'T BELONG HERE
HIS LEGS ARE SUPER HAIRY
NOOOO...

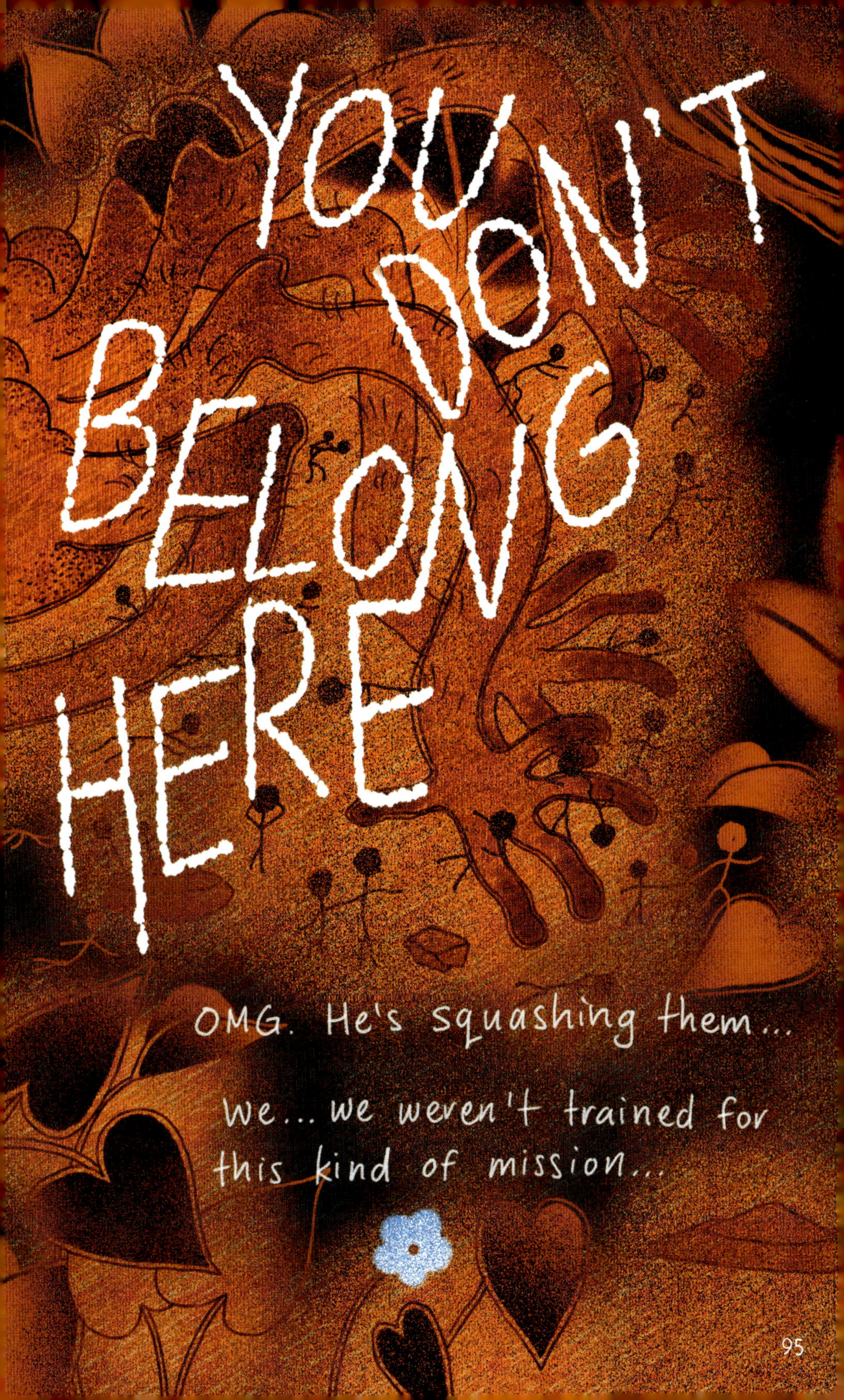
YOU DON'T BELONG HERE
OMG. He's squashing them...
We... we weren't trained for this kind of mission...

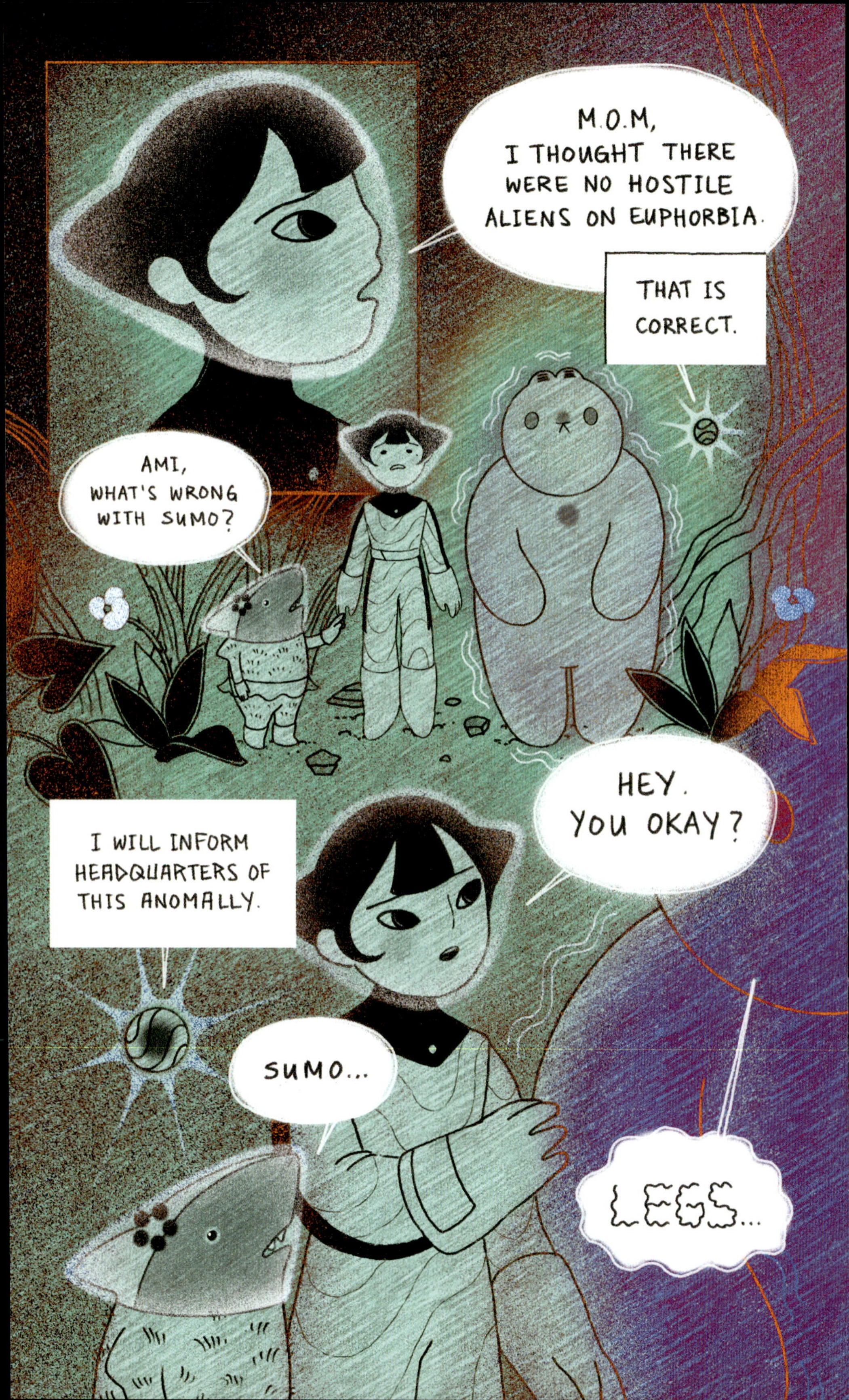
M.O.M,
I THOUGHT THERE WERE NO HOSTILE ALIENS ON EUPHORBIA.
THAT IS CORRECT.
AMI, WHAT'S WRONG WITH SUMO?
HEY. YOU OKAY?
I WILL INFORM HEADQUARTERS OF THIS ANOMALLY.
SUMO...
LEGS...

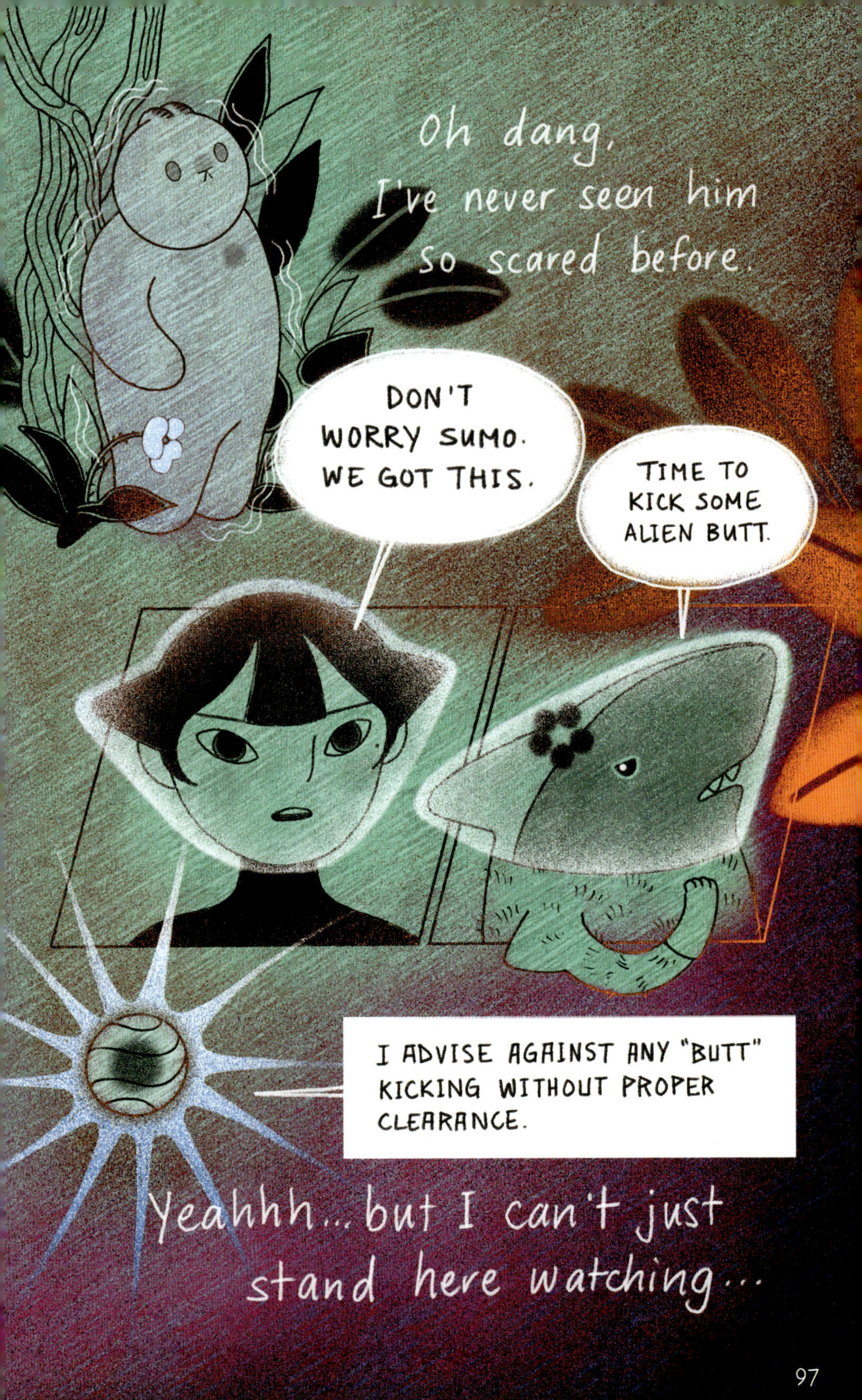
Oh dang,
I've never seen him
so scared before.
DON'T WORRY SUMO. WE GOT THIS.
TIME TO KICK SOME ALIEN BUTT.
I ADVISE AGAINST ANY "BUTT" KICKING WITHOUT PROPER CLEARANCE.
Yeahhh... but I can't just
stand here watching...

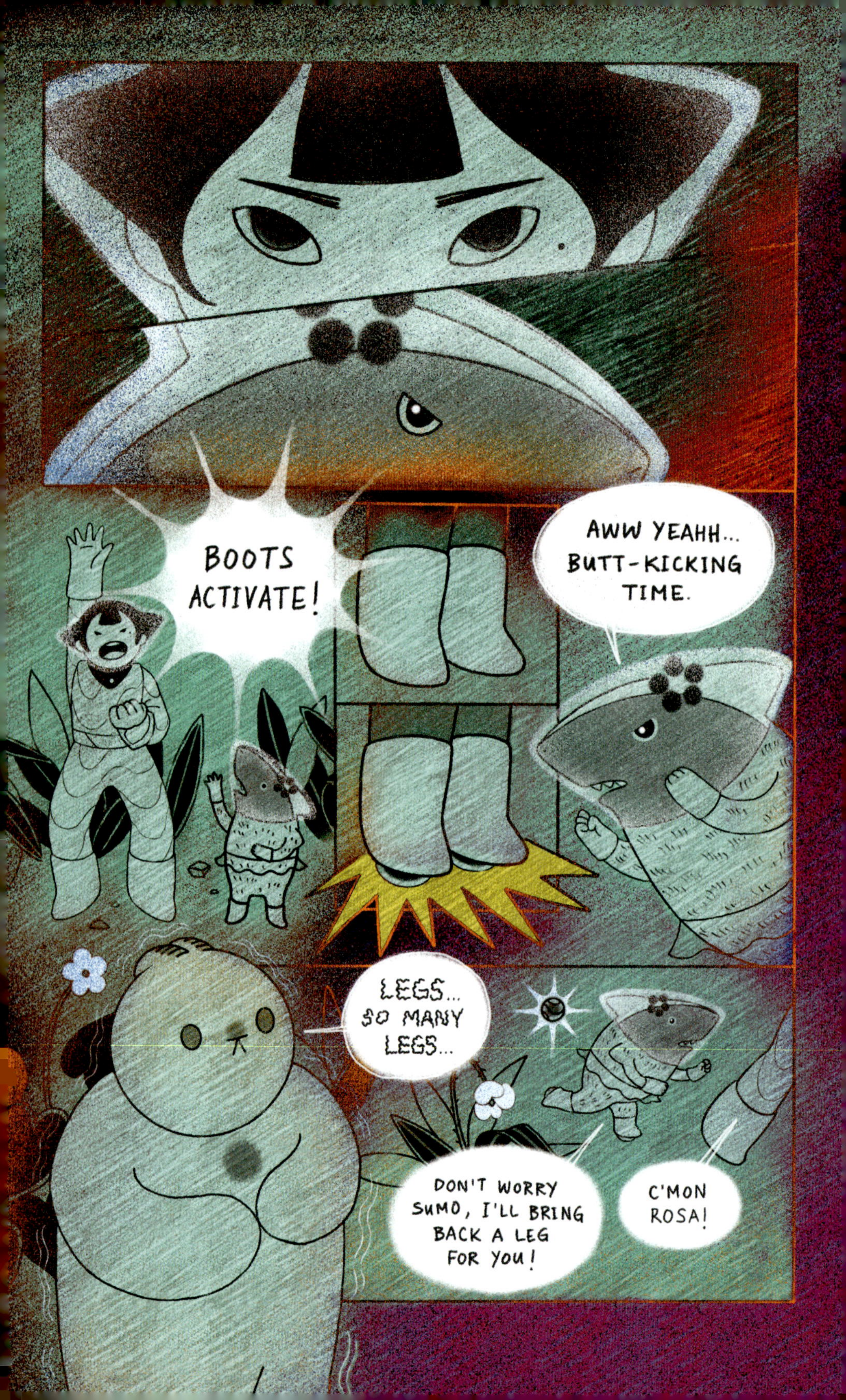
BOOTS ACTIVATE!
AWW YEAHH... BUTT-KICKING TIME.
LEGS... SO MANY LEGS...
DON'T WORRY SUMO, I'LL BRING BACK A LEG FOR YOU!
C'MON ROSA!

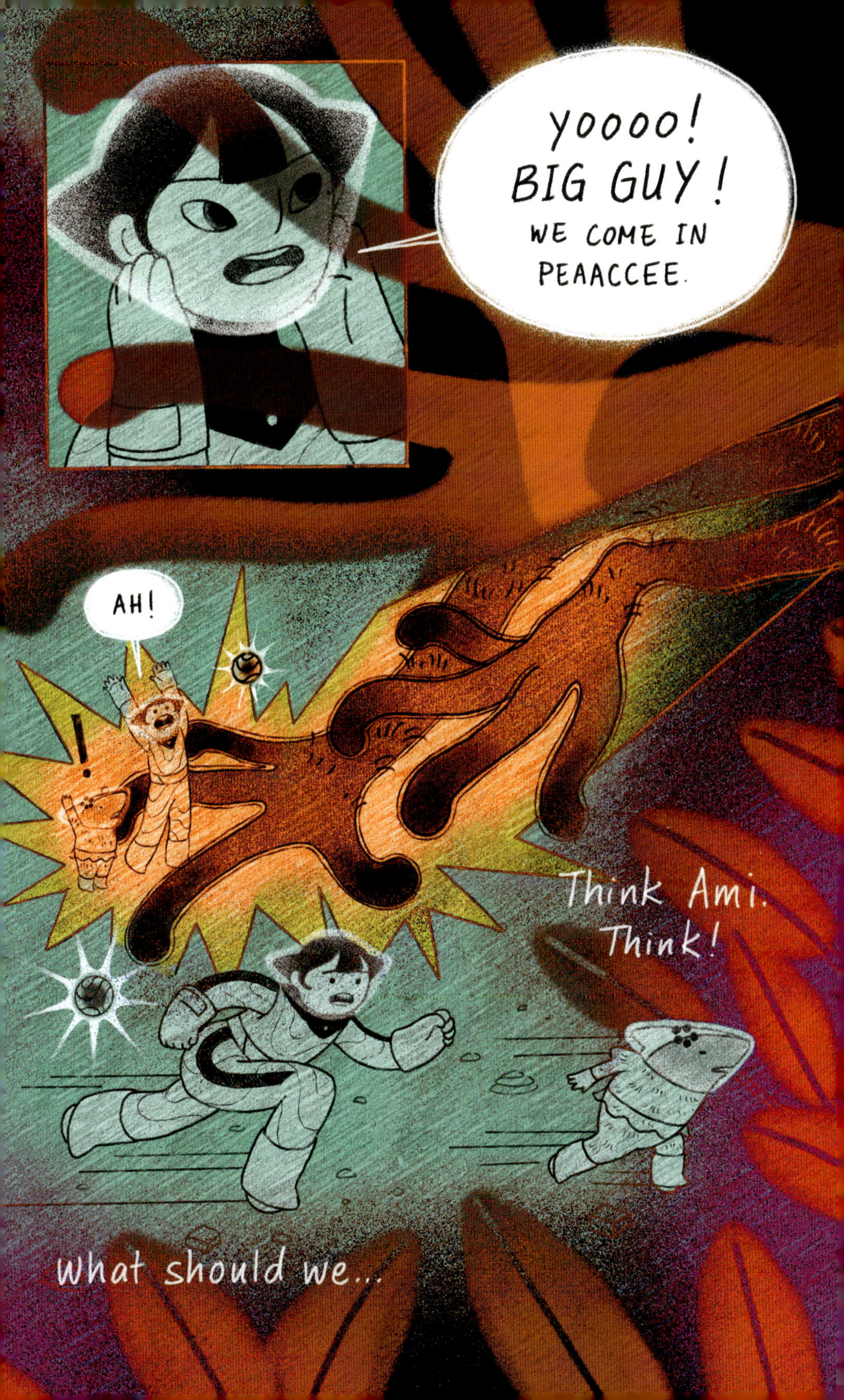
yoooo! BIG GUY! WE COME IN PEAACCEE.
AH!
!
Think Ami. Think!
What should we...

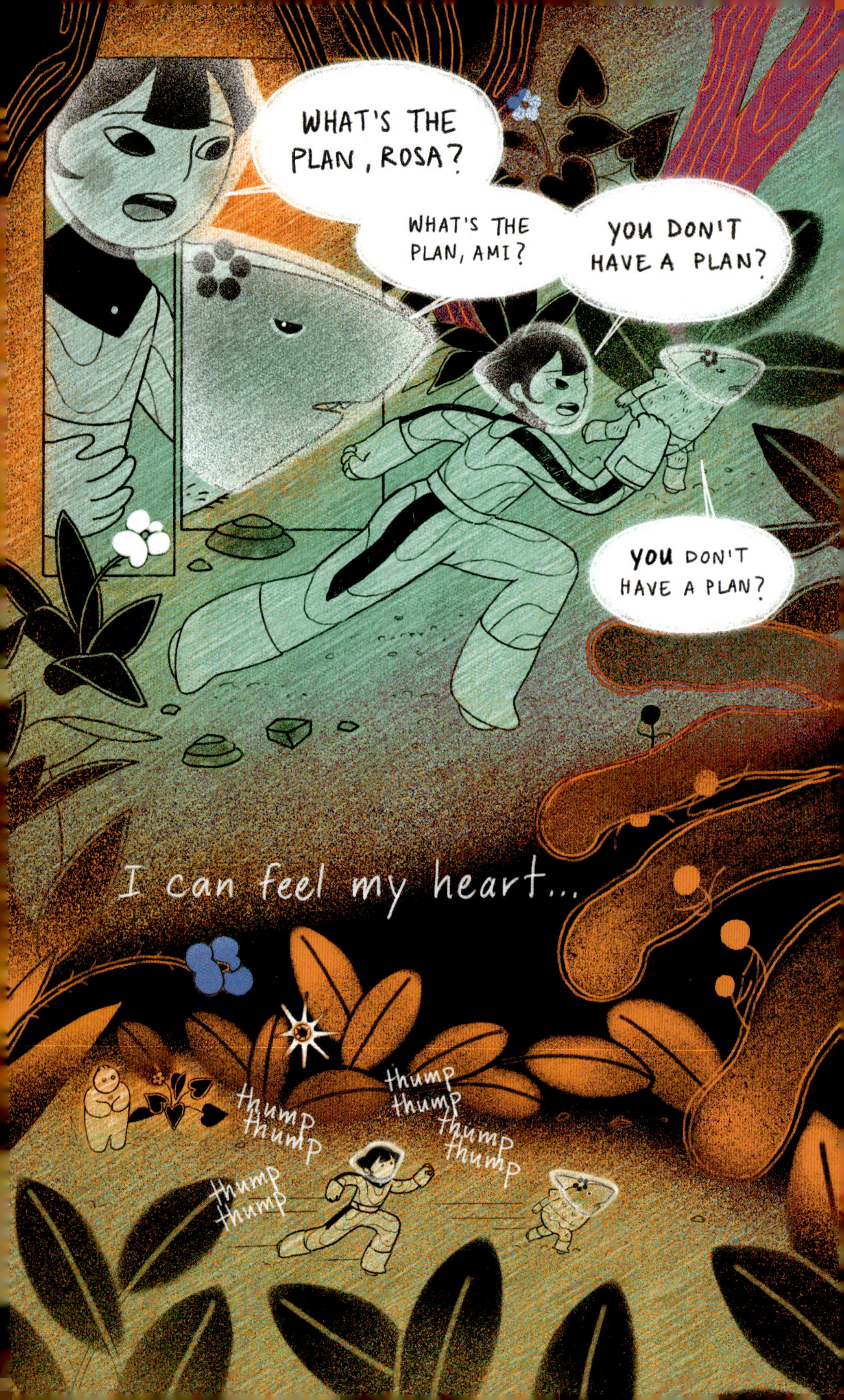
WHAT'S THE PLAN, ROSA?
WHAT'S THE PLAN, AMI?
YOU DON'T HAVE A PLAN?
YOU DON'T HAVE A PLAN?
I can feel my heart...
thump thump
thump thump
thump thump
thump thump

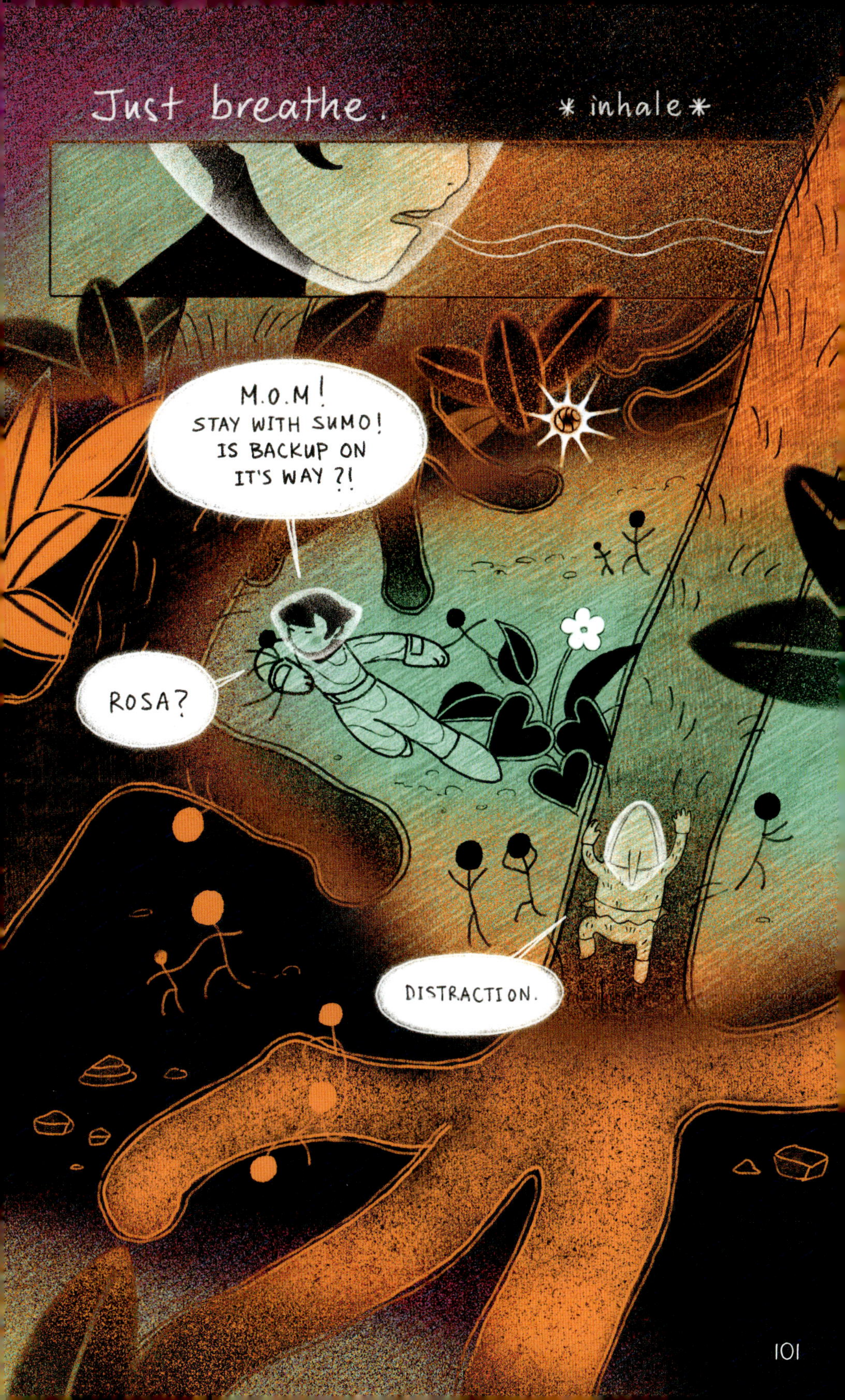
Just breathe.
inhale
M.O.M!
STAY WITH SUMO!
IS BACKUP ON
IT'S WAY ?!
ROSA?
DISTRACTION.

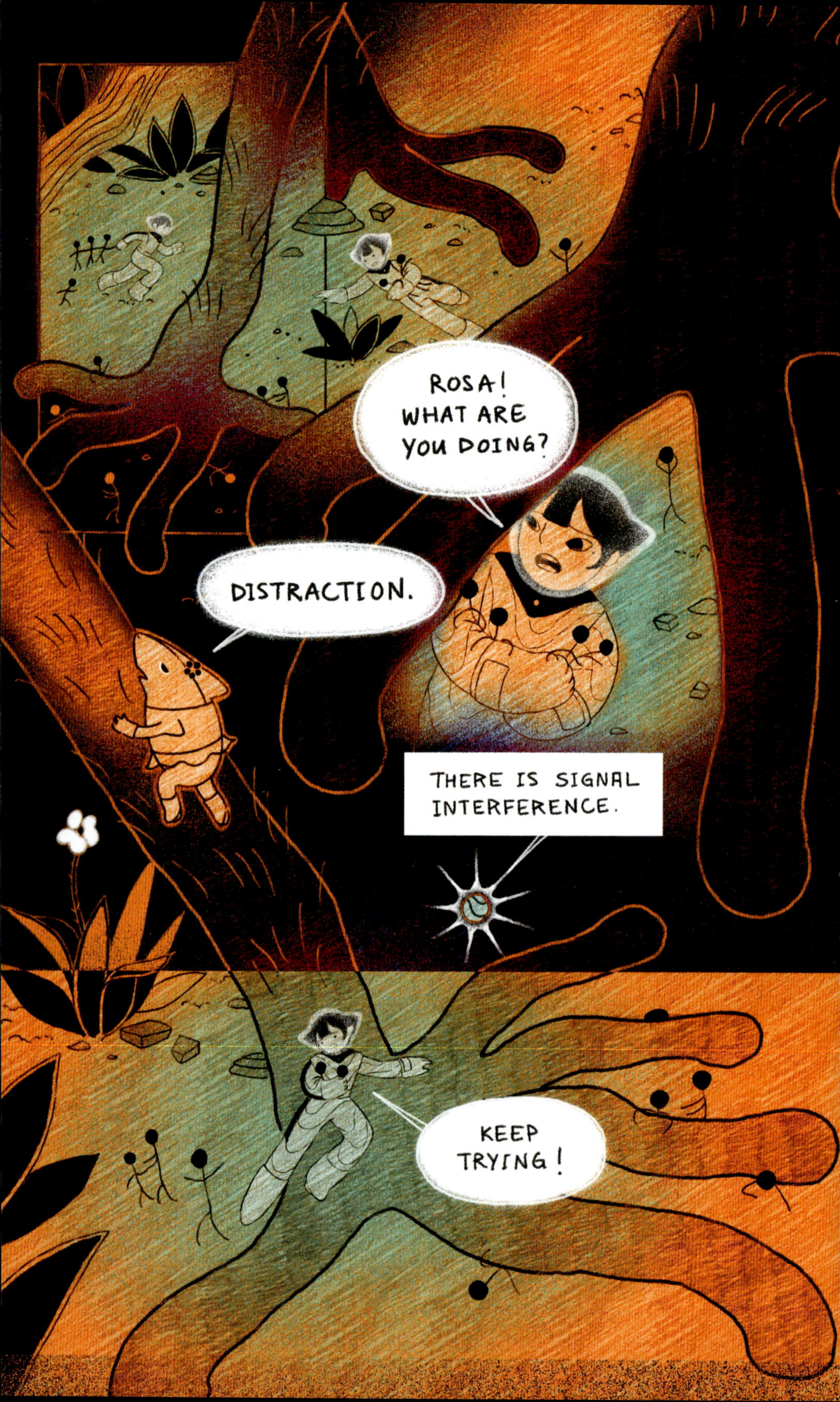
ROSA! WHAT ARE YOU DOING?
DISTRACTION.
THERE IS SIGNAL INTERFERENCE.
KEEP TRYING!

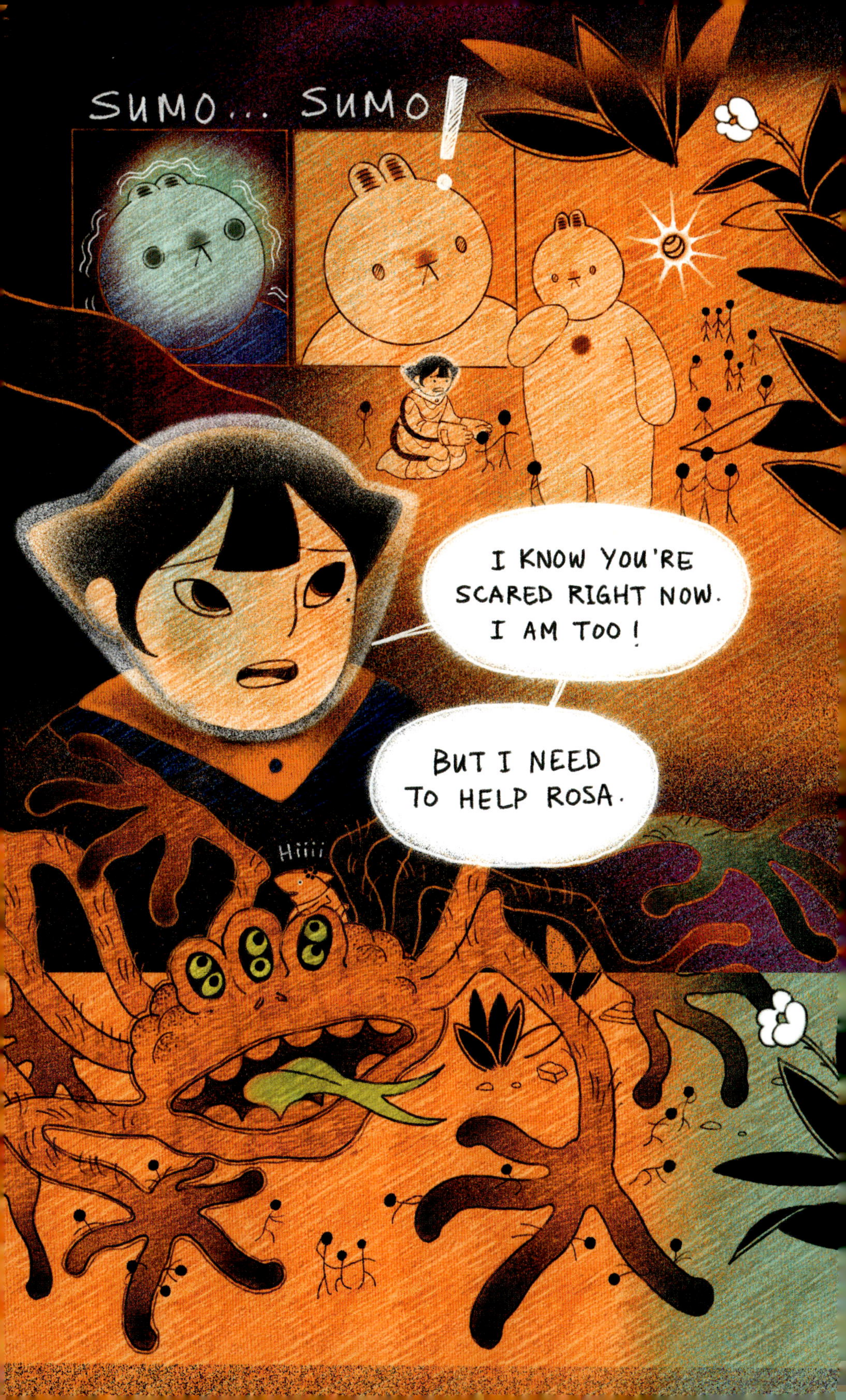
SUMO... SUMO!
I KNOW YOU'RE SCARED RIGHT NOW. I AM TOO!
BUT I NEED TO HELP ROSA.
Hiiii

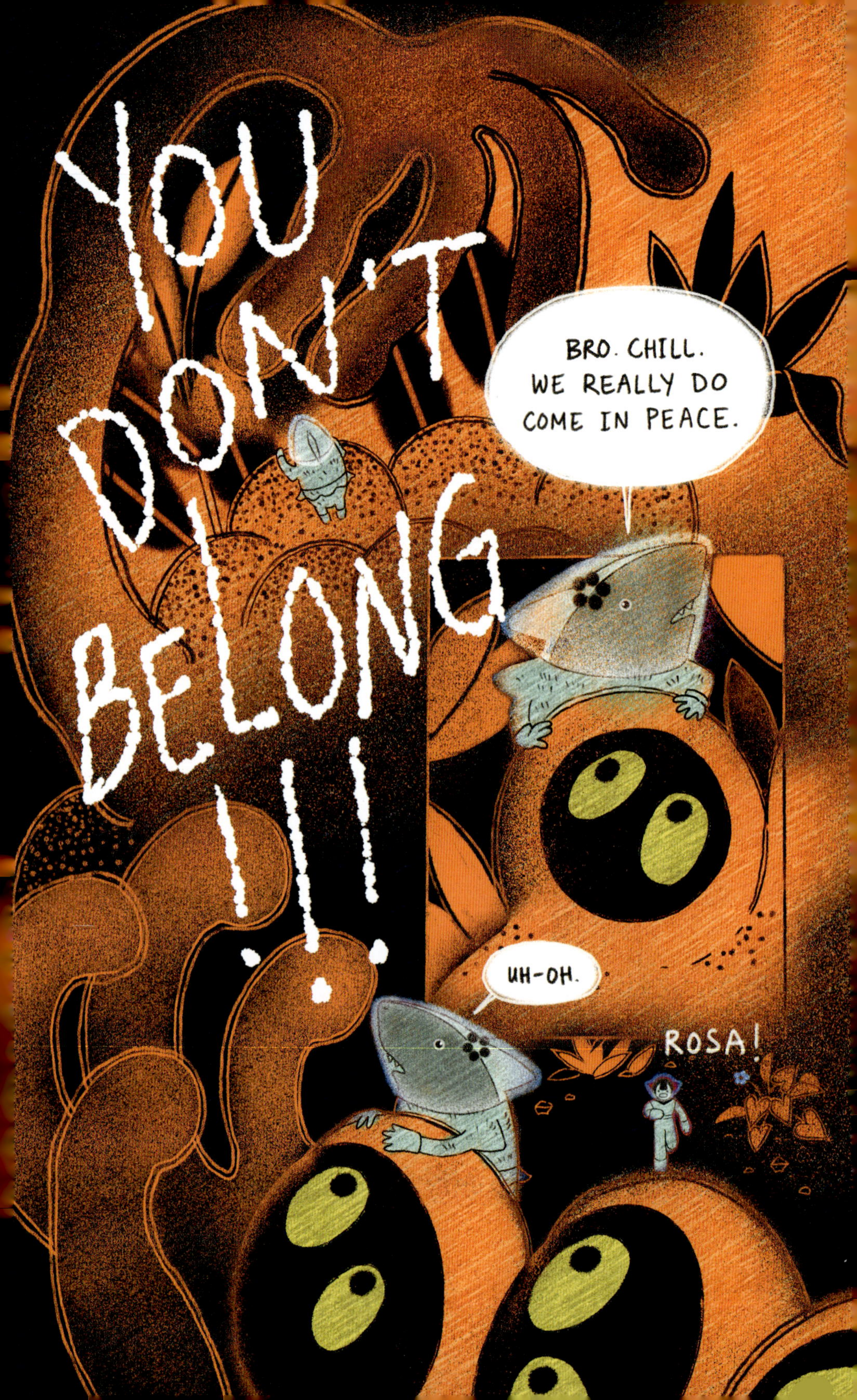
YOU DON'T BELONG!!!
BRO. CHILL. WE REALLY DO COME IN PEACE.
UH-OH.
ROSA!

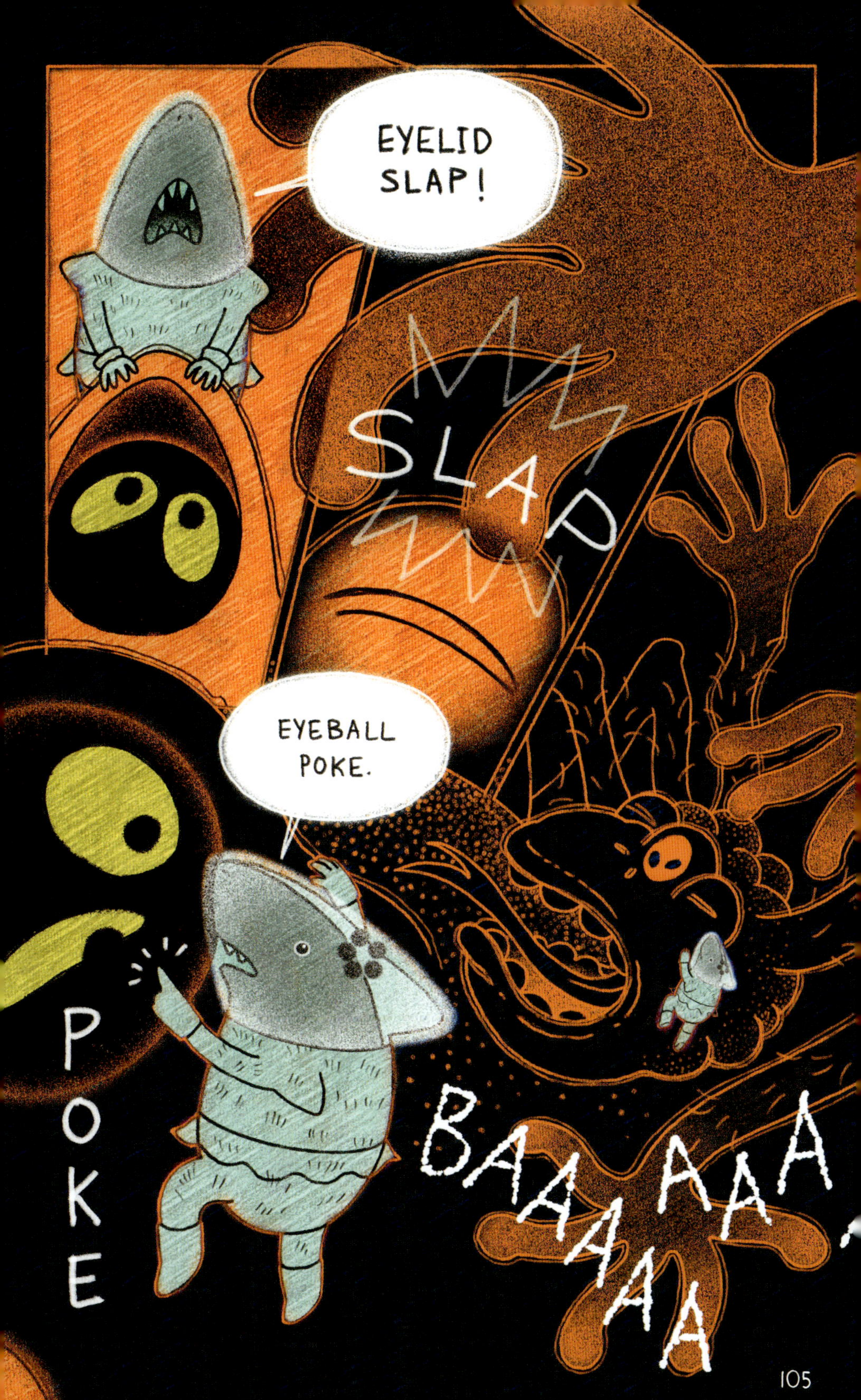
EYELID SLAP!
SLAP
EYEBALL POKE.
POKE
BAAAAAAAA

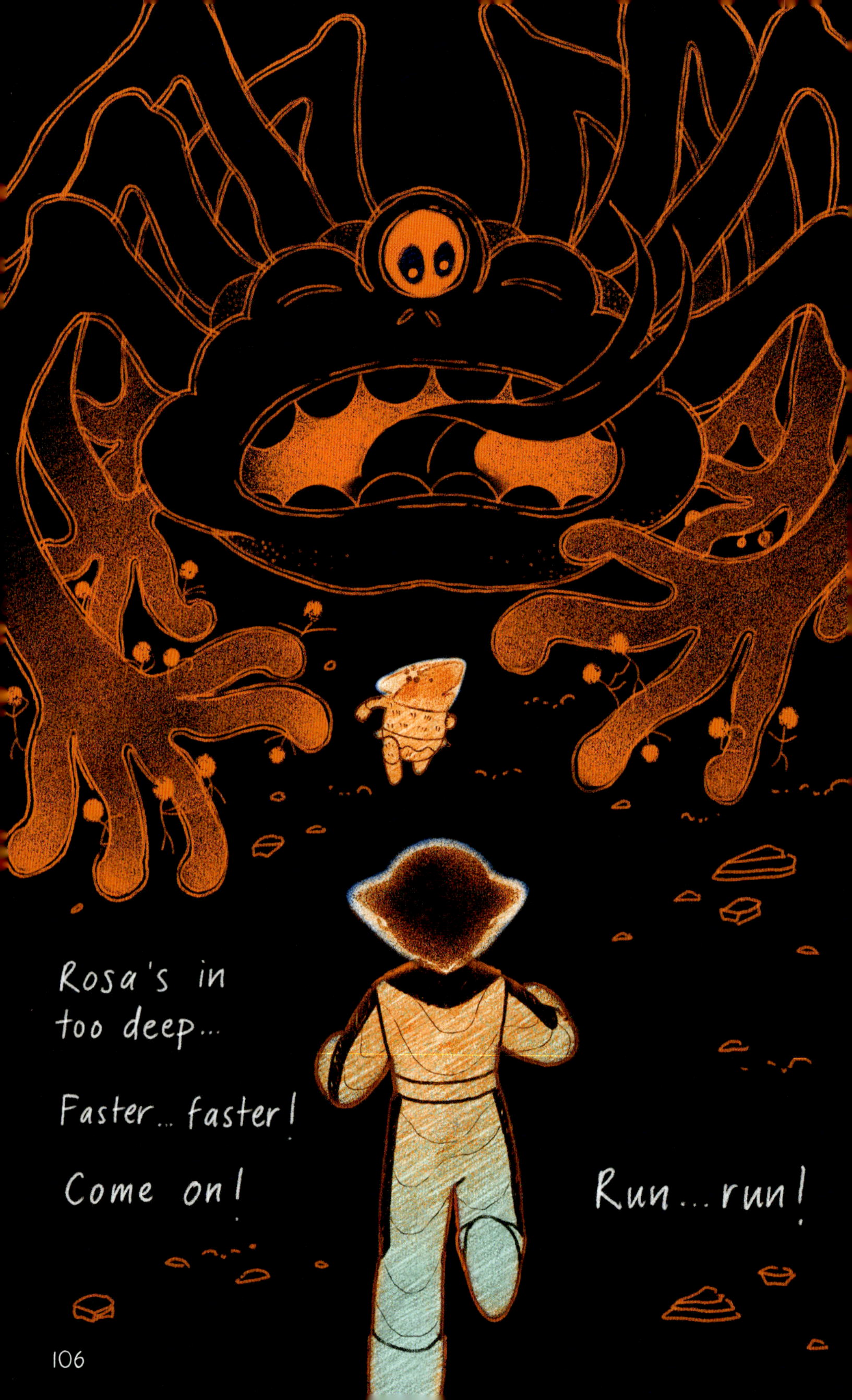
Rosa's in too deep...
Faster... faster!
Come on!
Run... run!

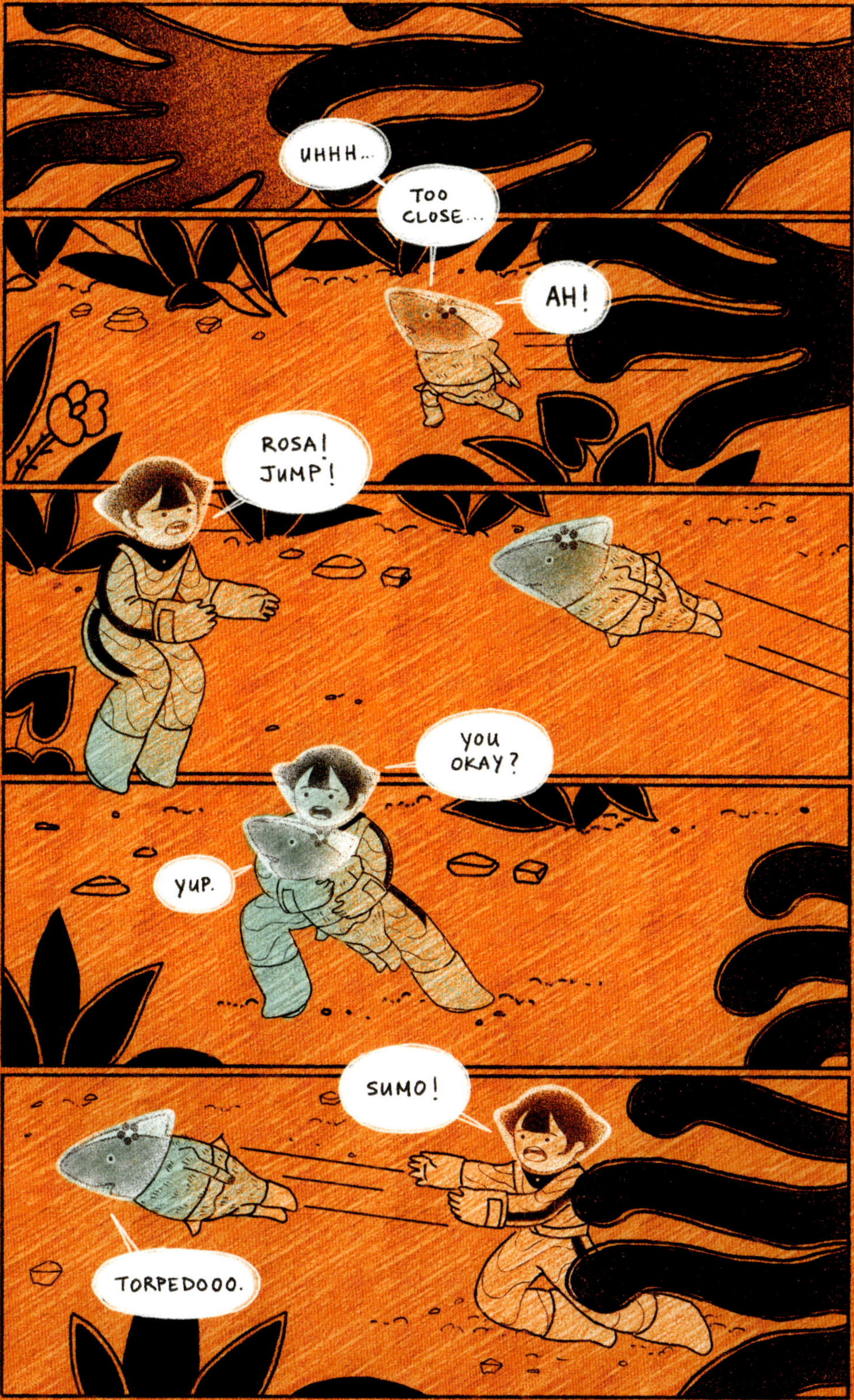
UHHH...
TOO CLOSE...
AH!
ROSA! JUMP!
YOU OKAY?
YUP.
SUMO!
TORPEDOOO.

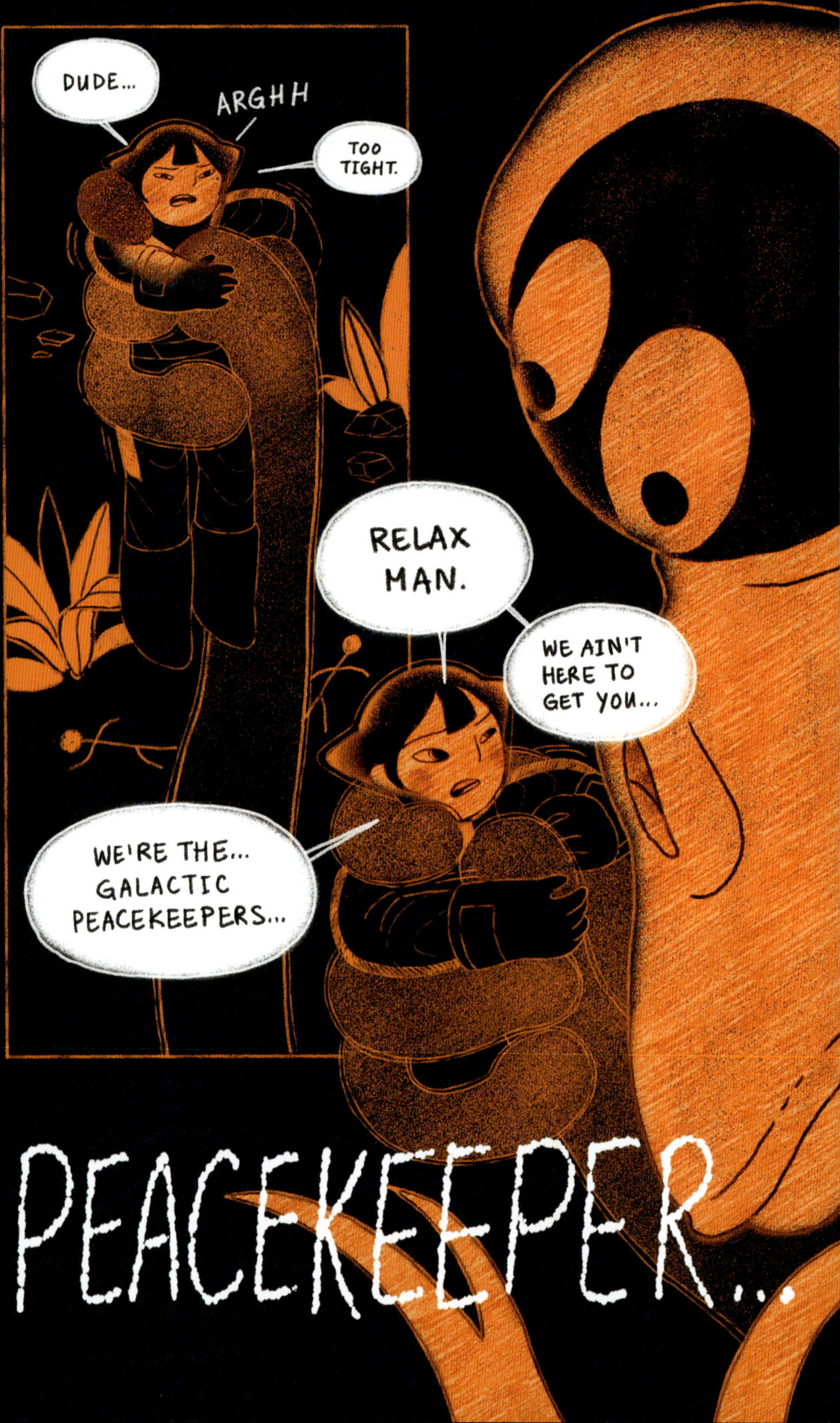
DUDE...
ARGHH
TOO TIGHT.
RELAX MAN.
WE AIN'T HERE TO GET YOU...
WE'RE THE... GALACTIC PEACEKEEPERS...
PEACEKEEPER...

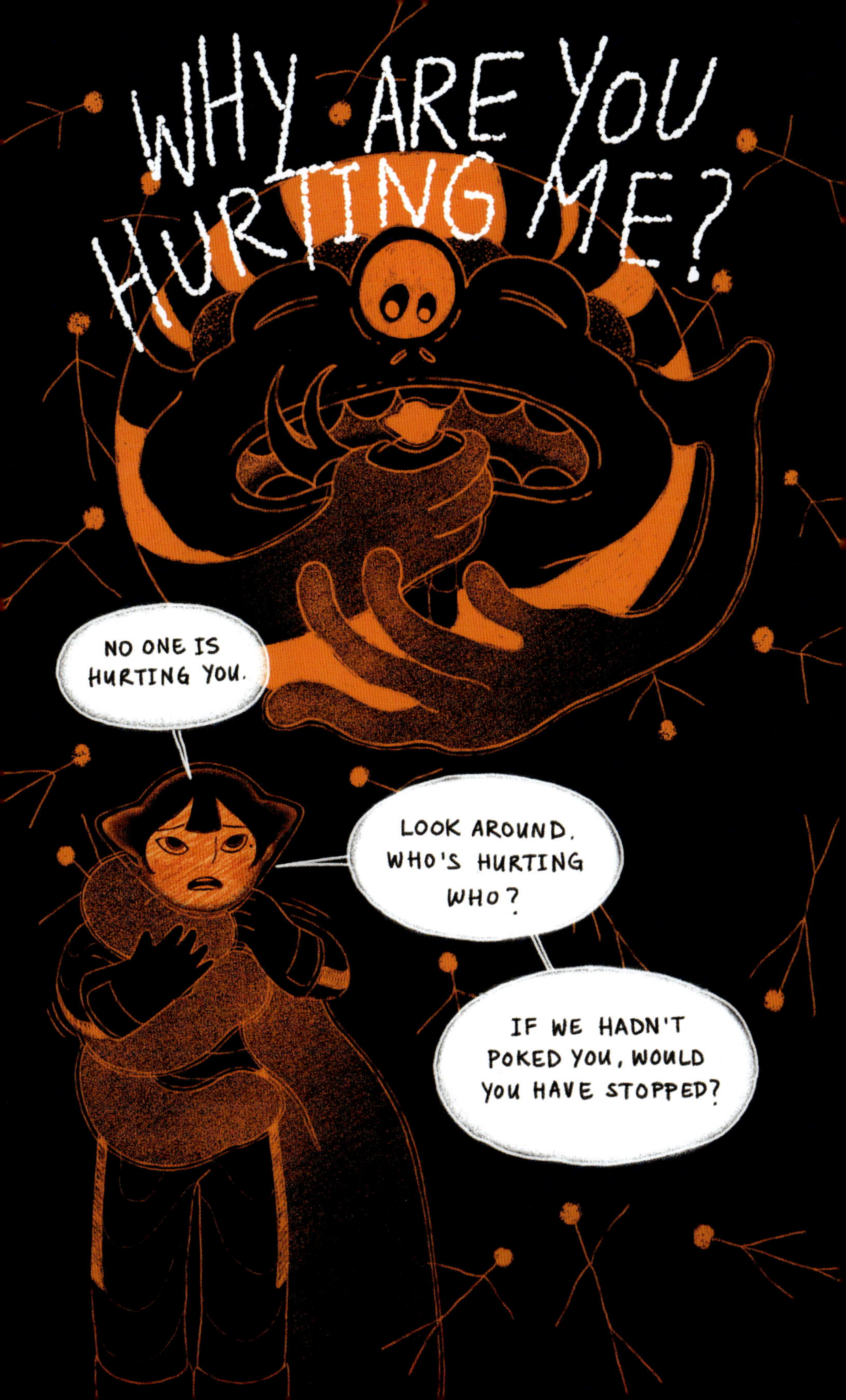
WHY ARE YOU HURTING ME?
NO ONE IS HURTING YOU.
LOOK AROUND. WHO'S HURTING WHO?
IF WE HADN'T POKED YOU, WOULD YOU HAVE STOPPED?

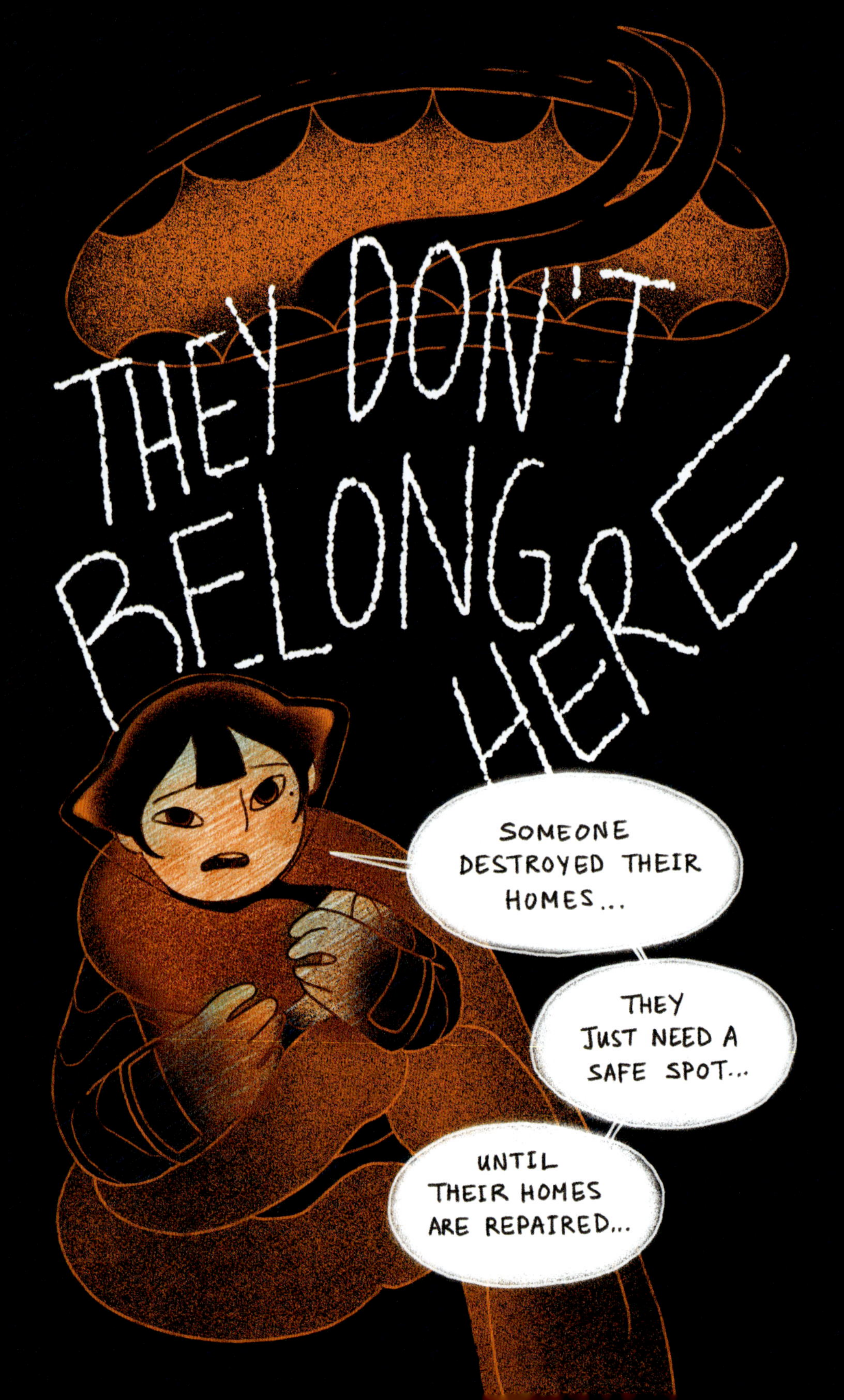
THEY DON'T BELONG HERE
SOMEONE DESTROYED THEIR HOMES...
THEY JUST NEED A SAFE SPOT...
UNTIL THEIR HOMES ARE REPAIRED...

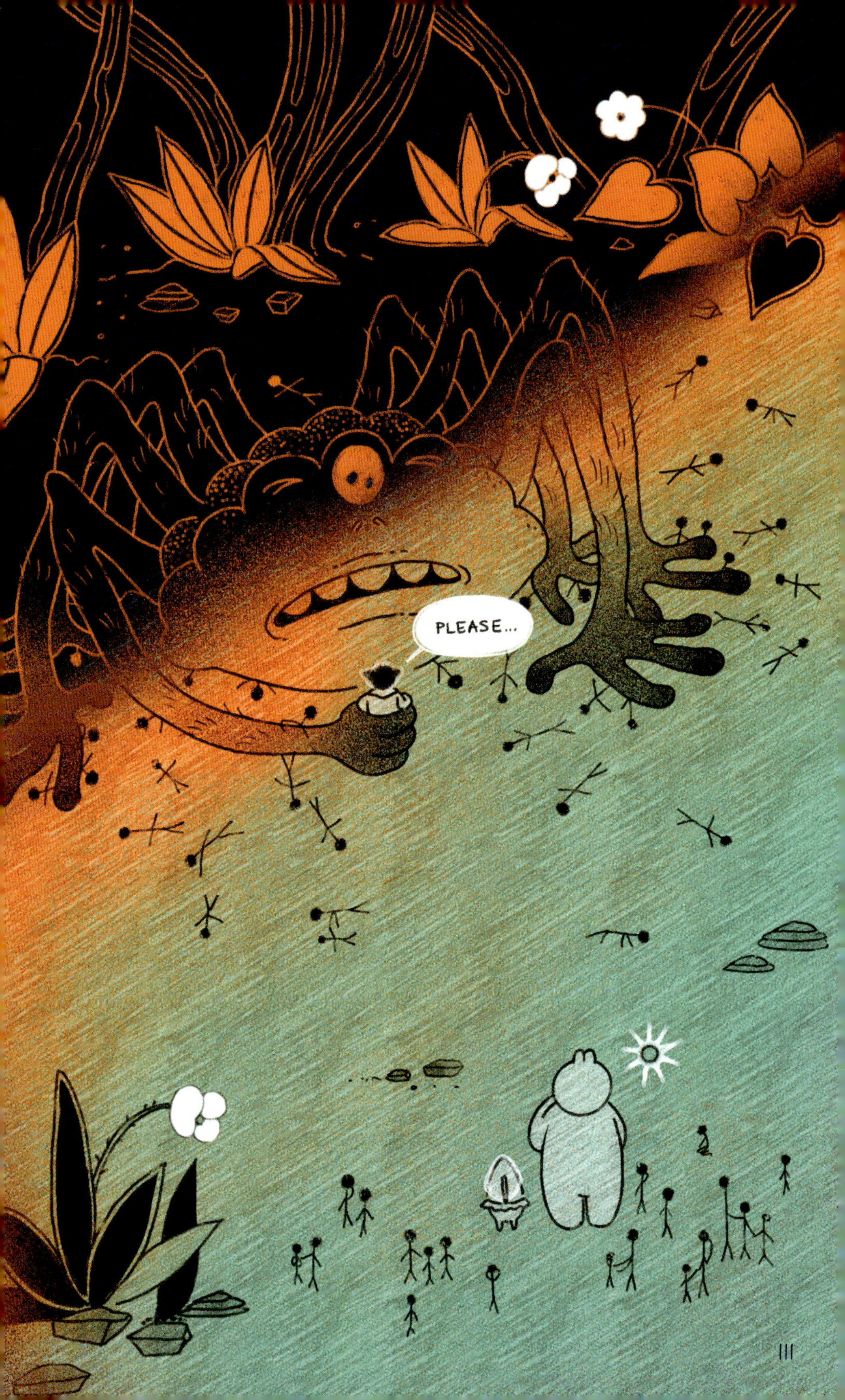
PLEASE...

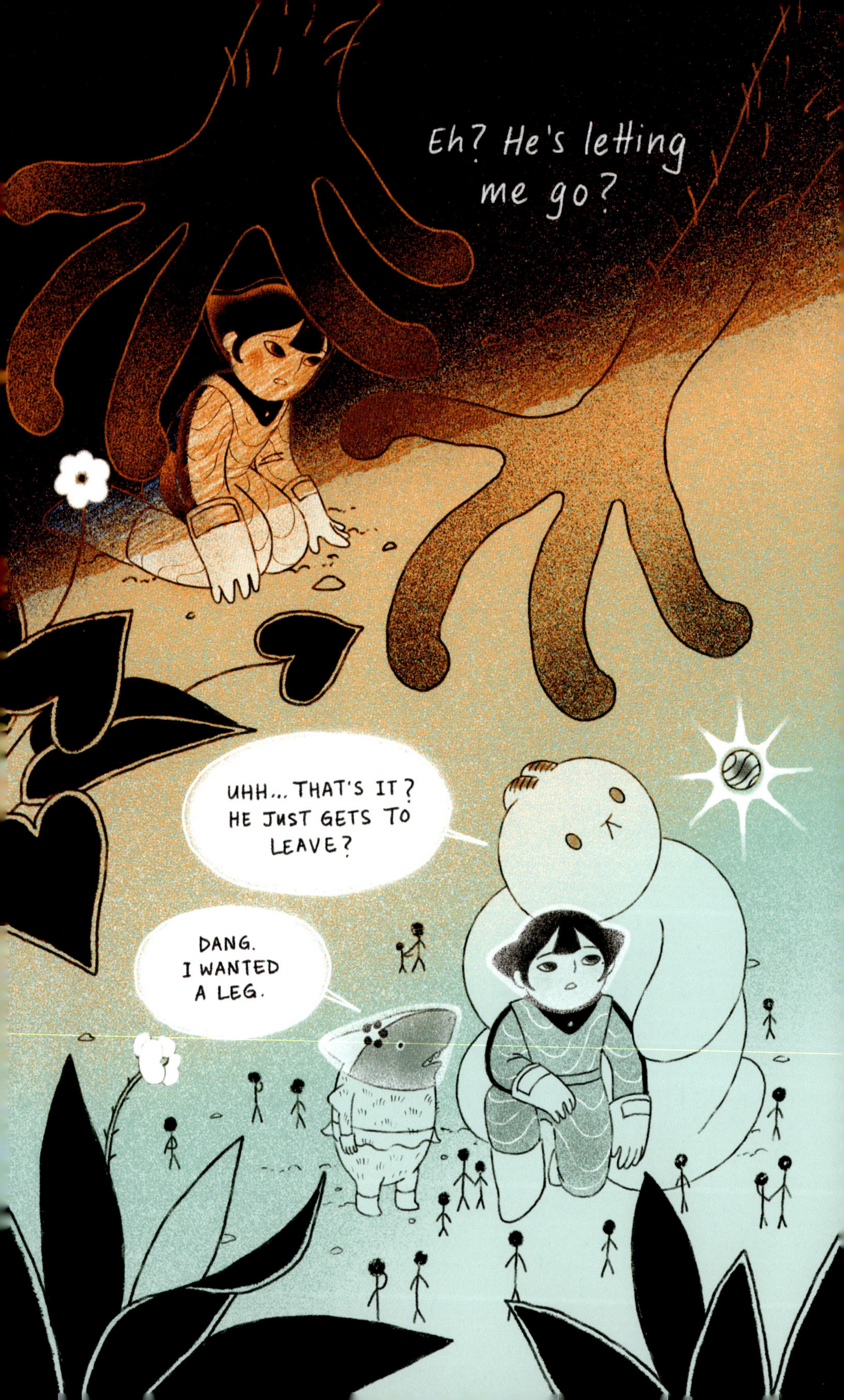
Eh? He's letting me go?
UHH... THAT'S IT? HE JUST GETS TO LEAVE?
DANG. I WANTED A LEG.

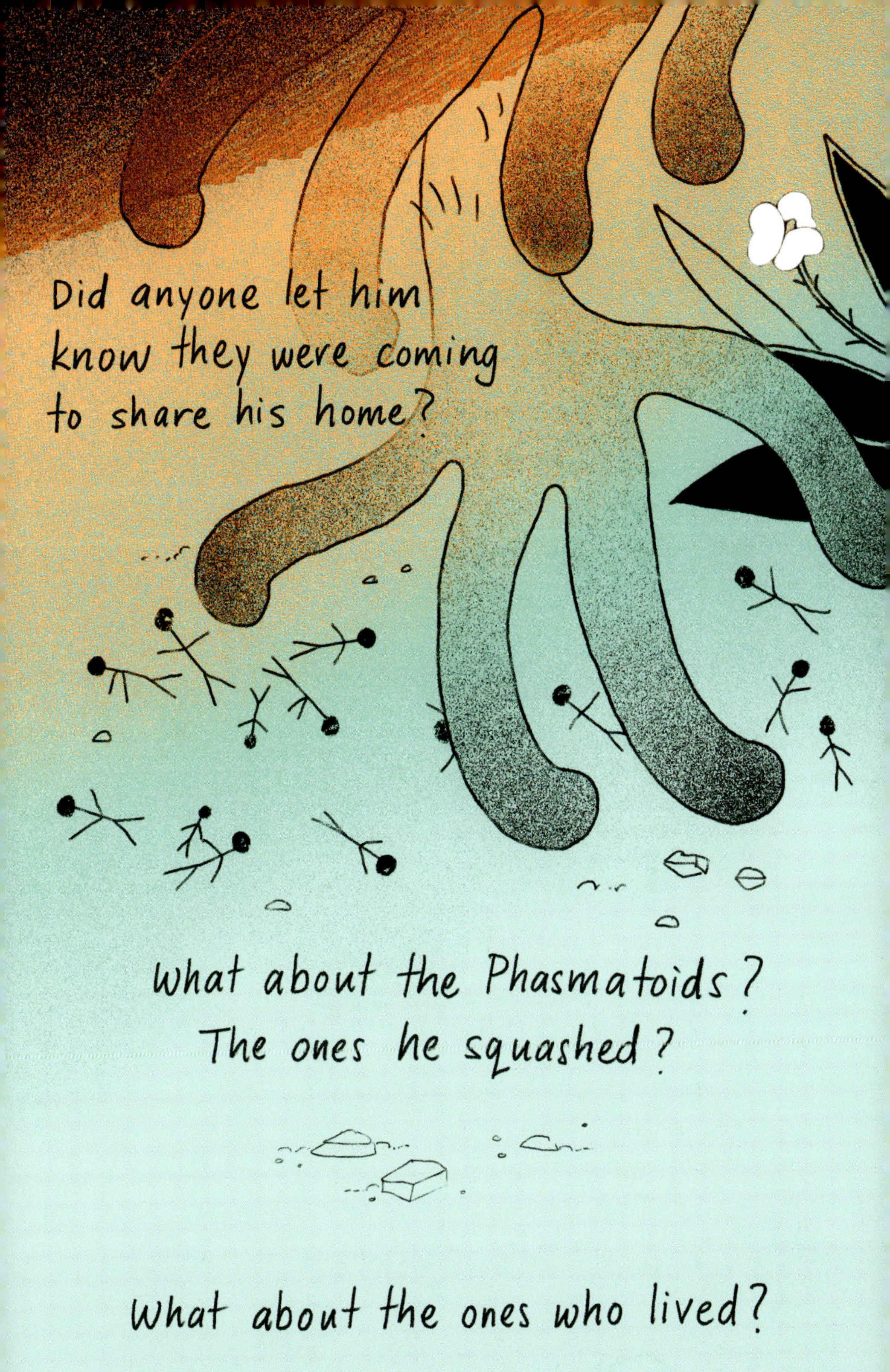
Did anyone let him know they were coming to share his home?
What about the Phasmatoids? The ones he squashed?
What about the ones who lived?

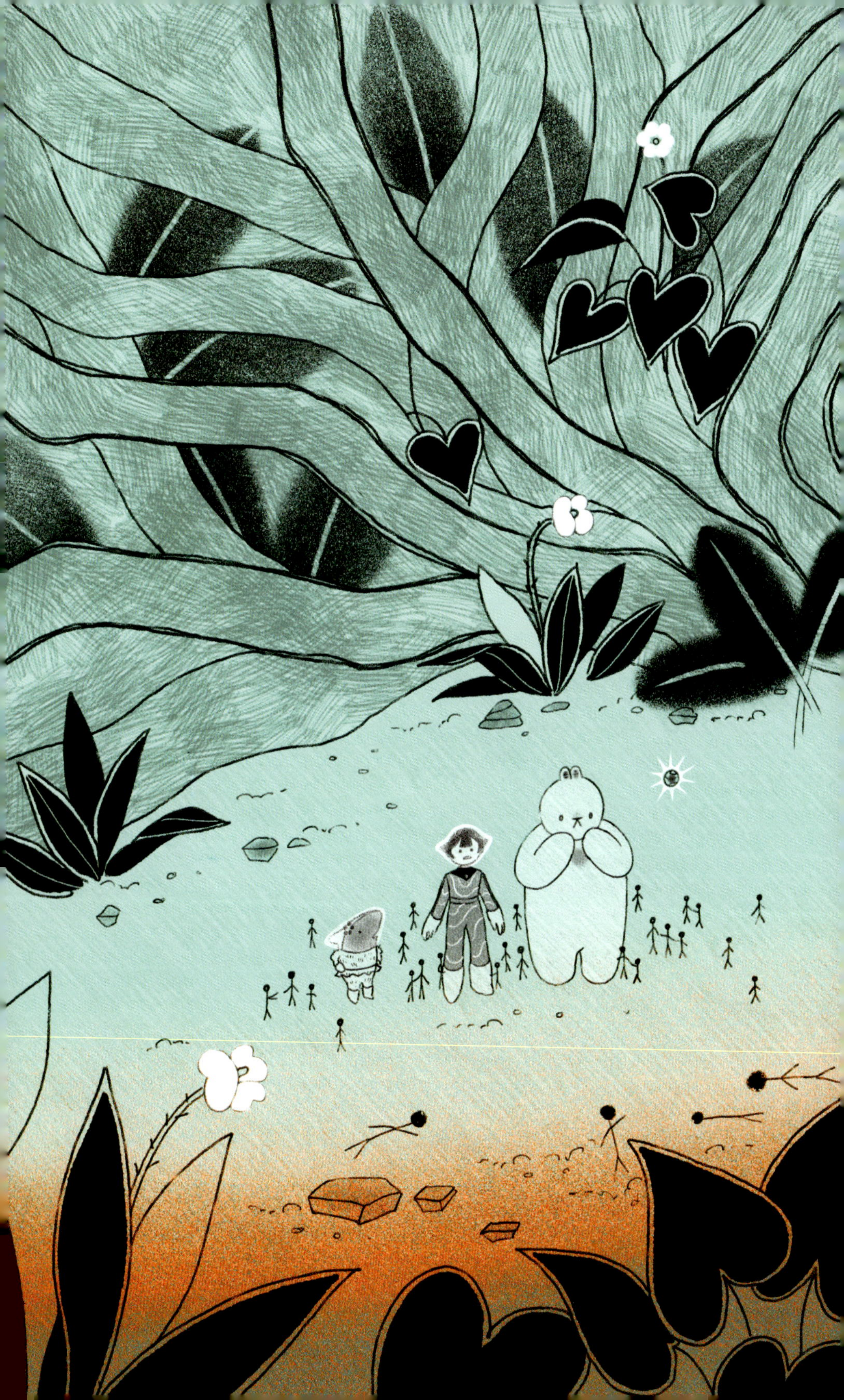

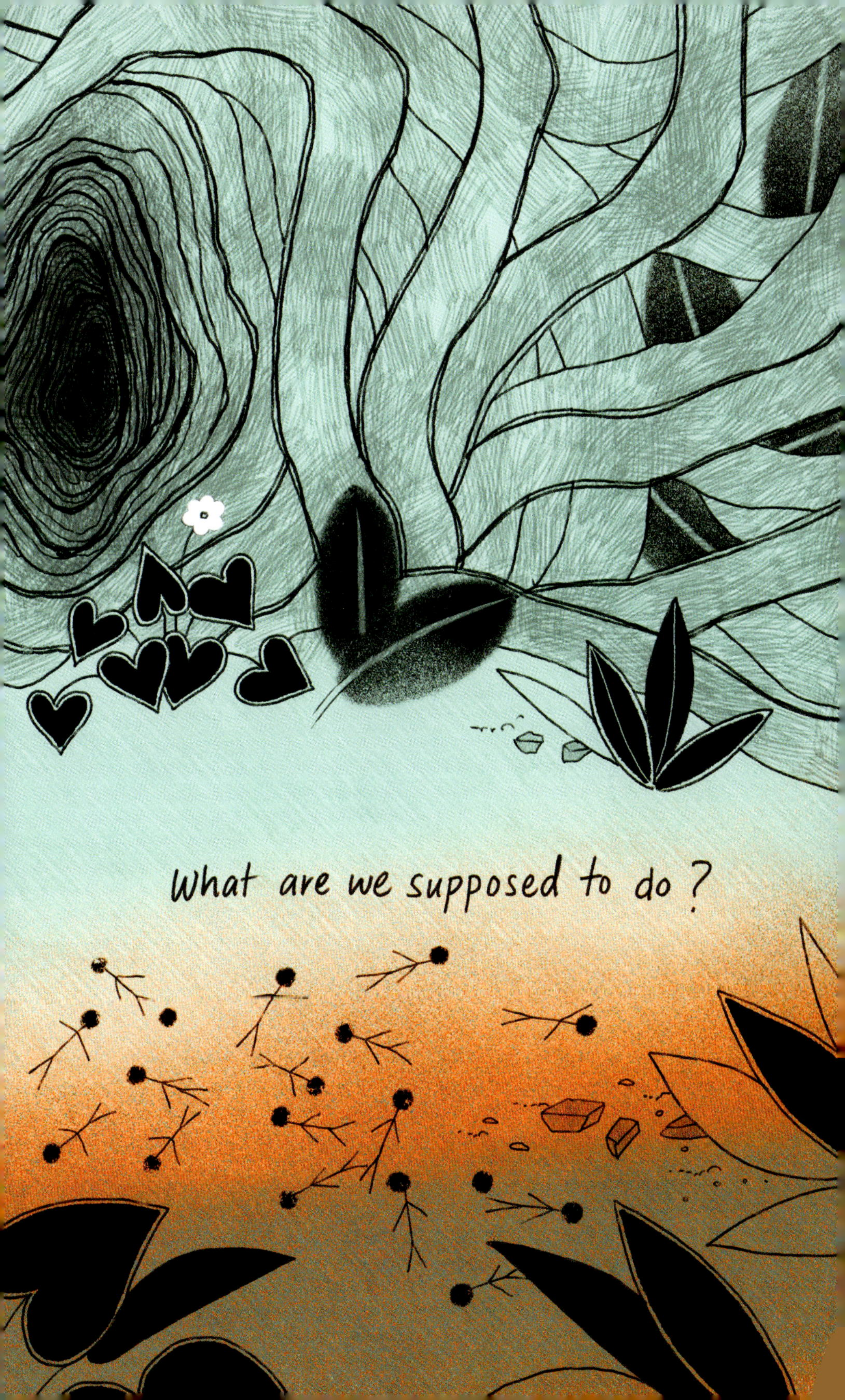
What are we supposed to do?

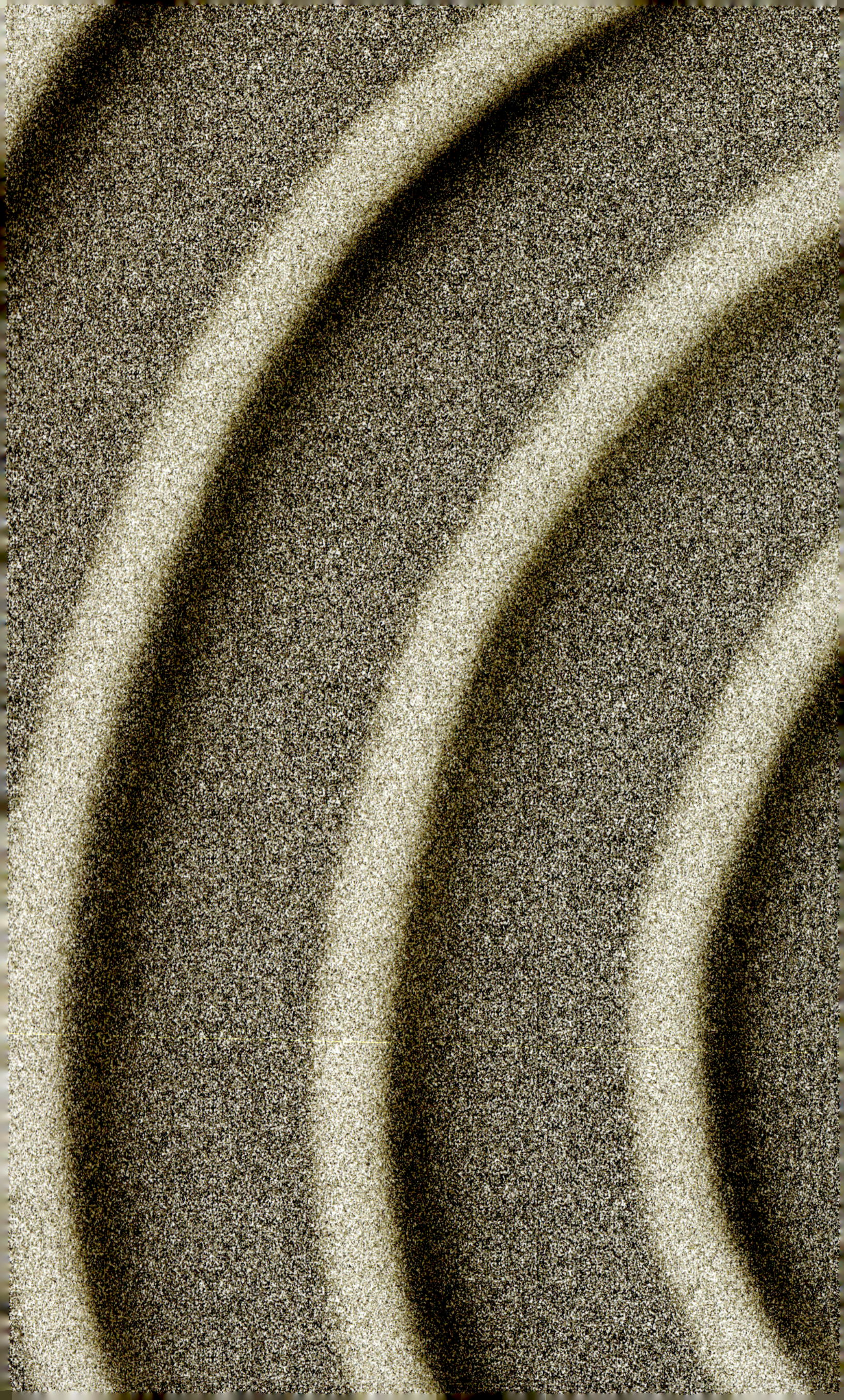

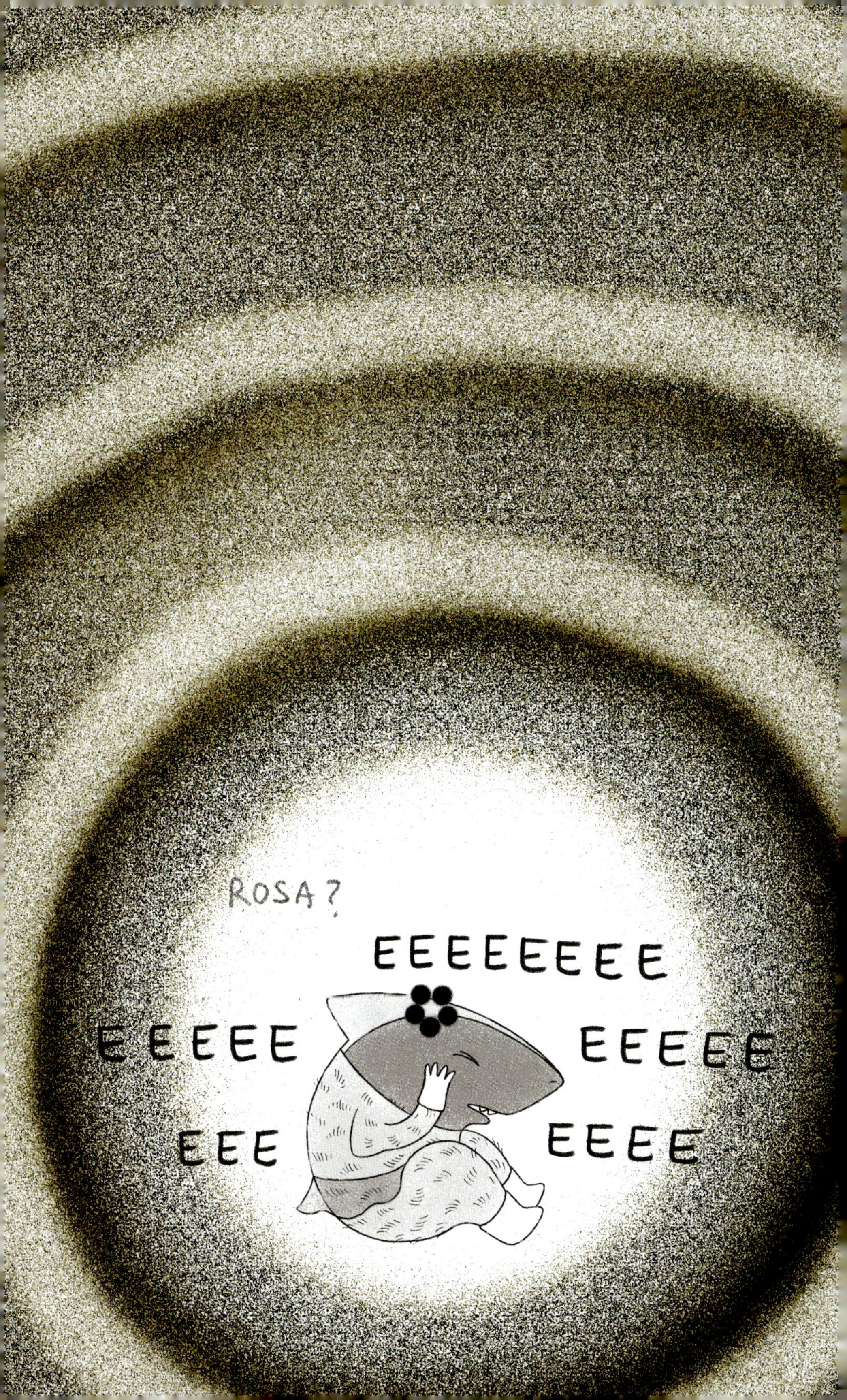
ROSA?
EEEEEEEEE
EEEEE
EEEEE
EEE
EEEE

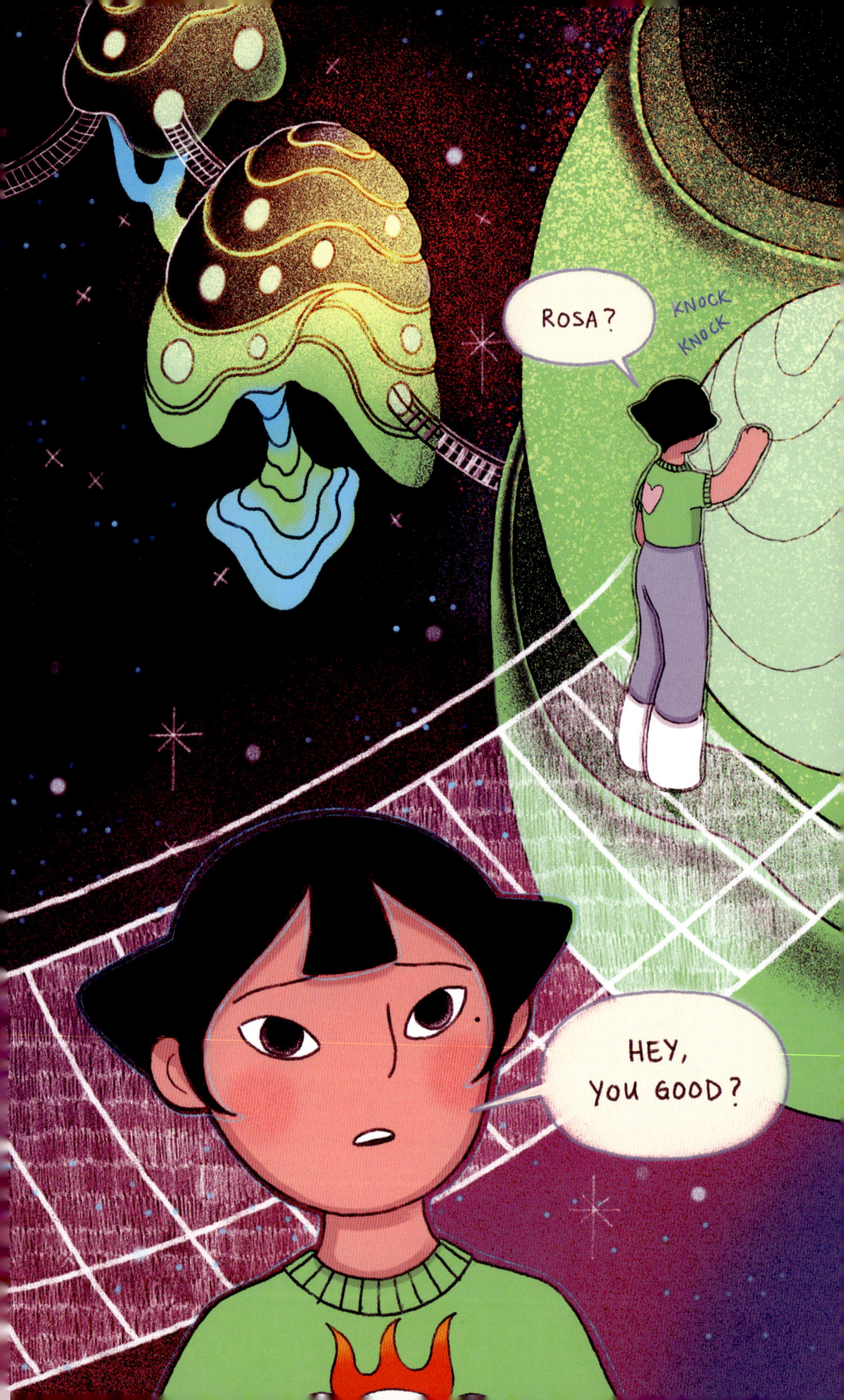
ROSA?
KNOCK
KNOCK
HEY,
YOU GOOD?

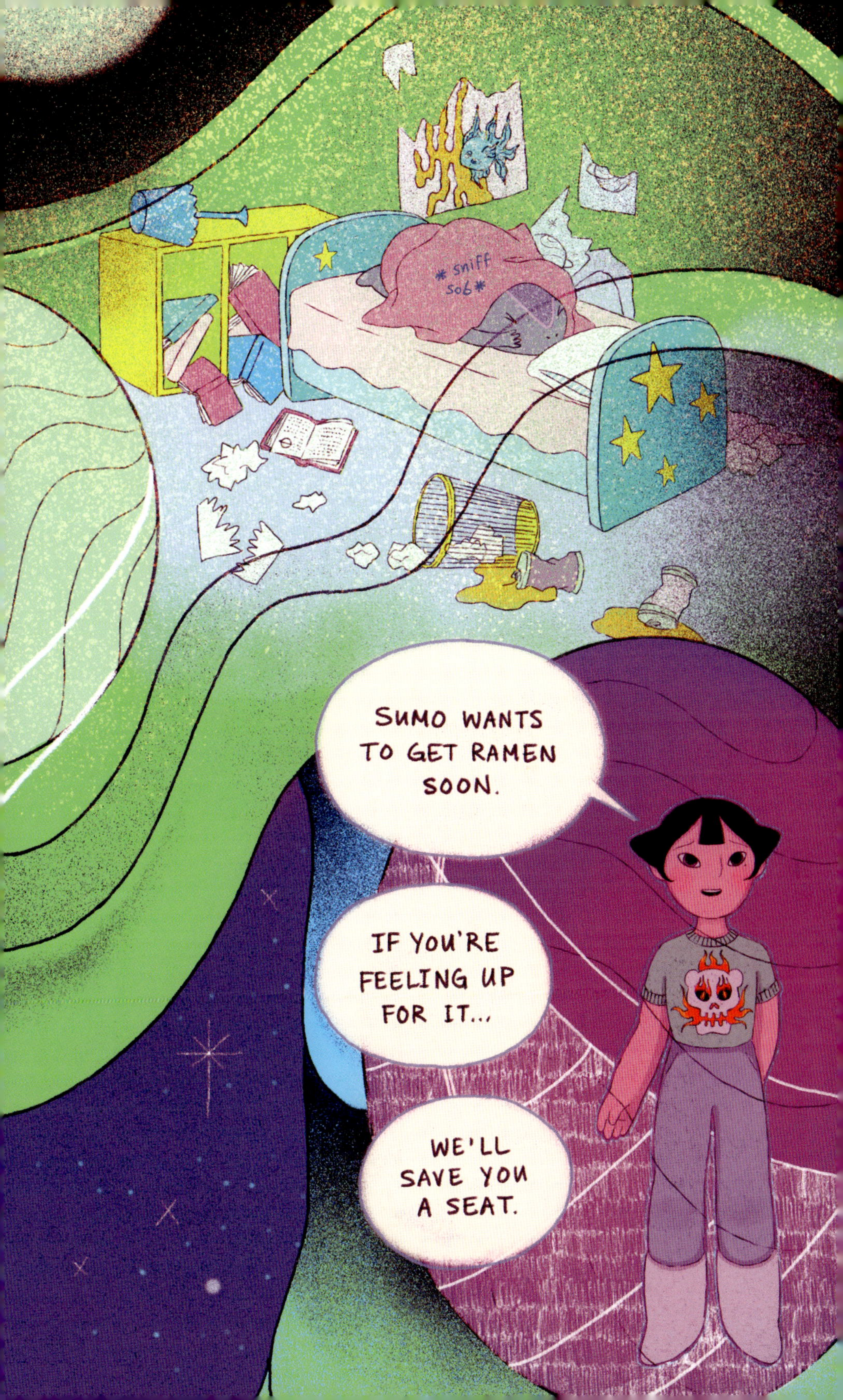
sniff sob
SUMO WANTS TO GET RAMEN SOON.
IF YOU'RE FEELING UP FOR IT...
WE'LL SAVE YOU A SEAT.

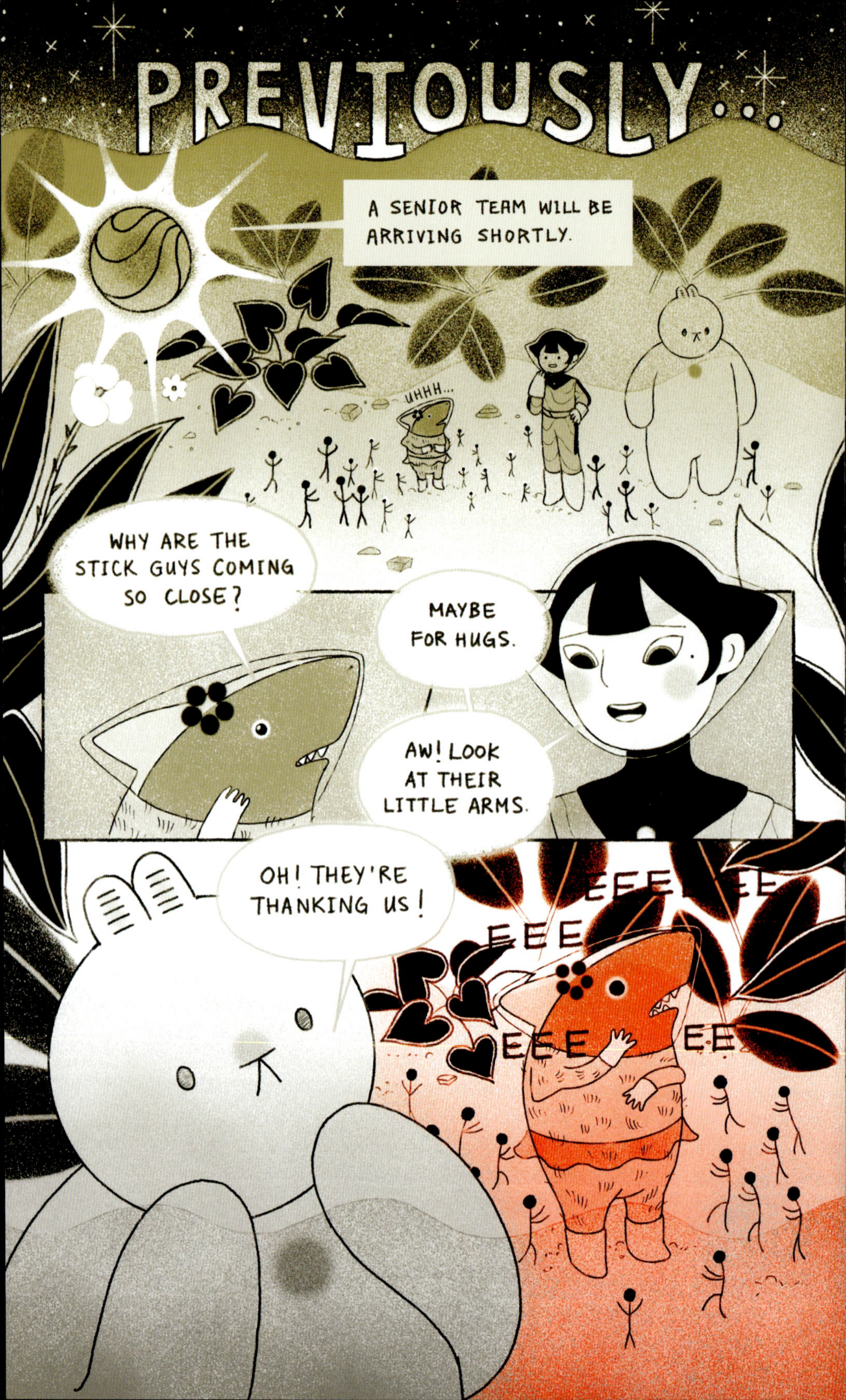
PREVIOUSLY...
A SENIOR TEAM WILL BE ARRIVING SHORTLY.
UHHH...
WHY ARE THE STICK GUYS COMING SO CLOSE?
MAYBE FOR HUGS.
AW! LOOK AT THEIR LITTLE ARMS.
OH! THEY'RE THANKING US!
EEE
EEE
EEE
EE

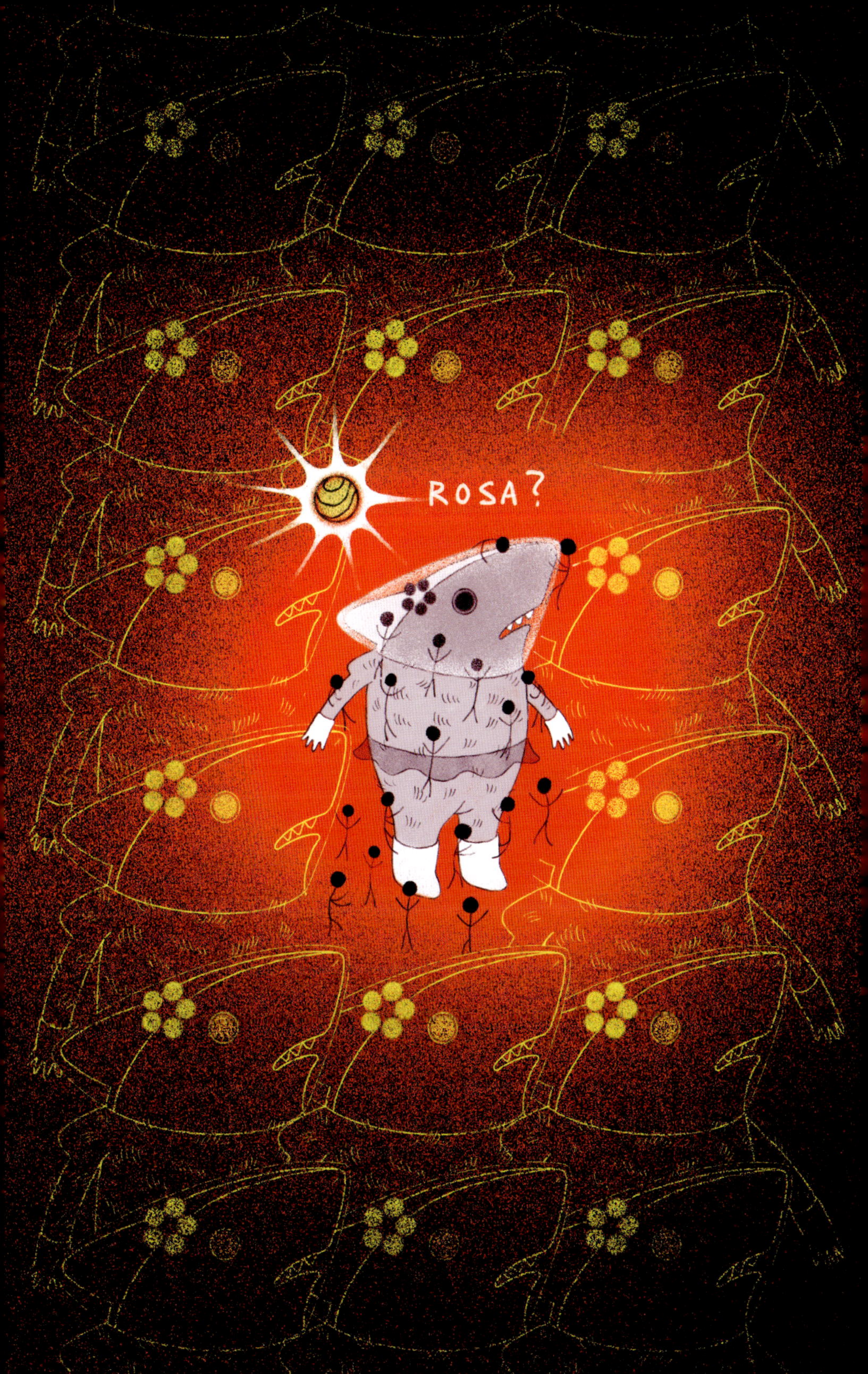
ROSA?

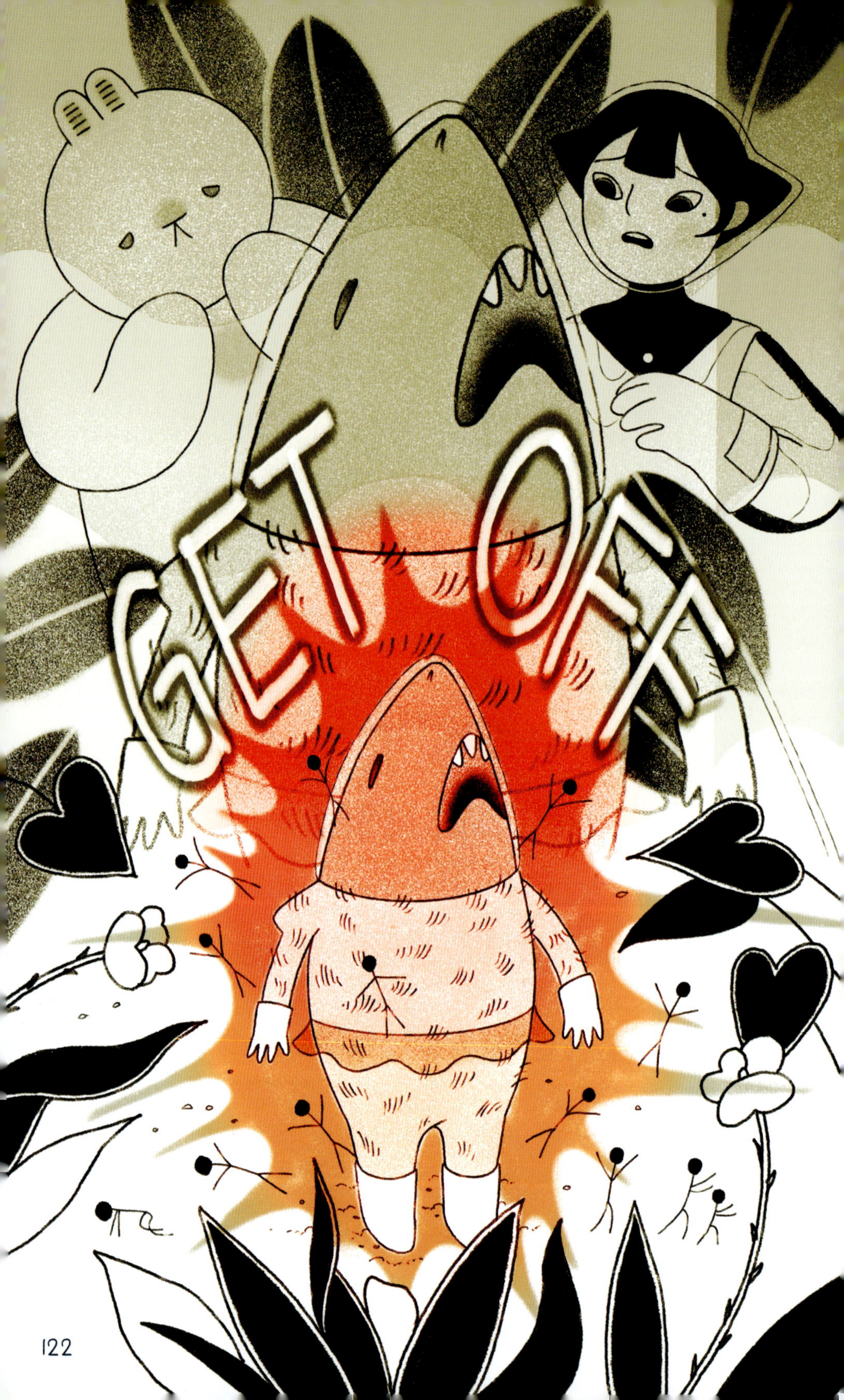
GET OFF

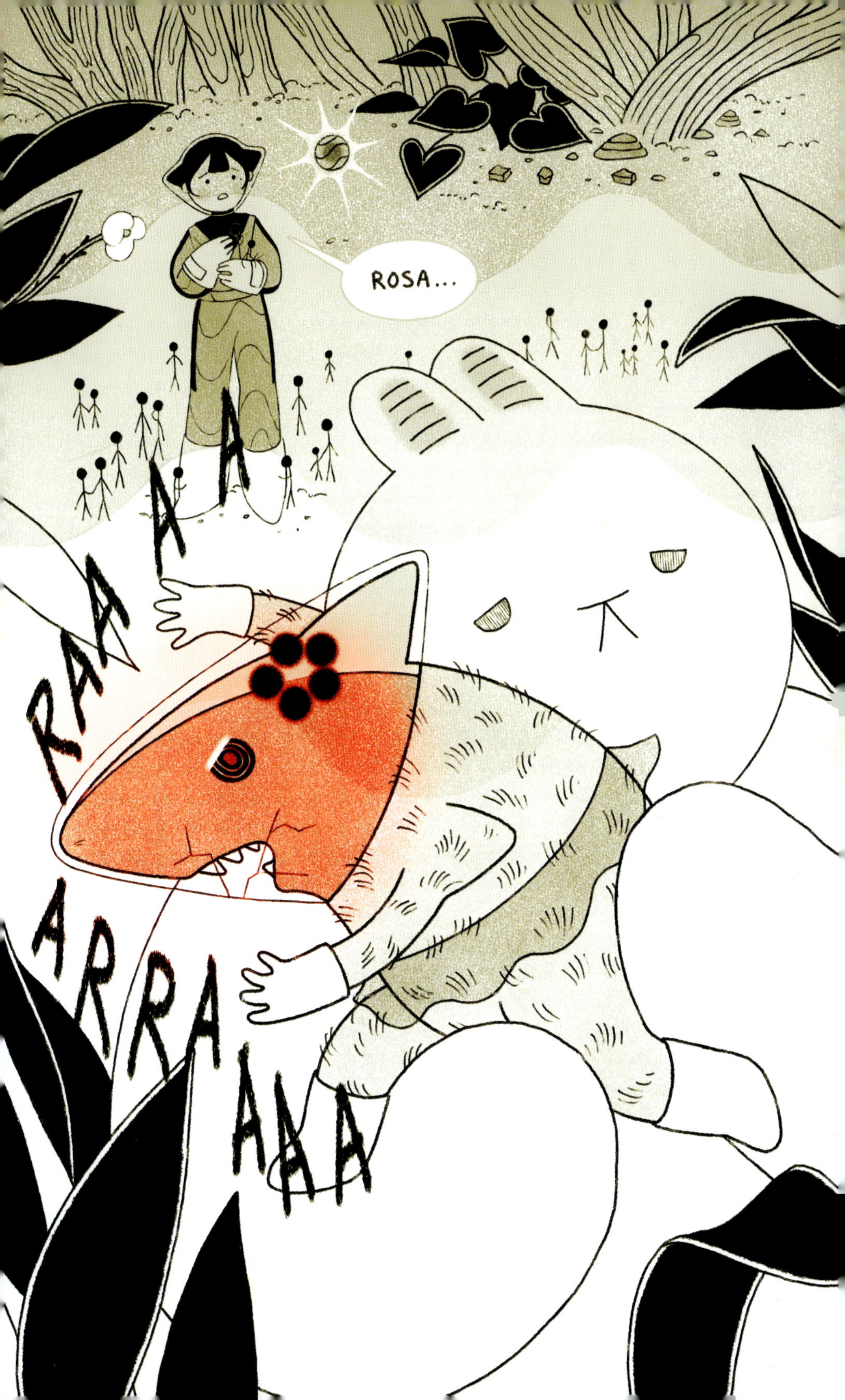
ROSA...
RAAAAA
ARRAAAA

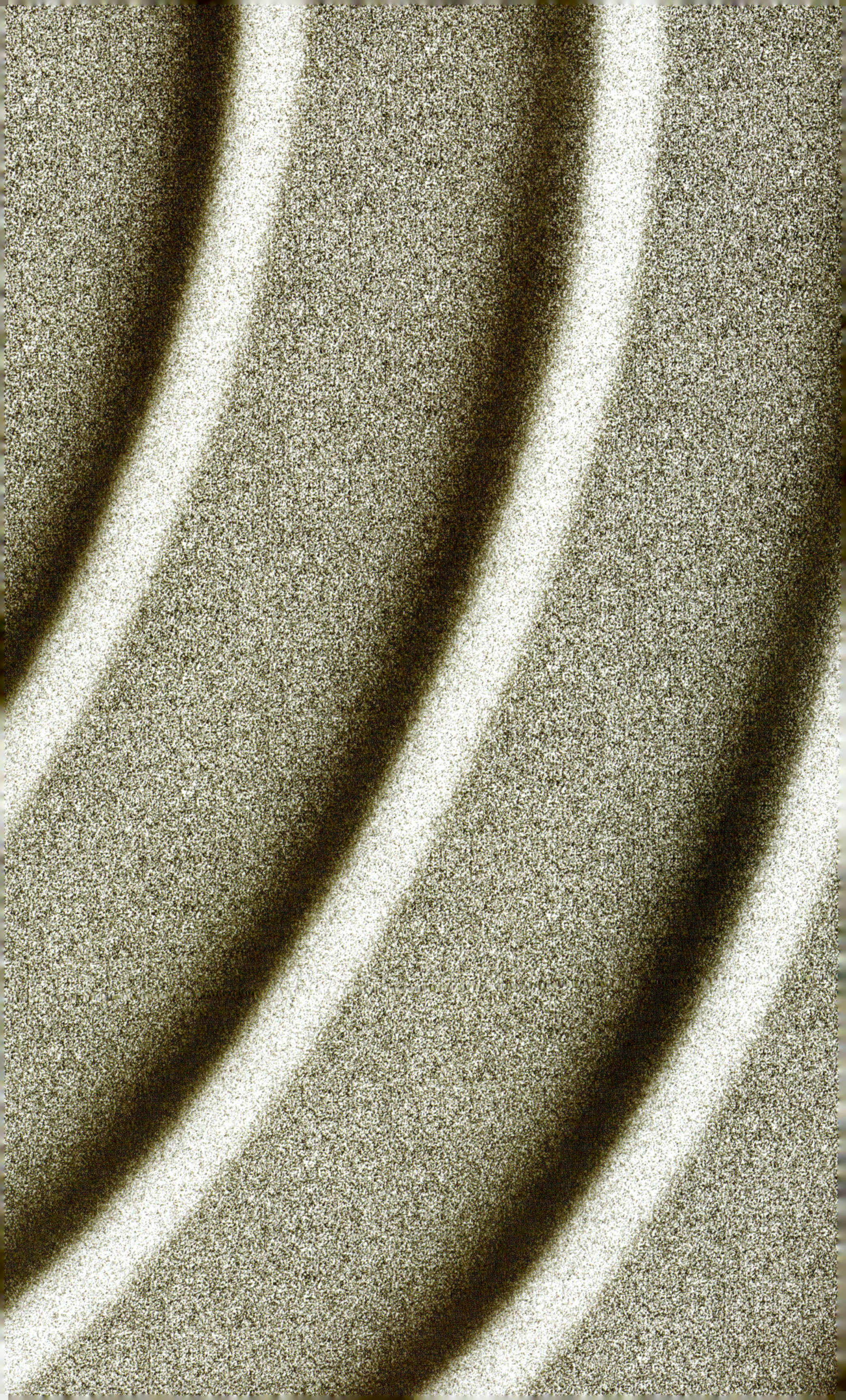

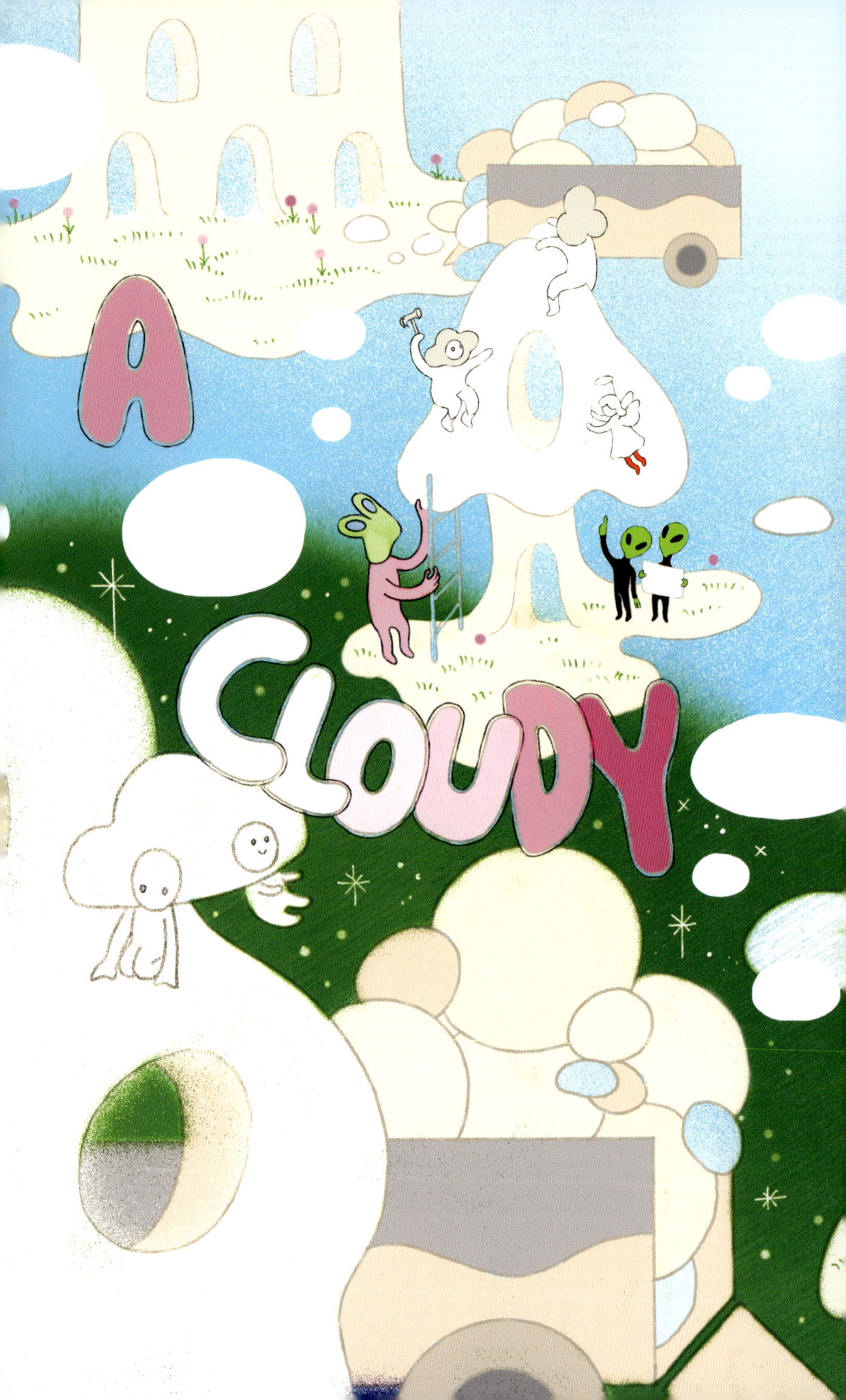
A
CLOUDY

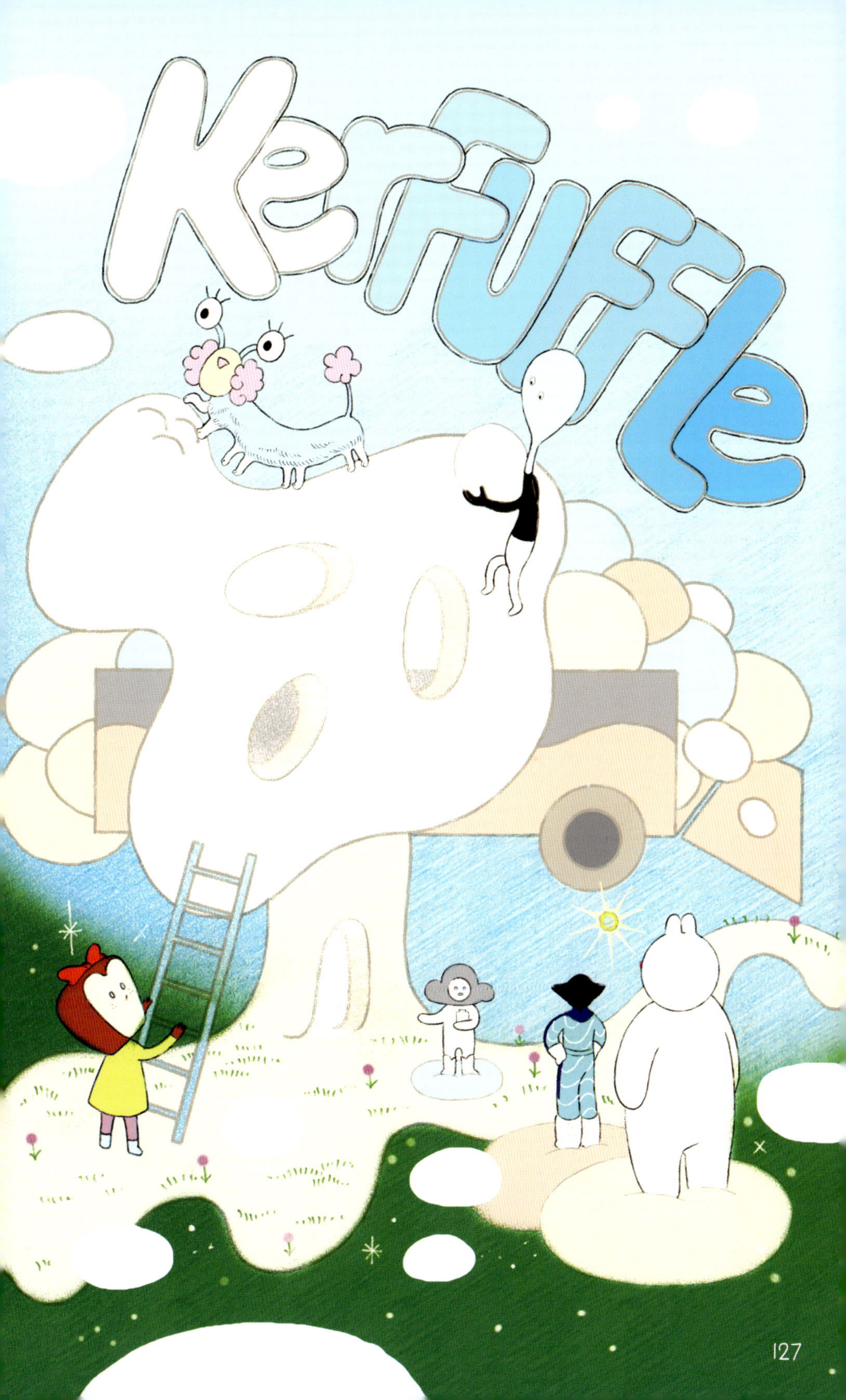
Kerfuffle

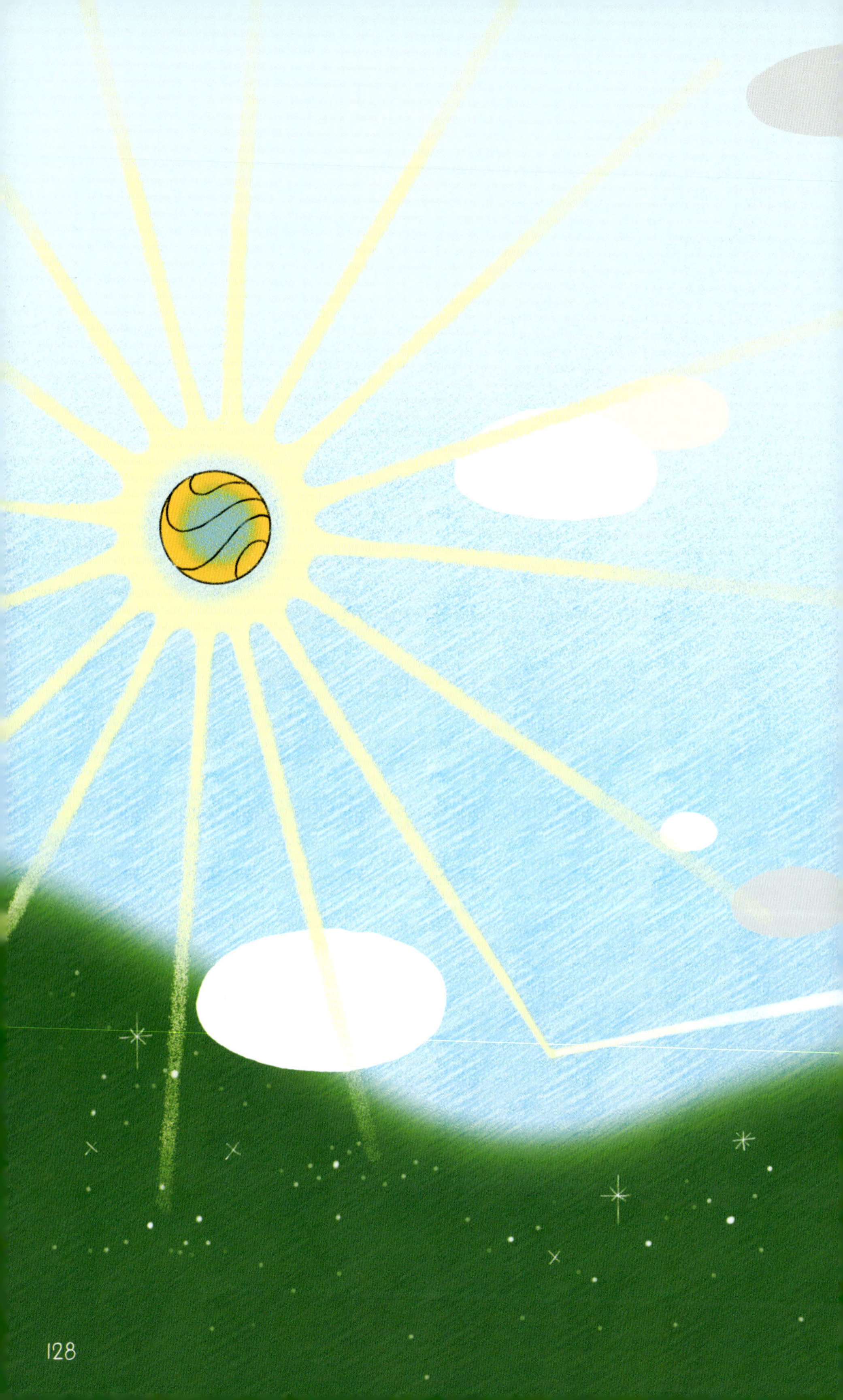

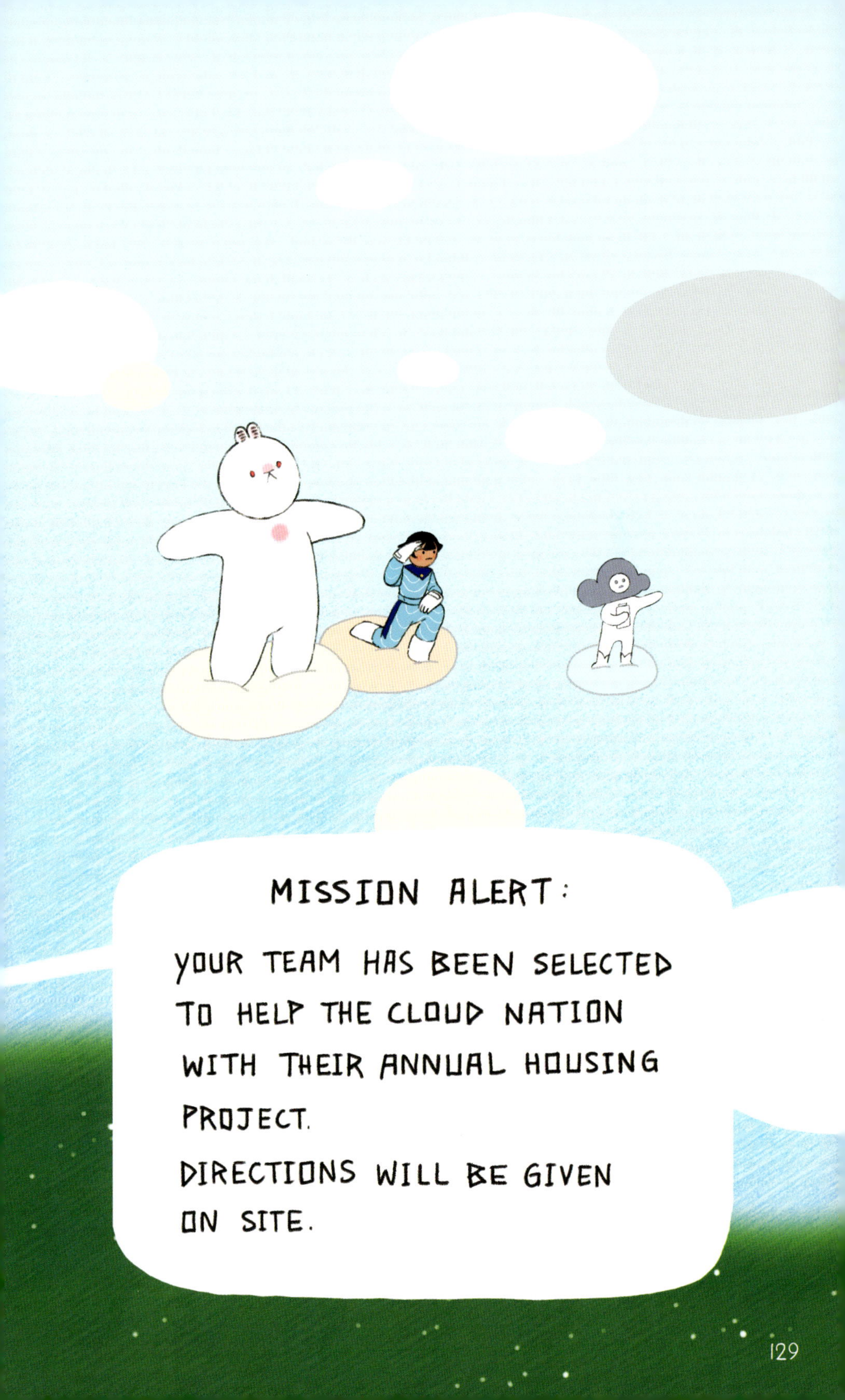
MISSION ALERT:
YOUR TEAM HAS BEEN SELECTED TO HELP THE CLOUD NATION WITH THEIR ANNUAL HOUSING PROJECT.
DIRECTIONS WILL BE GIVEN ON SITE.

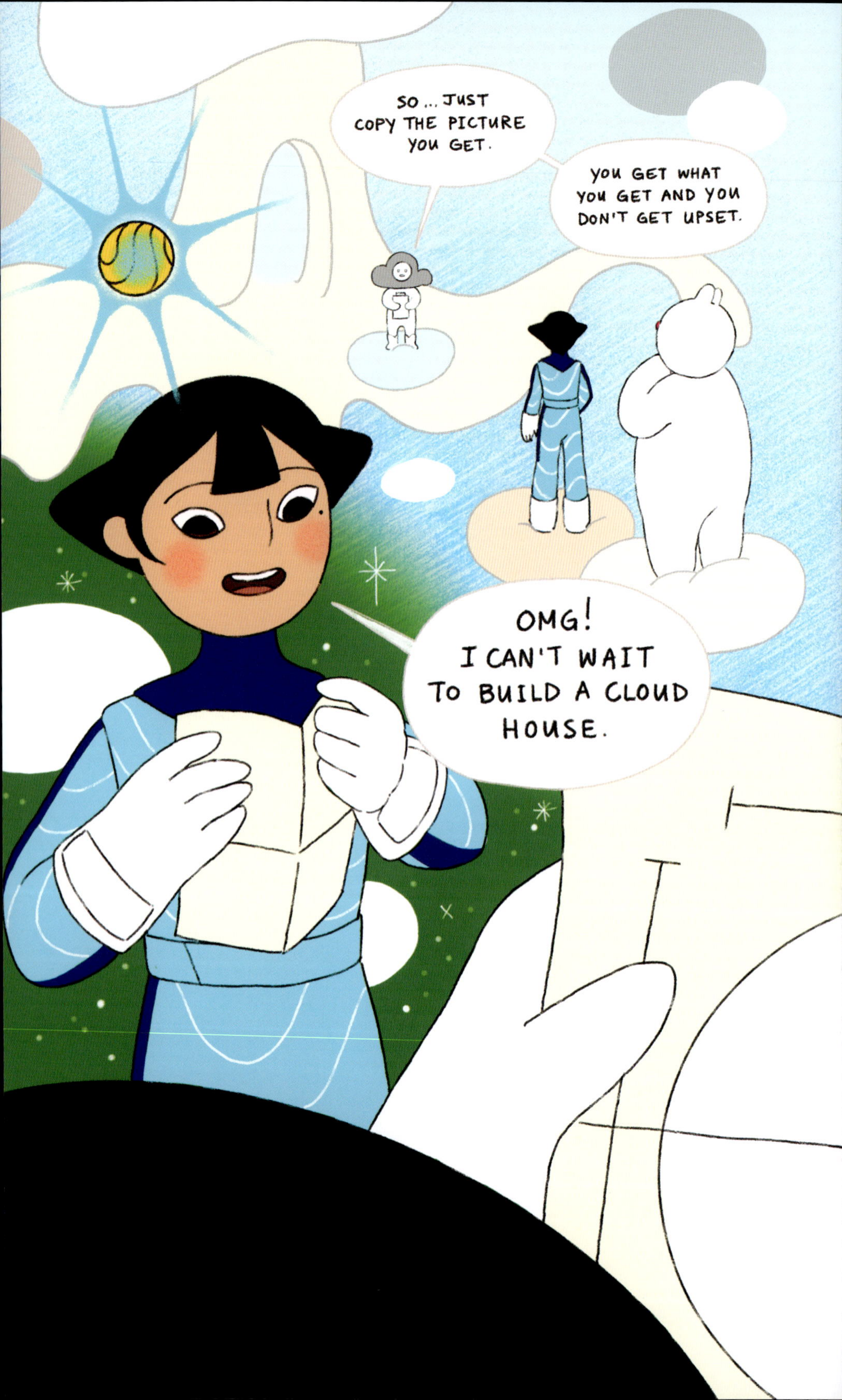
SO ... JUST COPY THE PICTURE YOU GET.
YOU GET WHAT YOU GET AND YOU DON'T GET UPSET.
OMG! I CAN'T WAIT TO BUILD A CLOUD HOUSE.

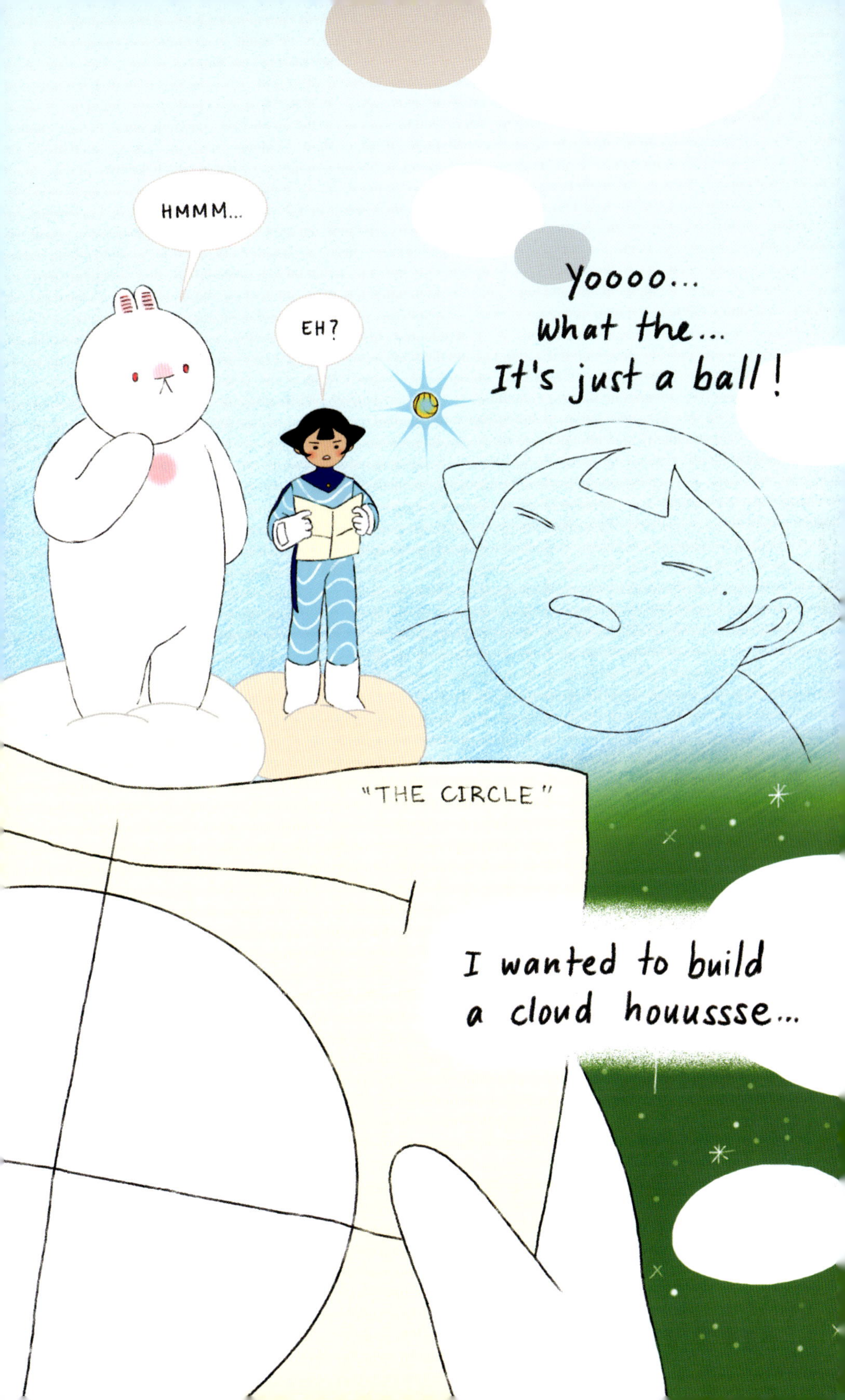
HMMM...
EH?
Yoooo...
what the...
It's just a ball!
"THE CIRCLE"
I wanted to build
a cloud houussse...

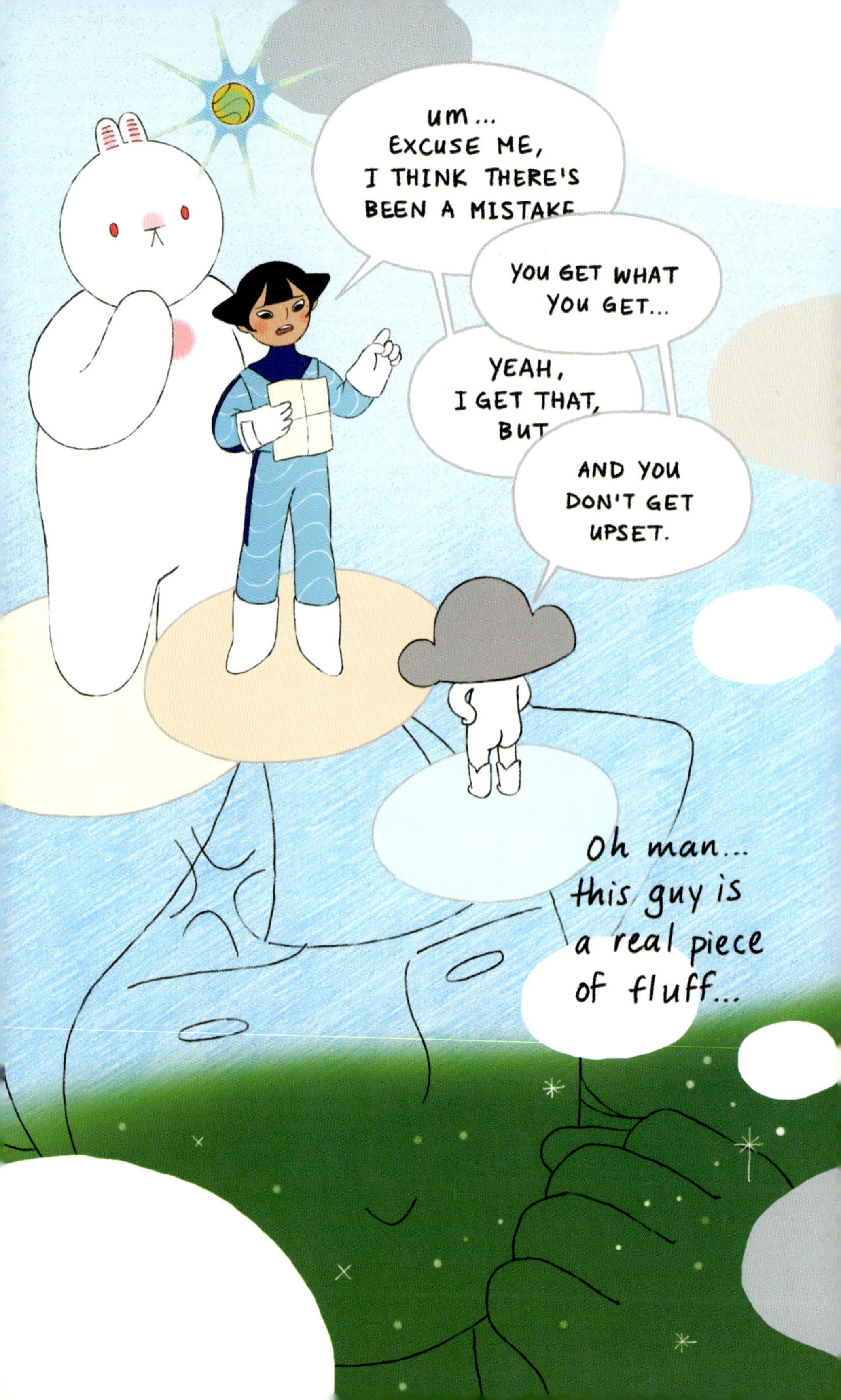
um... EXCUSE ME, I THINK THERE'S BEEN A MISTAKE
YOU GET WHAT YOU GET...
YEAH, I GET THAT, BUT
AND YOU DON'T GET UPSET.
Oh man... this guy is a real piece of fluff...

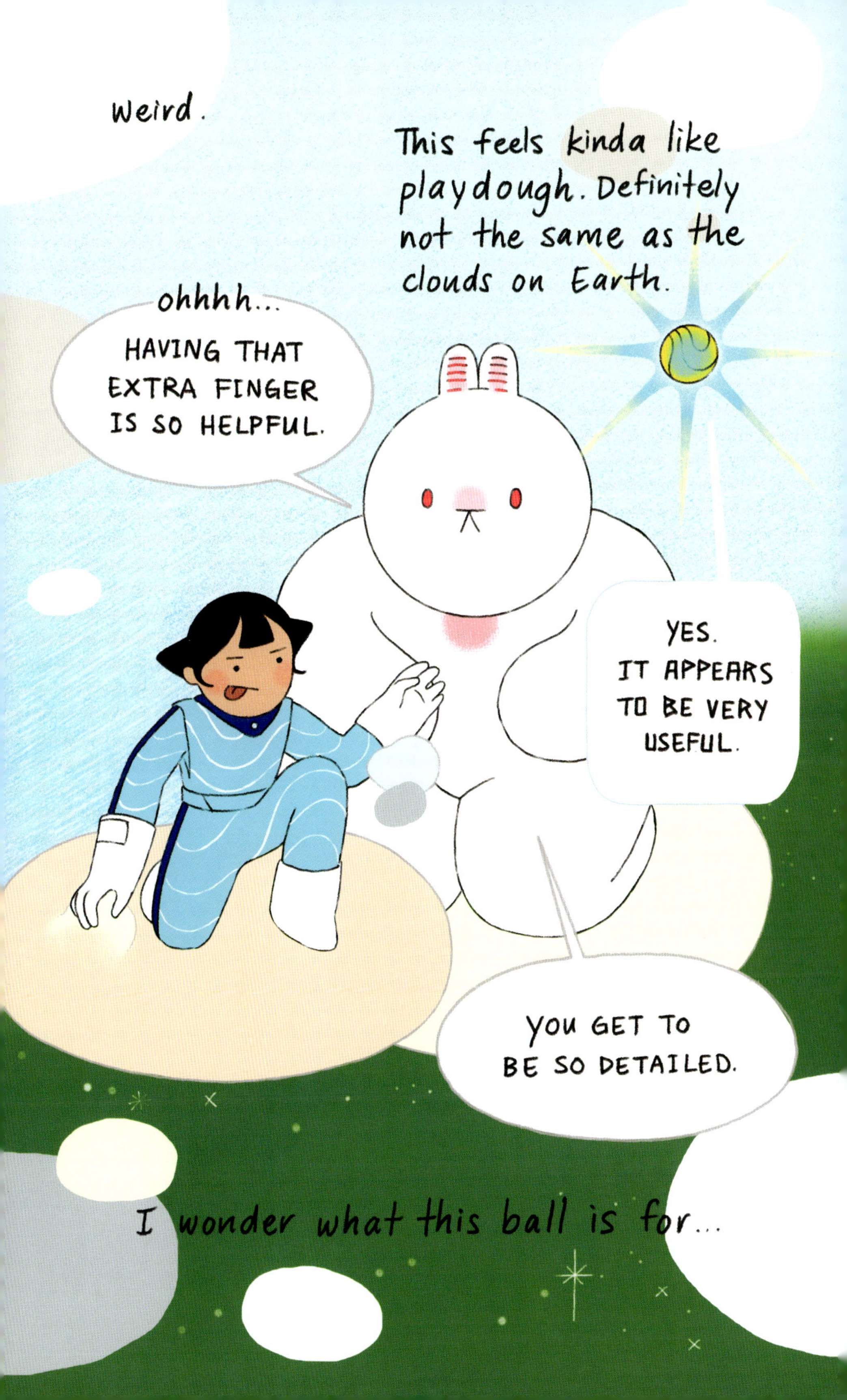
weird.
This feels kinda like playdough. Definitely not the same as the clouds on Earth.
ohhhh...
HAVING THAT EXTRA FINGER IS SO HELPFUL.
YES. IT APPEARS TO BE VERY USEFUL.
YOU GET TO BE SO DETAILED.
I wonder what this ball is for...

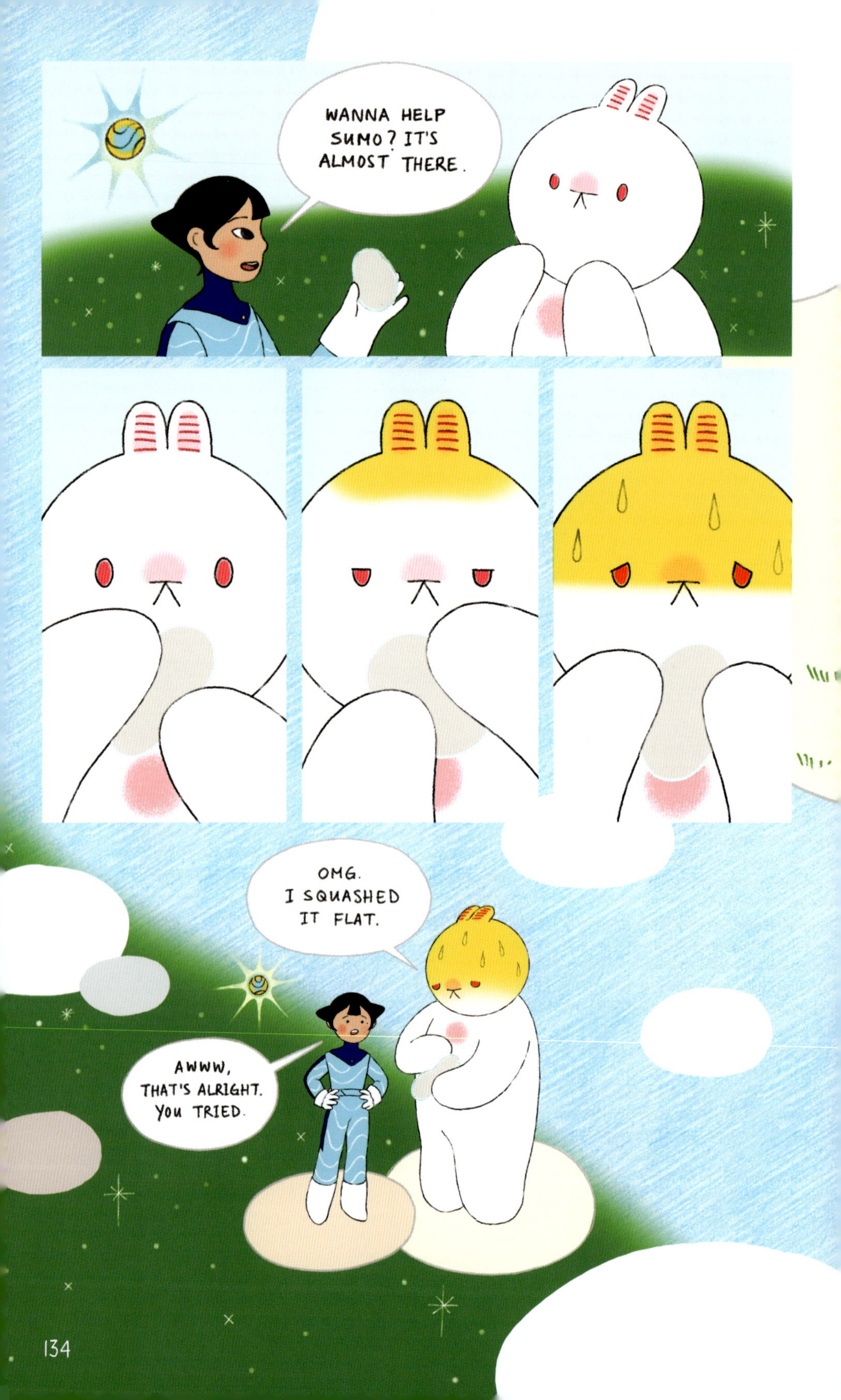
WANNA HELP SUMO? IT'S ALMOST THERE.
OMG. I SQUASHED IT FLAT.
AWWW, THAT'S ALRIGHT. YOU TRIED.

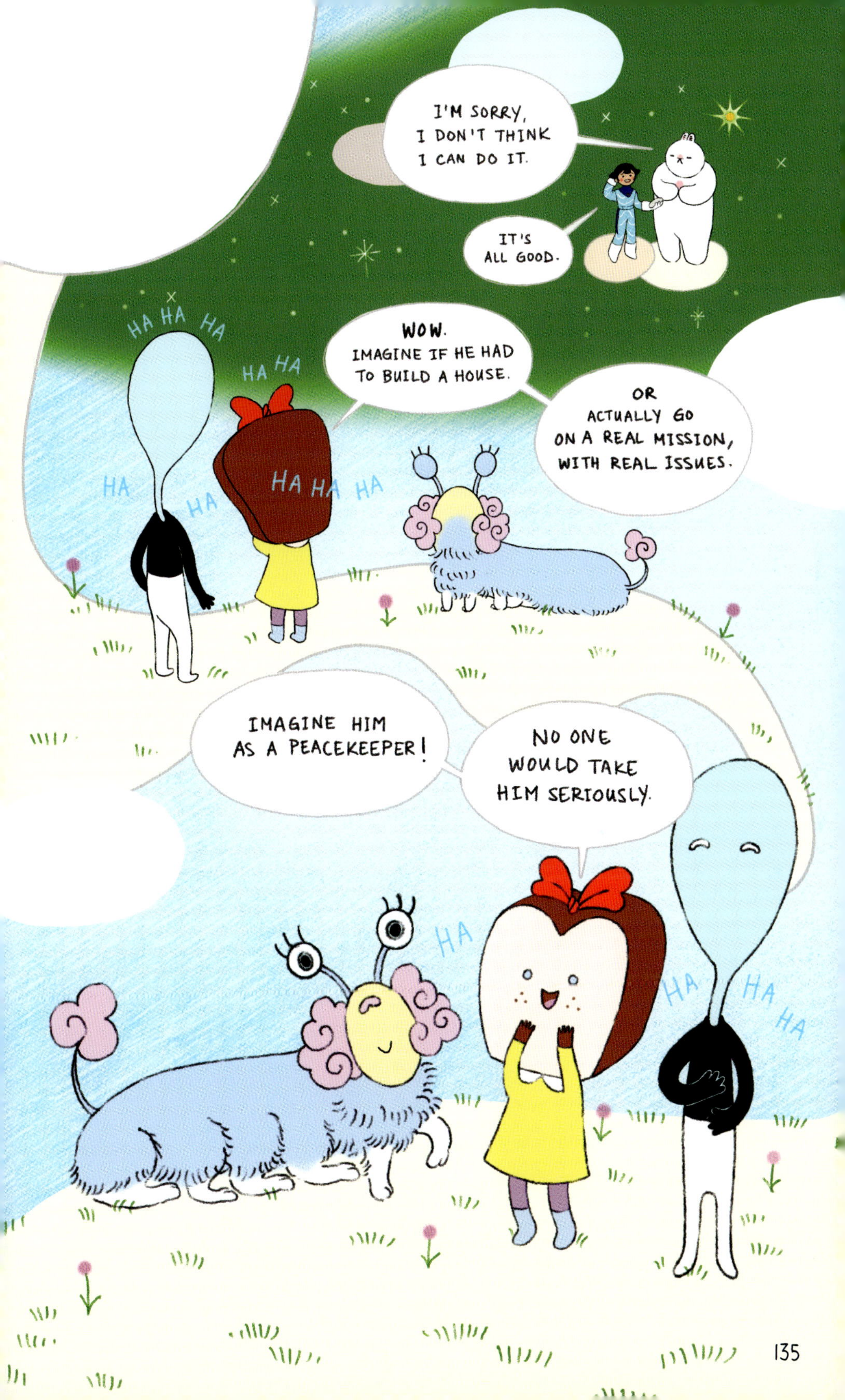
I'M SORRY, I DON'T THINK I CAN DO IT.
IT'S ALL GOOD.
HA HA HA
HA HA
WOW. IMAGINE IF HE HAD TO BUILD A HOUSE.
OR ACTUALLY GO ON A REAL MISSION, WITH REAL ISSUES.
HA
HA
HA HA HA
IMAGINE HIM AS A PEACEKEEPER!
NO ONE WOULD TAKE HIM SERIOUSLY.
HA
HA
HA
HA

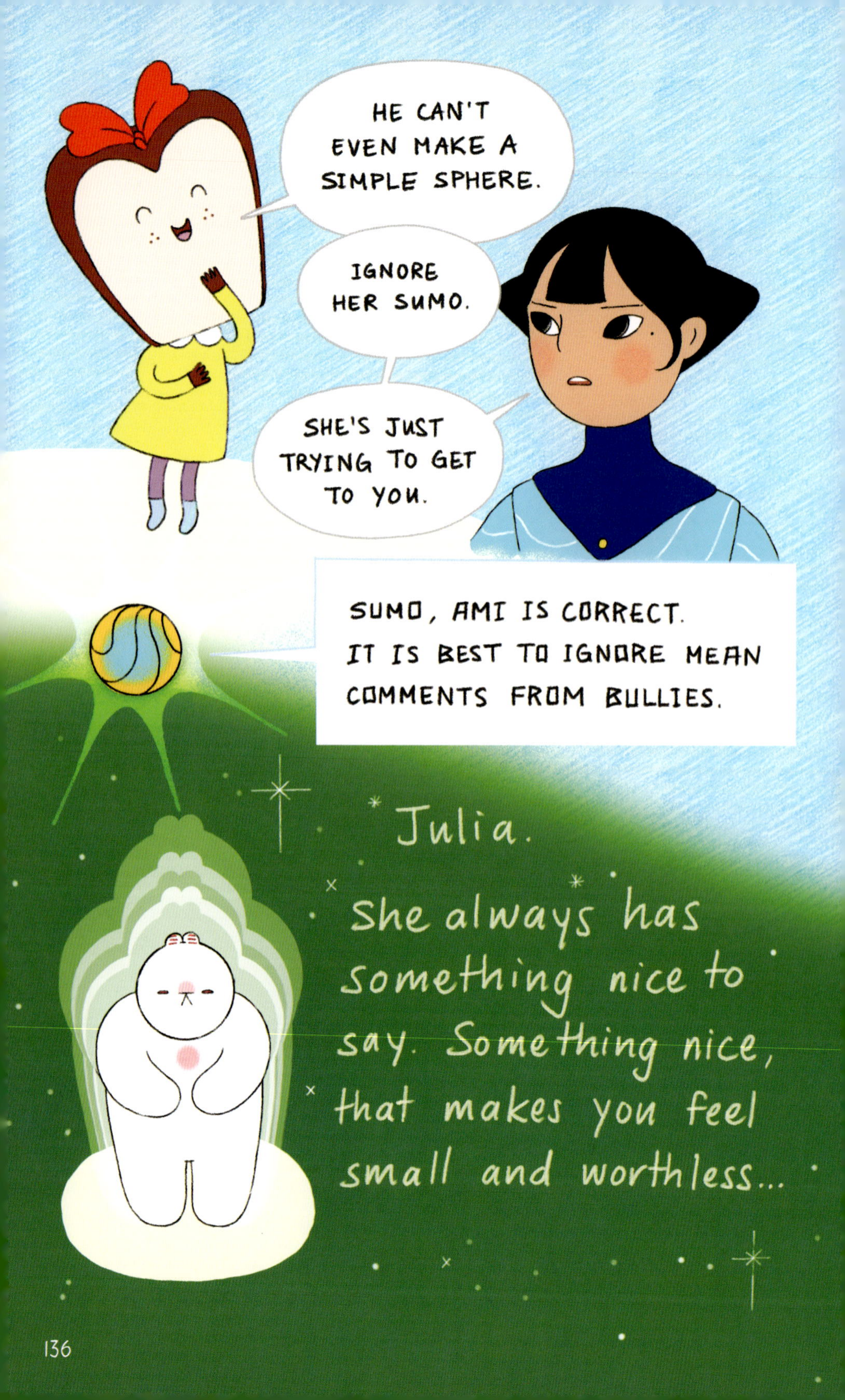
HE CAN'T EVEN MAKE A SIMPLE SPHERE.
IGNORE HER SUMO.
SHE'S JUST TRYING TO GET TO YOU.
SUMO, AMI IS CORRECT. IT IS BEST TO IGNORE MEAN COMMENTS FROM BULLIES.
Julia.
She always has something nice to say. Something nice, that makes you feel small and worthless...

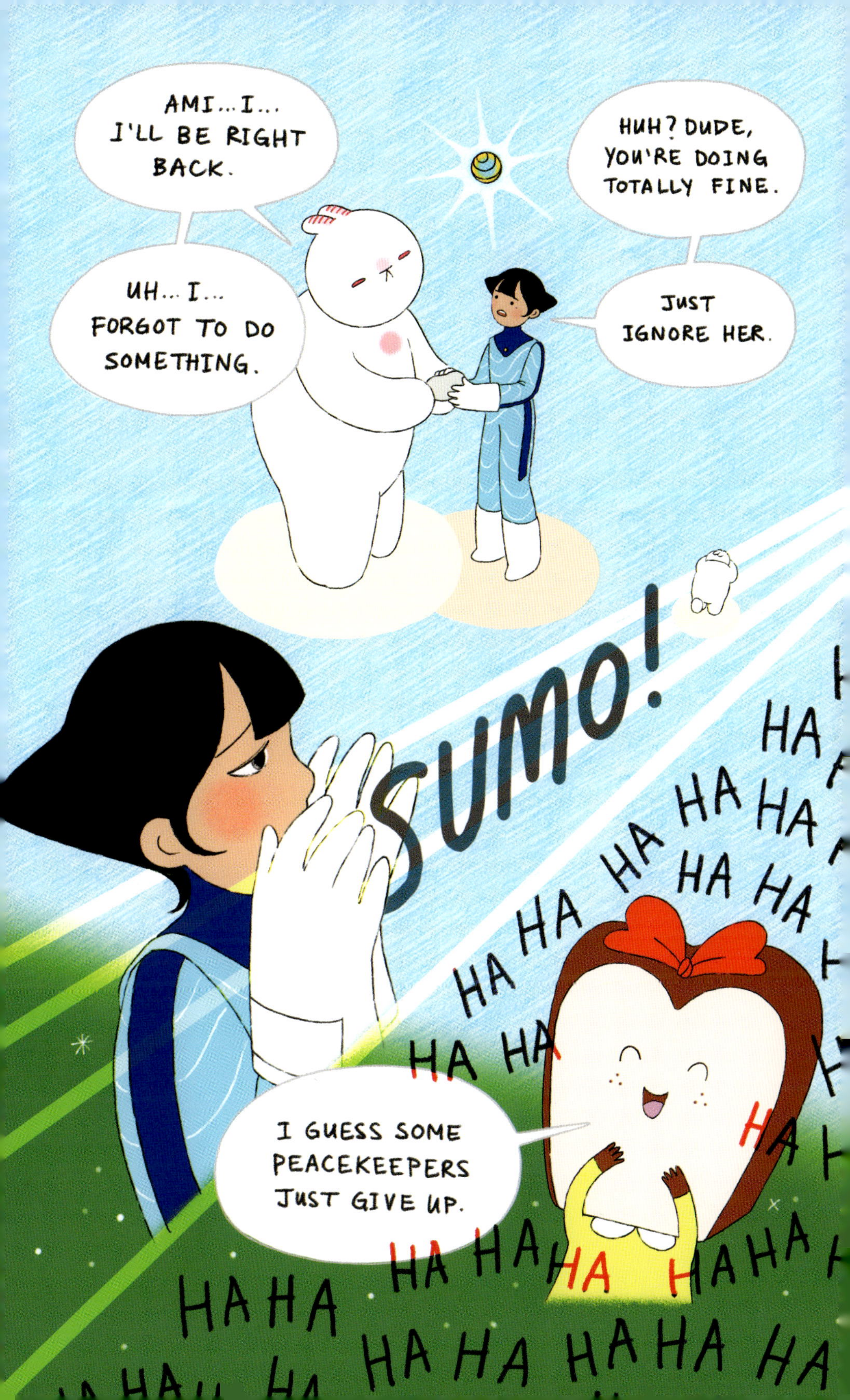
AMI... I...
I'LL BE RIGHT BACK.
UH... I...
FORGOT TO DO SOMETHING.
HUH? DUDE, YOU'RE DOING TOTALLY FINE.
JUST IGNORE HER.
SUMO!
HA HA HA HA HA HA HA HA HA
I GUESS SOME PEACEKEEPERS JUST GIVE UP.
HA HA HA HA HA HA HA HA HA HA HA HA HA

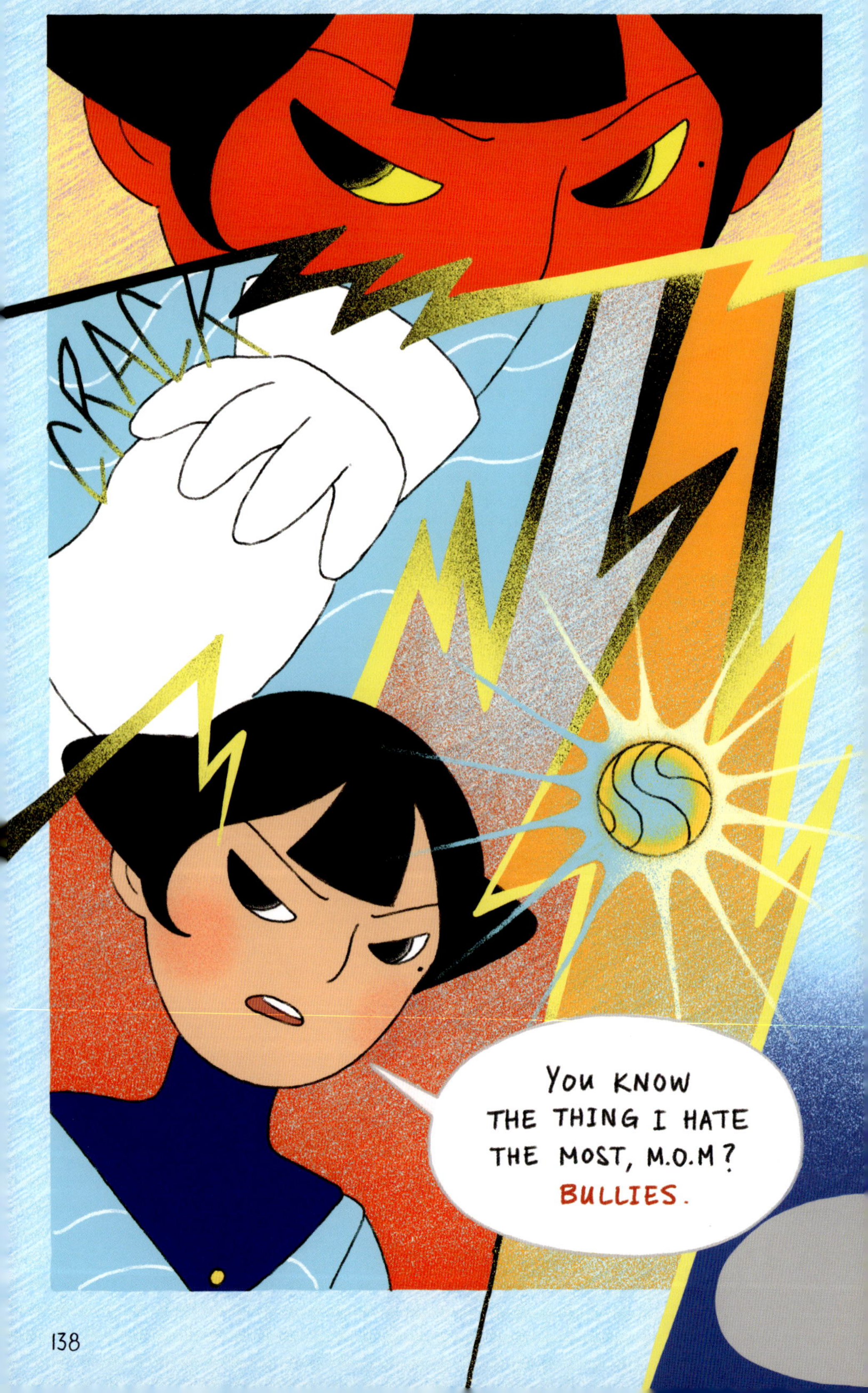
CRACK
YOU KNOW THE THING I HATE THE MOST, M.O.M? BULLIES.

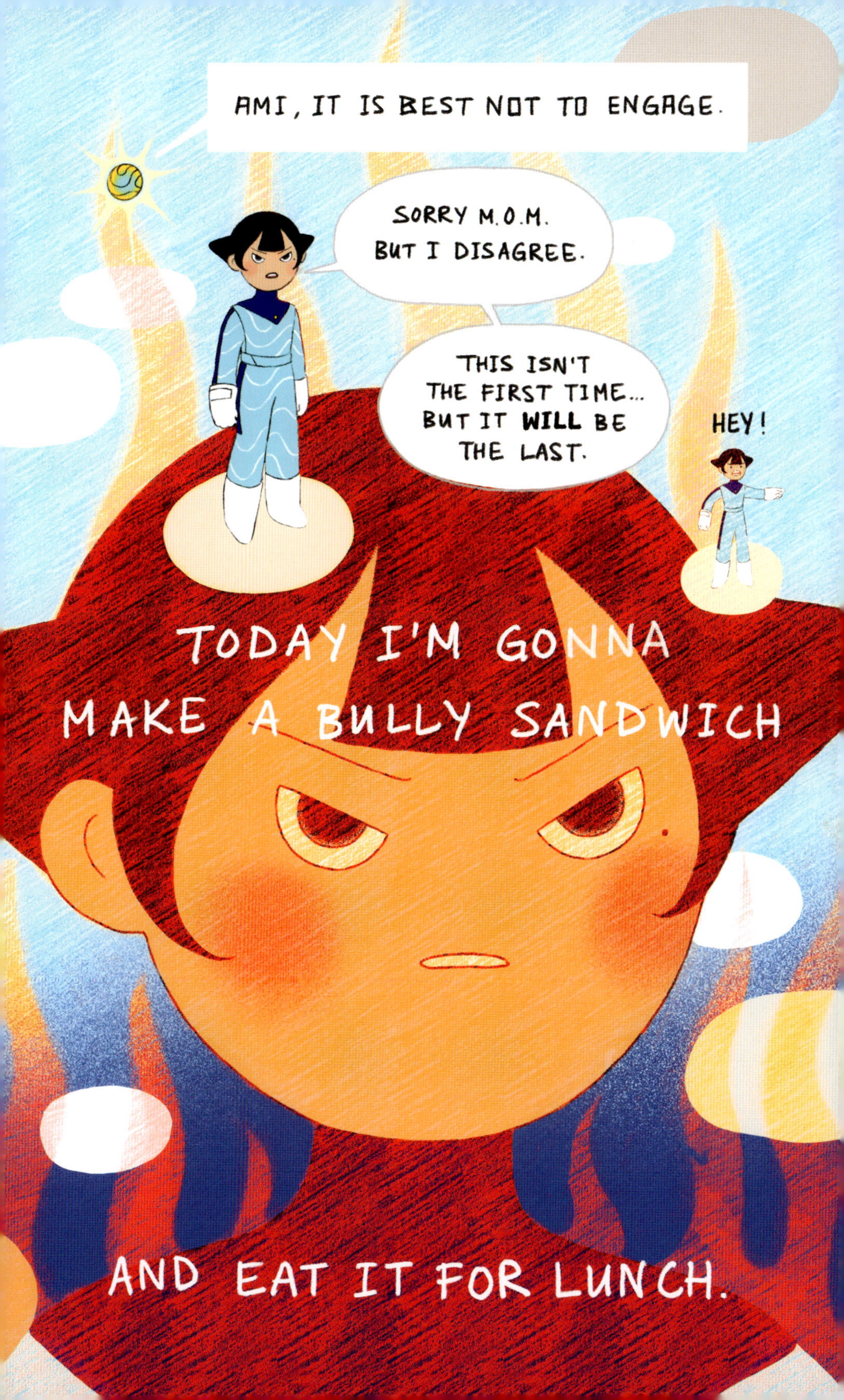
AMI, IT IS BEST NOT TO ENGAGE.
SORRY M.O.M. BUT I DISAGREE.
THIS ISN'T THE FIRST TIME... BUT IT **WILL** BE THE LAST.
HEY!
TODAY I'M GONNA MAKE A BULLY SANDWICH
AND EAT IT FOR LUNCH.

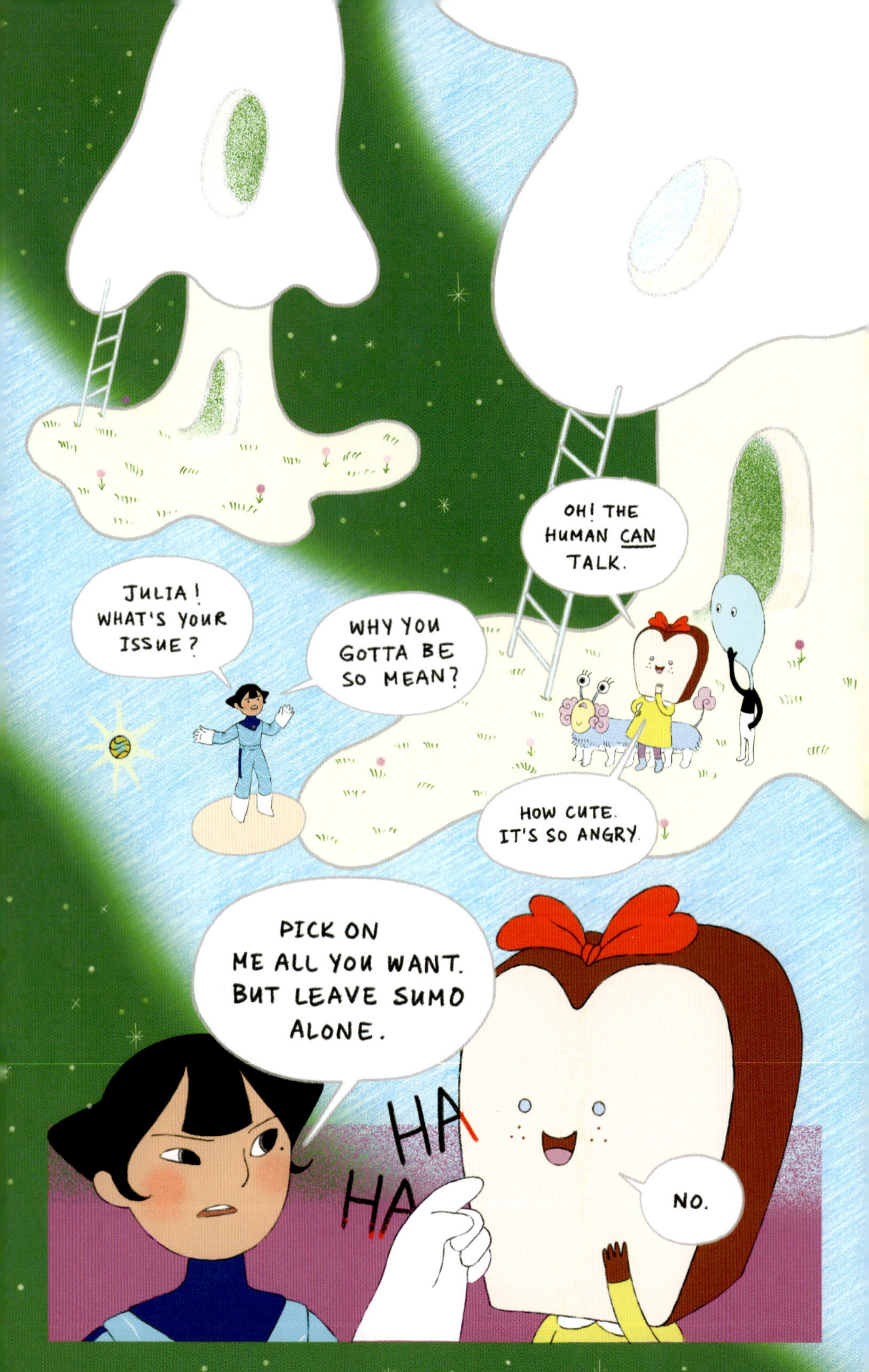
JULIA! WHAT'S YOUR ISSUE?
WHY YOU GOTTA BE SO MEAN?
OH! THE HUMAN CAN TALK.
HOW CUTE. IT'S SO ANGRY.
PICK ON ME ALL YOU WANT. BUT LEAVE SUMO ALONE.
HA HA
NO.

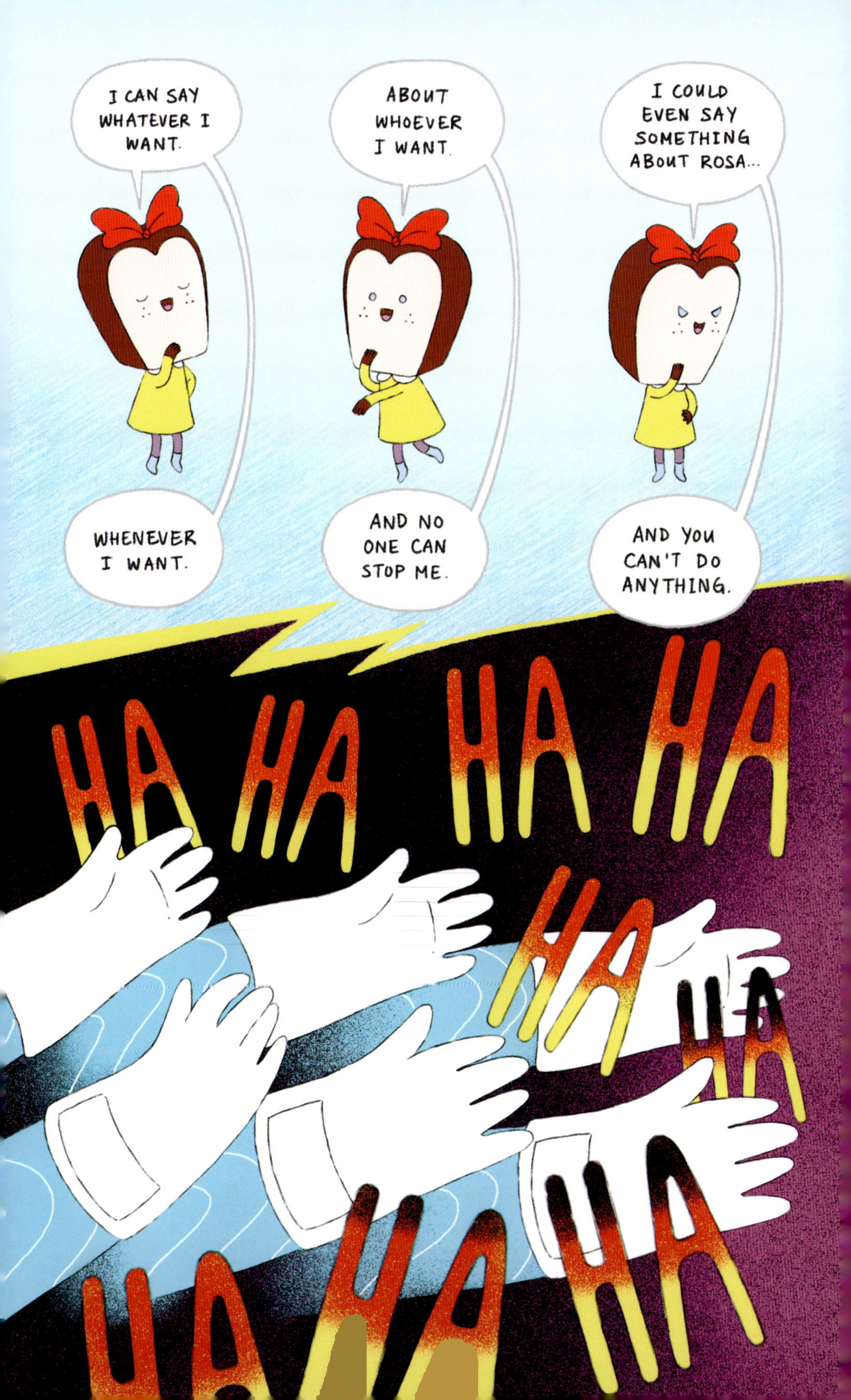
I CAN SAY WHATEVER I WANT.
WHENEVER I WANT.
ABOUT WHOEVER I WANT.
AND NO ONE CAN STOP ME.
I COULD EVEN SAY SOMETHING ABOUT ROSA...
AND YOU CAN'T DO ANYTHING.
HA HA HA HA
HA
HA
HA HA HA HA

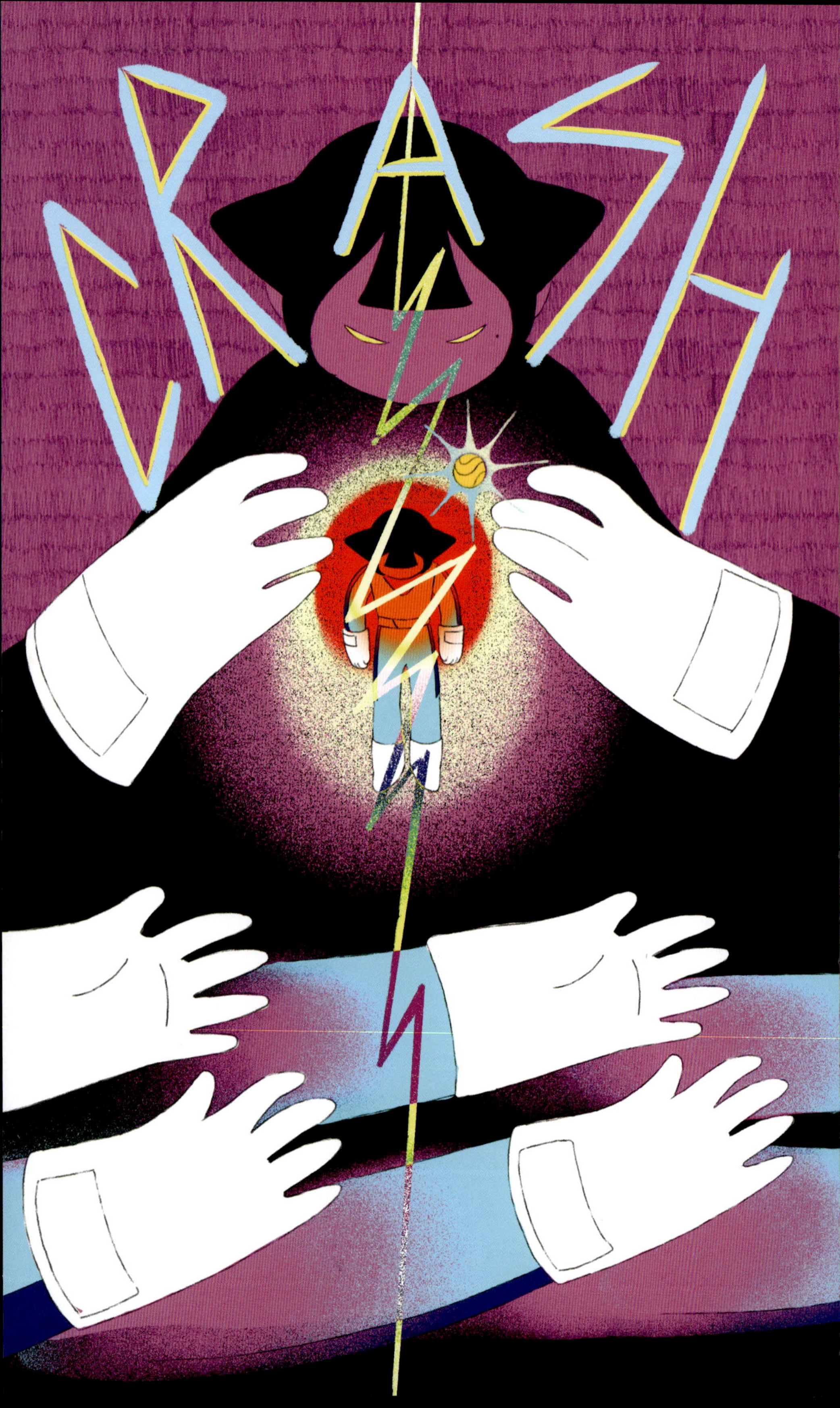
CRASH

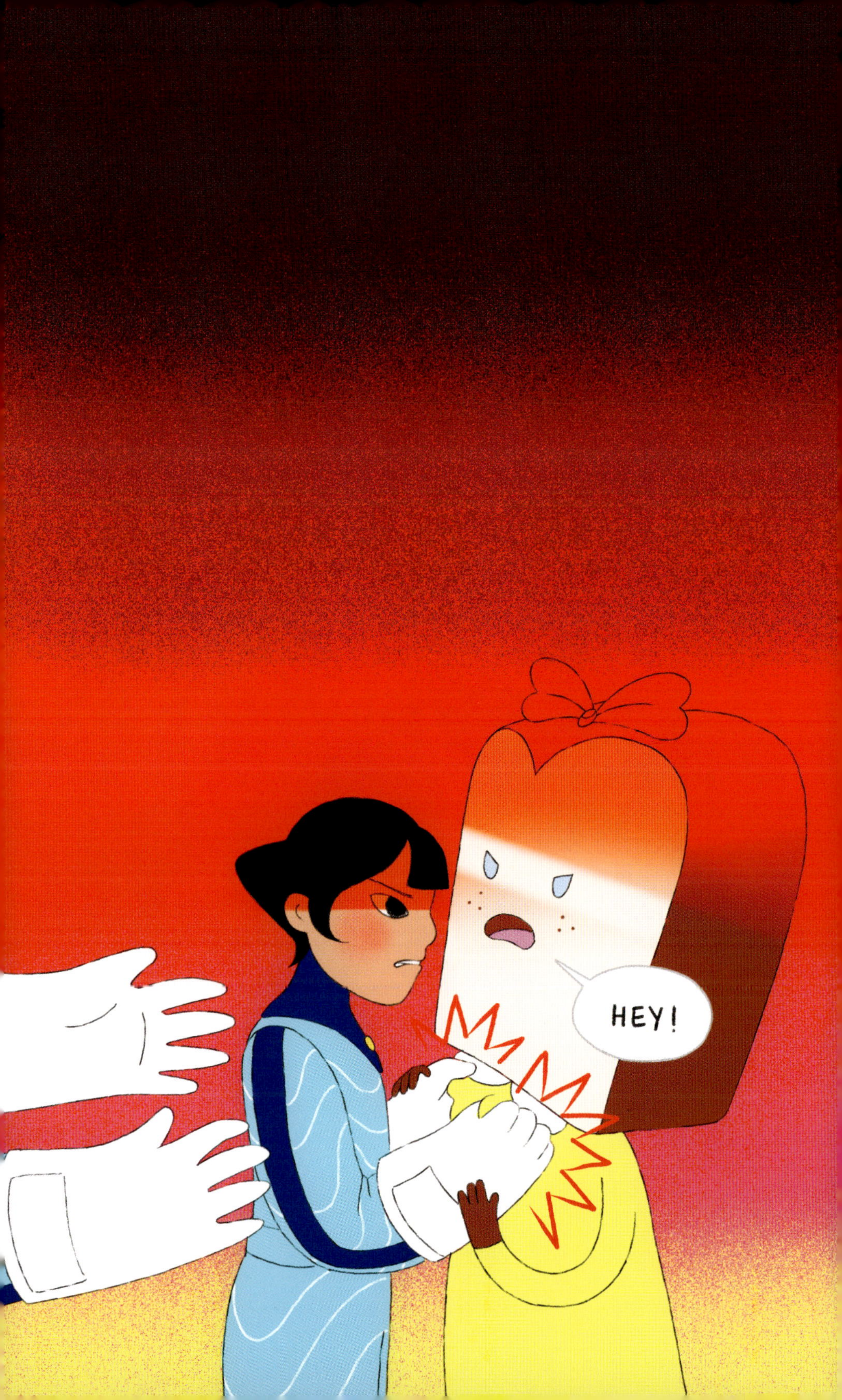
HEY!

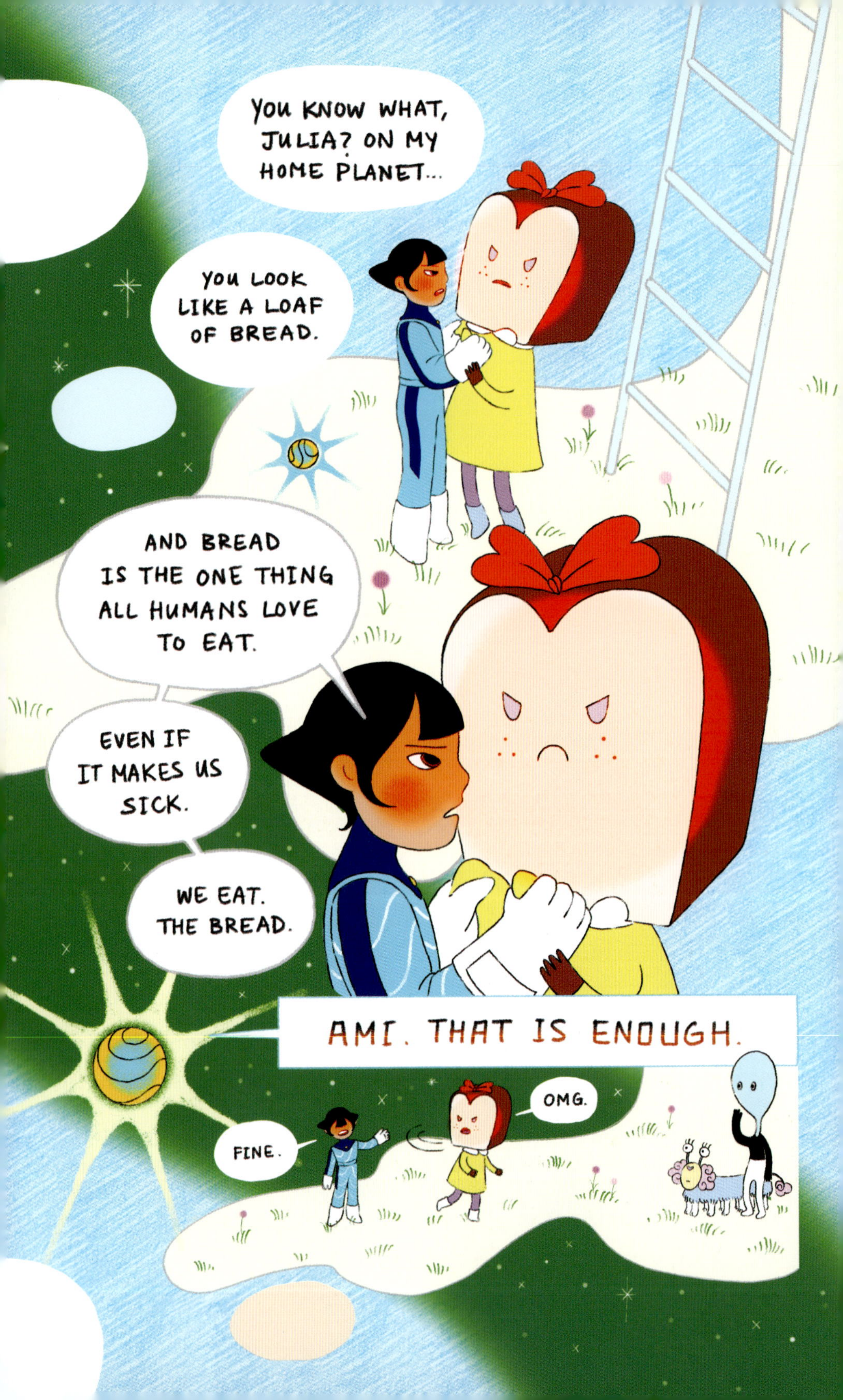

YOU KNOW WHAT, JULIA? ON MY HOME PLANET...
YOU LOOK LIKE A LOAF OF BREAD.
AND BREAD IS THE ONE THING ALL HUMANS LOVE TO EAT.
EVEN IF IT MAKES US SICK.
WE EAT. THE BREAD.
AMI. THAT IS ENOUGH.
FINE.
OMG.

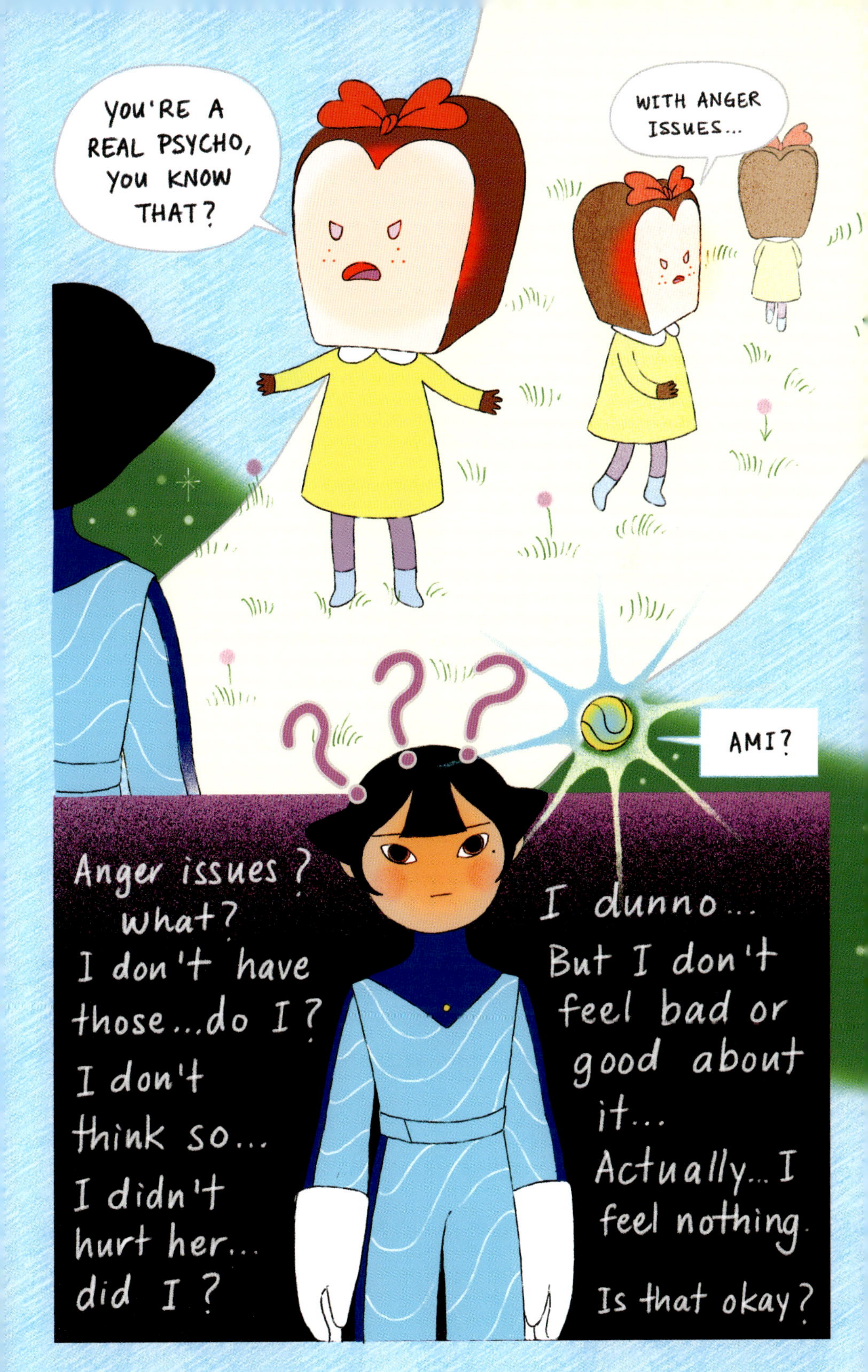
YOU'RE A REAL PSYCHO, YOU KNOW THAT?
WITH ANGER ISSUES...
AMI?
Anger issues? what? I don't have those...do I? I don't think so... I didn't hurt her... did I?
I dunno... But I don't feel bad or good about it... Actually... I feel nothing. Is that okay?

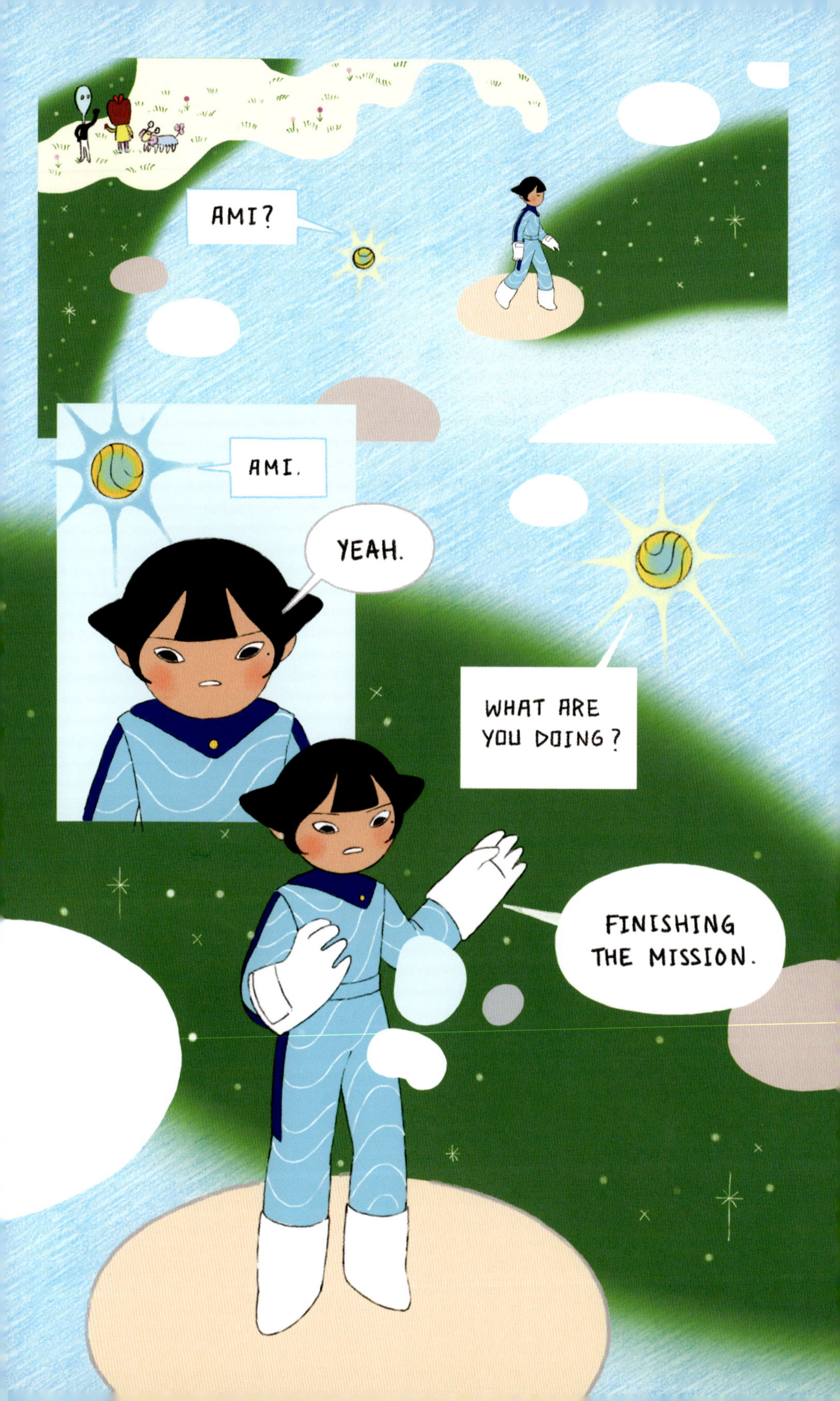
AMI?
AMI.
YEAH.
WHAT ARE YOU DOING?
FINISHING THE MISSION.

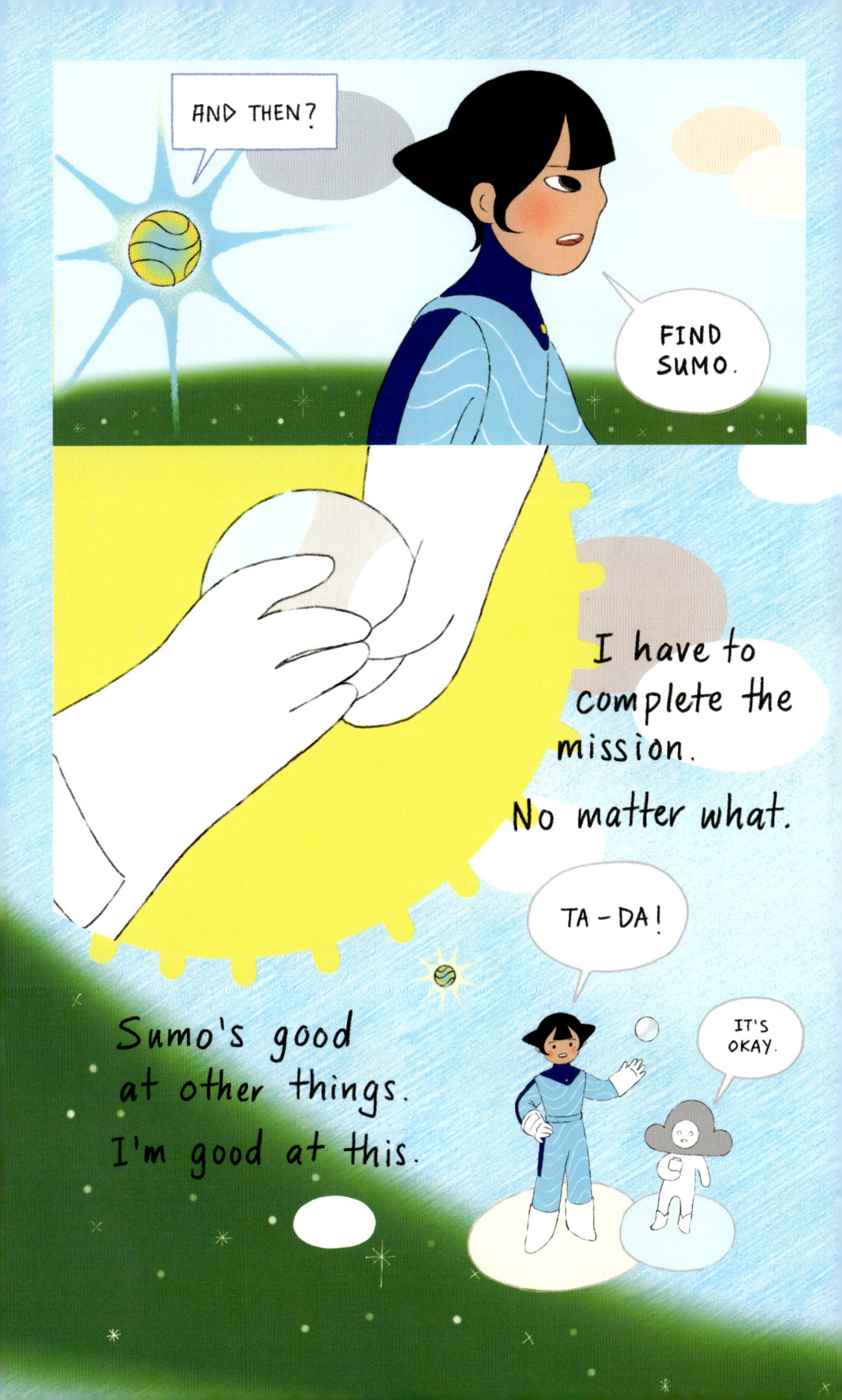
AND THEN?
FIND SUMO.
I have to complete the mission.
No matter what.
TA-DA!
IT'S OKAY.
Sumo's good at other things.
I'm good at this.

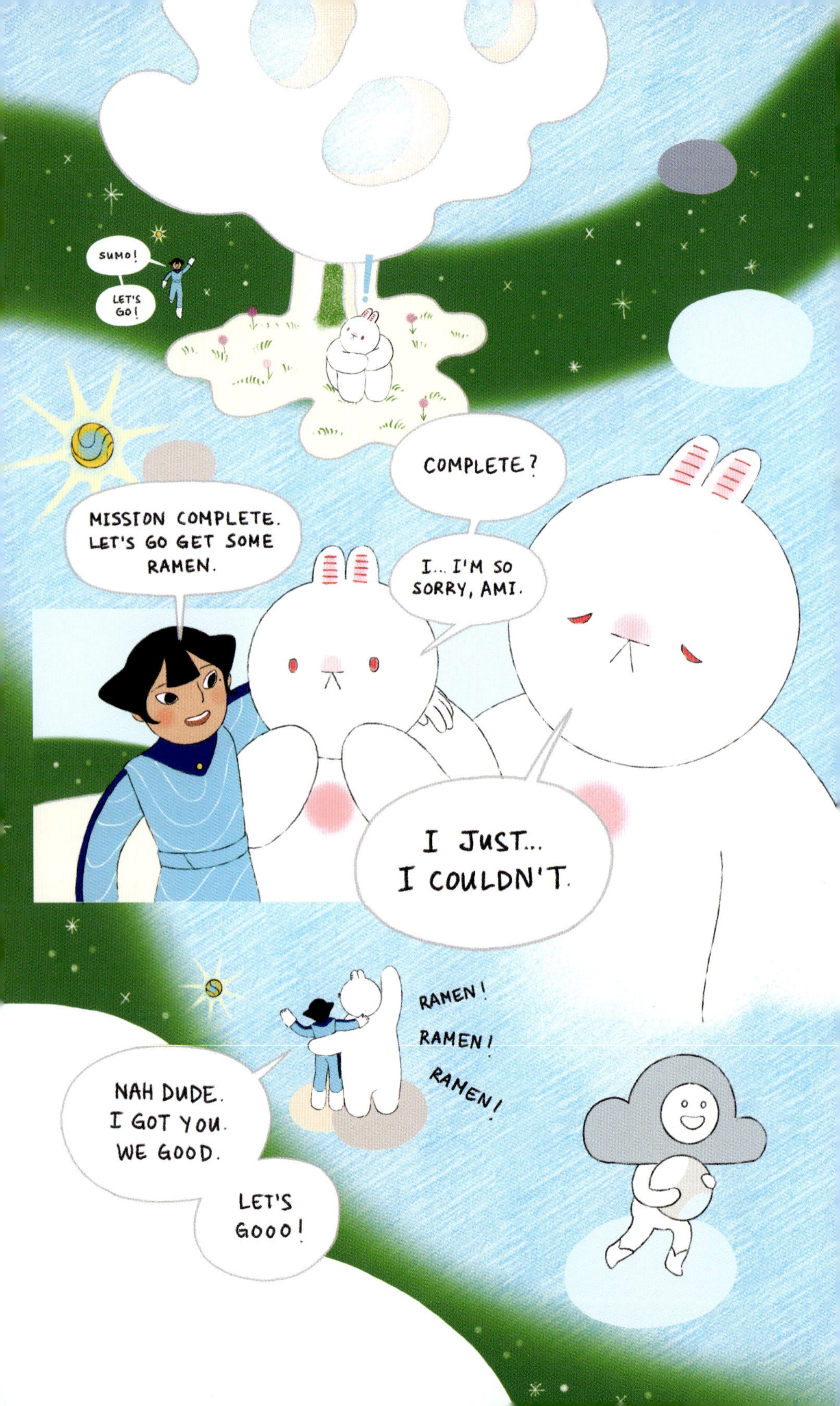
SUMO!
LET'S GO!
MISSION COMPLETE. LET'S GO GET SOME RAMEN.
COMPLETE?
I... I'M SO SORRY, AMI.
I JUST... I COULDN'T.
RAMEN!
RAMEN!
RAMEN!
NAH DUDE. I GOT YOU. WE GOOD.
LET'S GOOO!

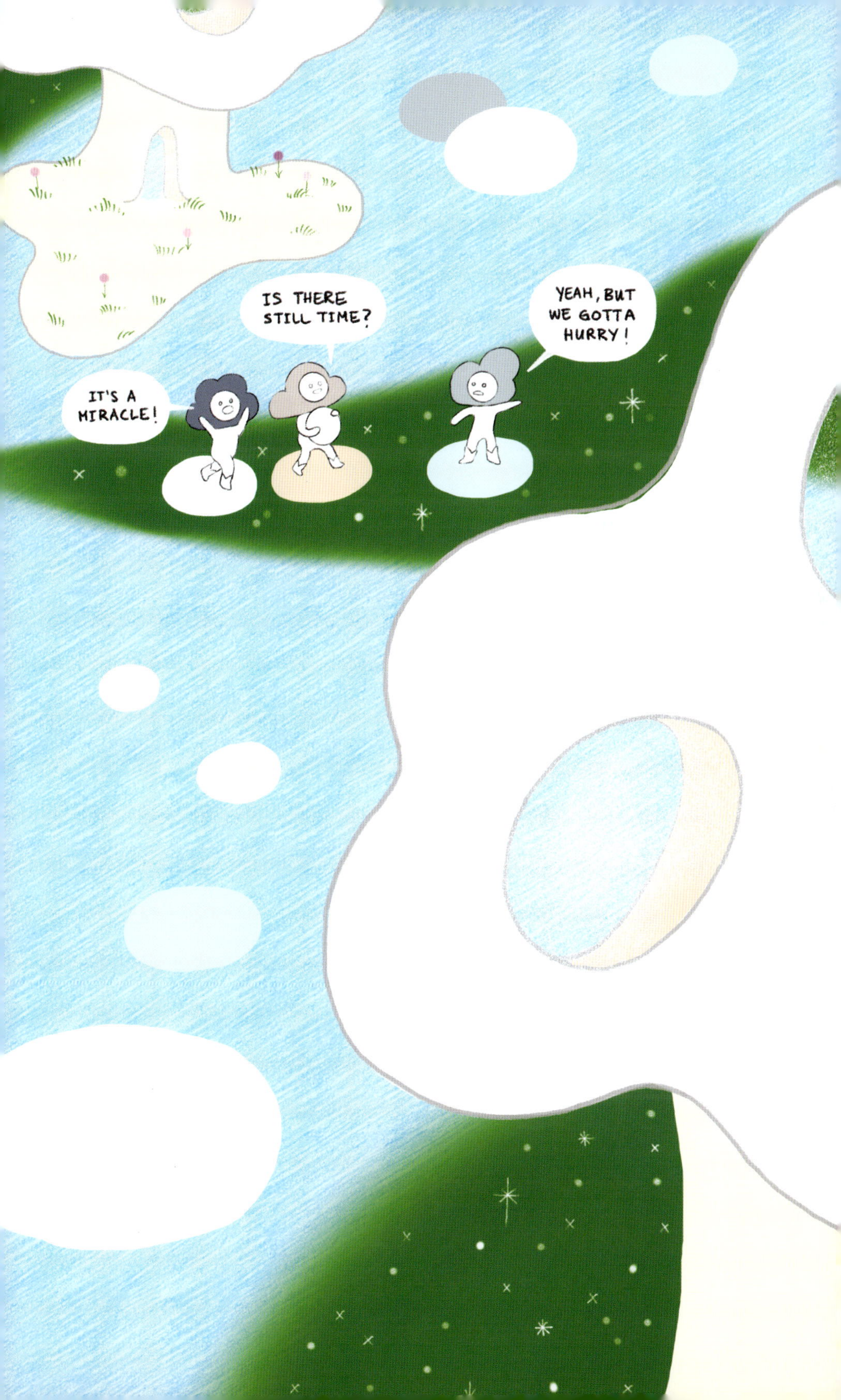
IT'S A MIRACLE!
IS THERE STILL TIME?
YEAH, BUT WE GOTTA HURRY!

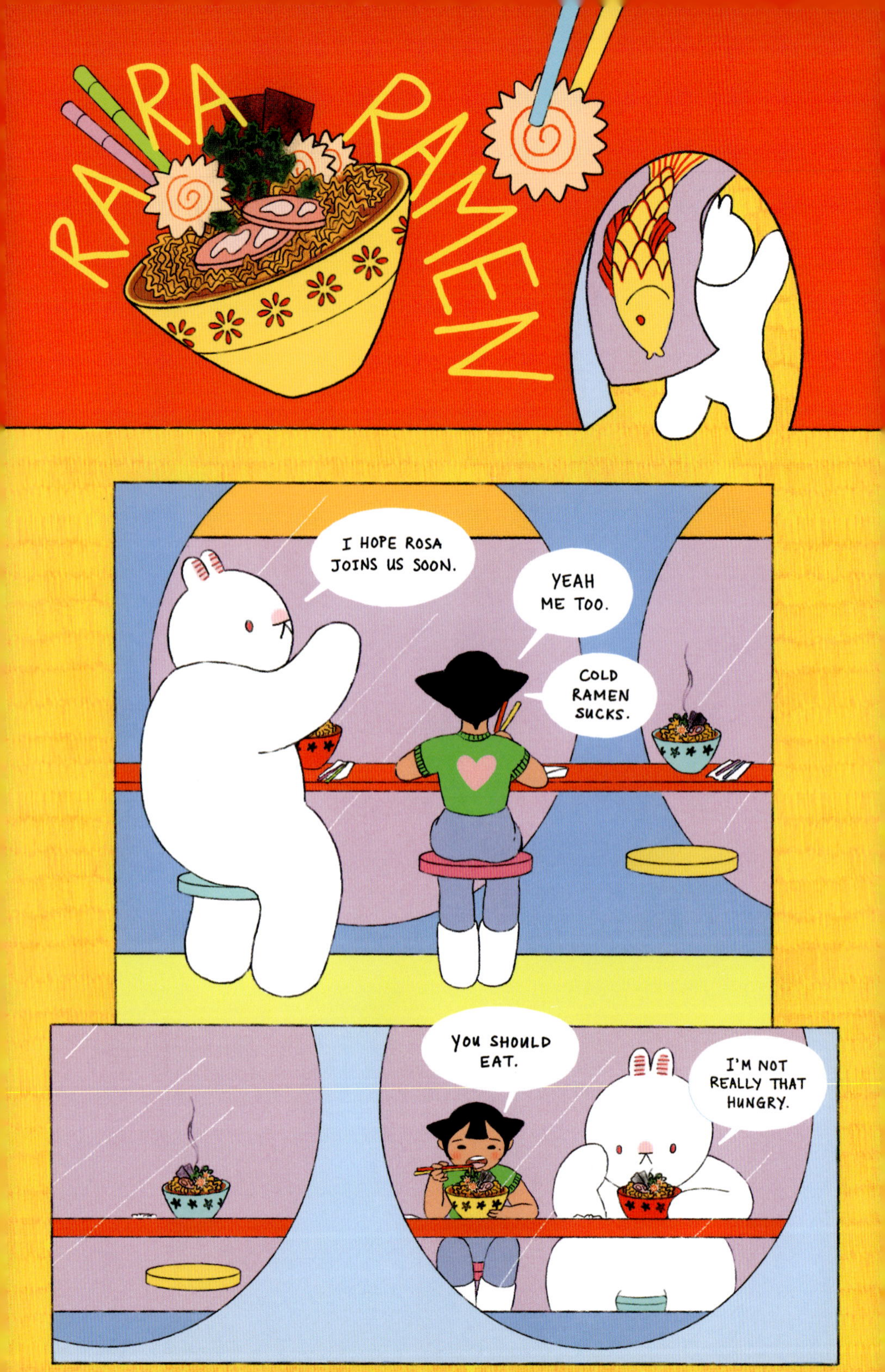
RA RA RAMEN
I HOPE ROSA JOINS US SOON.
YEAH ME TOO.
COLD RAMEN SUCKS.
YOU SHOULD EAT.
I'M NOT REALLY THAT HUNGRY.

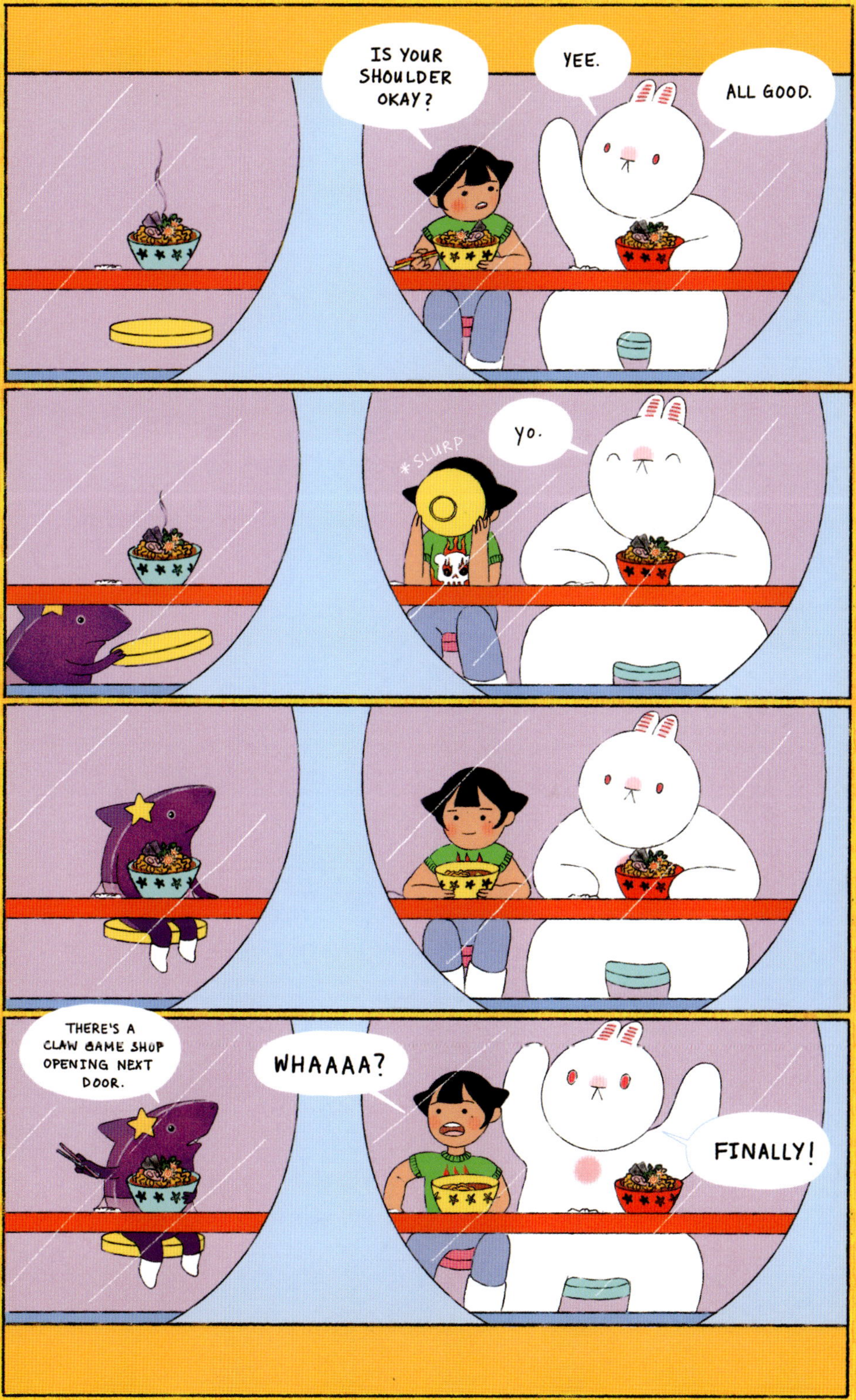
IS YOUR SHOULDER OKAY?
YEE.
ALL GOOD.
*SLURP
yo.
THERE'S A CLAW GAME SHOP OPENING NEXT DOOR.
WHAAAA?
FINALLY!

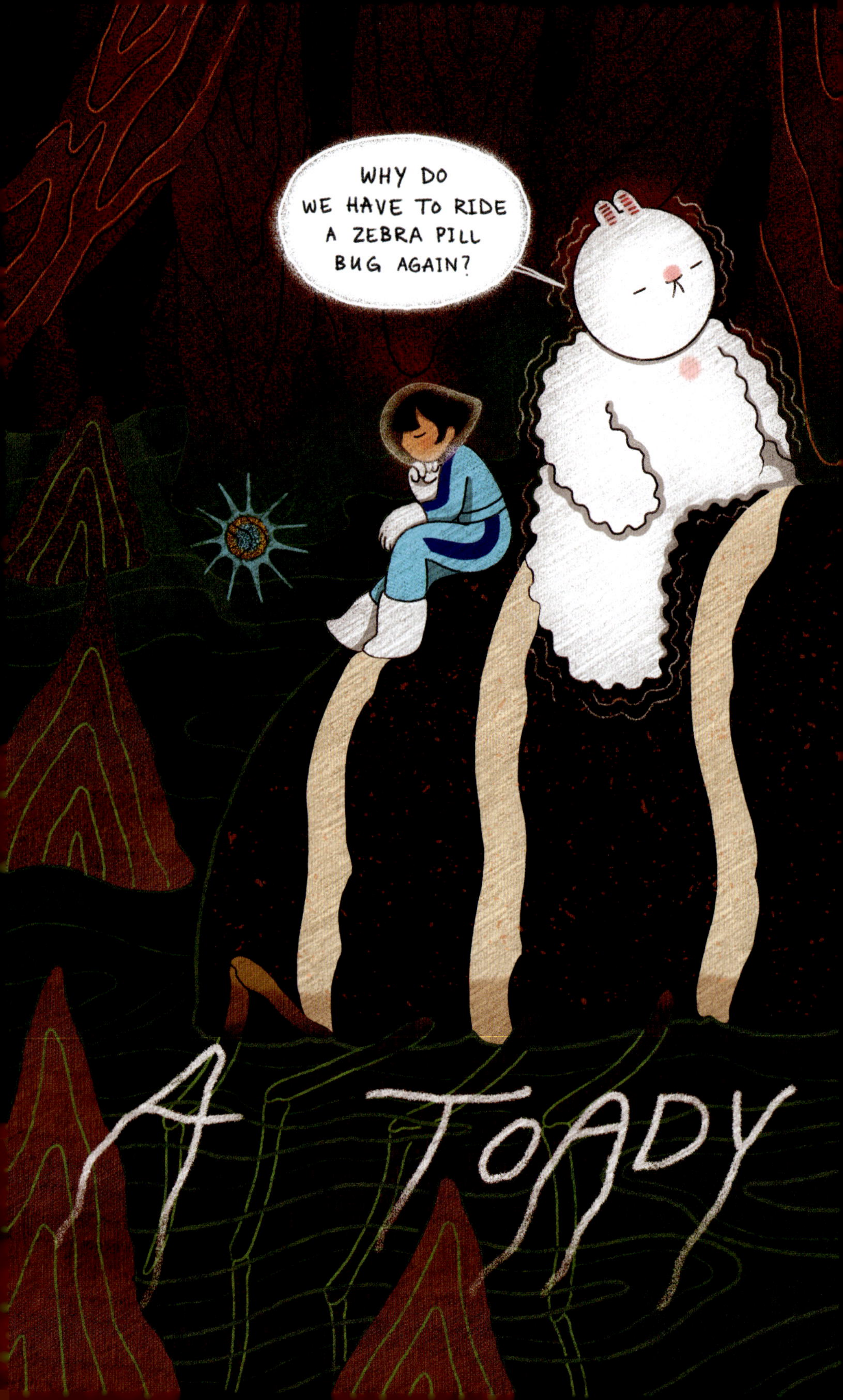
WHY DO WE HAVE TO RIDE A ZEBRA PILL BUG AGAIN?
A TOADY

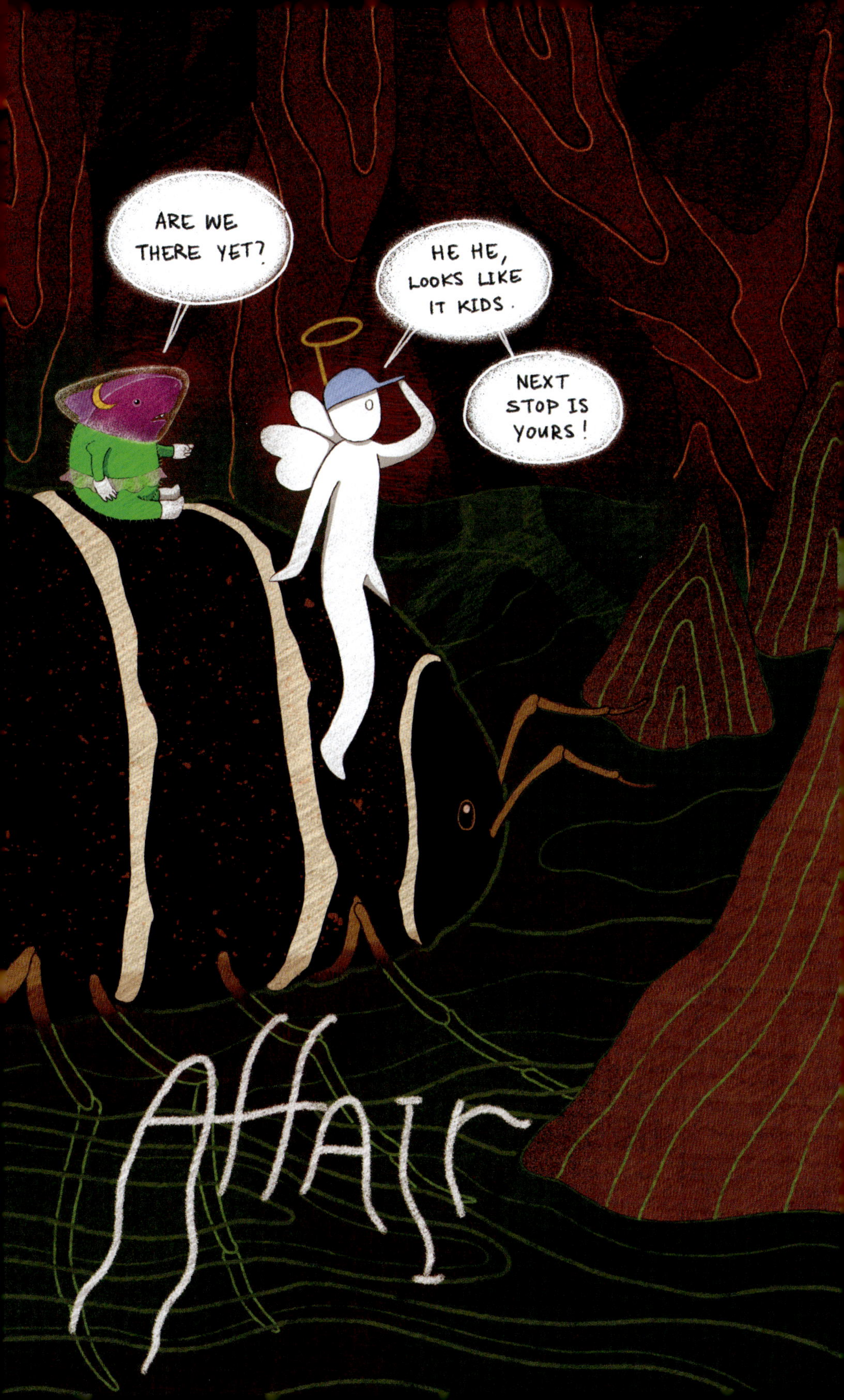
ARE WE THERE YET?
HE HE, LOOKS LIKE IT KIDS.
NEXT STOP IS YOURS!
Affair

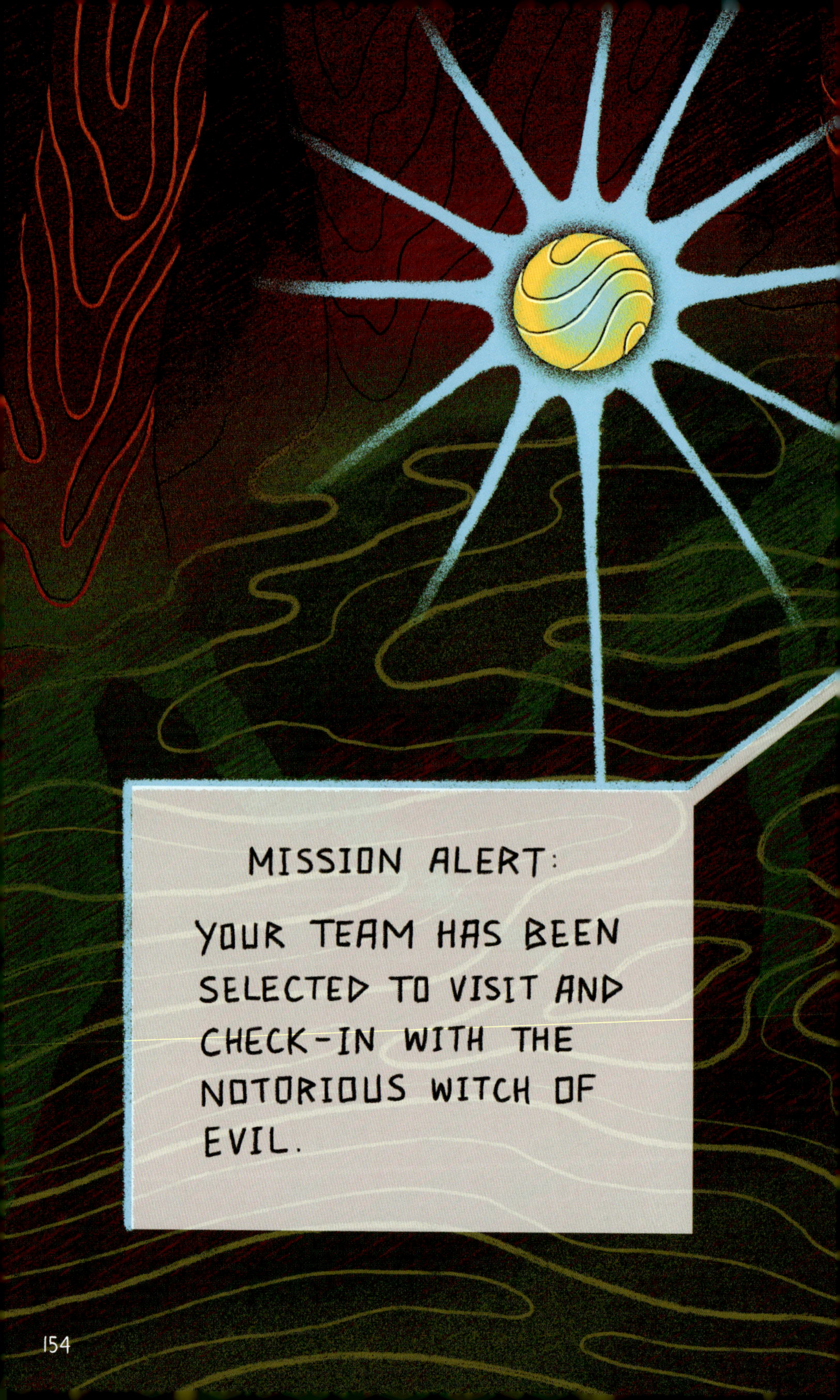
MISSION ALERT:
YOUR TEAM HAS BEEN SELECTED TO VISIT AND CHECK-IN WITH THE NOTORIOUS WITCH OF EVIL.

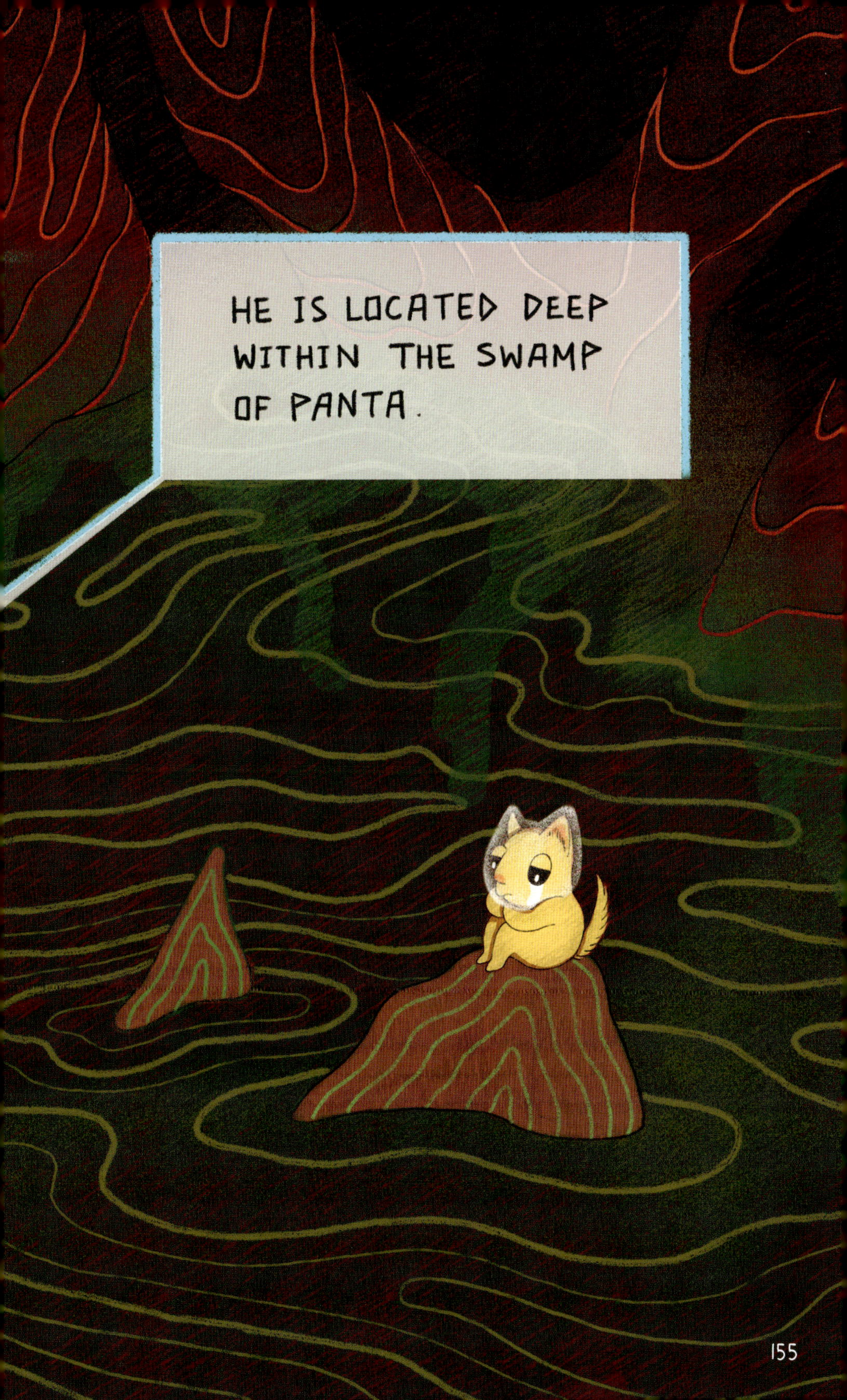
HE IS LOCATED DEEP WITHIN THE SWAMP OF PANTA.

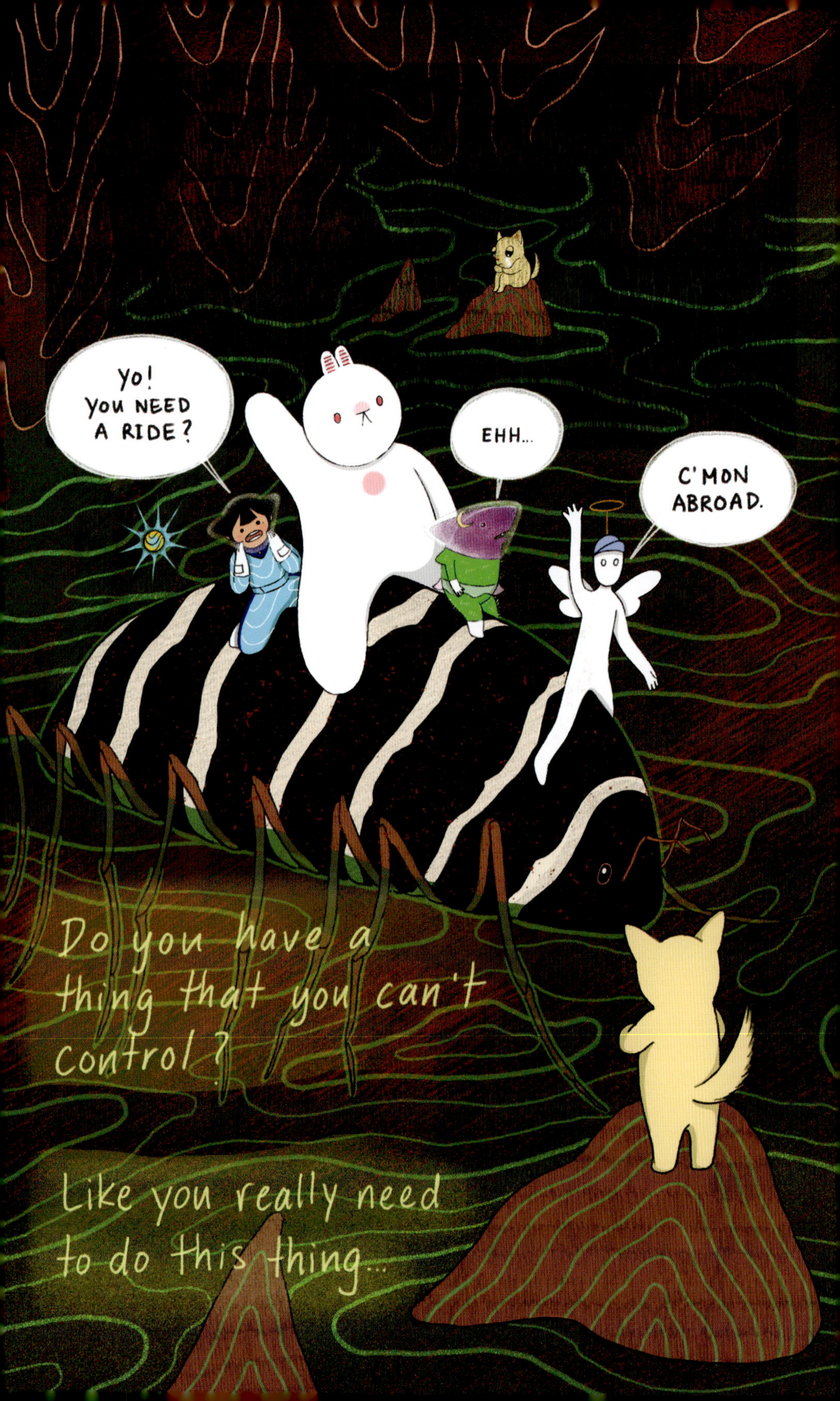
YO! YOU NEED A RIDE?
EHH...
C'MON ABROAD.
Do you have a thing that you can't control?
Like you really need to do this thing...

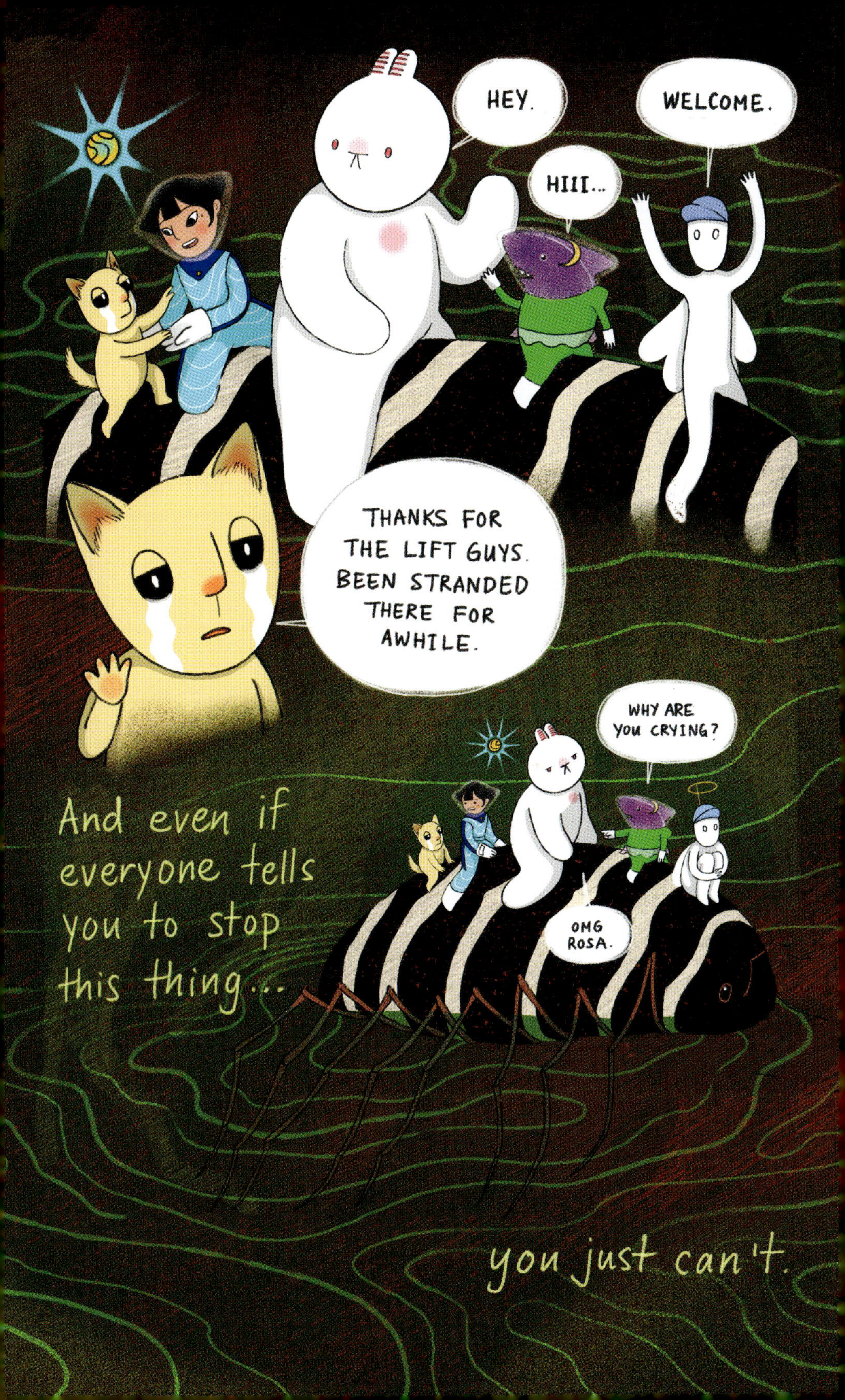
HEY.
HIII...
WELCOME.
THANKS FOR THE LIFT GUYS. BEEN STRANDED THERE FOR AWHILE.
And even if everyone tells you to stop this thing...
WHY ARE YOU CRYING?
OMG ROSA.
you just can't.

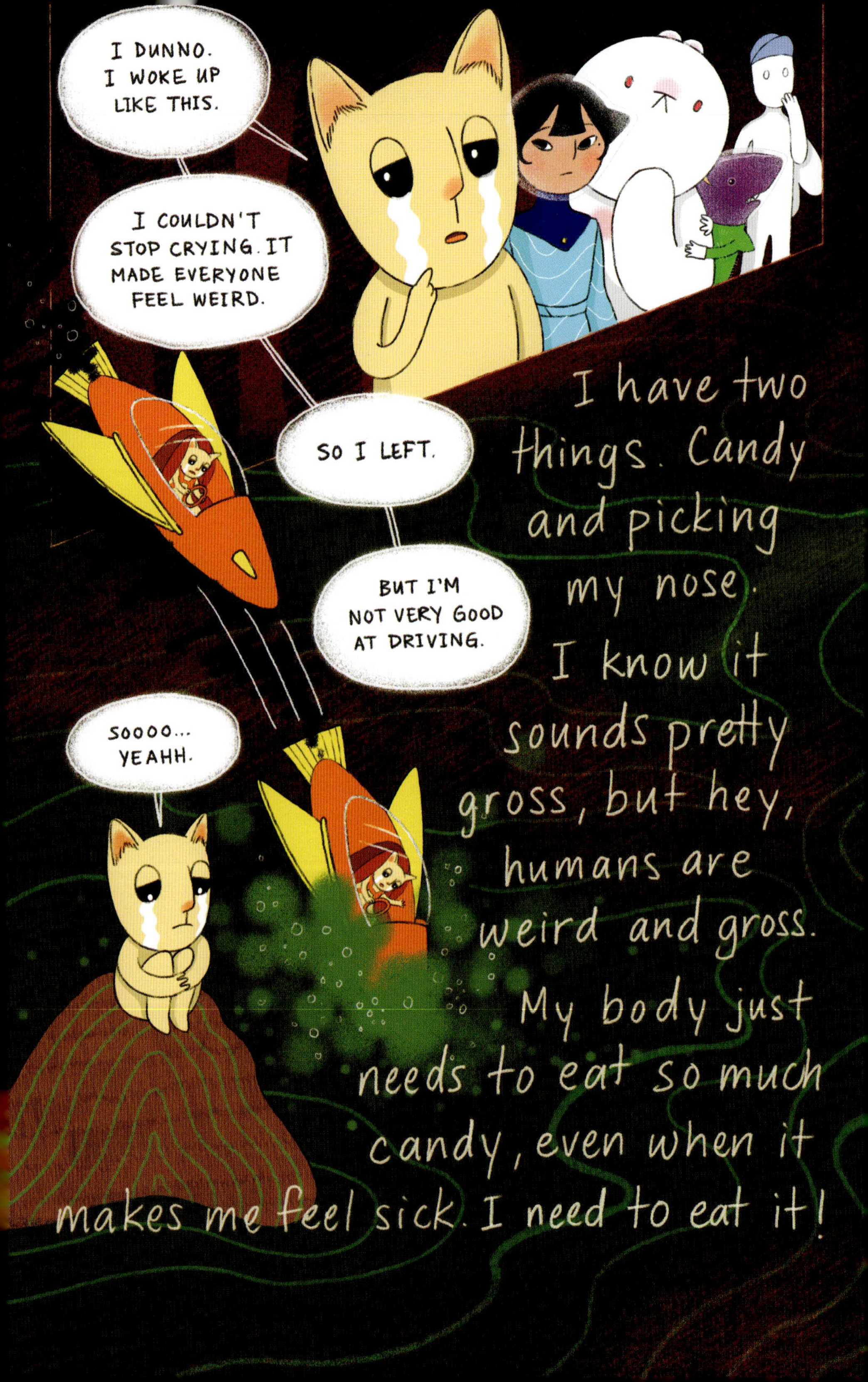
I DUNNO. I WOKE UP LIKE THIS.
I COULDN'T STOP CRYING. IT MADE EVERYONE FEEL WEIRD.
SO I LEFT.
BUT I'M NOT VERY GOOD AT DRIVING.
SOOOO... YEAHH.
I have two things. Candy and picking my nose. I know it sounds pretty gross, but hey, humans are weird and gross. My body just needs to eat so much candy, even when it makes me feel sick. I need to eat it!

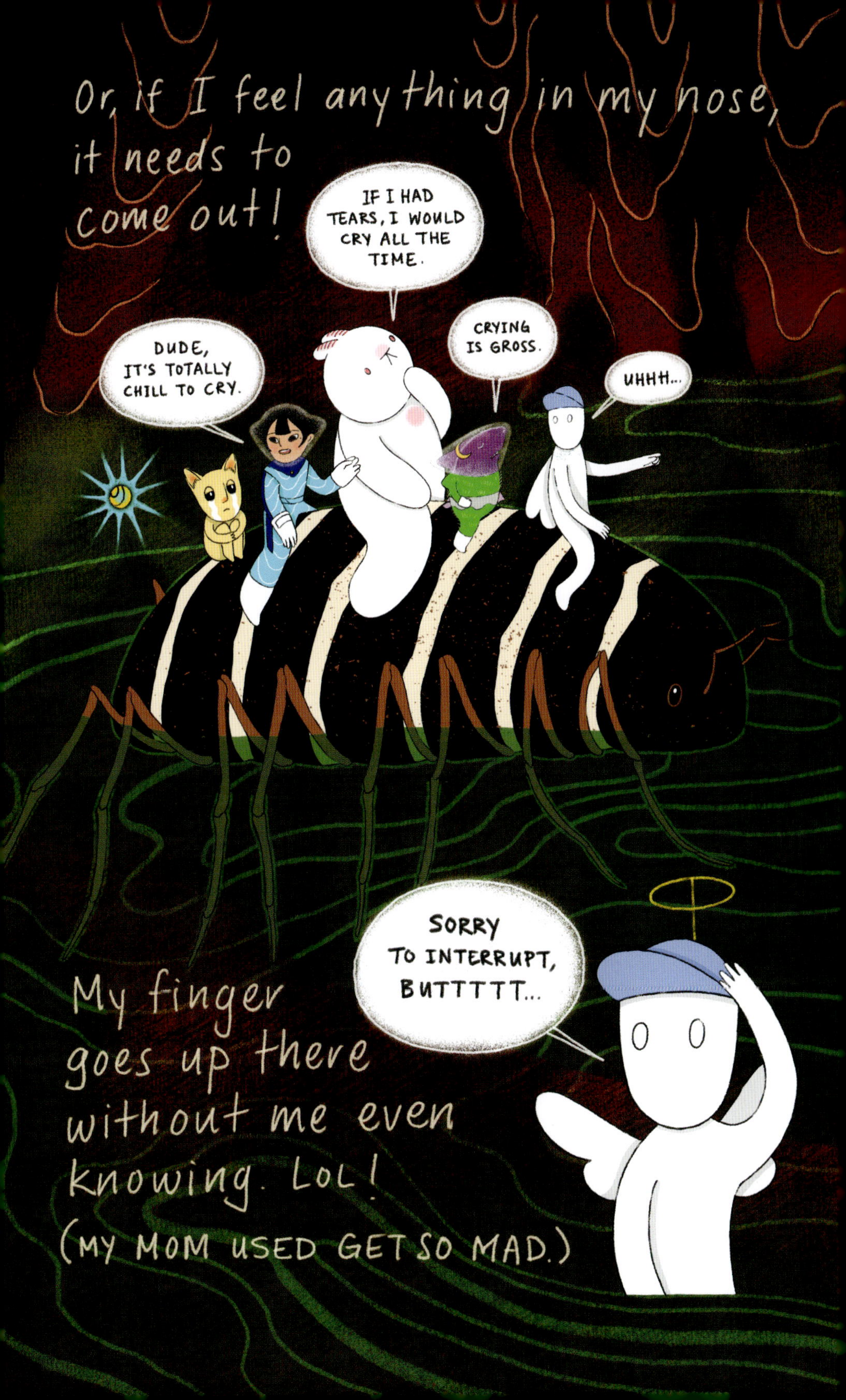
Or, if I feel anything in my nose, it needs to come out!
DUDE, IT'S TOTALLY CHILL TO CRY.
IF I HAD TEARS, I WOULD CRY ALL THE TIME.
CRYING IS GROSS.
UHHH...
My finger goes up there without me even knowing. LOL!
(MY MOM USED GET SO MAD.)
SORRY TO INTERRUPT, BUTTTTT...

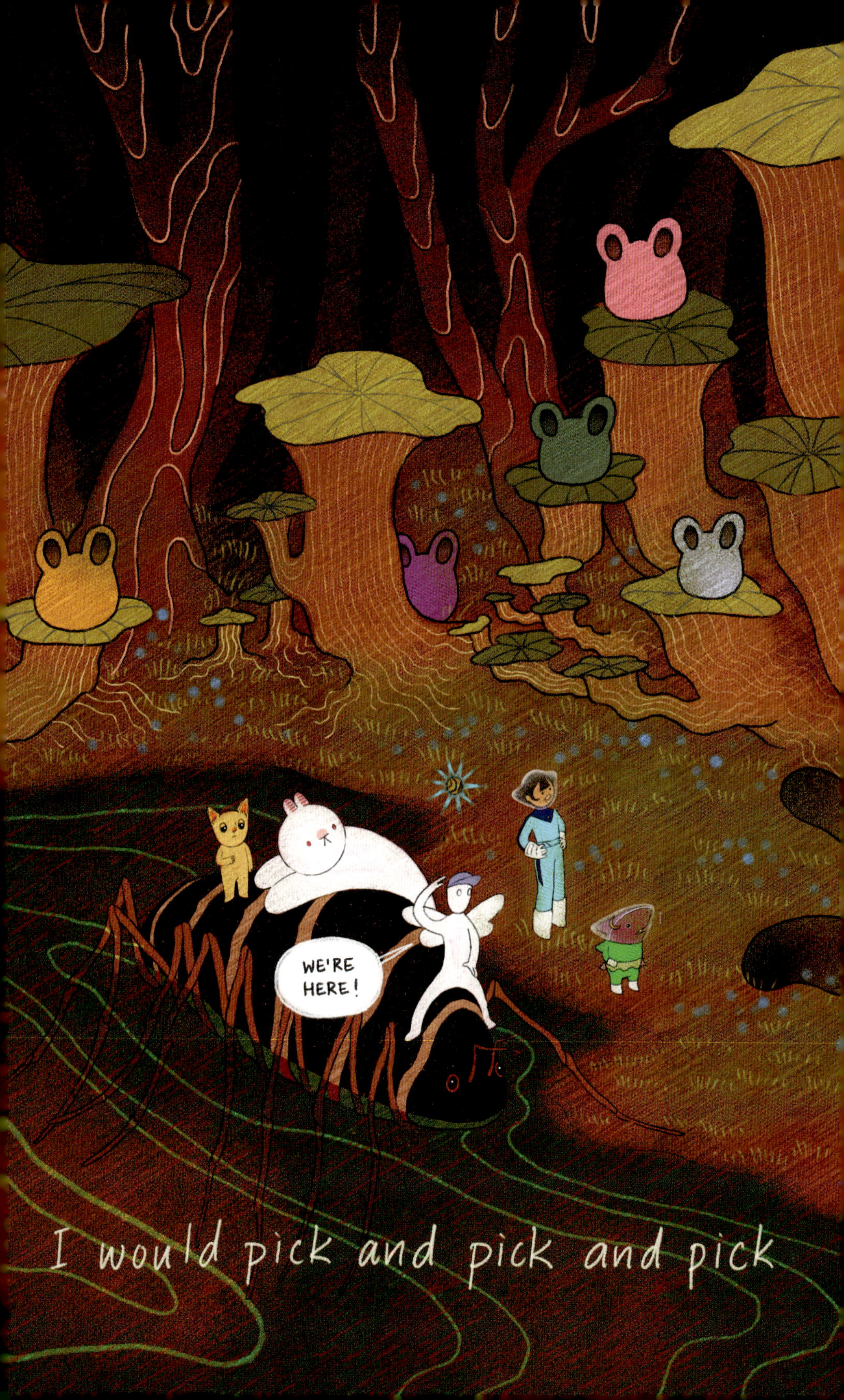
WE'RE HERE!

I would pick and pick and pick

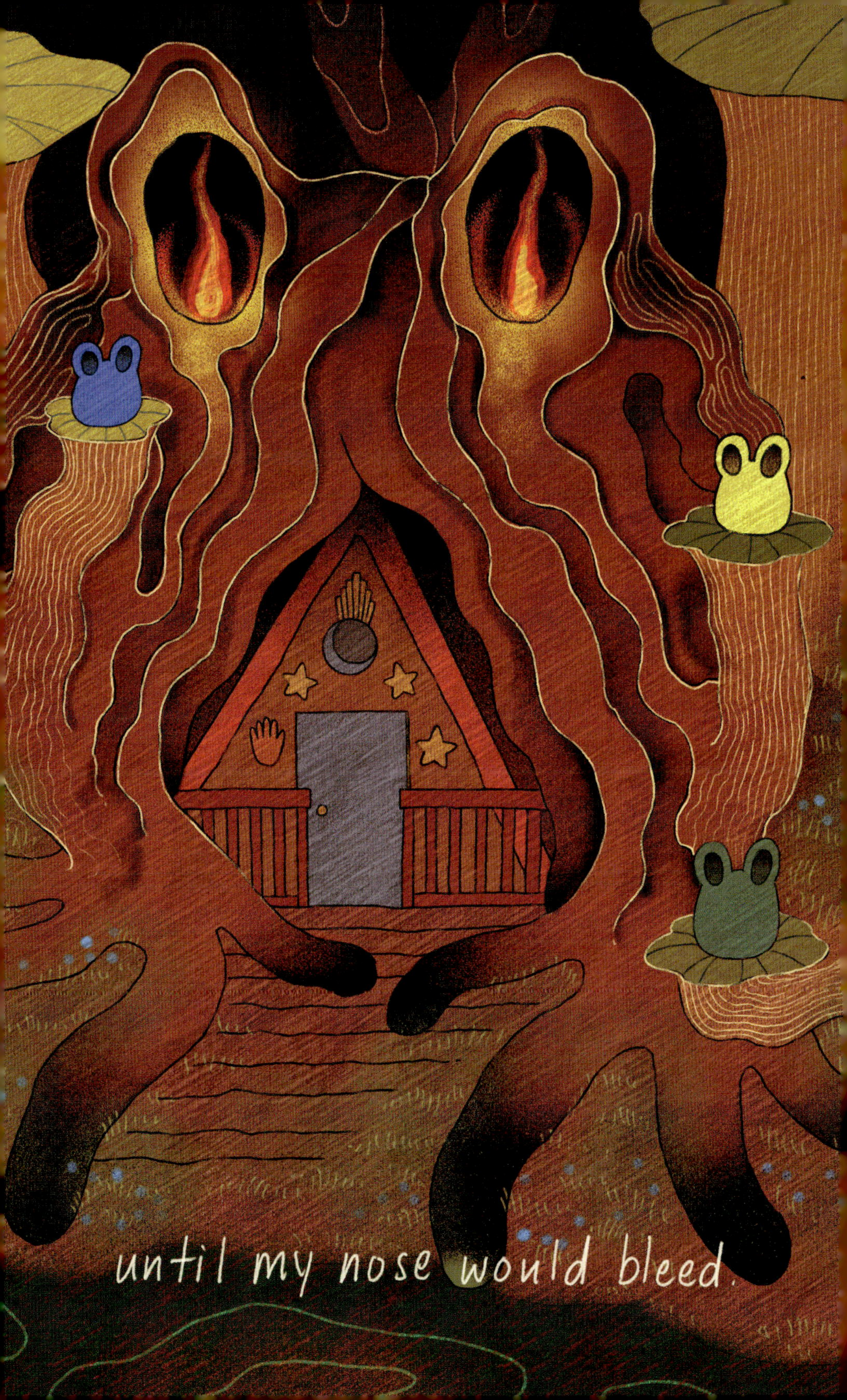
until my nose would bleed.

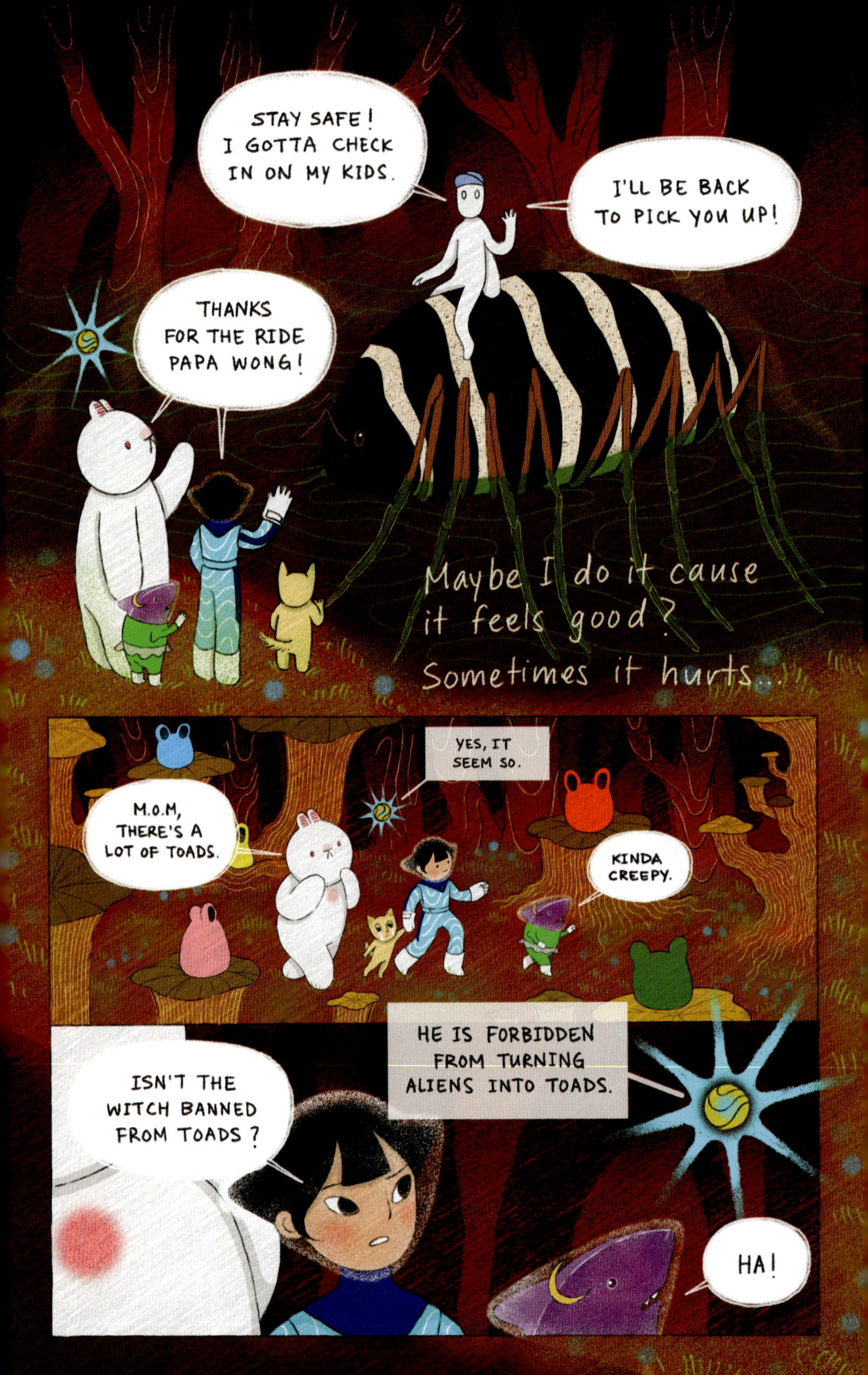
STAY SAFE! I GOTTA CHECK IN ON MY KIDS.
I'LL BE BACK TO PICK YOU UP!
THANKS FOR THE RIDE PAPA WONG!
Maybe I do it cause it feels good? Sometimes it hurts...
YES, IT SEEM SO.
M.O.M, THERE'S A LOT OF TOADS.
KINDA CREEPY.
HE IS FORBIDDEN FROM TURNING ALIENS INTO TOADS.
ISN'T THE WITCH BANNED FROM TOADS?
HA!

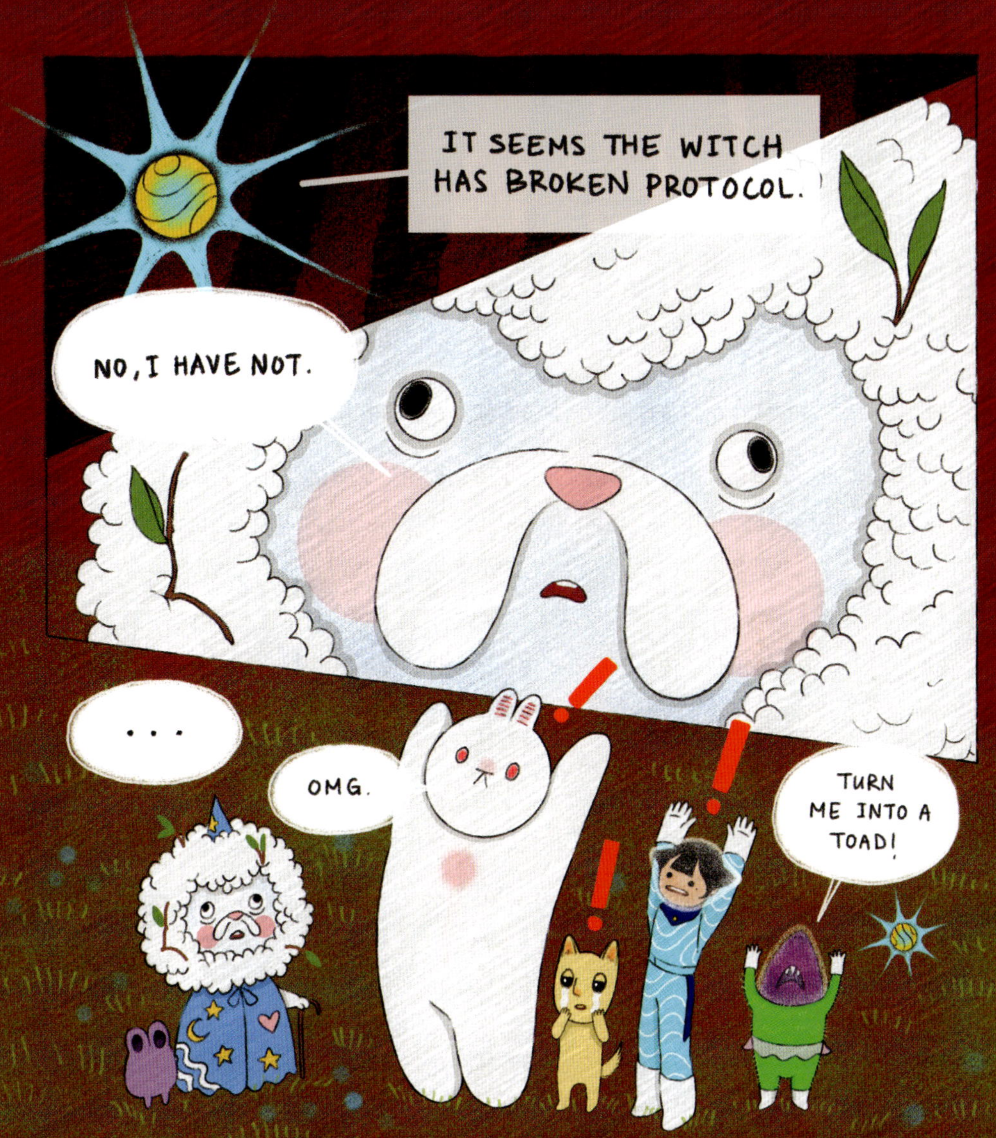
IT SEEMS THE WITCH HAS BROKEN PROTOCOL.
NO, I HAVE NOT.
...
OMG.
TURN ME INTO A TOAD!

Since arriving in Andromeda, I've been trying to eat a little less candy and pick a little less too. I'm not sure why I didn't try and stop before...

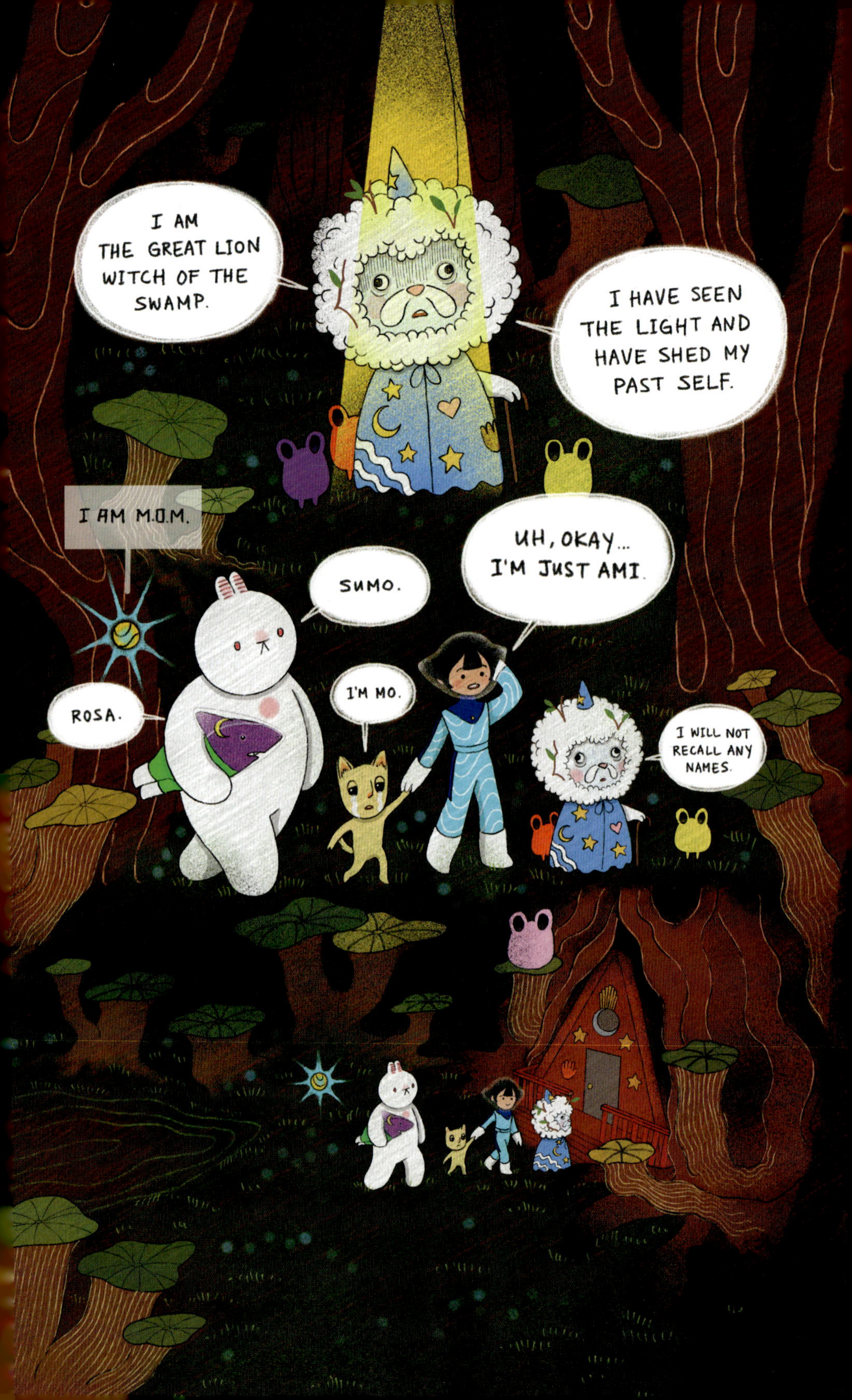
I AM THE GREAT LION WITCH OF THE SWAMP.
I HAVE SEEN THE LIGHT AND HAVE SHED MY PAST SELF.
I AM M.O.M.
SUMO.
UH, OKAY... I'M JUST AMI.
ROSA.
I'M MO.
I WILL NOT RECALL ANY NAMES.

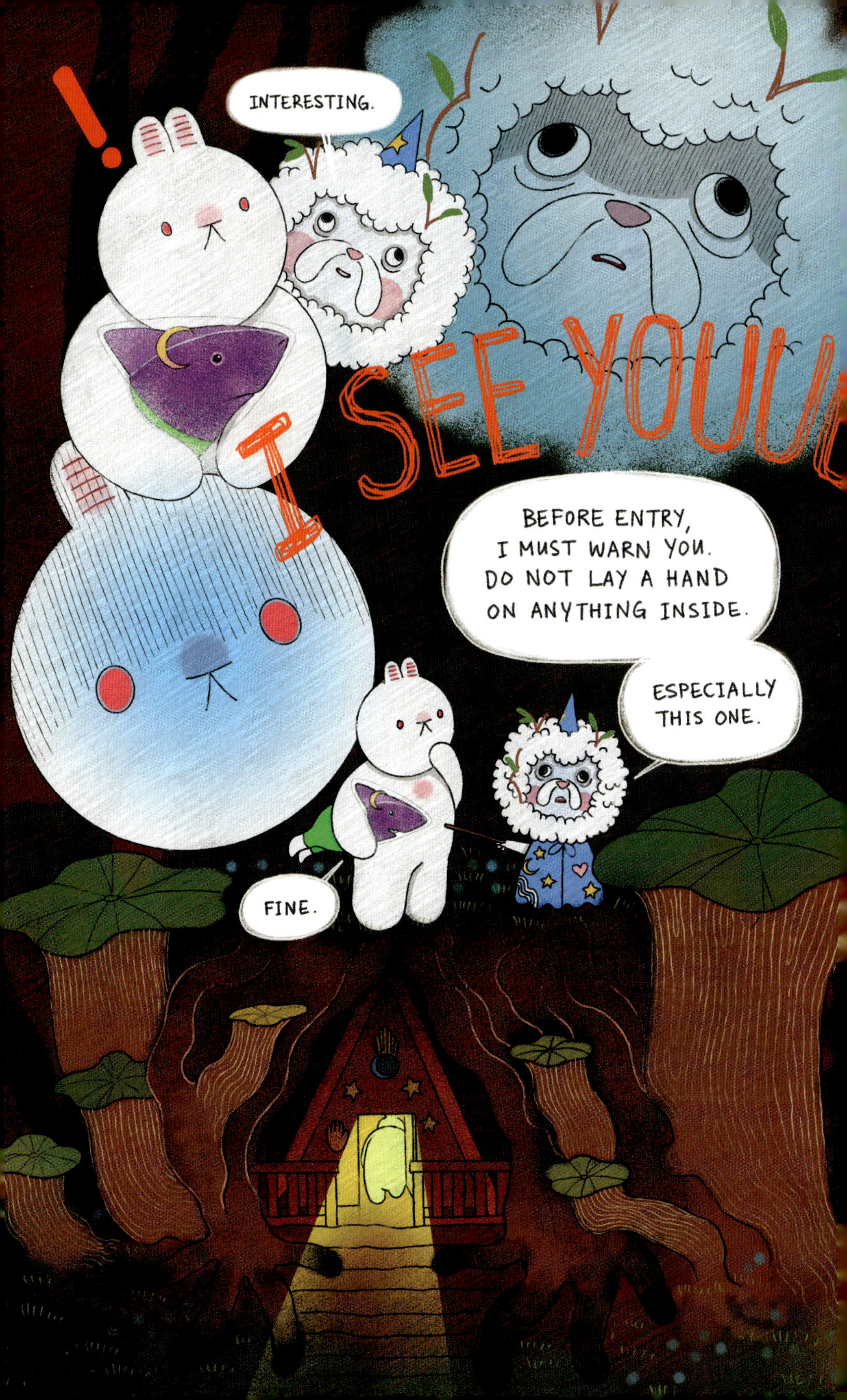
!
INTERESTING.
I SEE YOUUU
BEFORE ENTRY, I MUST WARN YOU. DO NOT LAY A HAND ON ANYTHING INSIDE.
ESPECIALLY THIS ONE.
FINE.

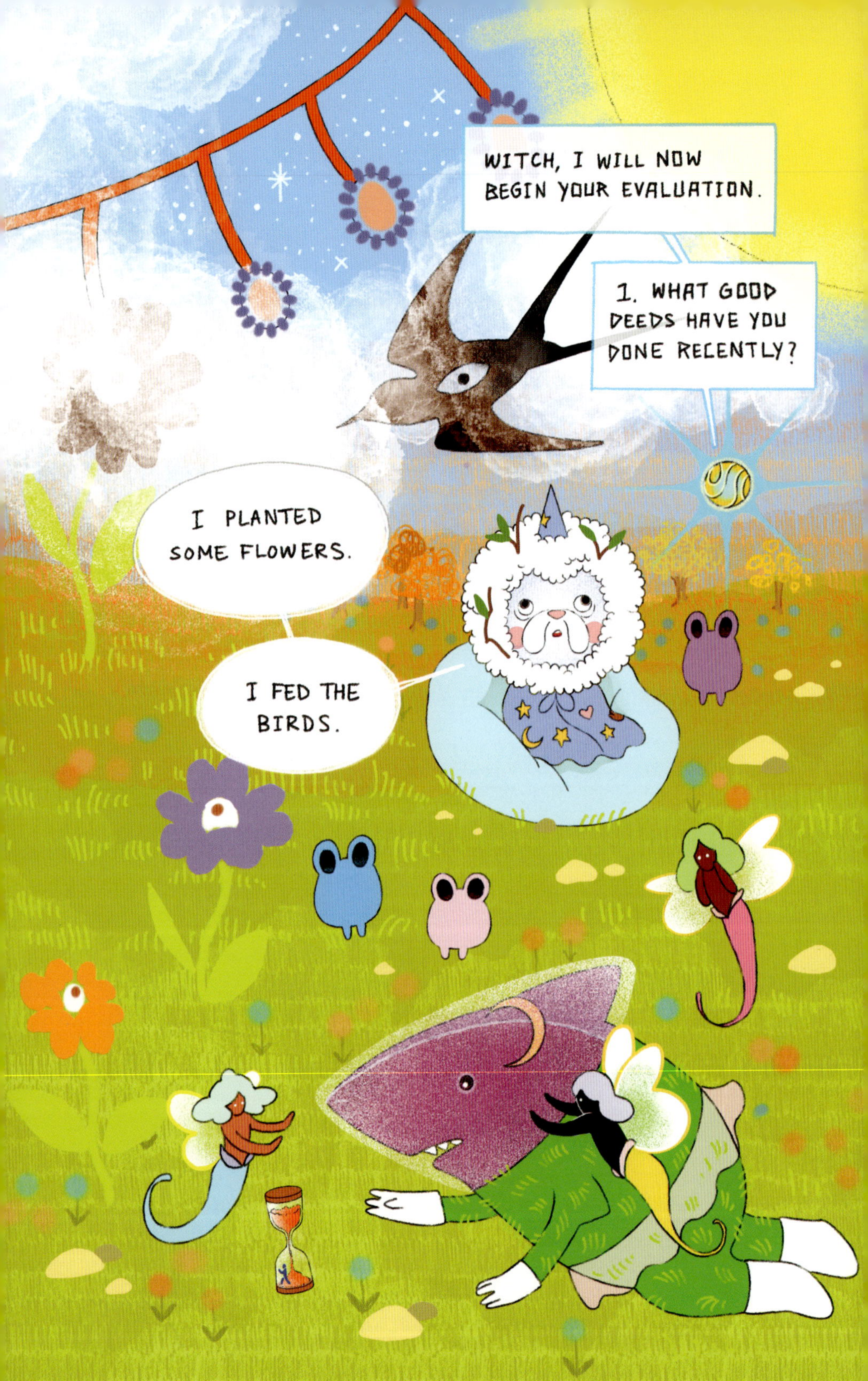
WITCH, I WILL NOW BEGIN YOUR EVALUATION.
1. WHAT GOOD DEEDS HAVE YOU DONE RECENTLY?
I PLANTED SOME FLOWERS.
I FED THE BIRDS.

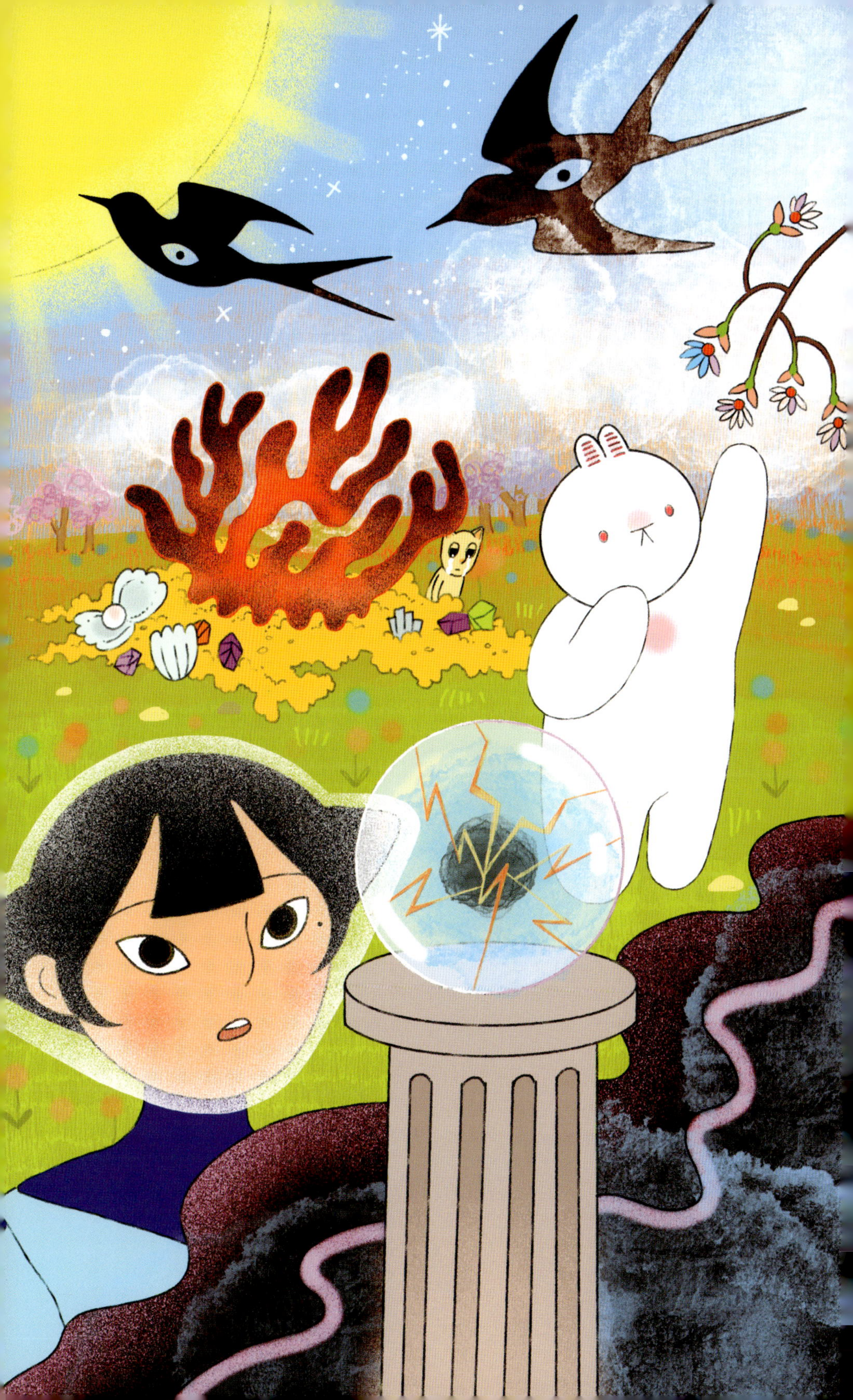

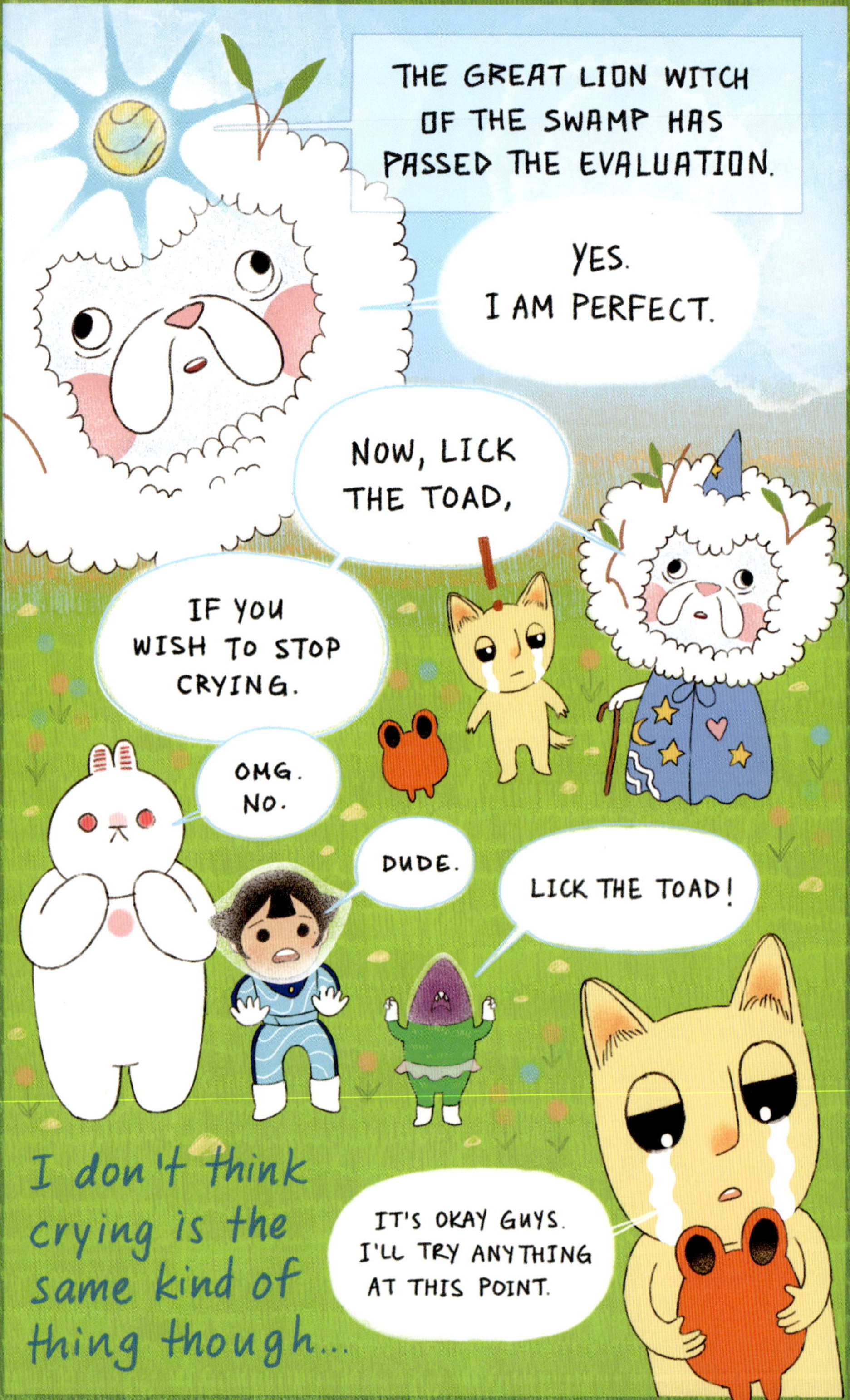
THE GREAT LION WITCH OF THE SWAMP HAS PASSED THE EVALUATION.
YES. I AM PERFECT.
NOW, LICK THE TOAD,
IF YOU WISH TO STOP CRYING.
OMG. NO.
DUDE.
LICK THE TOAD!
I don't think crying is the same kind of thing though...
IT'S OKAY GUYS. I'LL TRY ANYTHING AT THIS POINT.

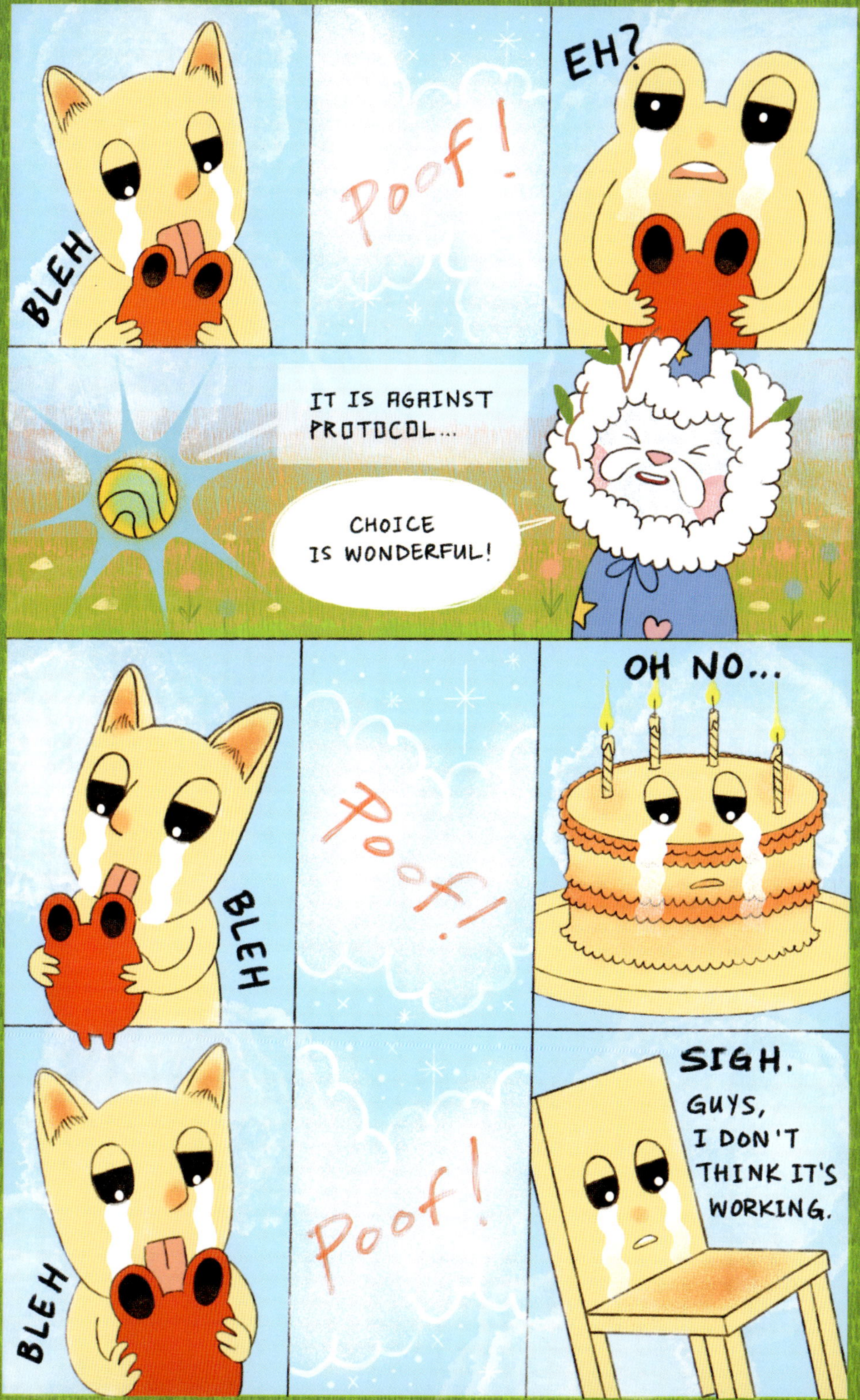
BLEH
Poof!
EH?
IT IS AGAINST PROTOCOL...
CHOICE IS WONDERFUL!
BLEH
Poof!
OH NO...
BLEH
Poof!
SIGH.
GUYS, I DON'T THINK IT'S WORKING.

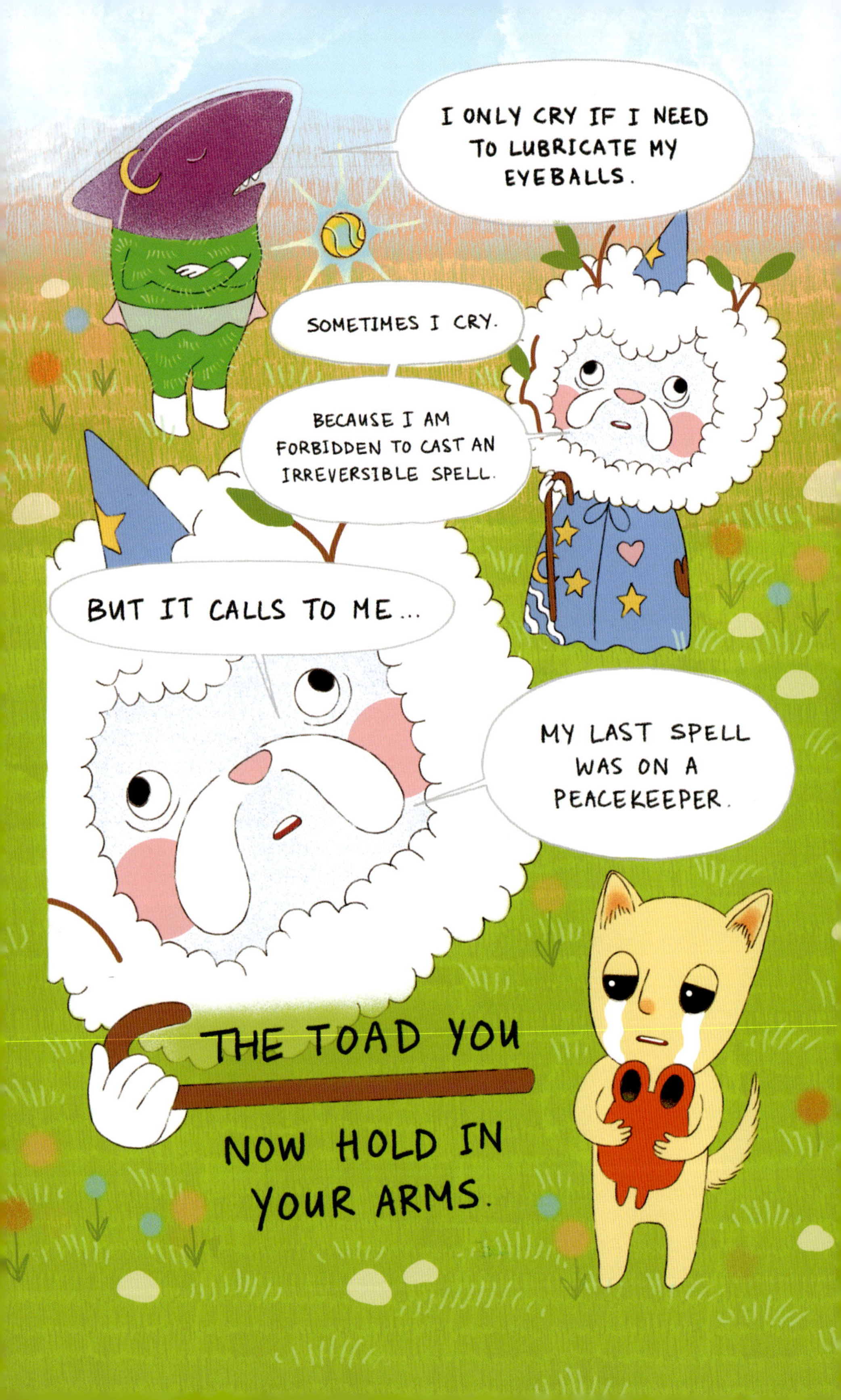

I ONLY CRY IF I NEED TO LUBRICATE MY EYEBALLS.
SOMETIMES I CRY.
BECAUSE I AM FORBIDDEN TO CAST AN IRREVERSIBLE SPELL.
BUT IT CALLS TO ME...
MY LAST SPELL WAS ON A PEACEKEEPER.
THE TOAD YOU NOW HOLD IN YOUR ARMS.

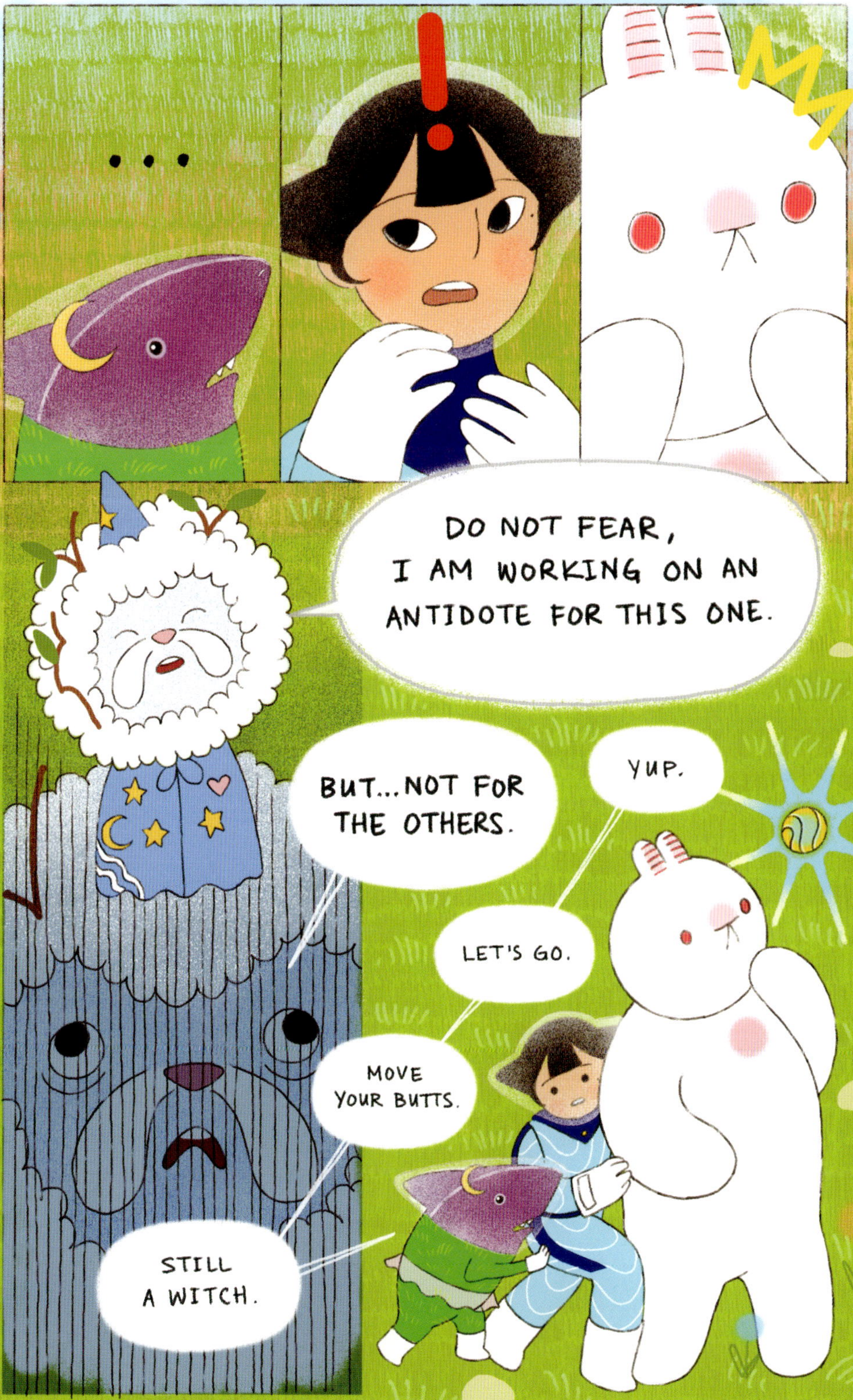
...
!
DO NOT FEAR, I AM WORKING ON AN ANTIDOTE FOR THIS ONE.
BUT...NOT FOR THE OTHERS.
YUP.
LET'S GO.
MOVE YOUR BUTTS.
STILL A WITCH.

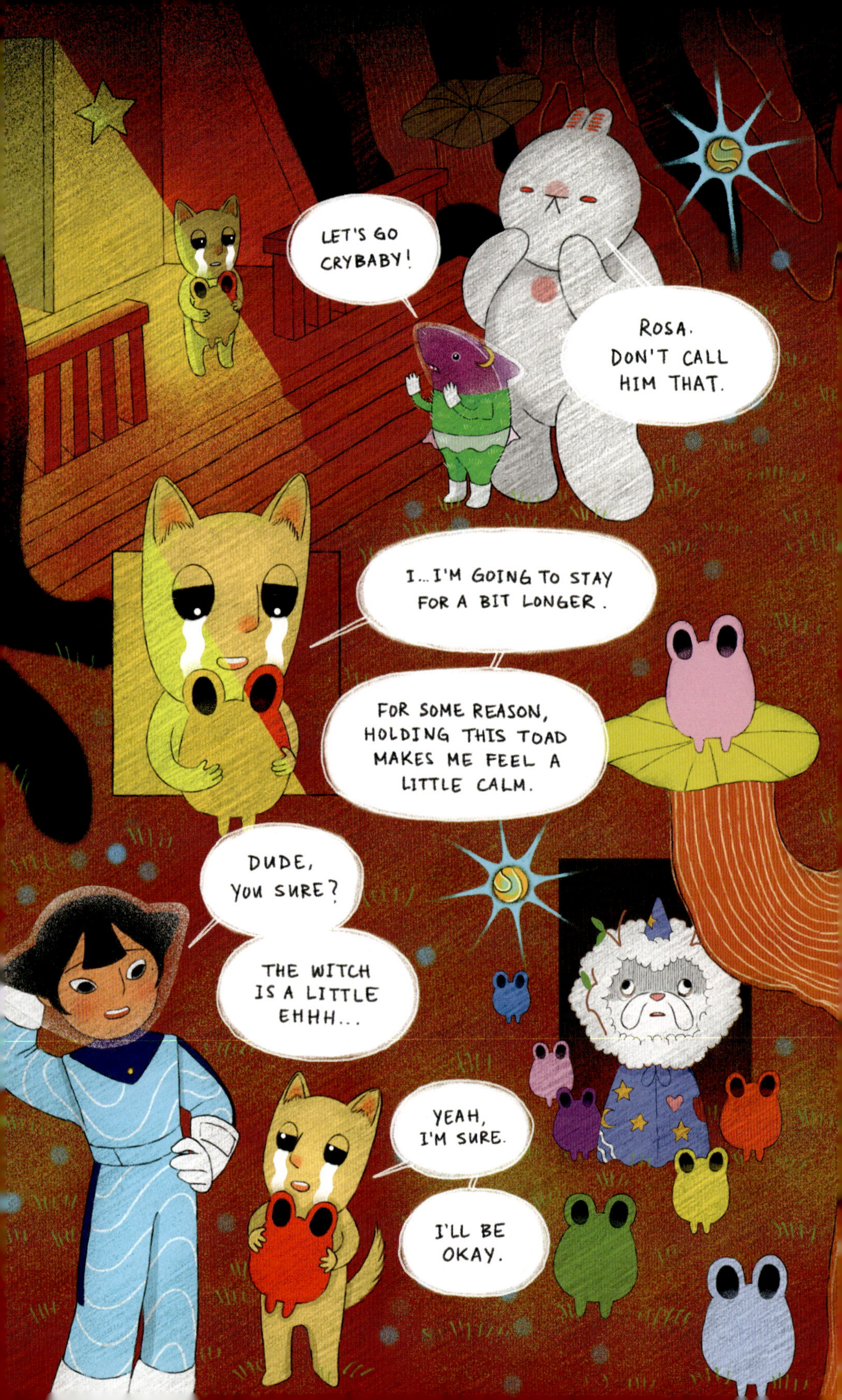

LET'S GO CRYBABY!
ROSA. DON'T CALL HIM THAT.
I... I'M GOING TO STAY FOR A BIT LONGER.
FOR SOME REASON, HOLDING THIS TOAD MAKES ME FEEL A LITTLE CALM.
DUDE, YOU SURE?
THE WITCH IS A LITTLE EHHH...
YEAH, I'M SURE.
I'LL BE OKAY.

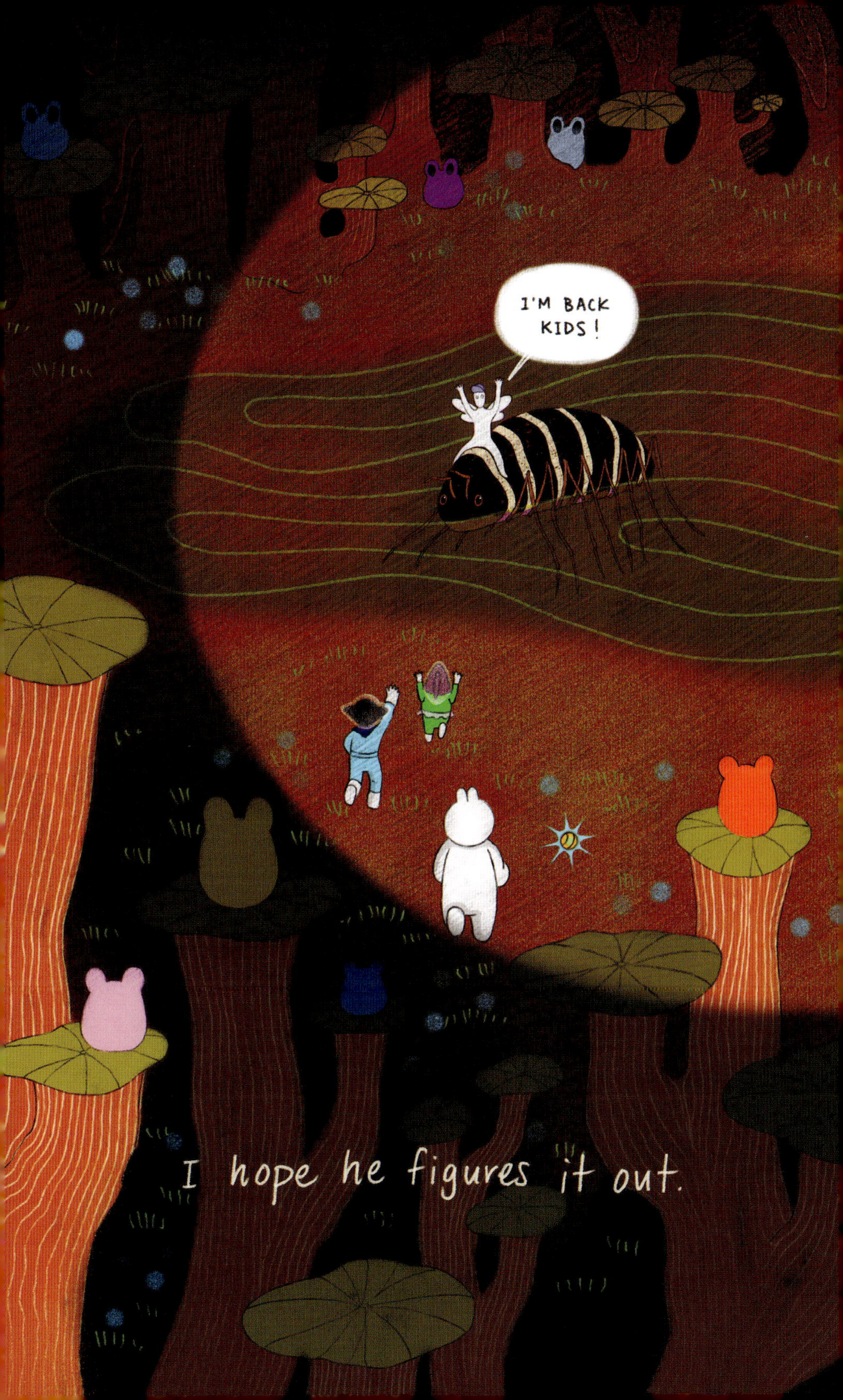
I'M BACK KIDS!
I hope he figures it out.

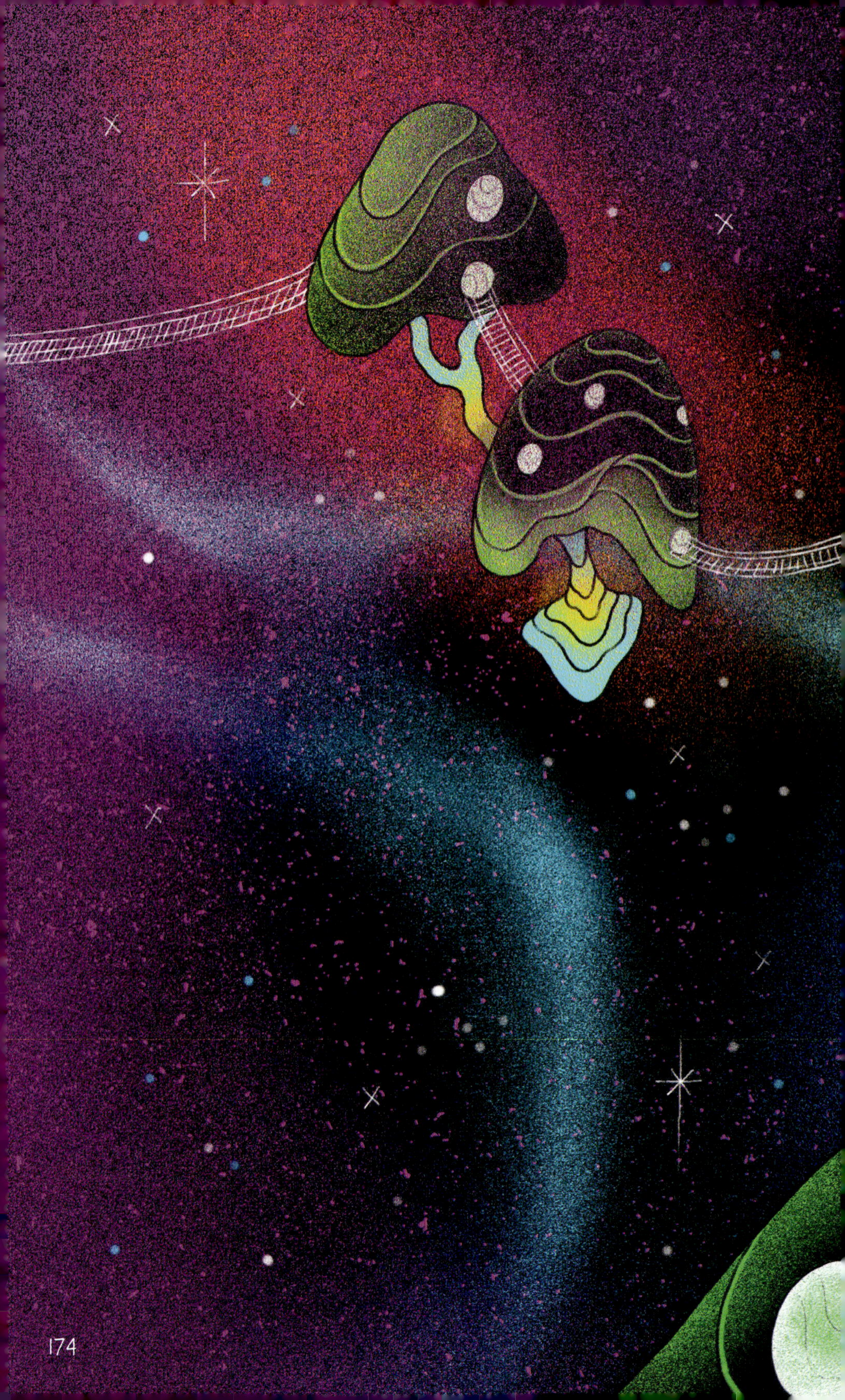

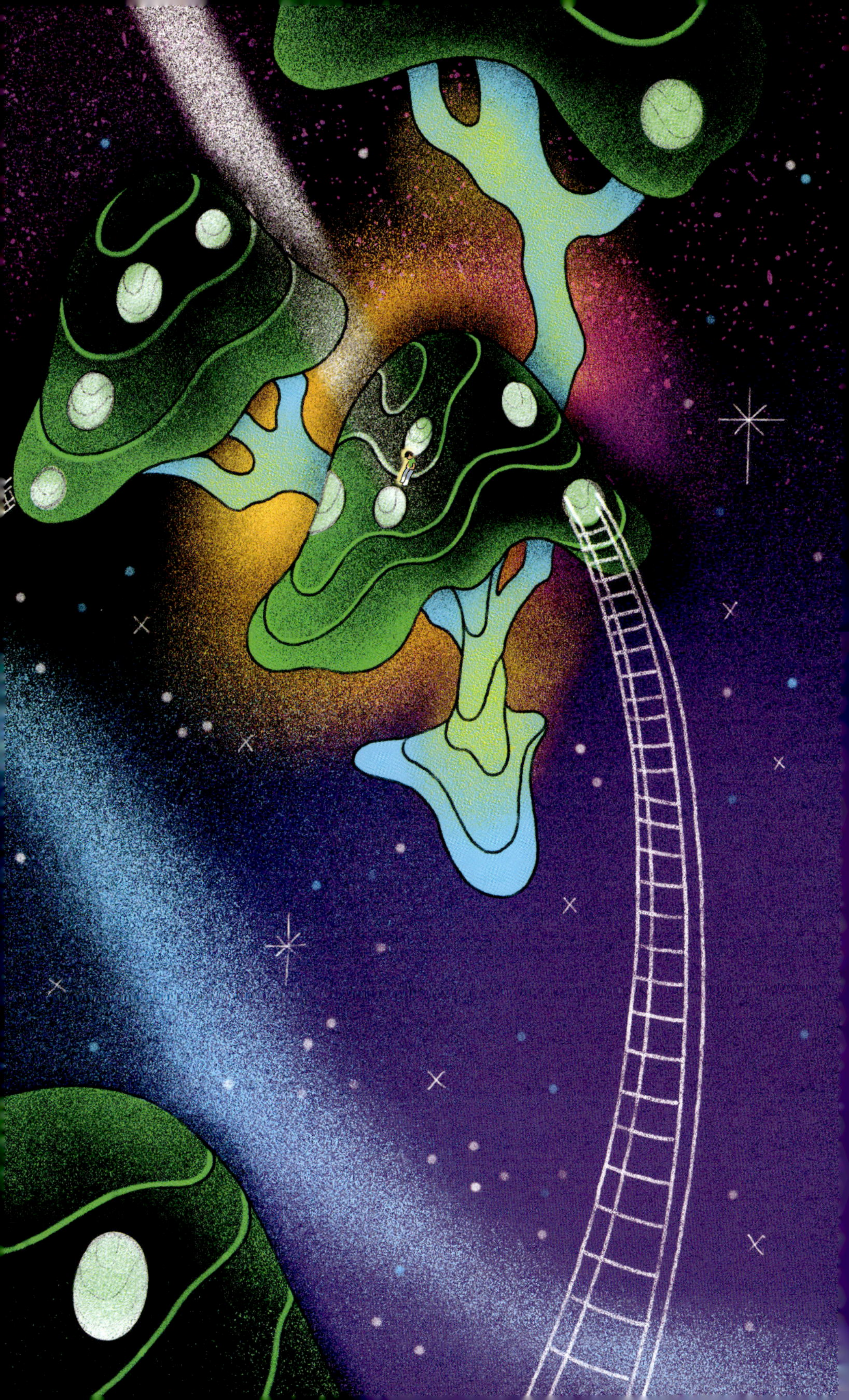

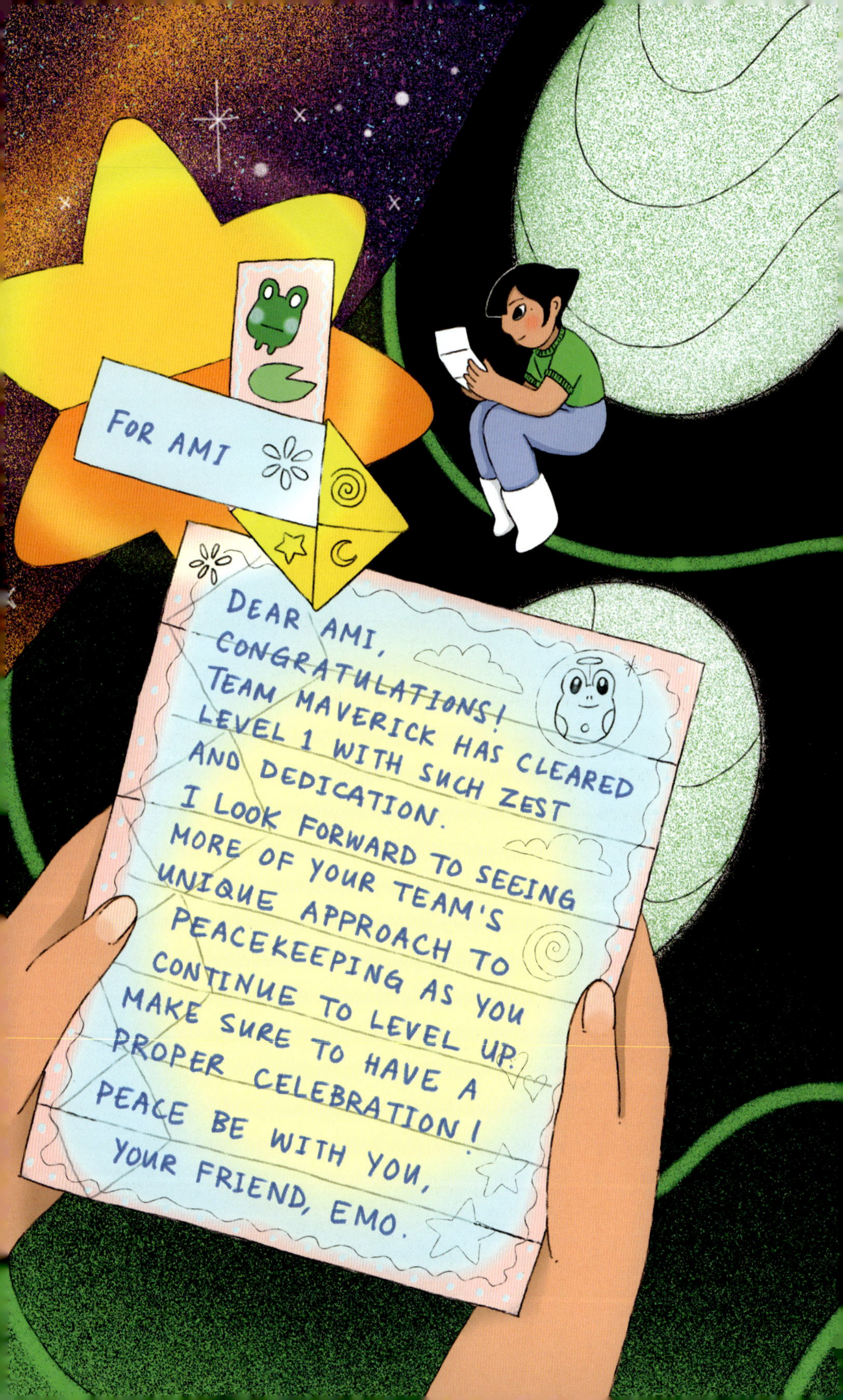
FOR AMI
DEAR AMI,
CONGRATULATIONS!
TEAM MAVERICK HAS CLEARED
LEVEL 1 WITH SUCH ZEST
AND DEDICATION.
I LOOK FORWARD TO SEEING
MORE OF YOUR TEAM'S
UNIQUE APPROACH TO
PEACEKEEPING AS YOU
CONTINUE TO LEVEL UP.
MAKE SURE TO HAVE A
PROPER CELEBRATION!
PEACE BE WITH YOU,
YOUR FRIEND, EMO.

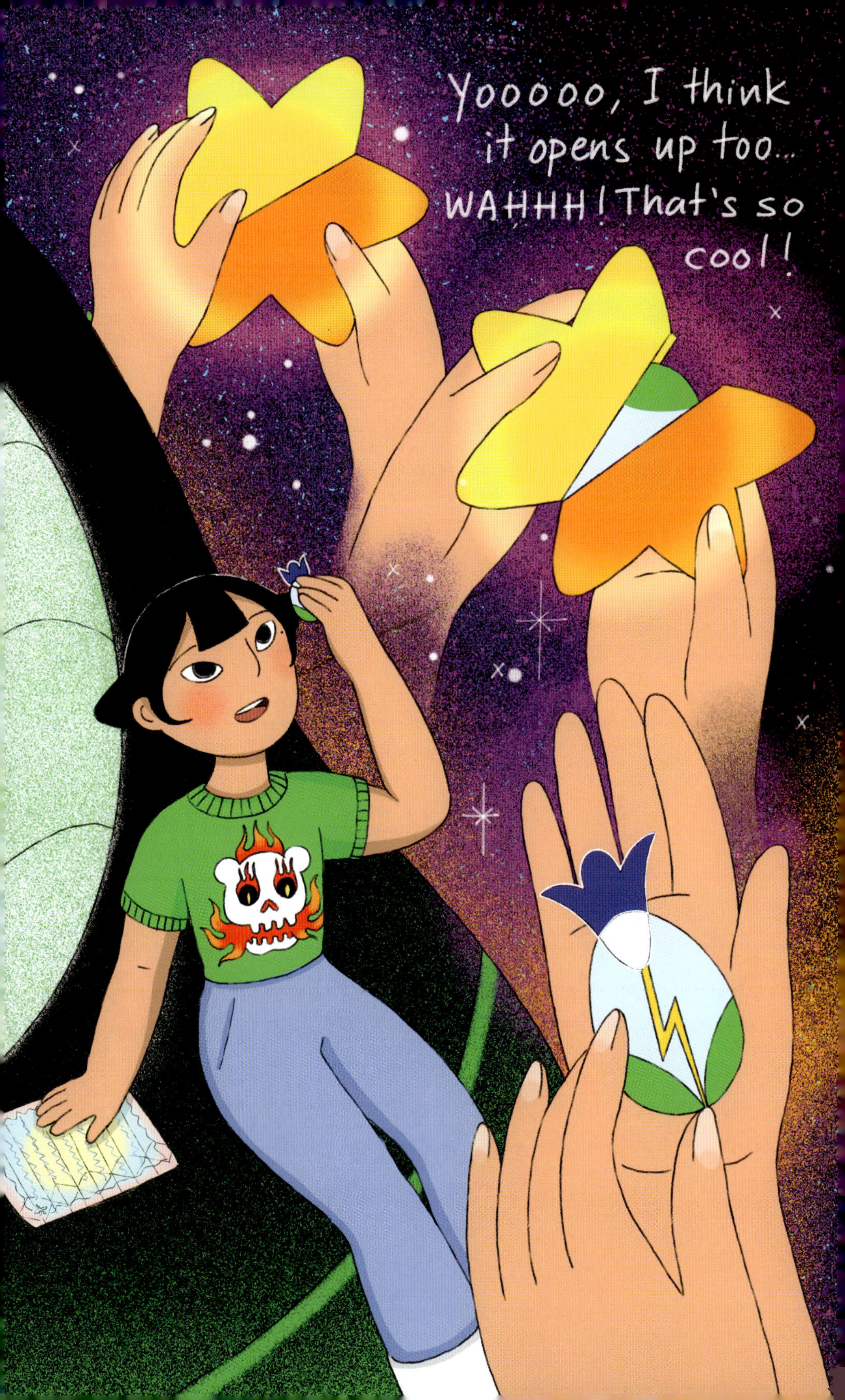
Yooooo, I think it opens up too... WAHHH! That's so cool!

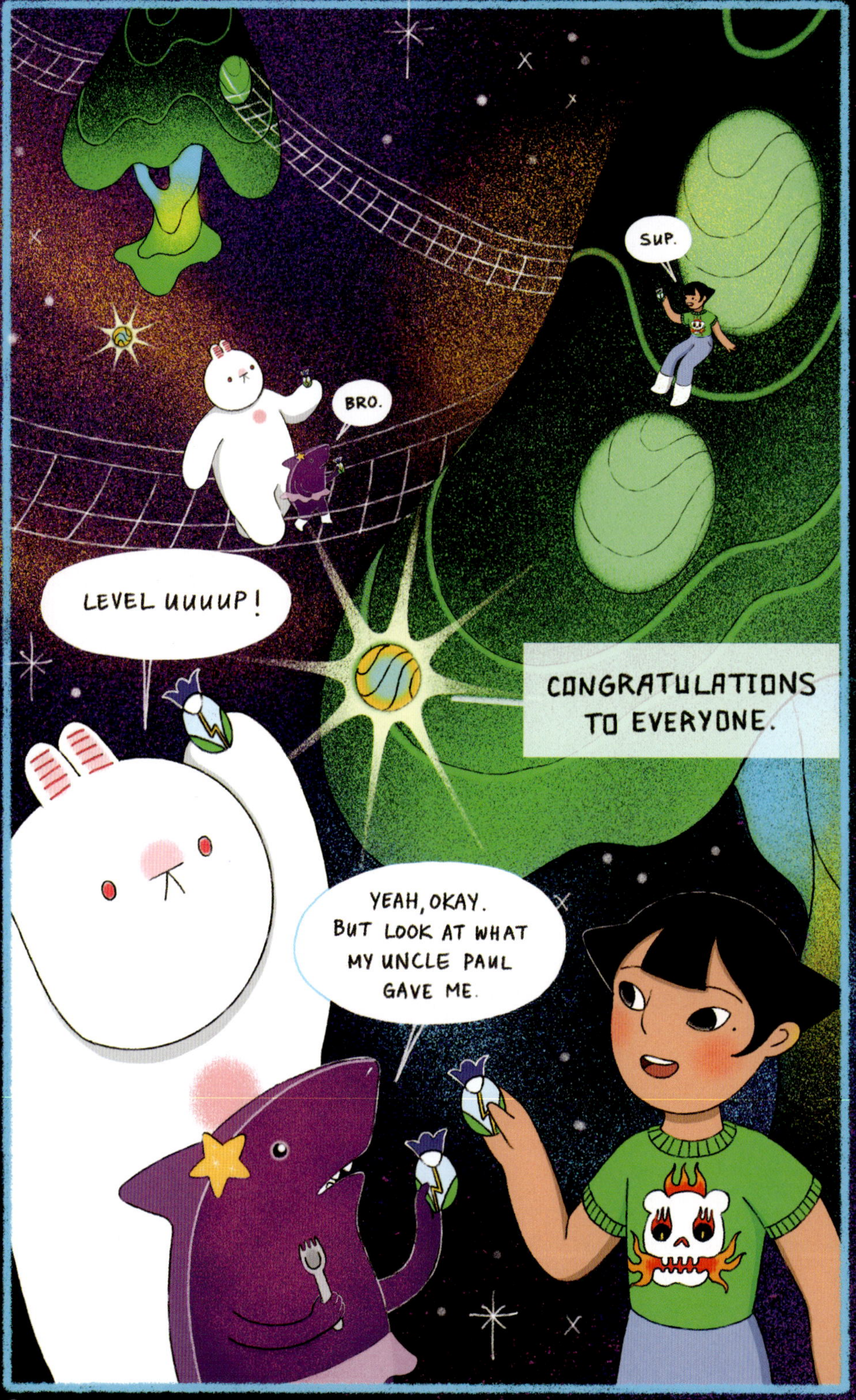
SUP.
BRO.
LEVEL UUUUP!
CONGRATULATIONS TO EVERYONE.
YEAH, OKAY. BUT LOOK AT WHAT MY UNCLE PAUL GAVE ME.

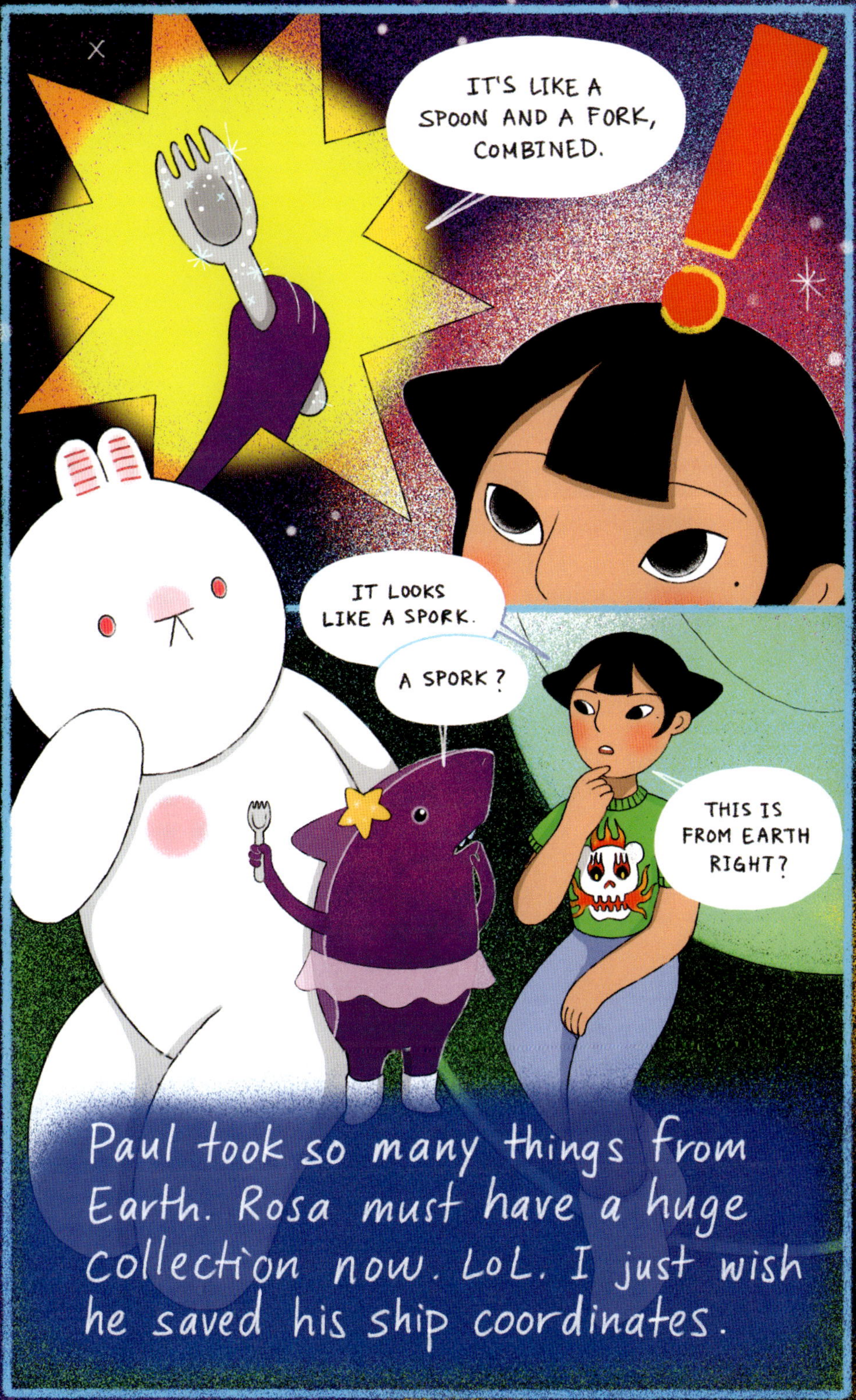
IT'S LIKE A SPOON AND A FORK, COMBINED.
IT LOOKS LIKE A SPORK.
A SPORK?
THIS IS FROM EARTH RIGHT?
Paul took so many things from Earth. Rosa must have a huge collection now. LoL. I just wish he saved his ship coordinates.

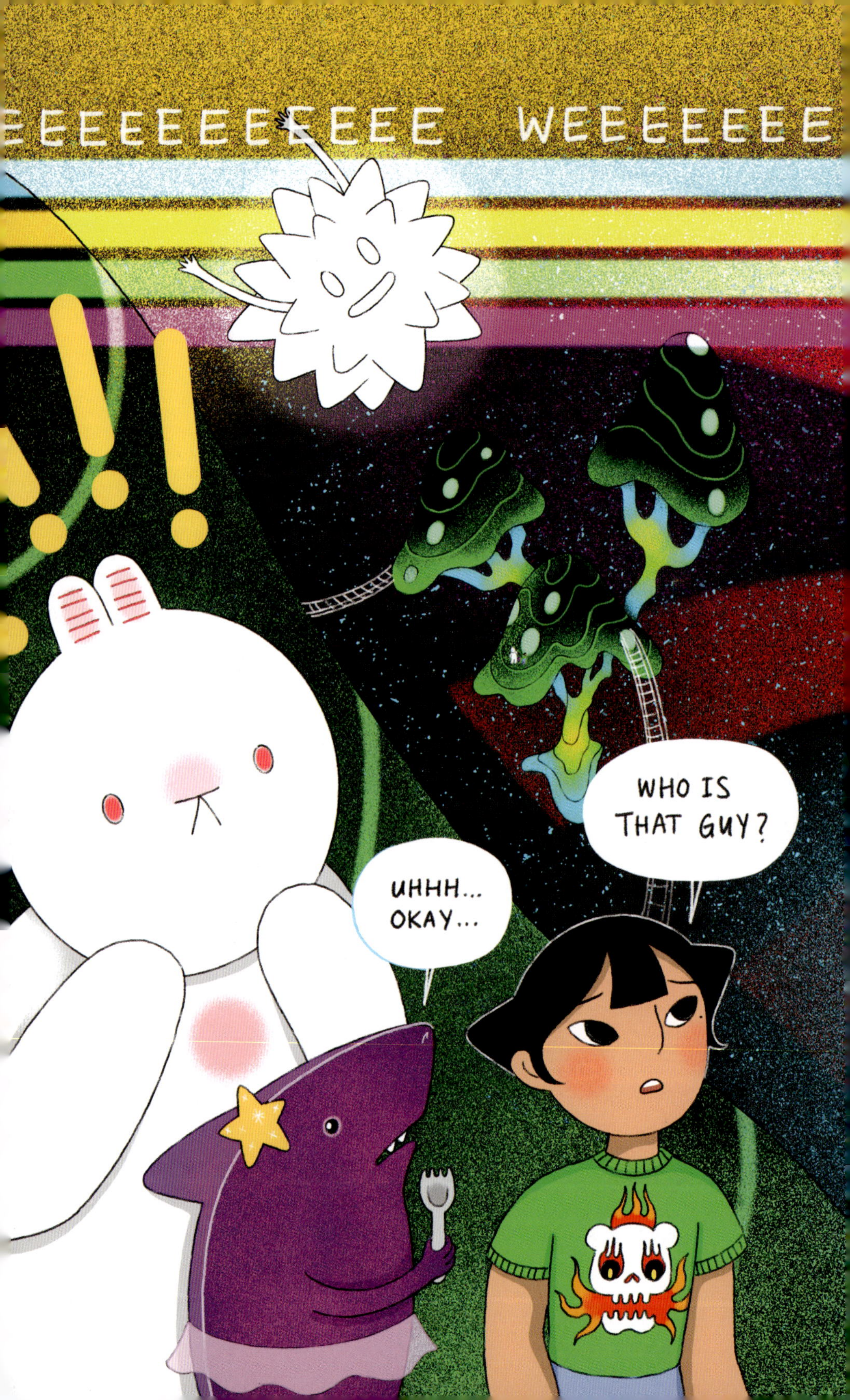
EEEEEEEEEEE WEEEEEEEE
!!!
UHHH... OKAY...
WHO IS THAT GUY?

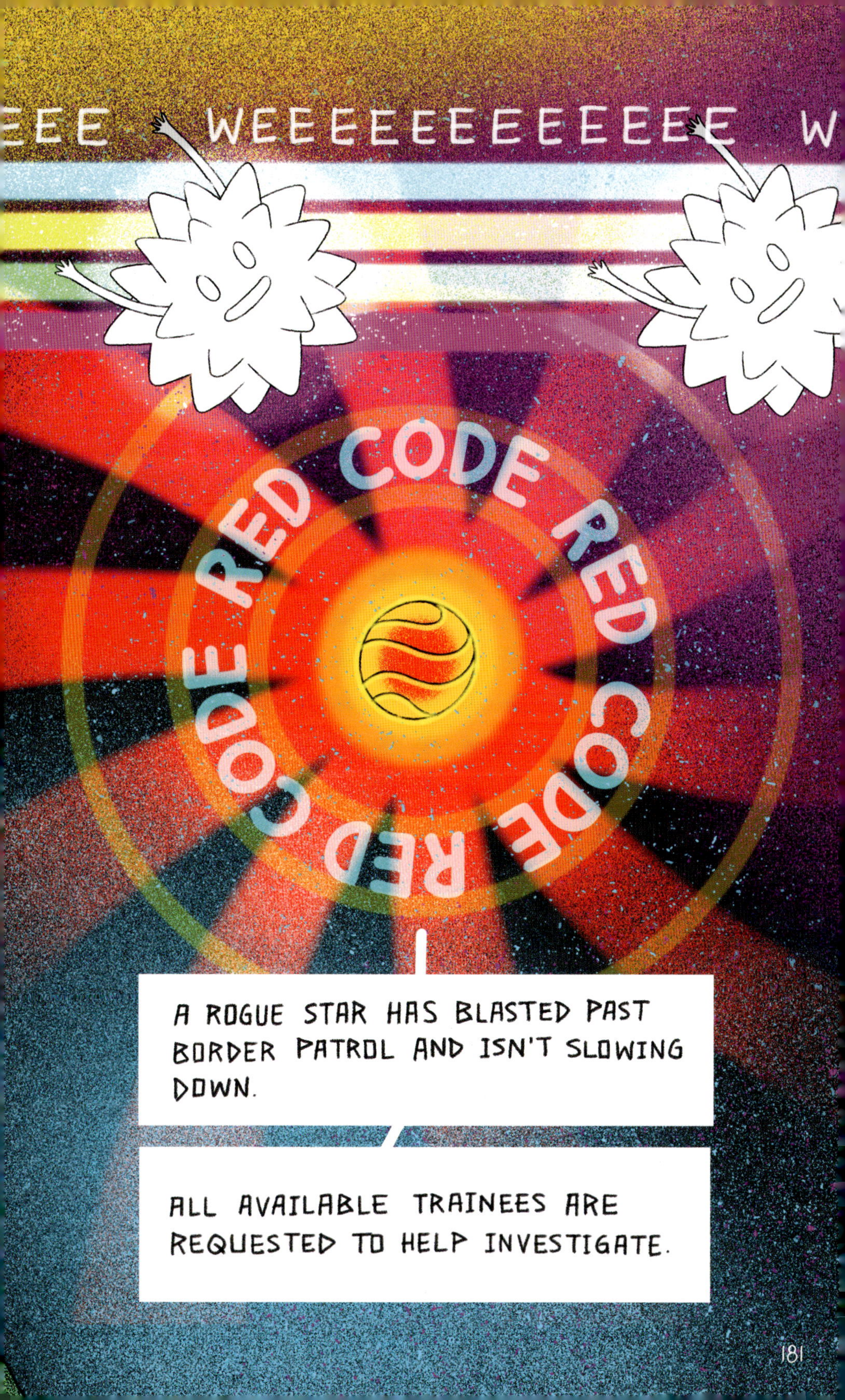
EEE WEEEEEEEEEEEEE W
RED CODE RED CODE RED CODE RED CODE
A ROGUE STAR HAS BLASTED PAST BORDER PATROL AND ISN'T SLOWING DOWN.
ALL AVAILABLE TRAINEES ARE REQUESTED TO HELP INVESTIGATE.

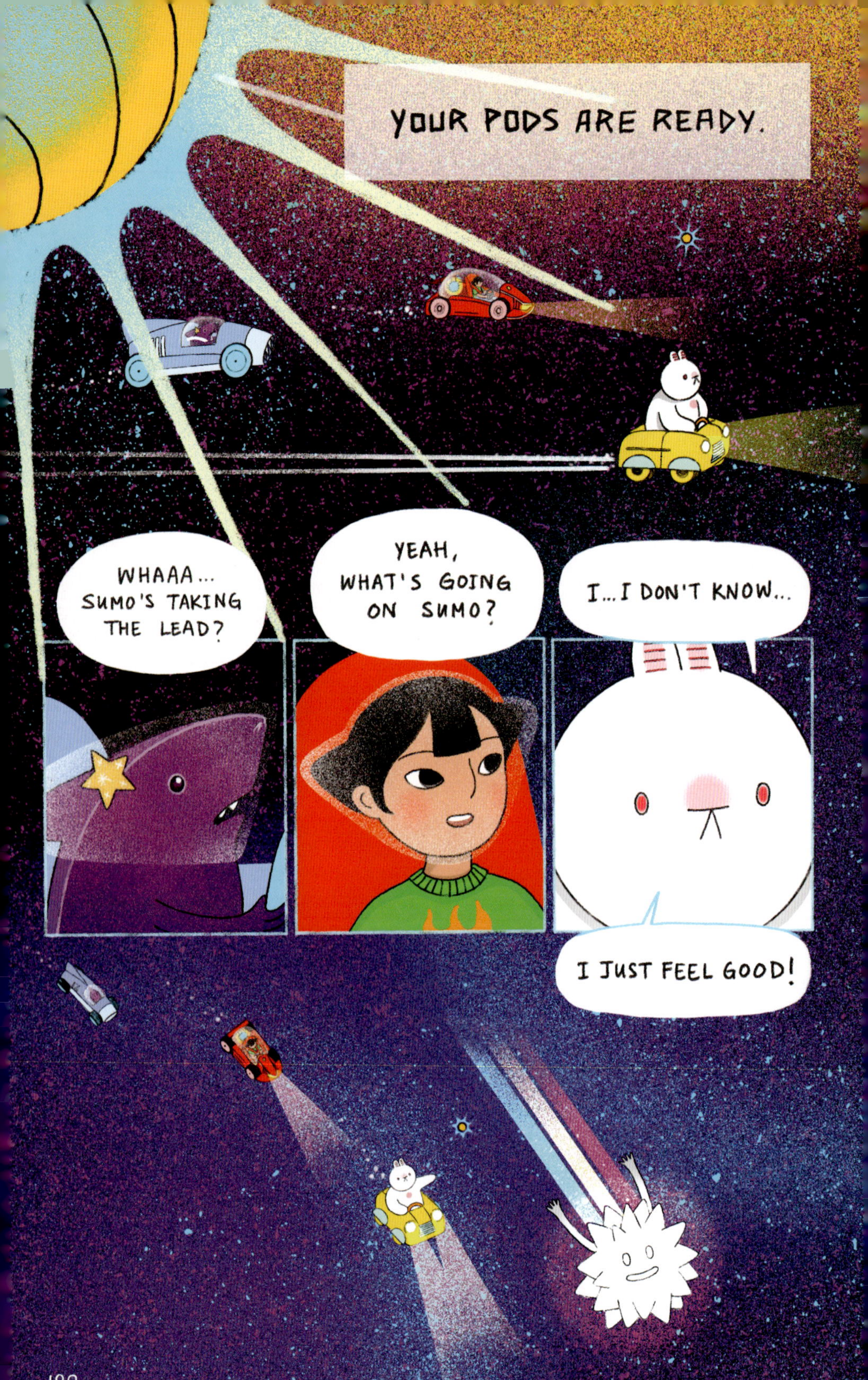
YOUR PODS ARE READY.
WHAAA... SUMO'S TAKING THE LEAD?
YEAH, WHAT'S GOING ON SUMO?
I...I DON'T KNOW...
I JUST FEEL GOOD!

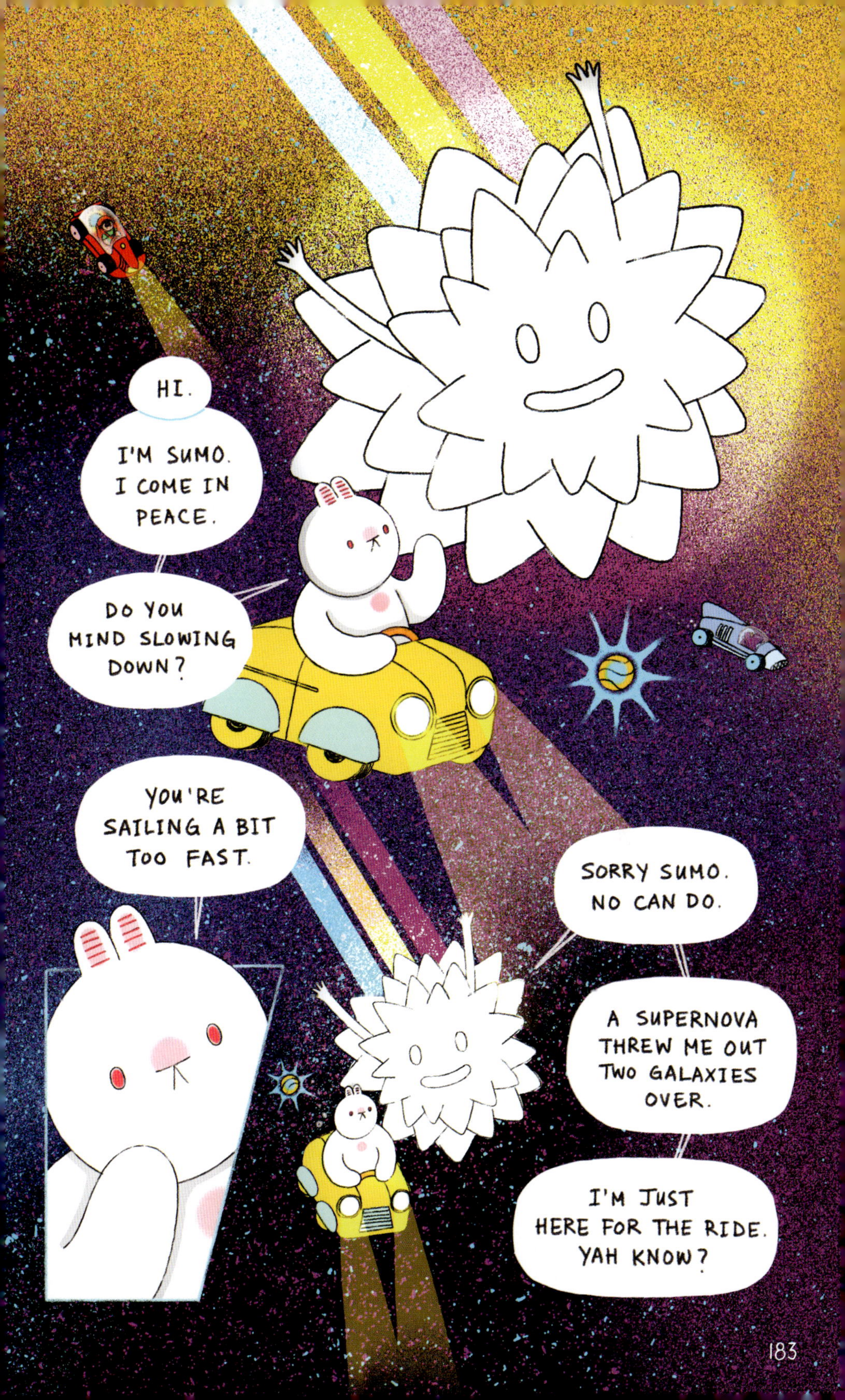
HI.
I'M SUMO. I COME IN PEACE.
DO YOU MIND SLOWING DOWN?
YOU'RE SAILING A BIT TOO FAST.
SORRY SUMO. NO CAN DO.
A SUPERNOVA THREW ME OUT TWO GALAXIES OVER.
I'M JUST HERE FOR THE RIDE. YAH KNOW?

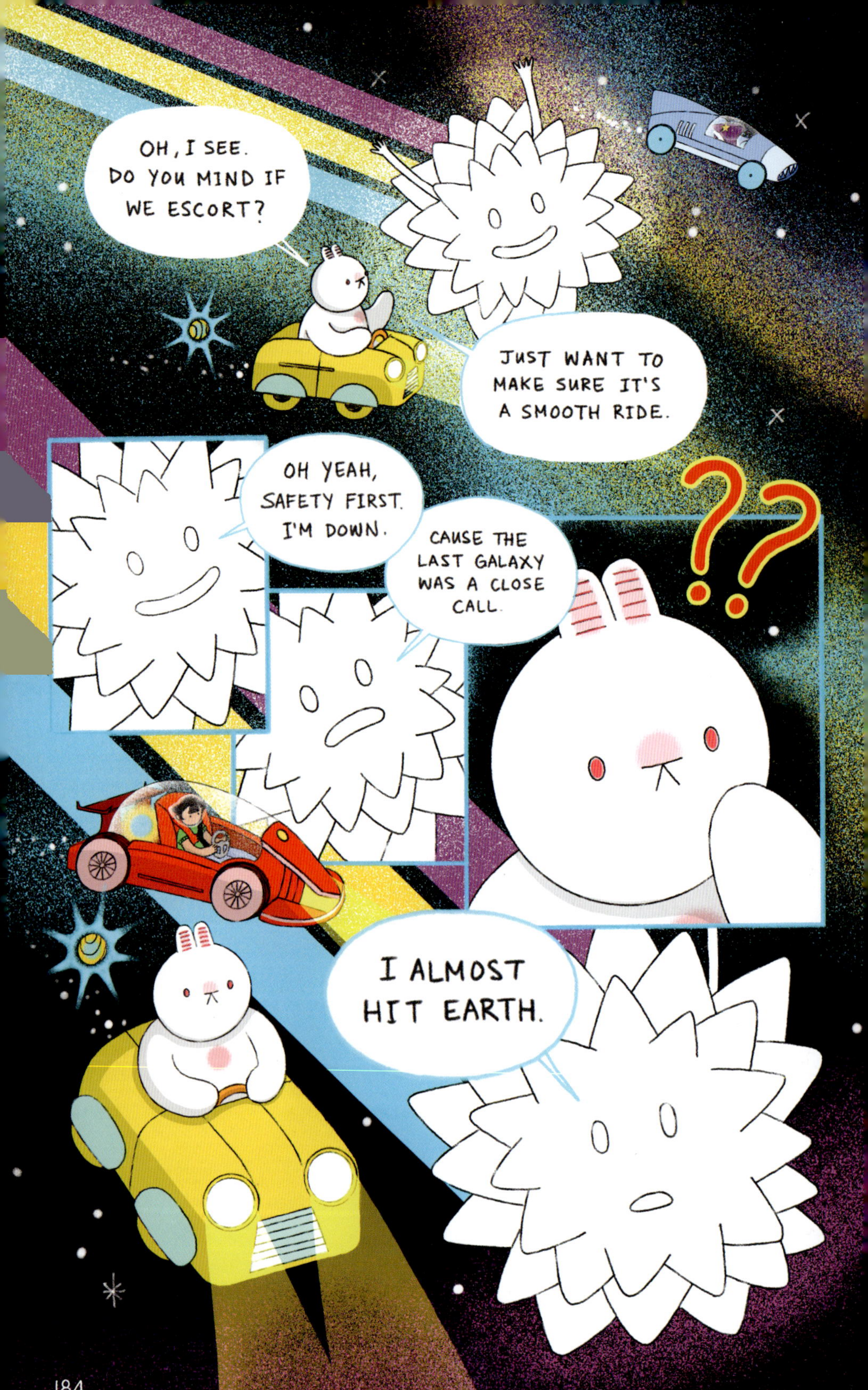
OH, I SEE. DO YOU MIND IF WE ESCORT?
JUST WANT TO MAKE SURE IT'S A SMOOTH RIDE.
OH YEAH, SAFETY FIRST. I'M DOWN.
CAUSE THE LAST GALAXY WAS A CLOSE CALL.
??
I ALMOST HIT EARTH.

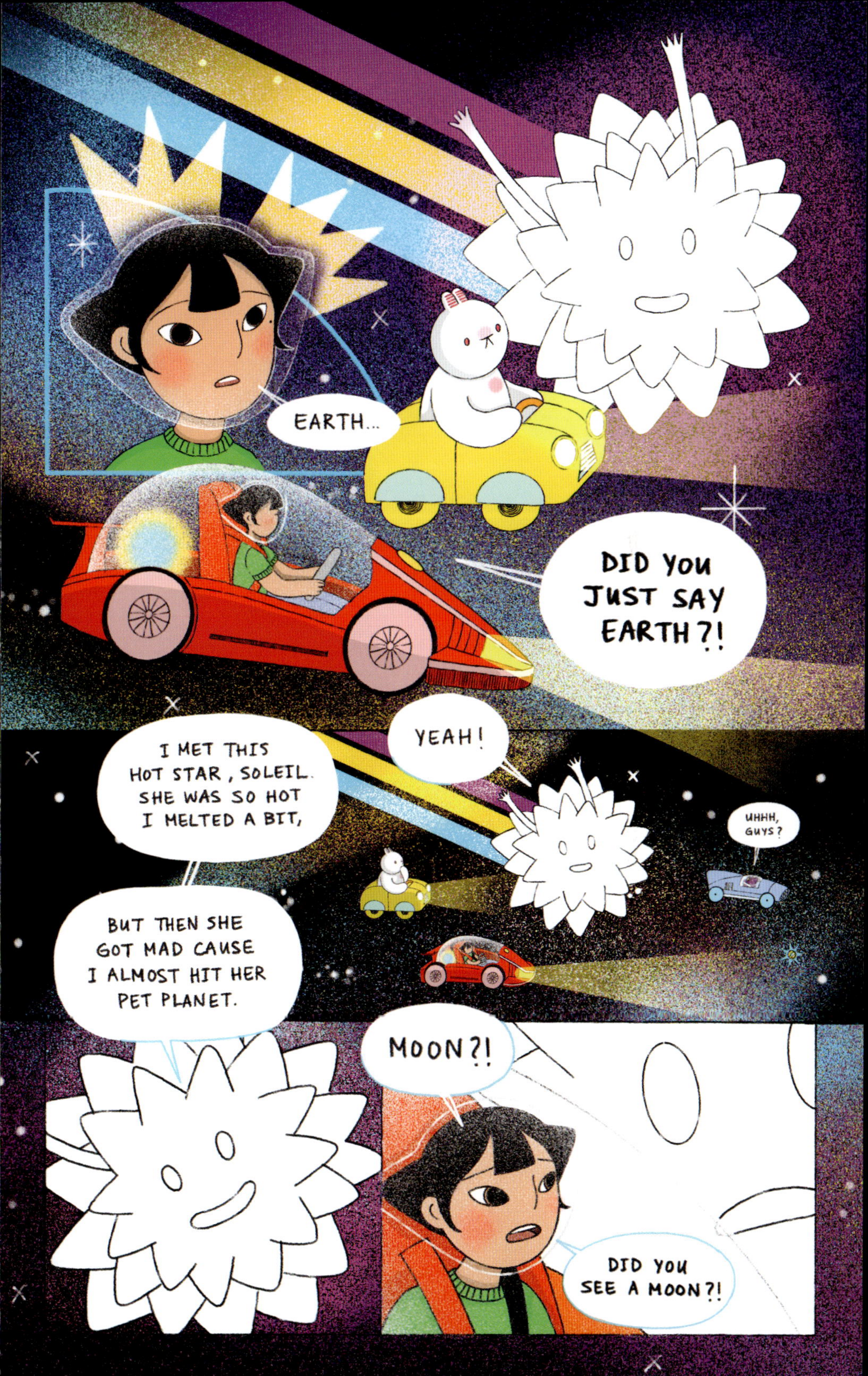
EARTH...
DID YOU JUST SAY EARTH?!
YEAH!
I MET THIS HOT STAR, SOLEIL. SHE WAS SO HOT I MELTED A BIT,
UHHH, GUYS?
BUT THEN SHE GOT MAD CAUSE I ALMOST HIT HER PET PLANET.
MOON?!
DID YOU SEE A MOON?!

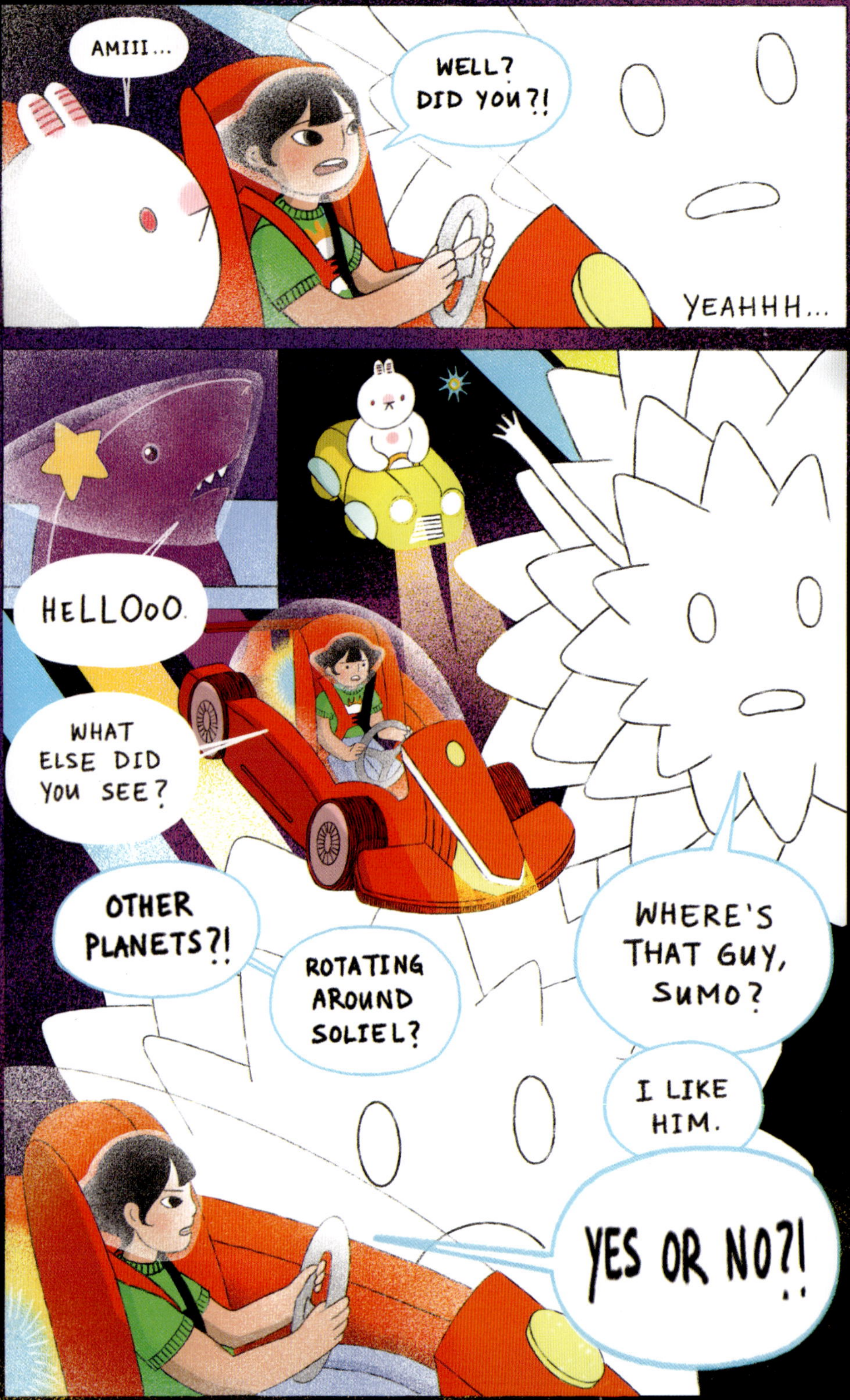
AMIII...
WELL? DID YOU?!
YEAHHH...
HELLOoO.
WHAT ELSE DID YOU SEE?
OTHER PLANETS?!
ROTATING AROUND SOLIEL?
WHERE'S THAT GUY, SUMO?
I LIKE HIM.
YES OR NO?!

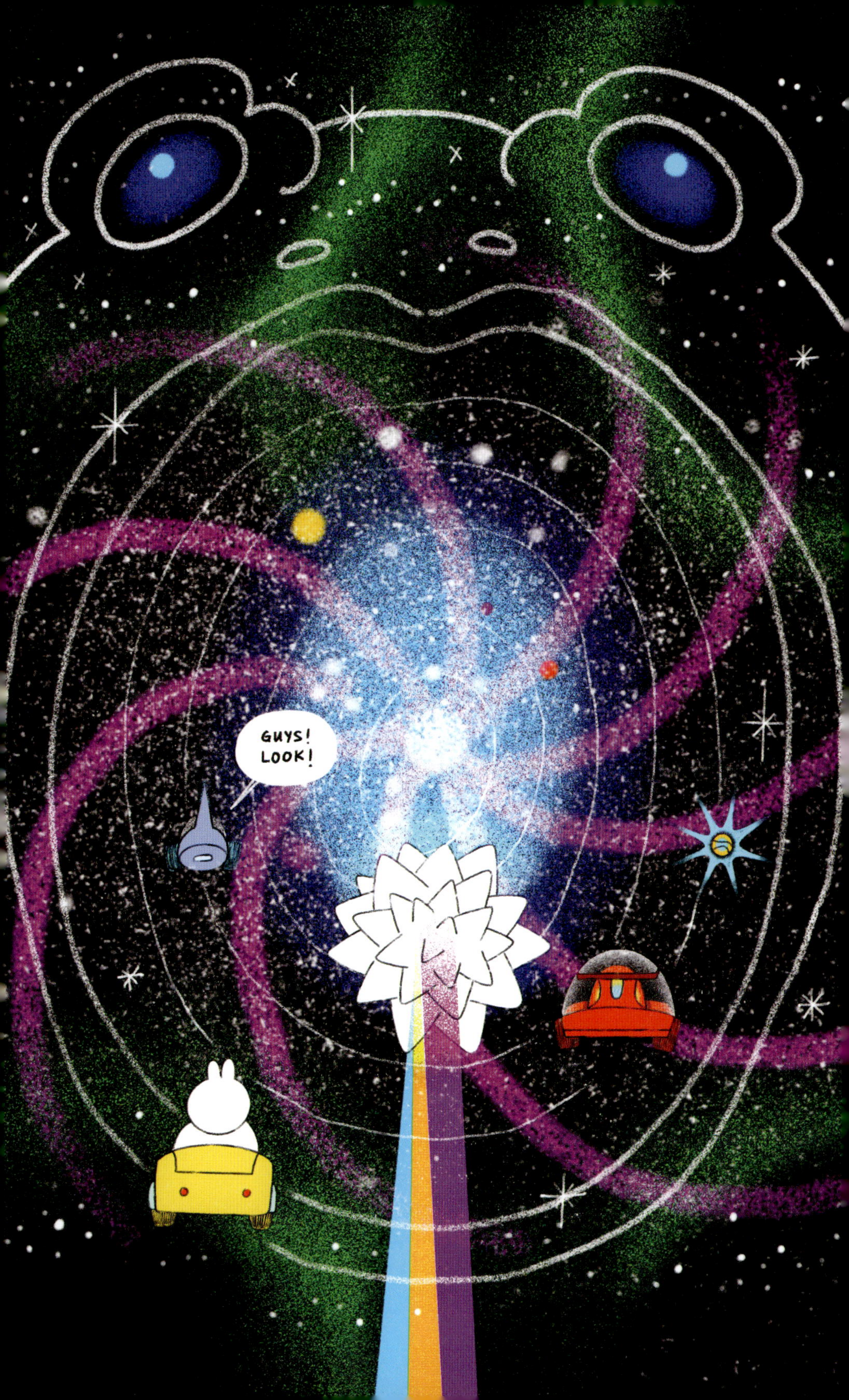
GUYS! LOOK!

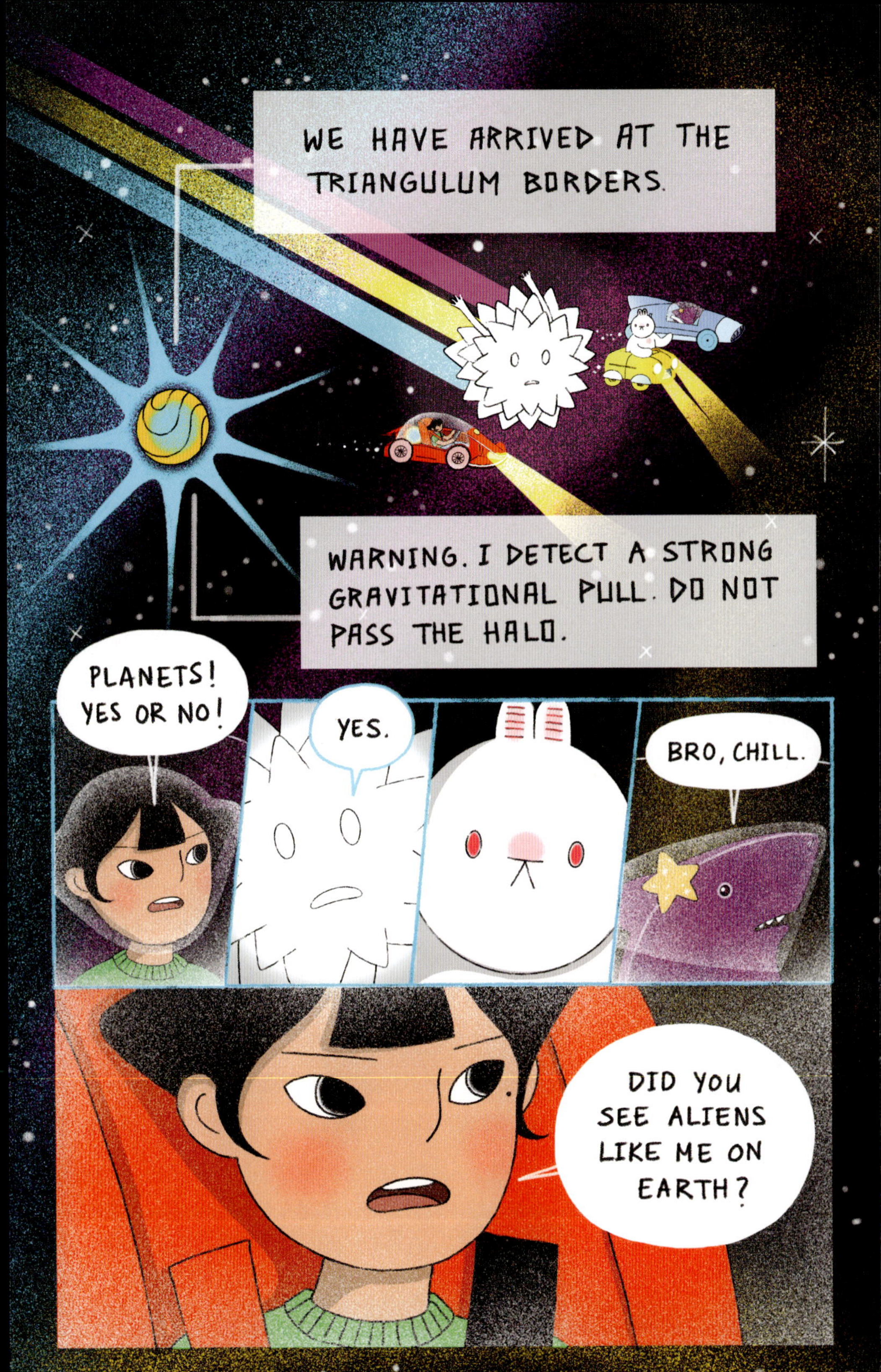
WE HAVE ARRIVED AT THE TRIANGULUM BORDERS.
WARNING. I DETECT A STRONG GRAVITATIONAL PULL. DO NOT PASS THE HALO.
PLANETS! YES OR NO!
YES.
BRO, CHILL.
DID YOU SEE ALIENS LIKE ME ON EARTH?

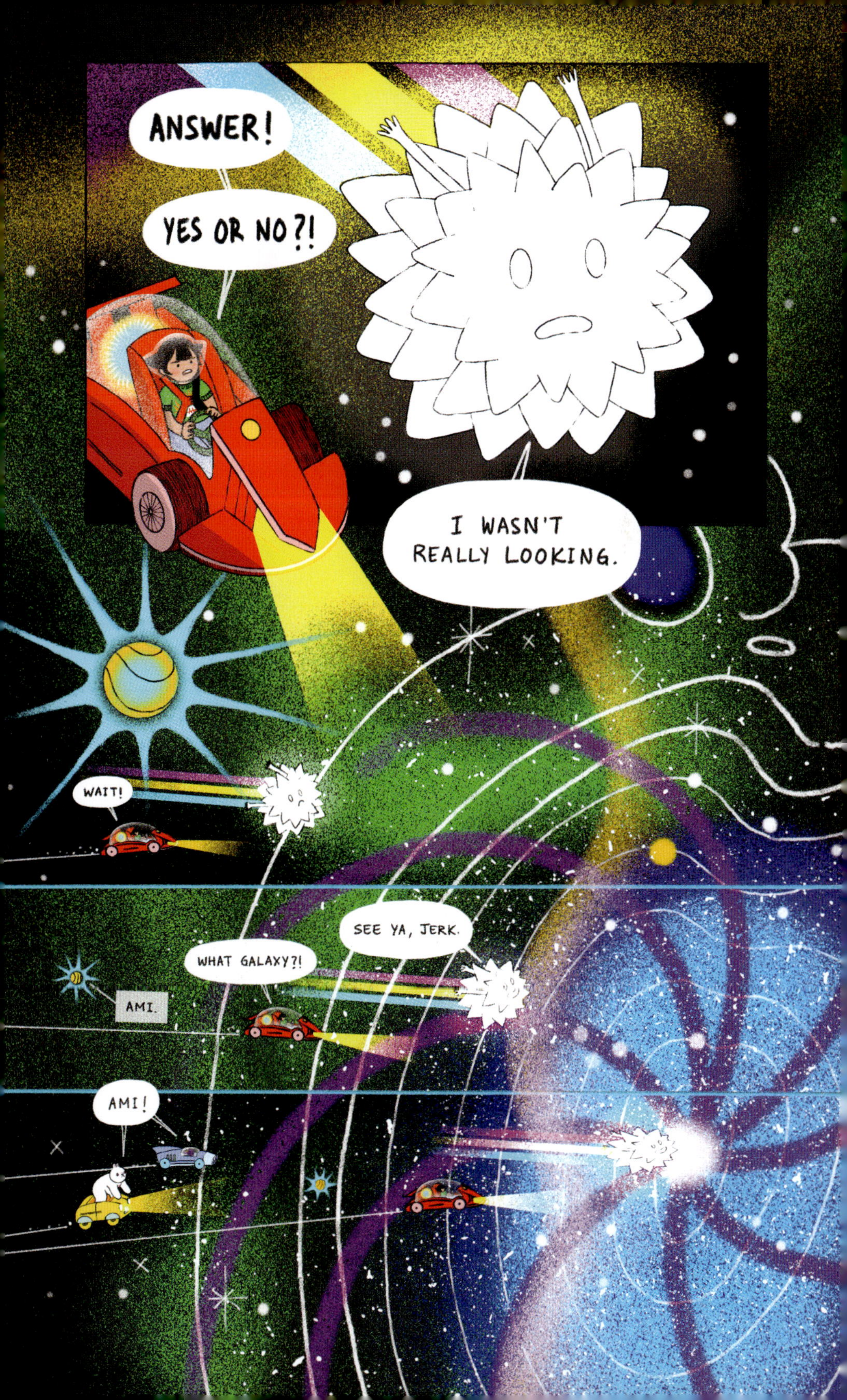
ANSWER!
YES OR NO?!
I WASN'T REALLY LOOKING.
WAIT!
WHAT GALAXY?!
SEE YA, JERK.
AMI.
AMI!

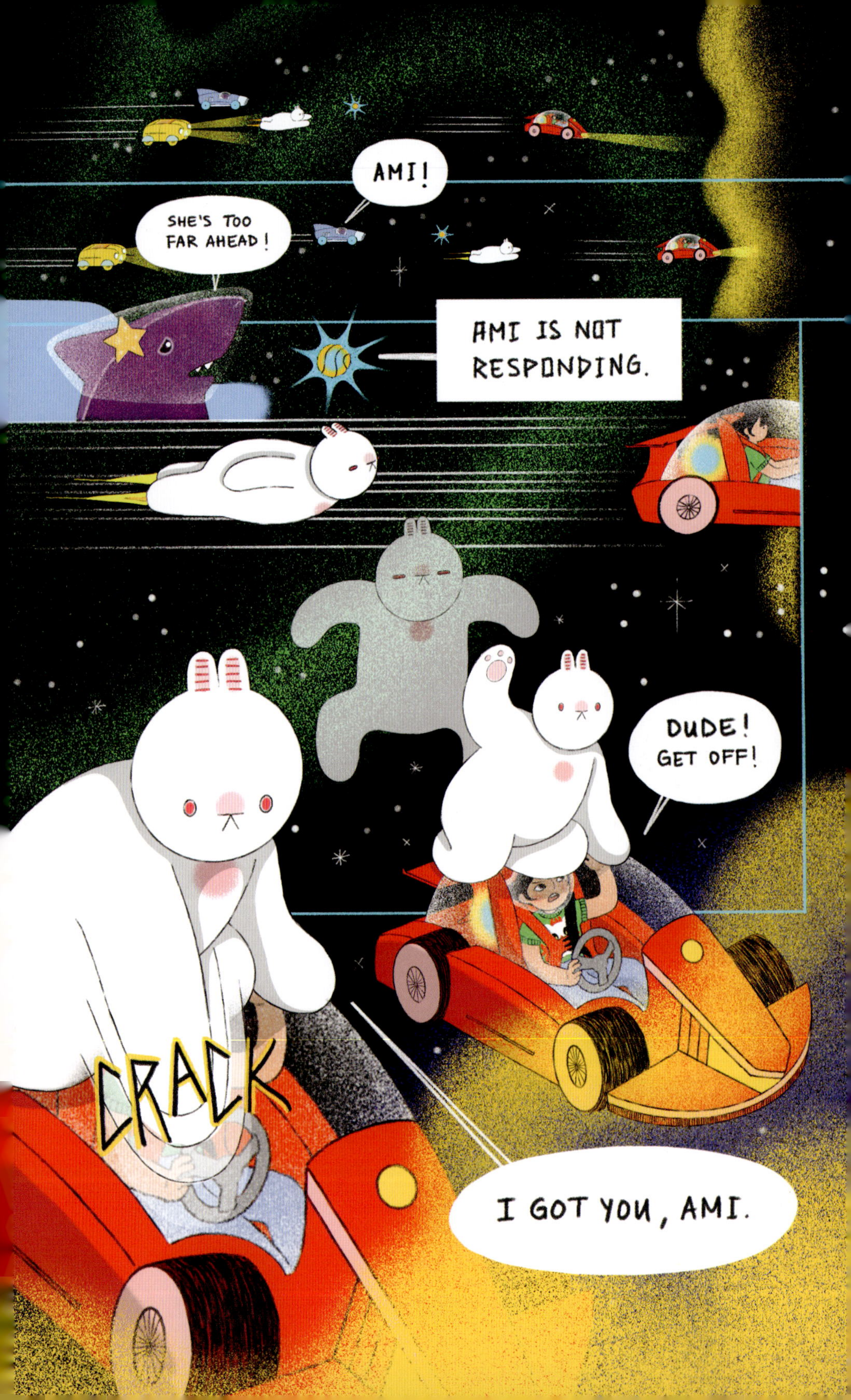
AMI!
SHE'S TOO FAR AHEAD!
AMI IS NOT RESPONDING.
DUDE! GET OFF!
CRACK
I GOT YOU, AMI.

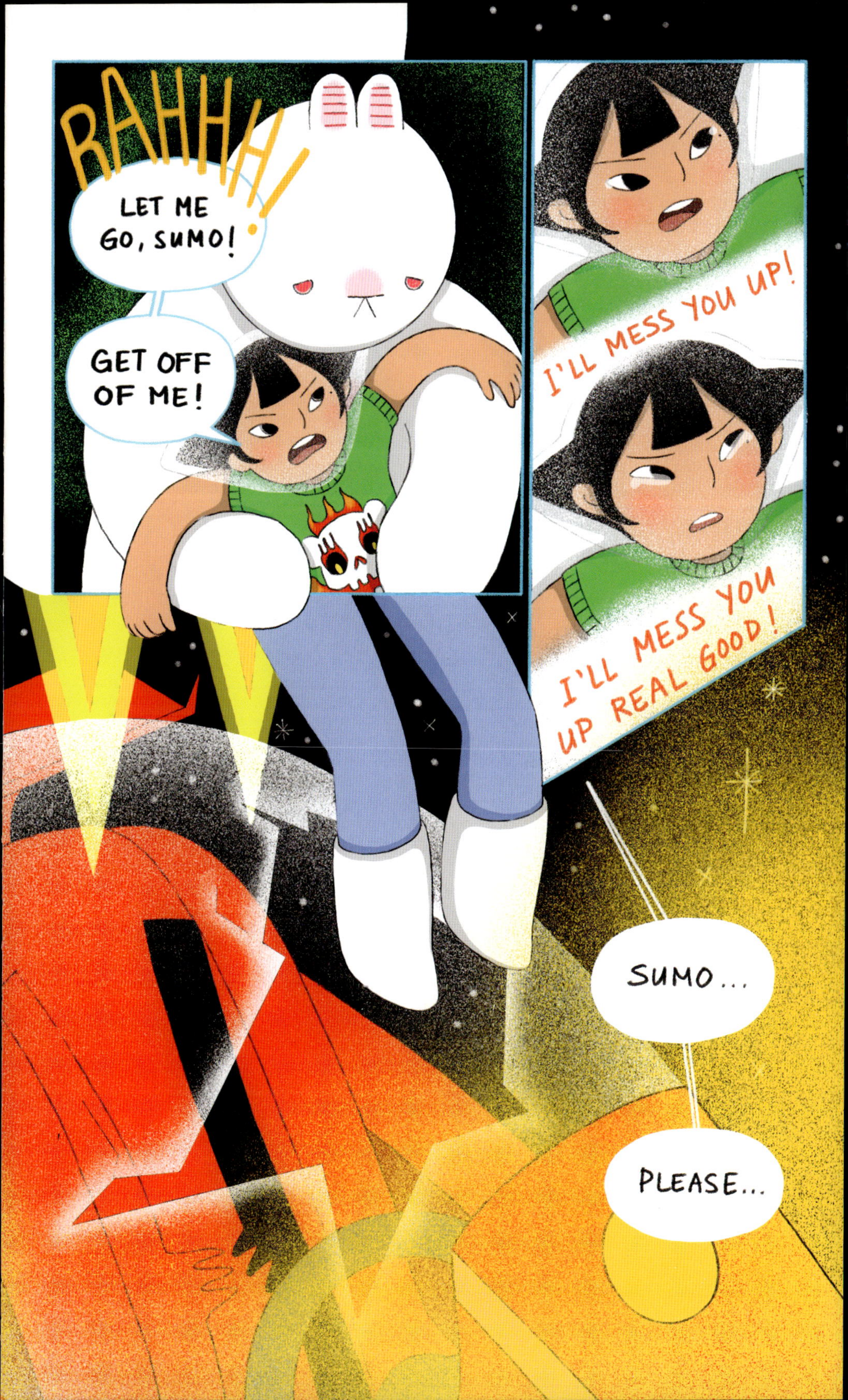
RAHHH!
LET ME GO, SUMO!
GET OFF OF ME!
I'LL MESS YOU UP!
I'LL MESS YOU UP REAL GOOD!
SUMO...
PLEASE...

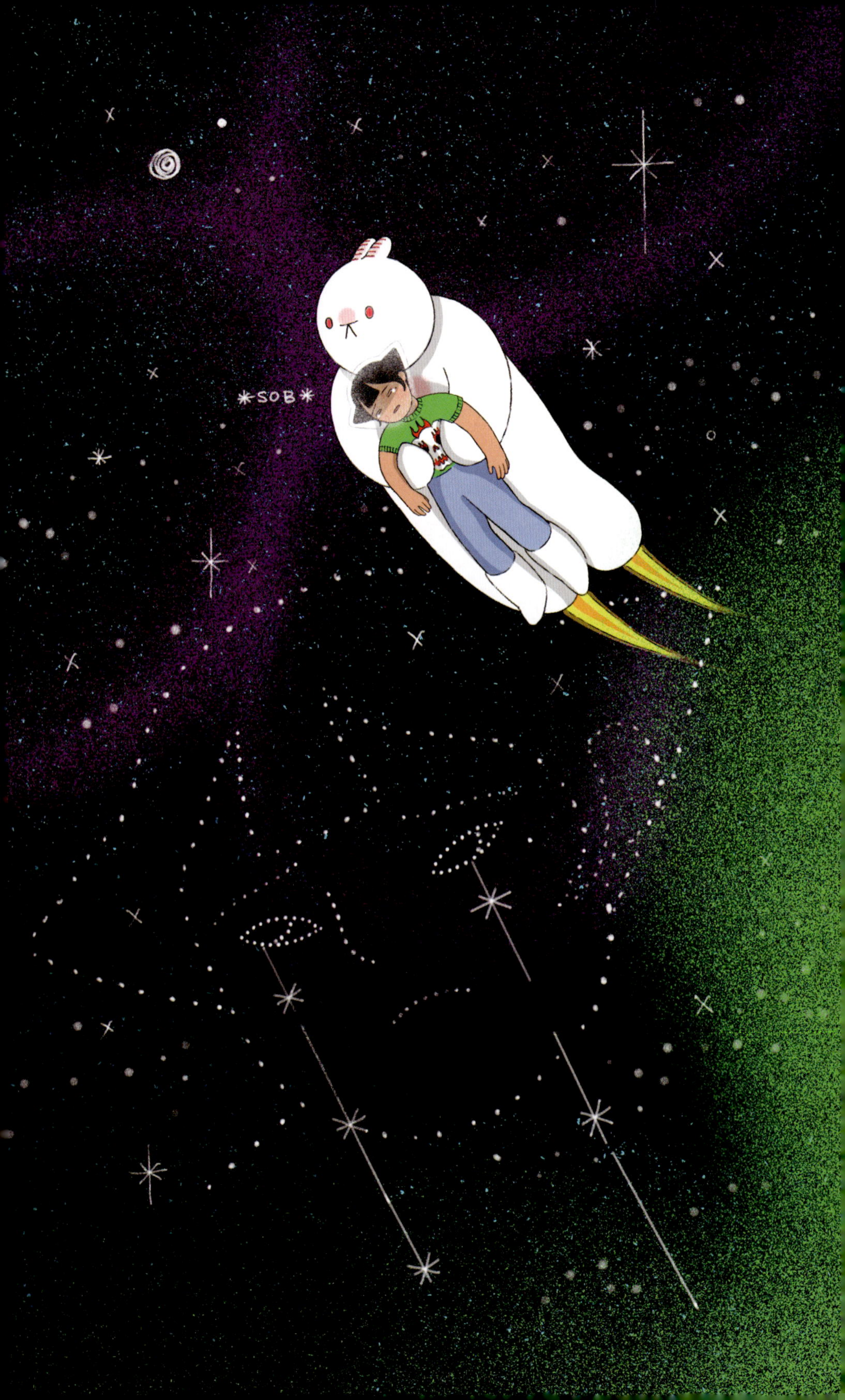
SOB

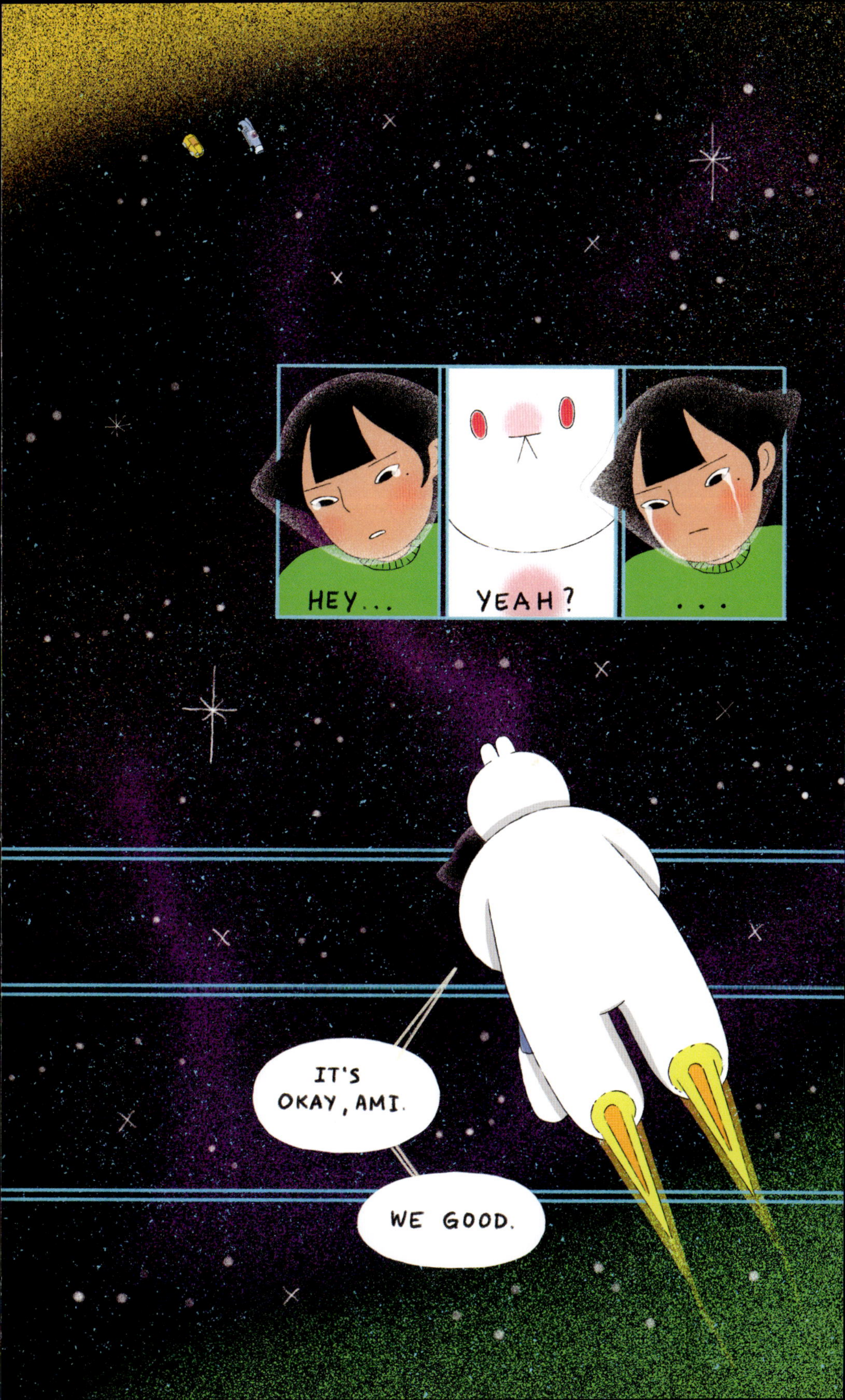
HEY...
YEAH?
...
IT'S OKAY, AMI.
WE GOOD.

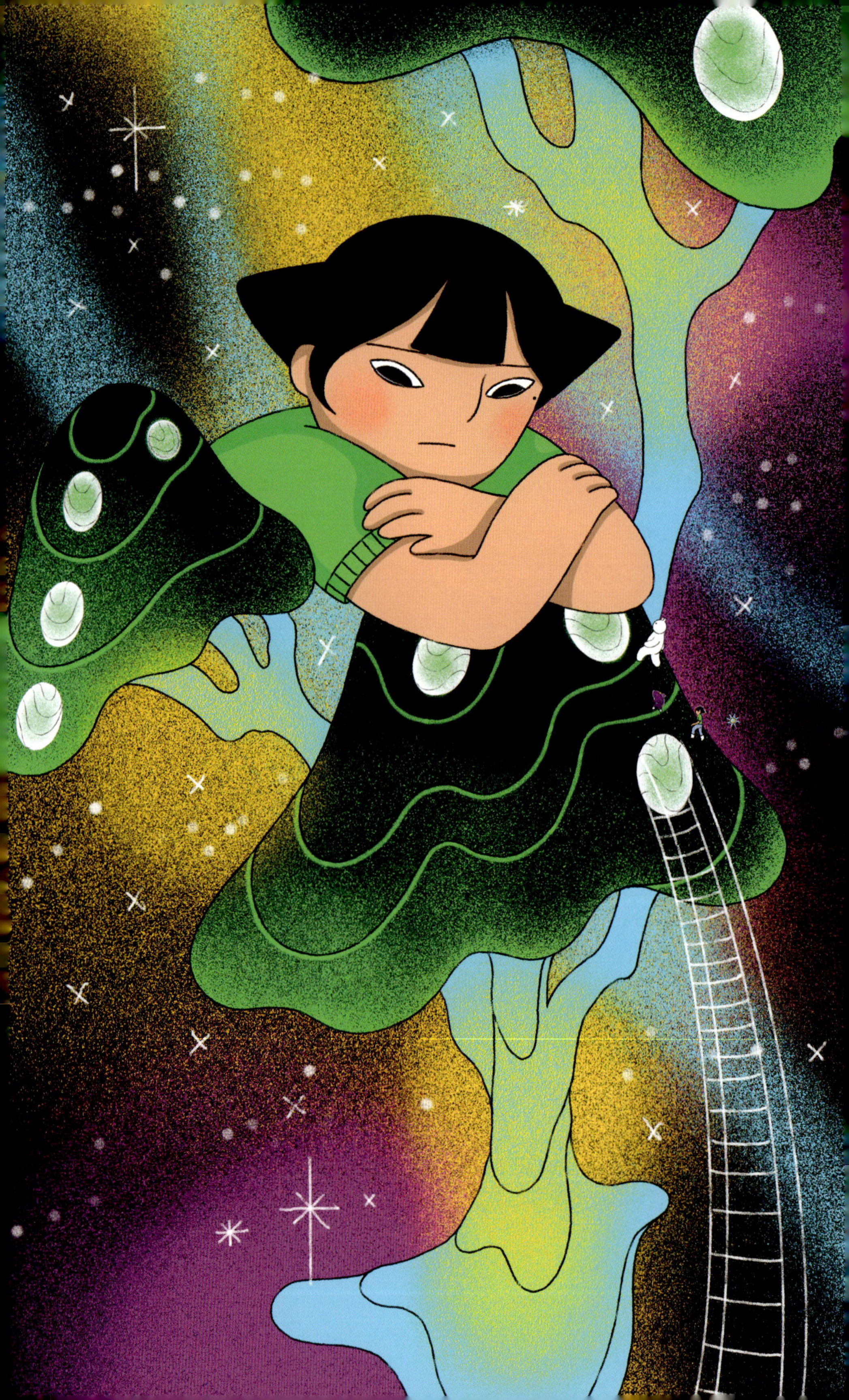

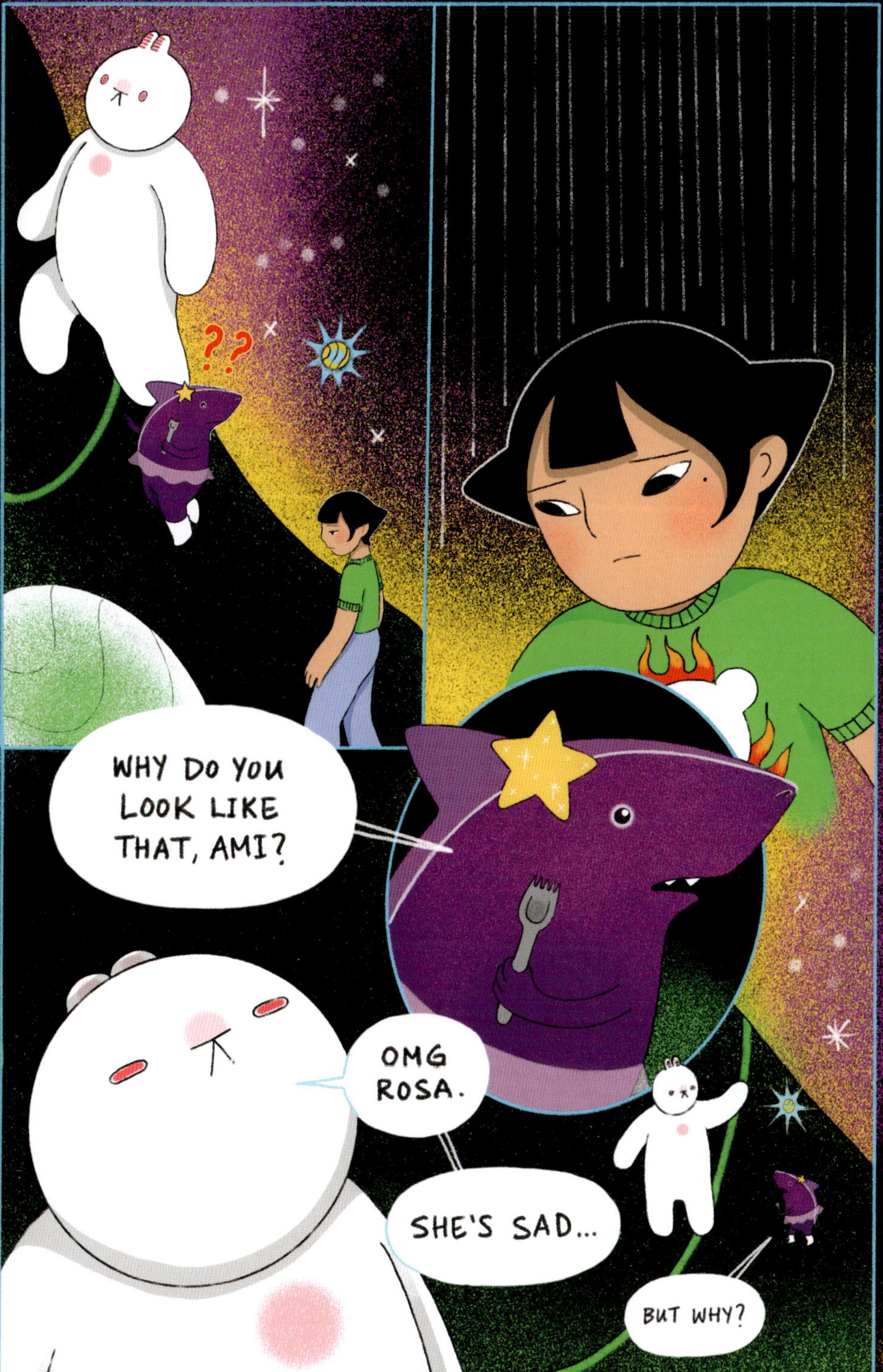
??
WHY DO YOU LOOK LIKE THAT, AMI?
OMG ROSA.
SHE'S SAD...
BUT WHY?

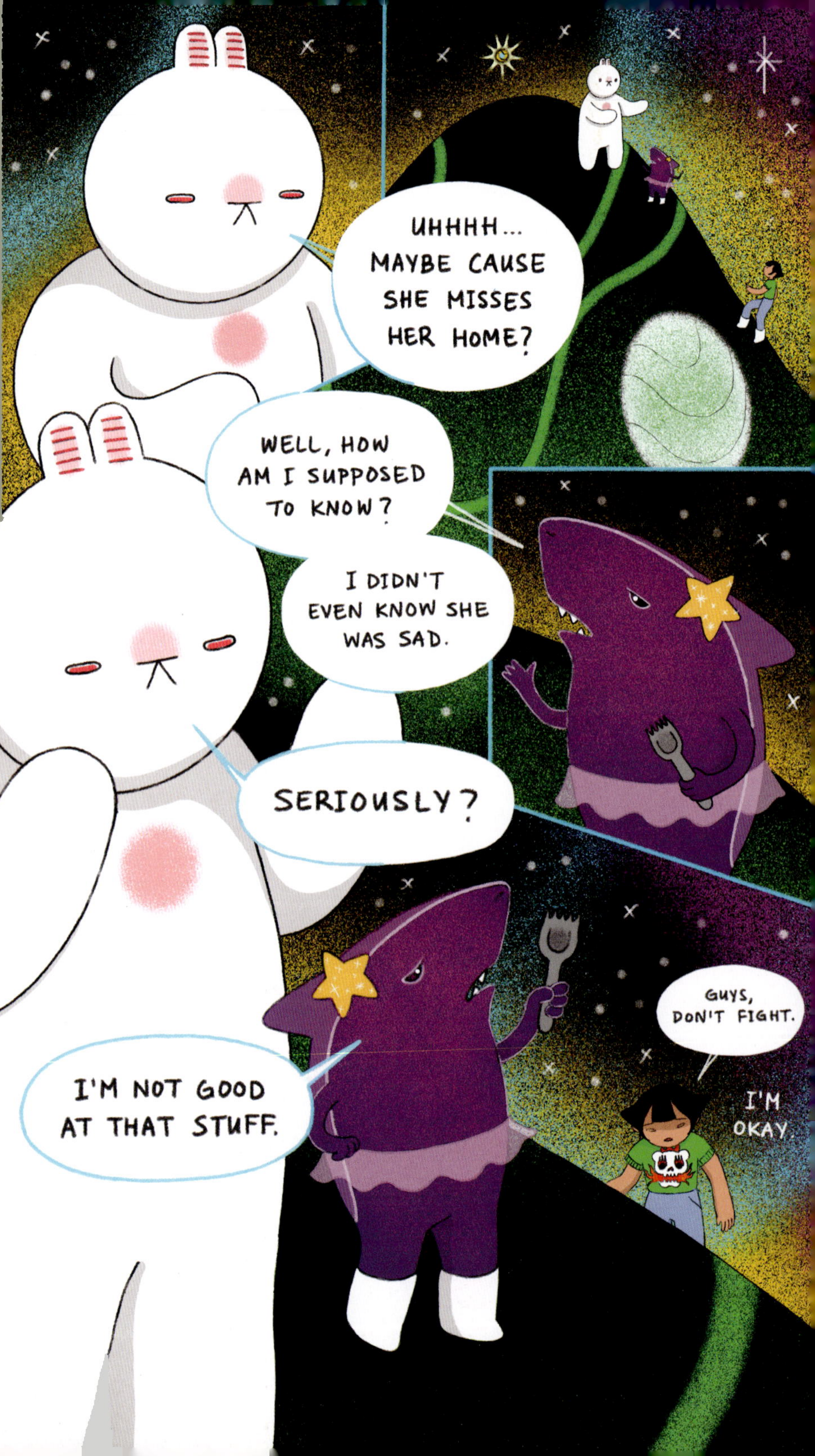
UHHHH... MAYBE CAUSE SHE MISSES HER HOME?
WELL, HOW AM I SUPPOSED TO KNOW?
I DIDN'T EVEN KNOW SHE WAS SAD.
SERIOUSLY?
I'M NOT GOOD AT THAT STUFF.
GUYS, DON'T FIGHT.
I'M OKAY.

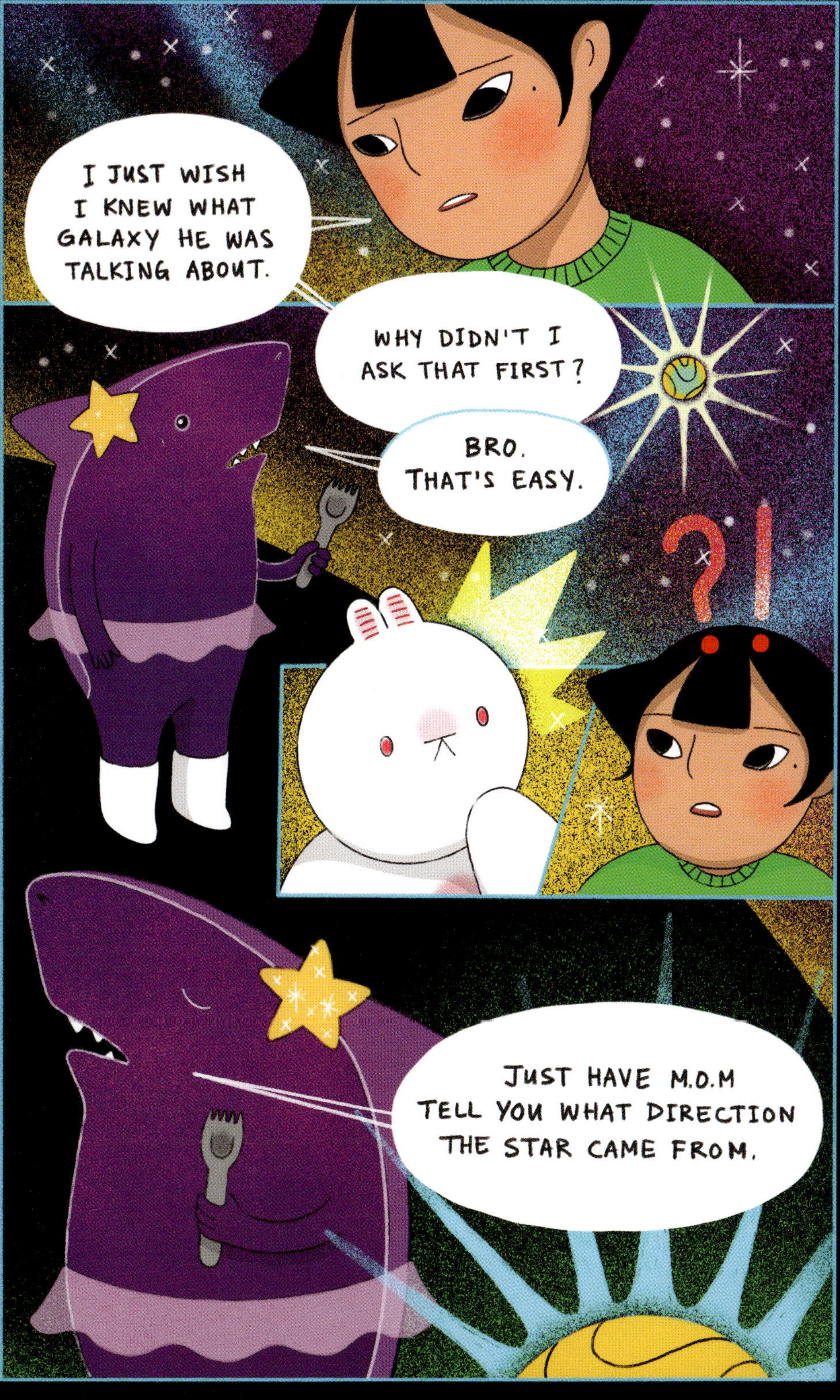
I JUST WISH I KNEW WHAT GALAXY HE WAS TALKING ABOUT.
WHY DIDN'T I ASK THAT FIRST?
BRO. THAT'S EASY.
?!
JUST HAVE M.O.M TELL YOU WHAT DIRECTION THE STAR CAME FROM.

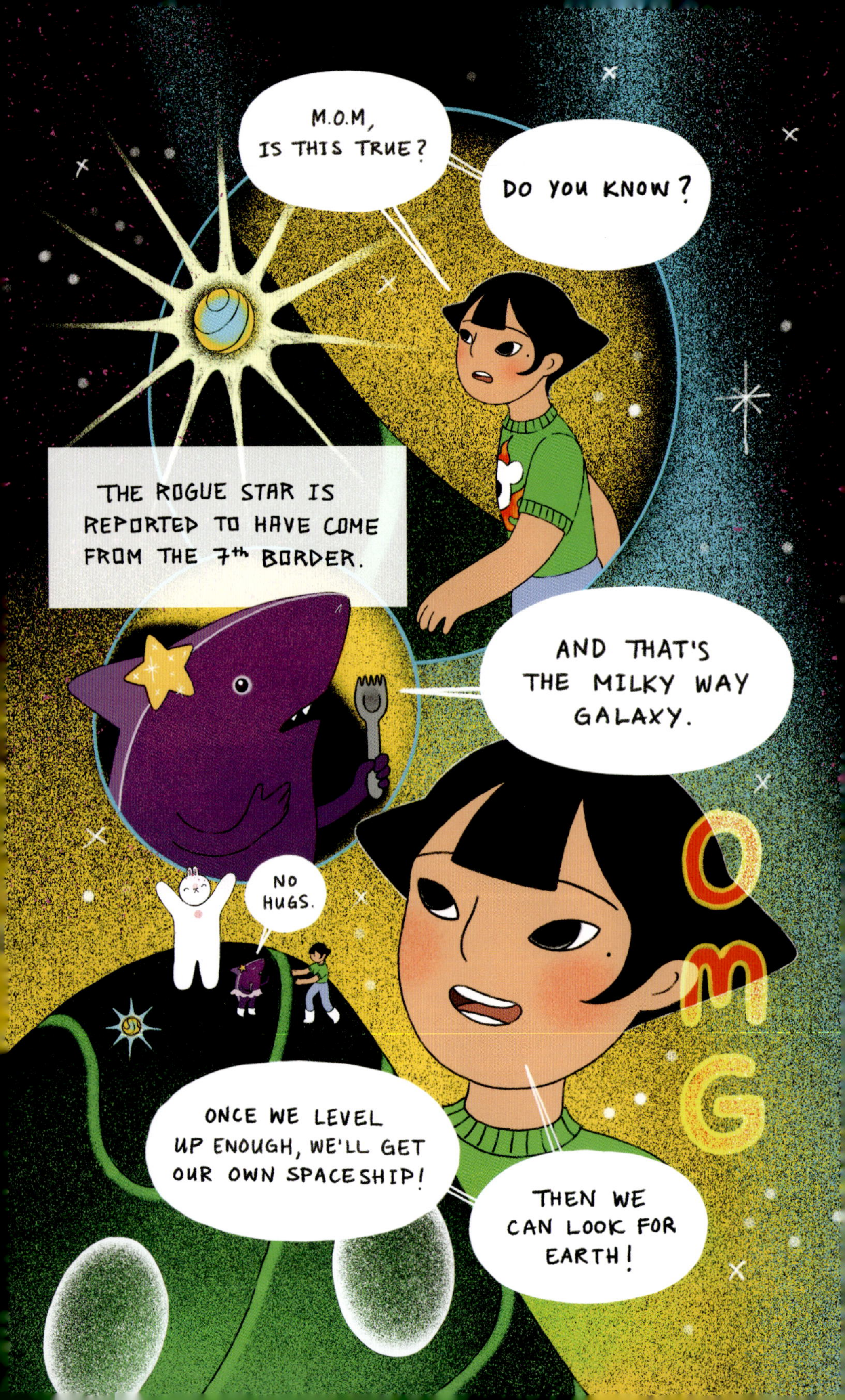
M.O.M,
IS THIS TRUE?
DO YOU KNOW?
THE ROGUE STAR IS REPORTED TO HAVE COME FROM THE 7th BORDER.
AND THAT'S THE MILKY WAY GALAXY.
OMG
NO HUGS.
ONCE WE LEVEL UP ENOUGH, WE'LL GET OUR OWN SPACESHIP!
THEN WE CAN LOOK FOR EARTH!

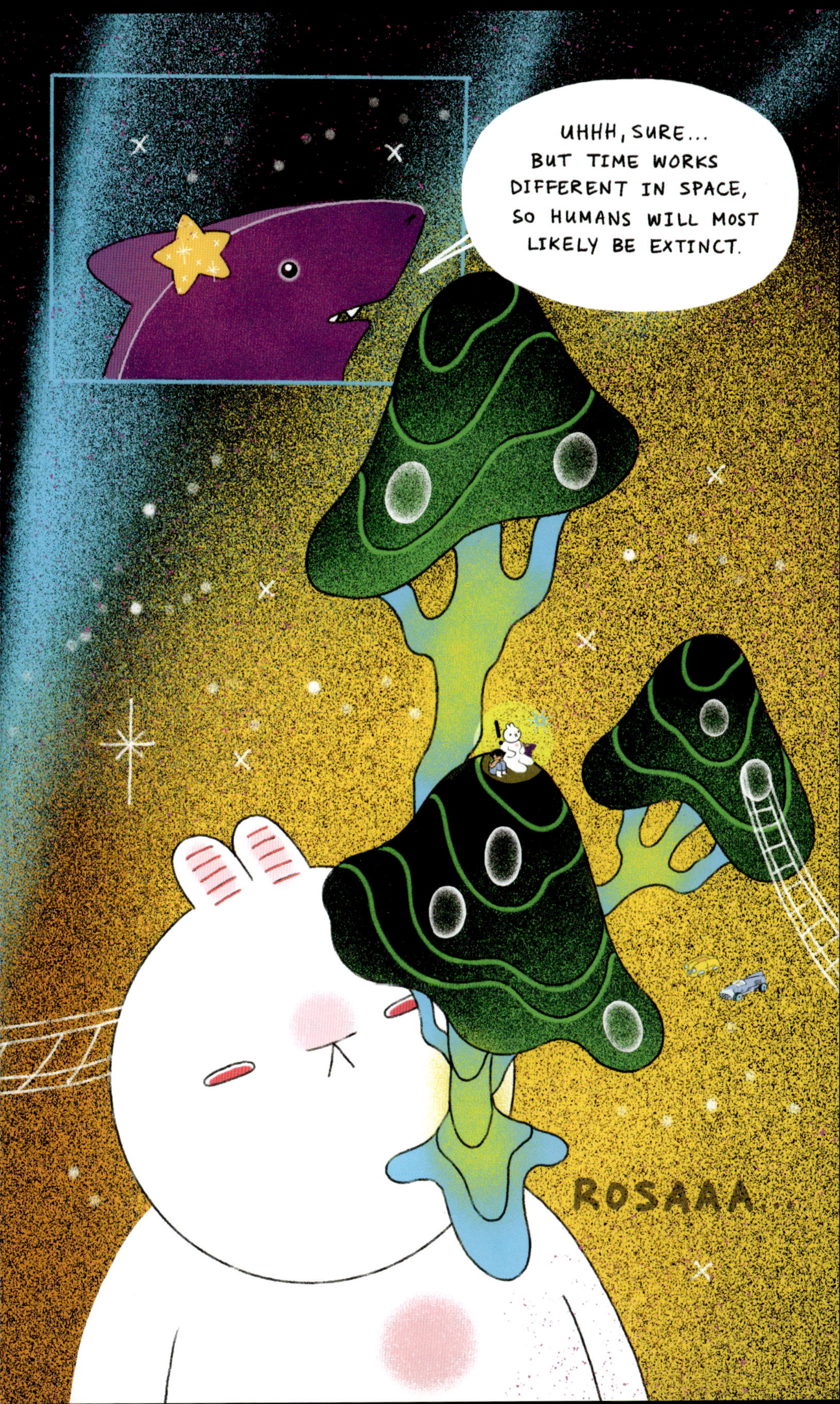
UHHH, SURE... BUT TIME WORKS DIFFERENT IN SPACE, SO HUMANS WILL MOST LIKELY BE EXTINCT.
ROSAAA...

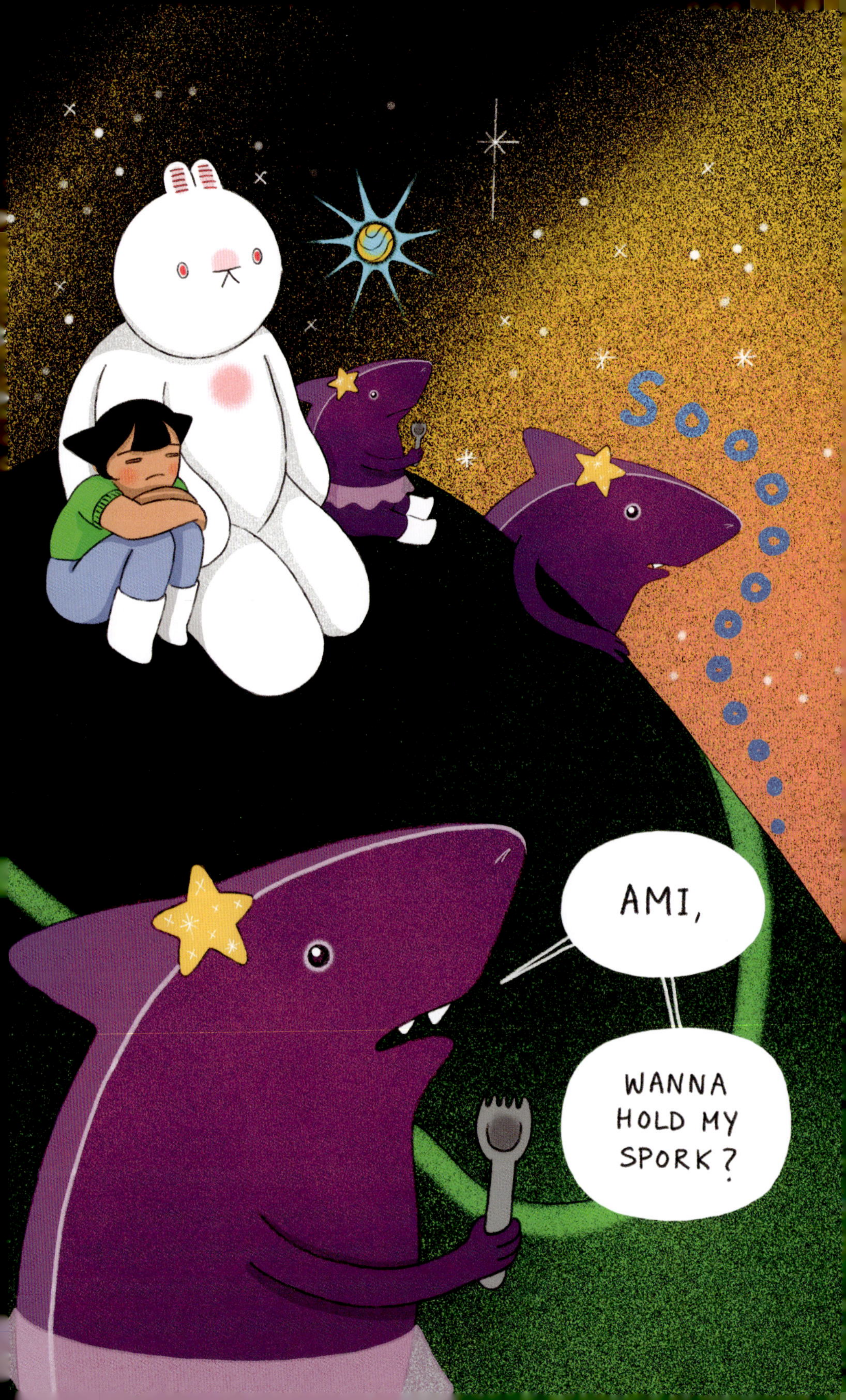
Soooooooo...
AMI,
WANNA HOLD MY SPORK?

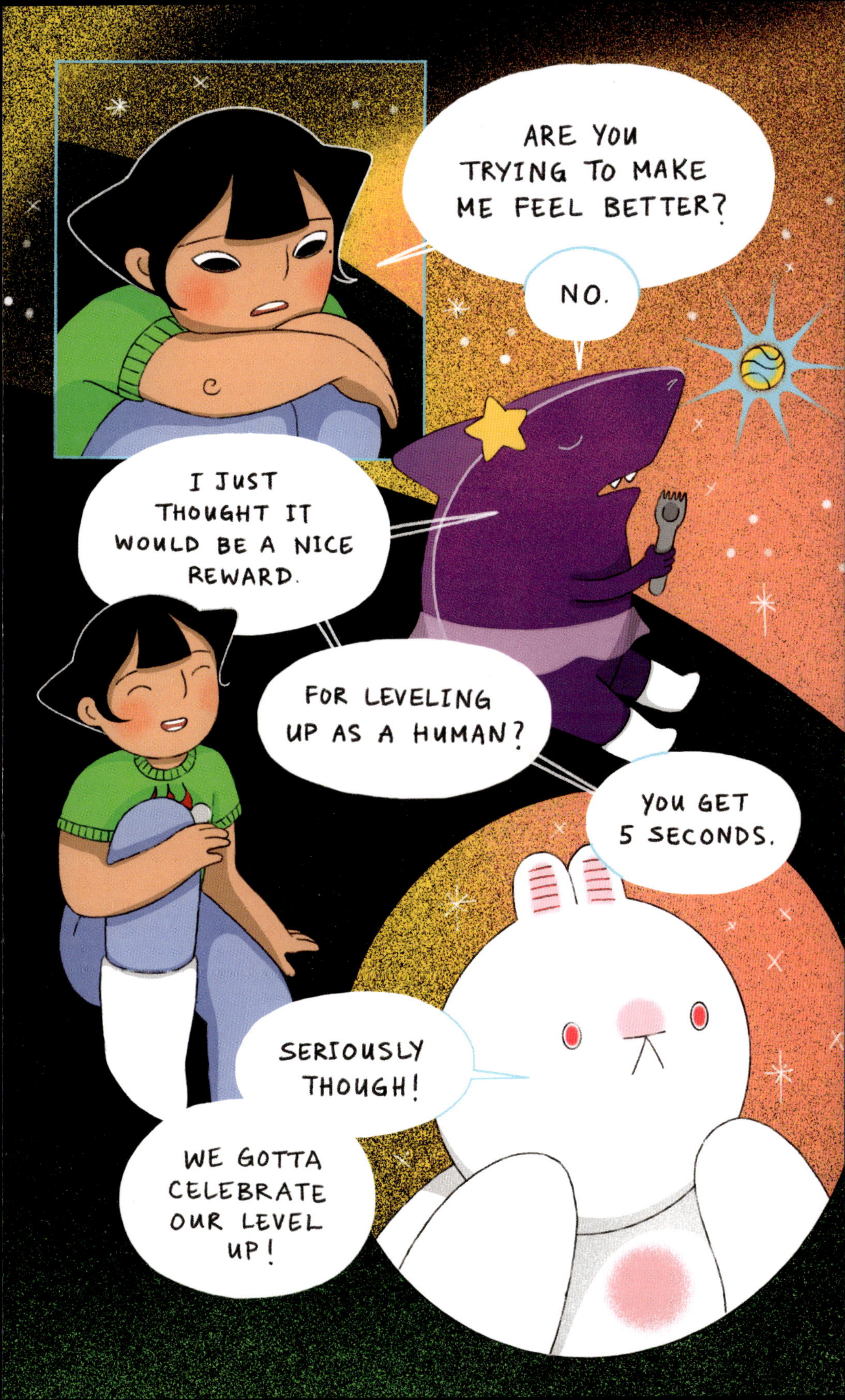
ARE YOU TRYING TO MAKE ME FEEL BETTER?
NO.
I JUST THOUGHT IT WOULD BE A NICE REWARD.
FOR LEVELING UP AS A HUMAN?
YOU GET 5 SECONDS.
SERIOUSLY THOUGH!
WE GOTTA CELEBRATE OUR LEVEL UP!

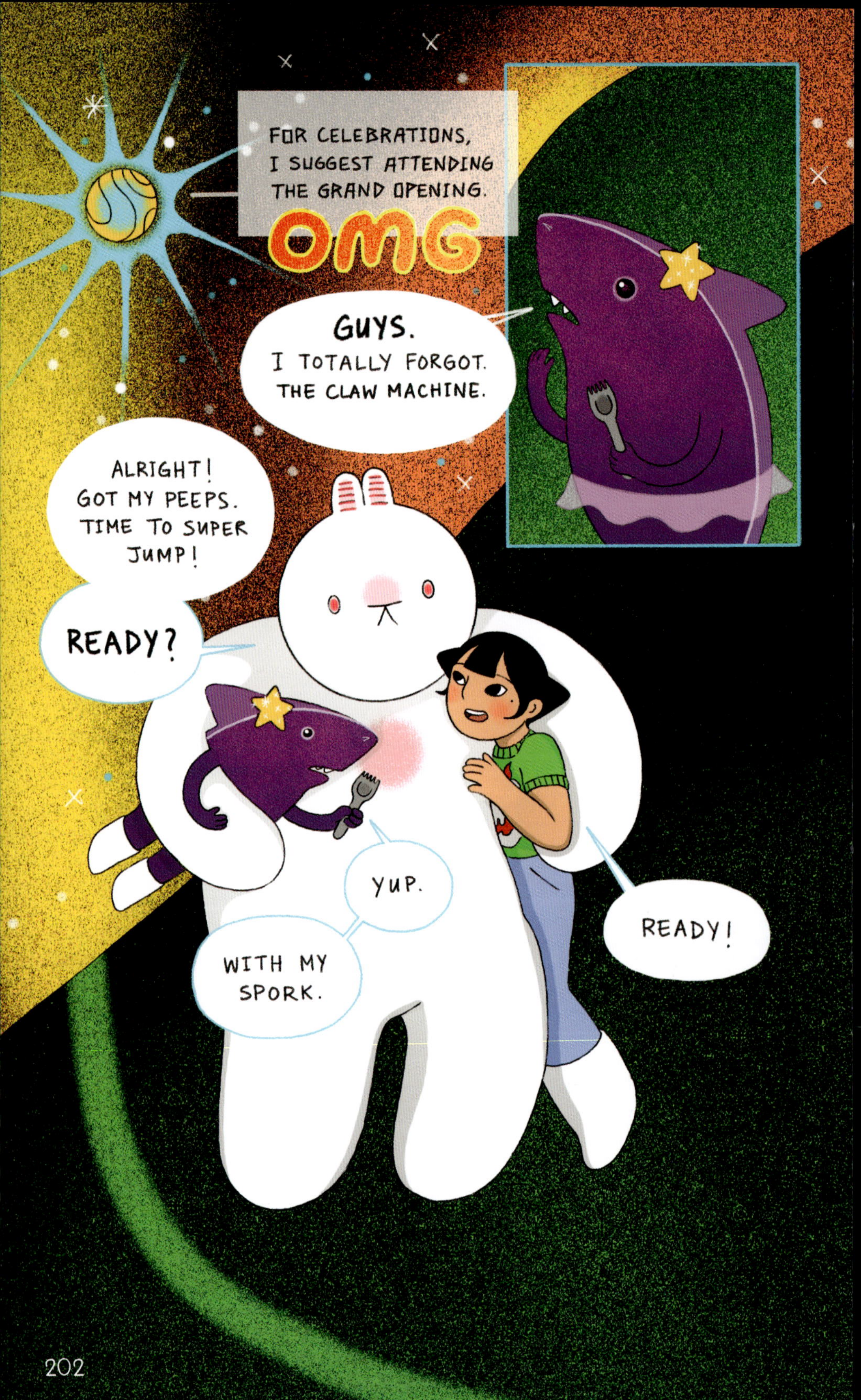
FOR CELEBRATIONS, I SUGGEST ATTENDING THE GRAND OPENING.
OMG
GUYS.
I TOTALLY FORGOT. THE CLAW MACHINE.
ALRIGHT! GOT MY PEEPS. TIME TO SUPER JUMP!
READY?
YUP.
WITH MY SPORK.
READY!

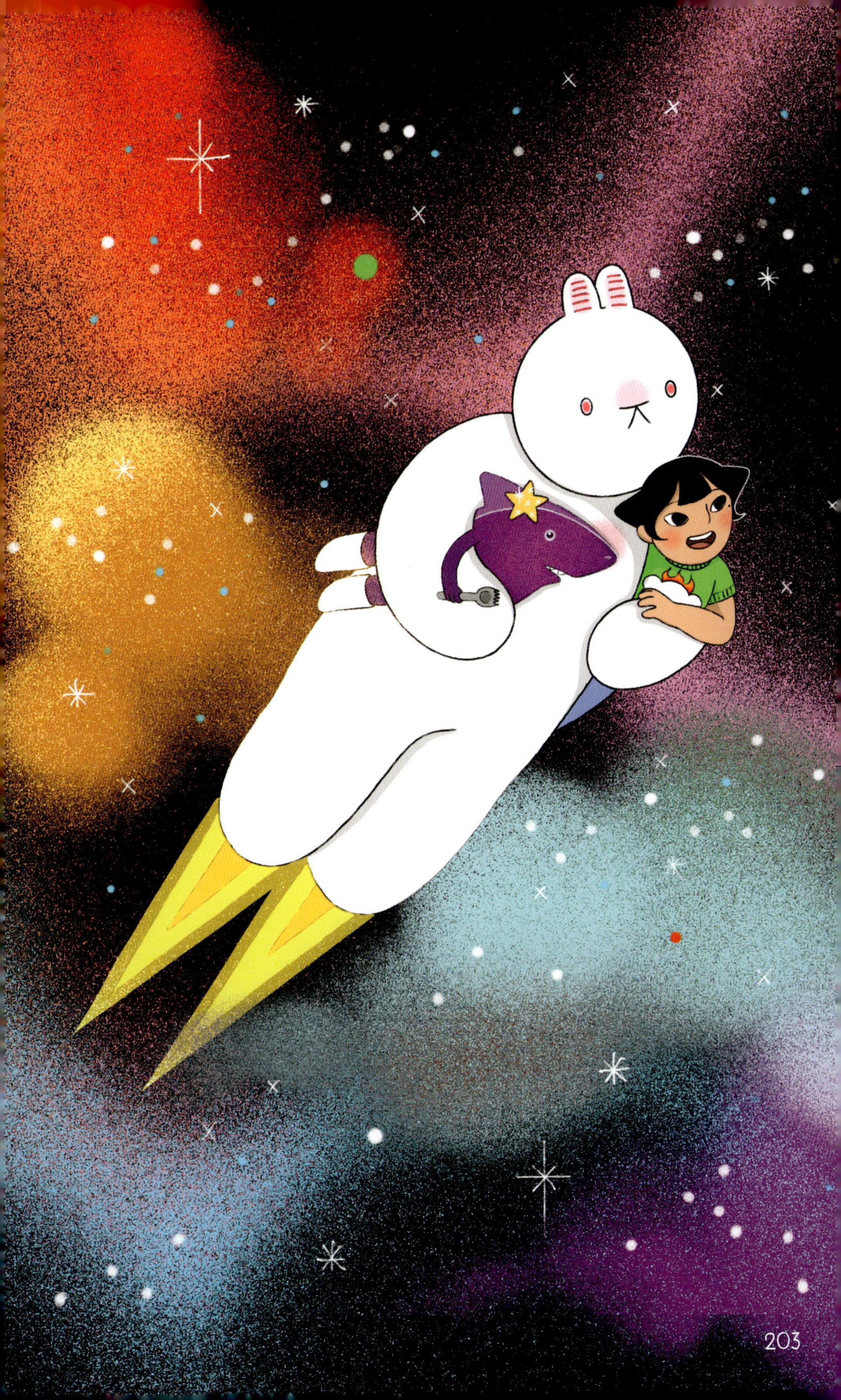

You know, after being away for so long... I realize I've never once thought about Earth as my home planet. But now that I'm not there, I think about it often.

I miss the way the sunset would paint the sky pastel, I miss the scream of cicadas on a hot summer day, the crunch of snow under my boots, and the smell of my mom's coffee in the mornings.

I miss my life on Earth...

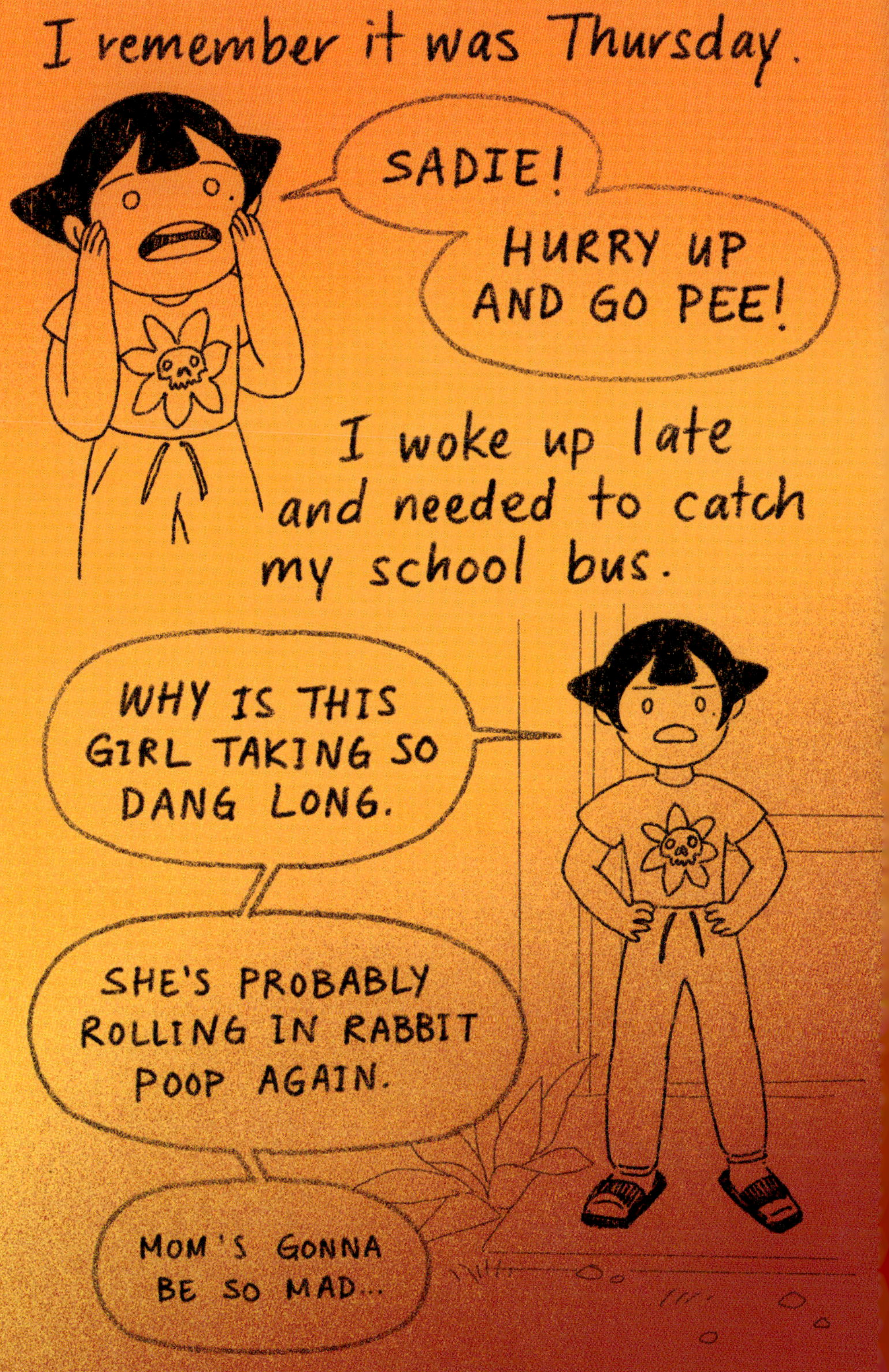

I remember it was Thursday.
SADIE!
HURRY UP AND GO PEE!
I woke up late and needed to catch my school bus.
WHY IS THIS GIRL TAKING SO DANG LONG.
SHE'S PROBABLY ROLLING IN RABBIT POOP AGAIN.
MOM'S GONNA BE SO MAD...

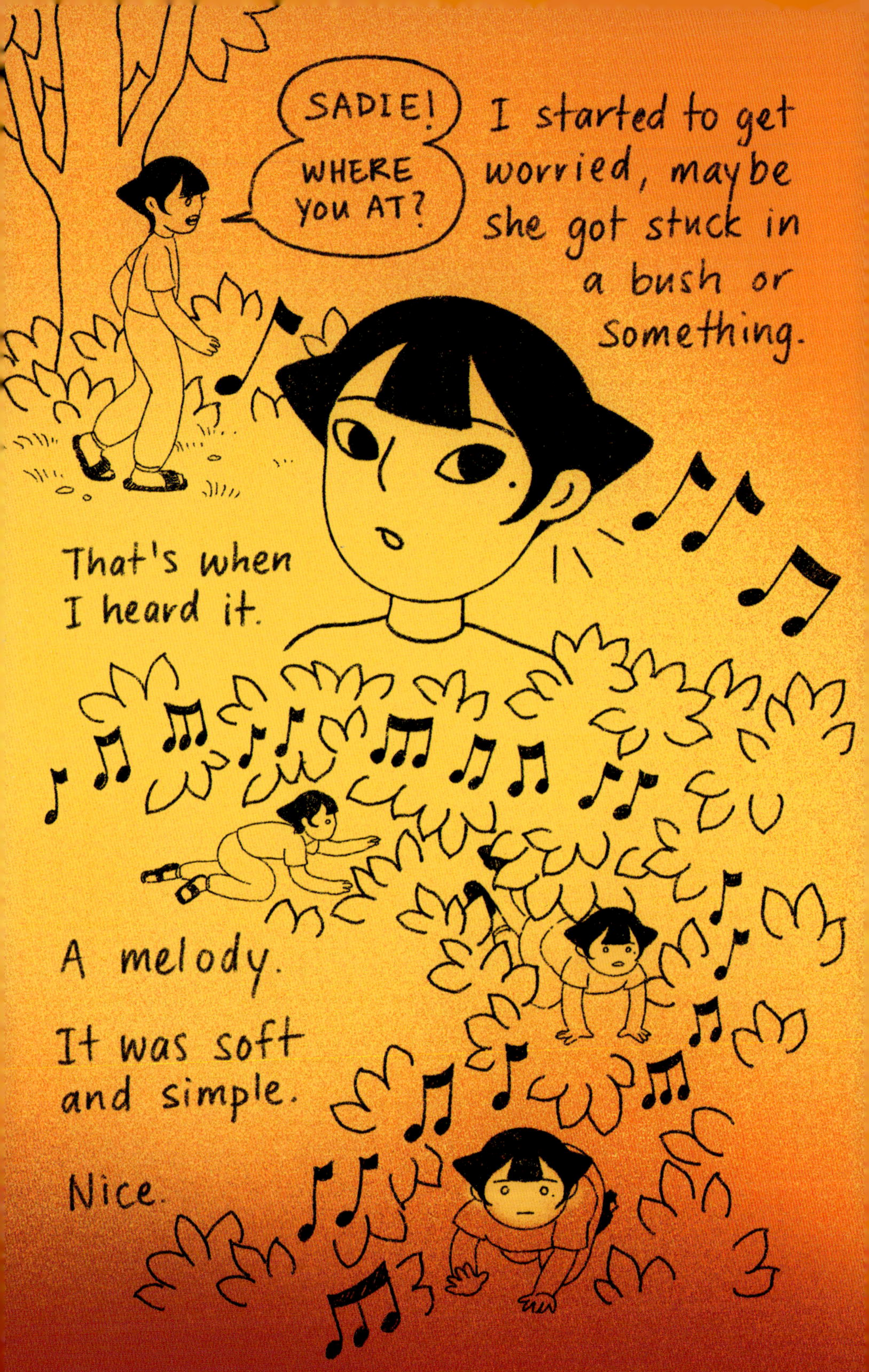
SADIE!
WHERE YOU AT?
I started to get worried, maybe she got stuck in a bush or something.
That's when I heard it.
A melody.
It was soft and simple.
Nice.

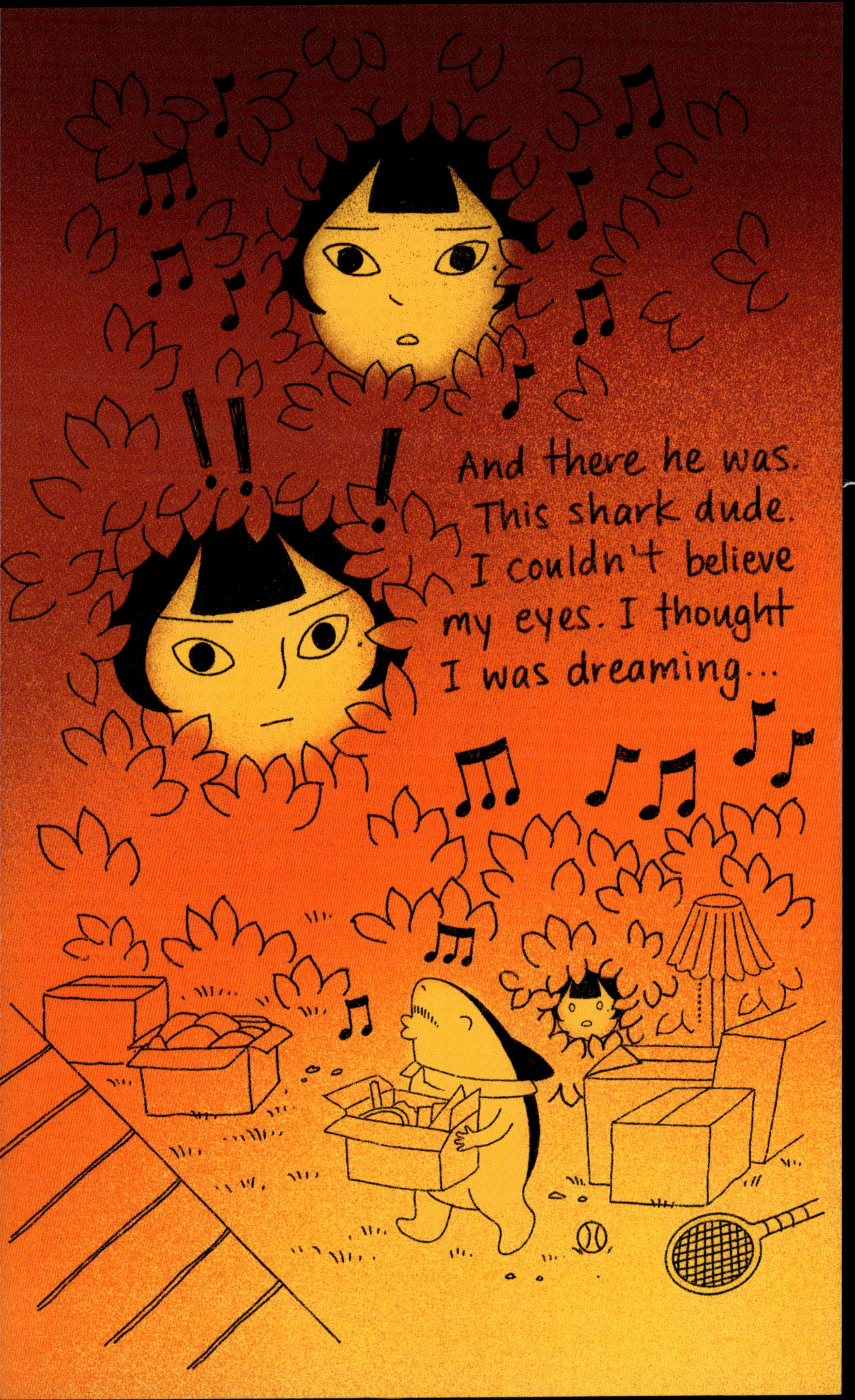
And there he was. This shark dude. I couldn't believe my eyes. I thought I was dreaming...

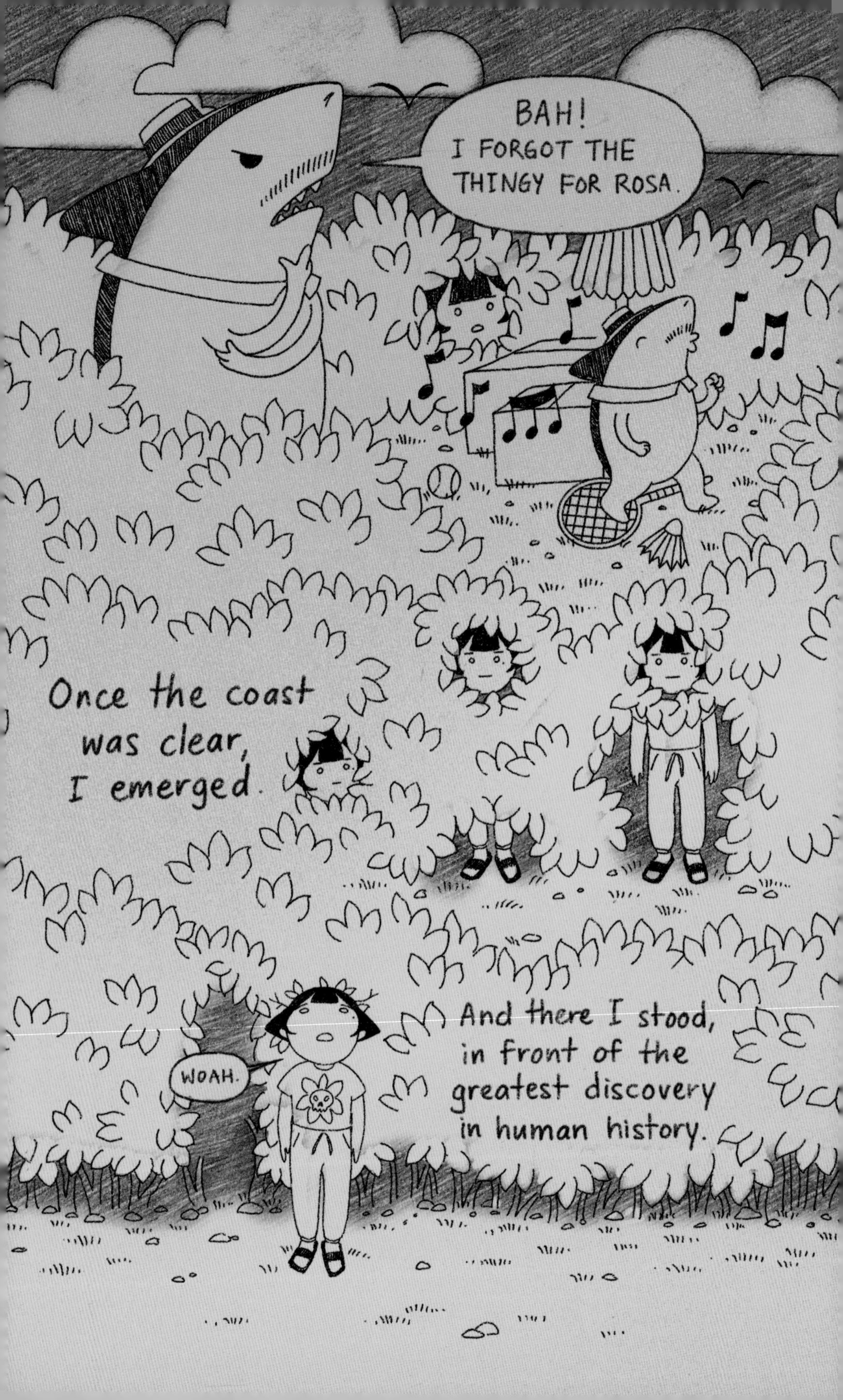
BAH! I FORGOT THE THINGY FOR ROSA.
Once the coast was clear, I emerged.
And there I stood, in front of the greatest discovery in human history.
WOAH.

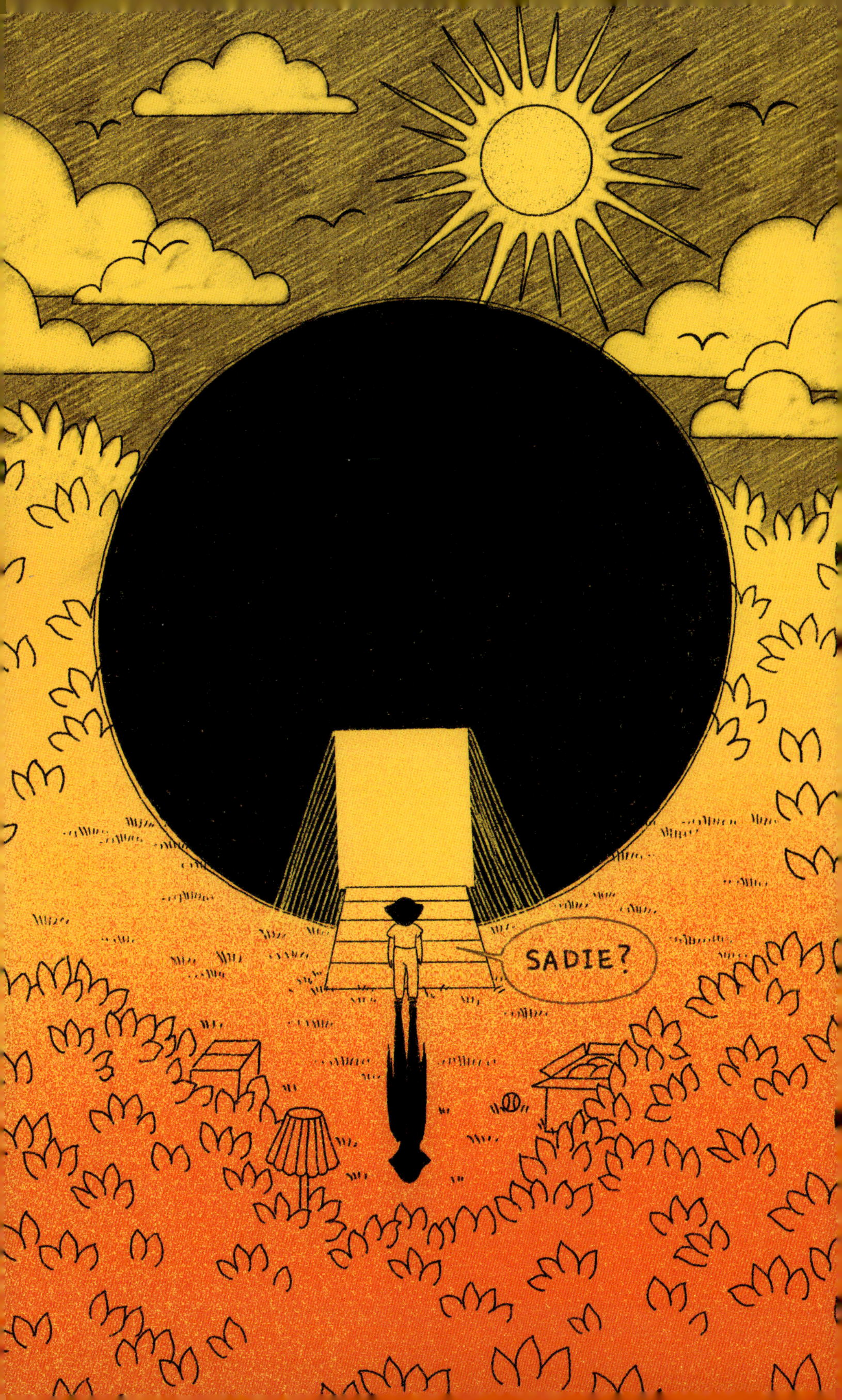
SADIE?

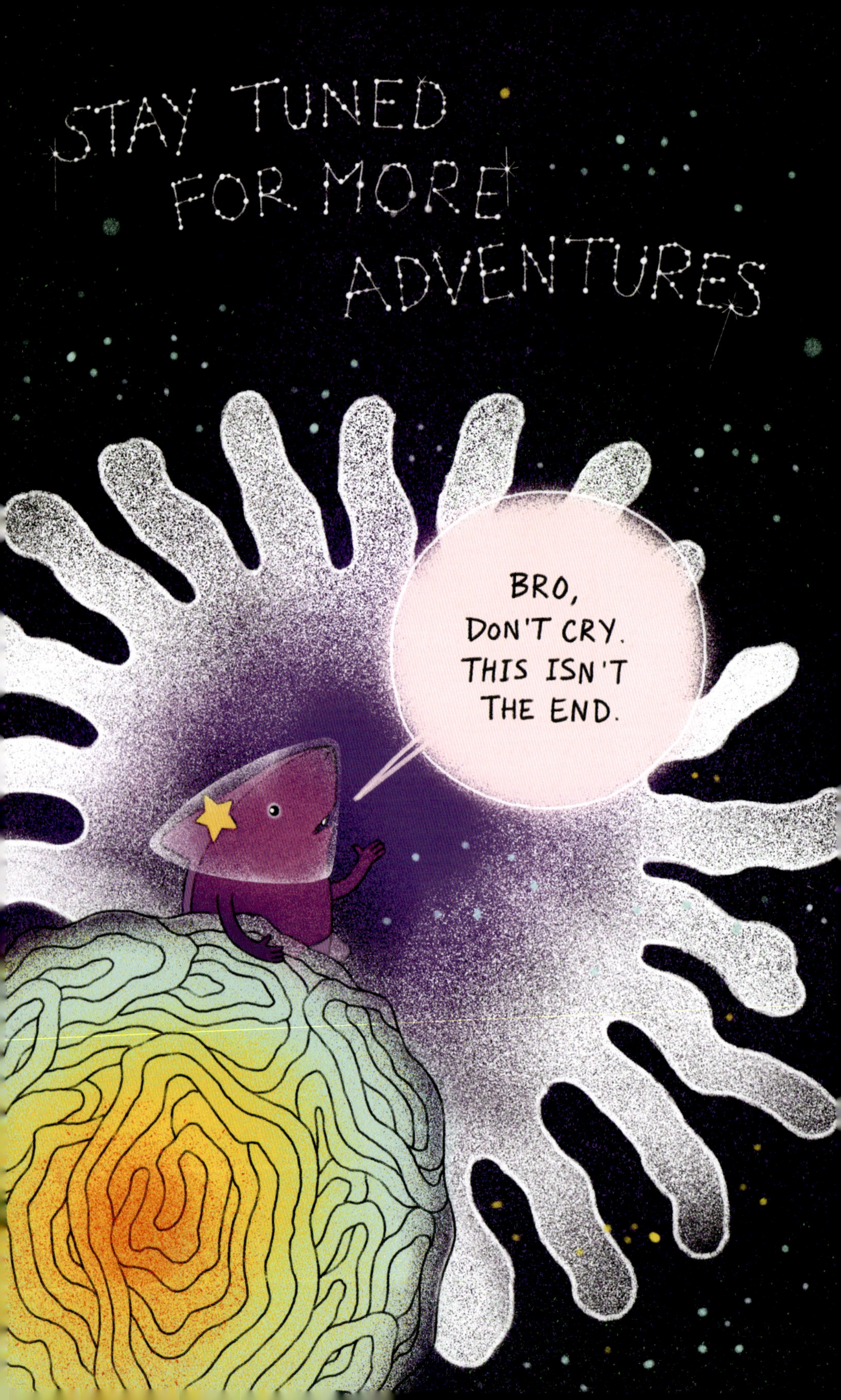
STAY TUNED
FOR MORE
ADVENTURES
BRO,
DON'T CRY.
THIS ISN'T
THE END.

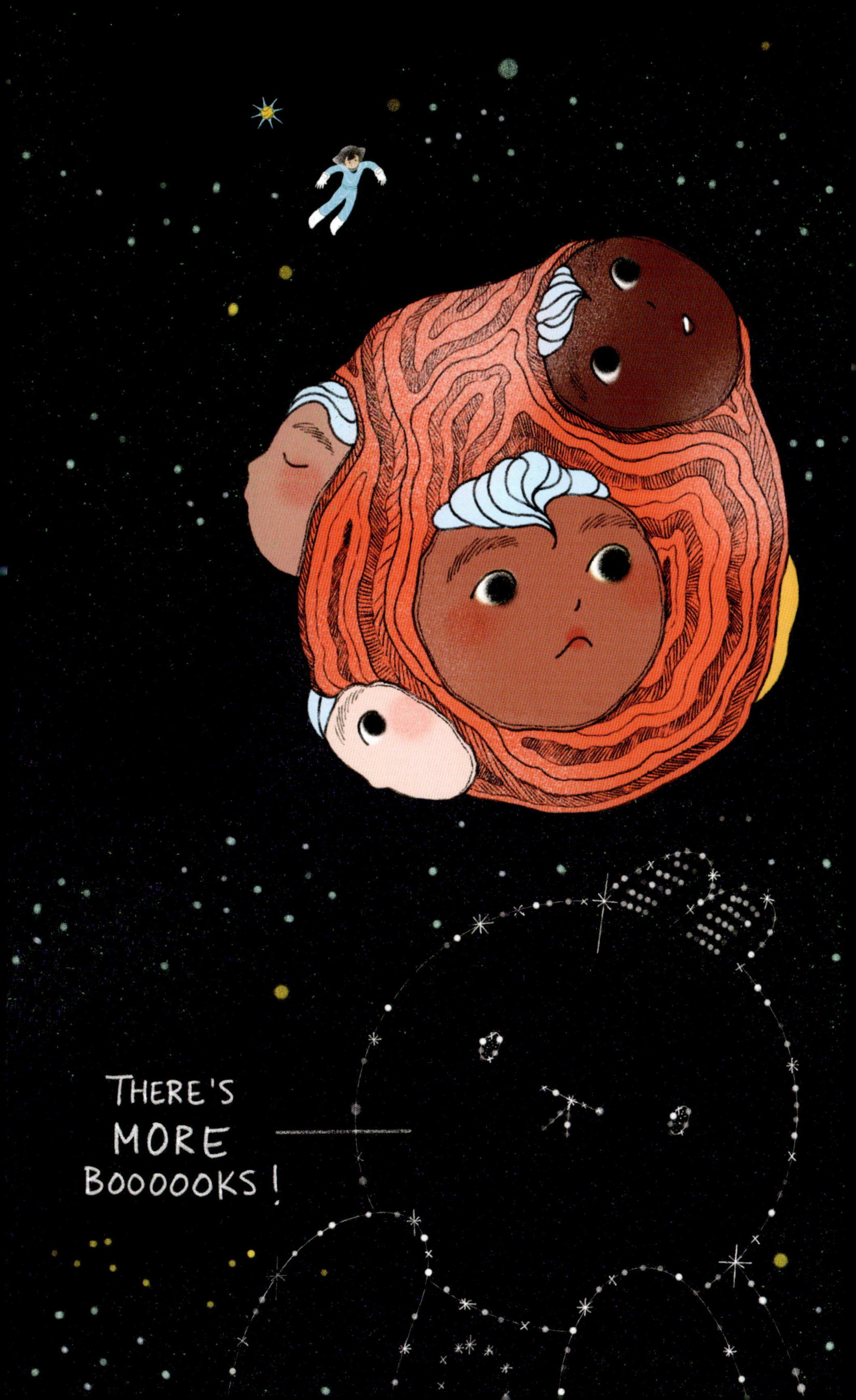
THERE'S MORE BOOOOOKS!

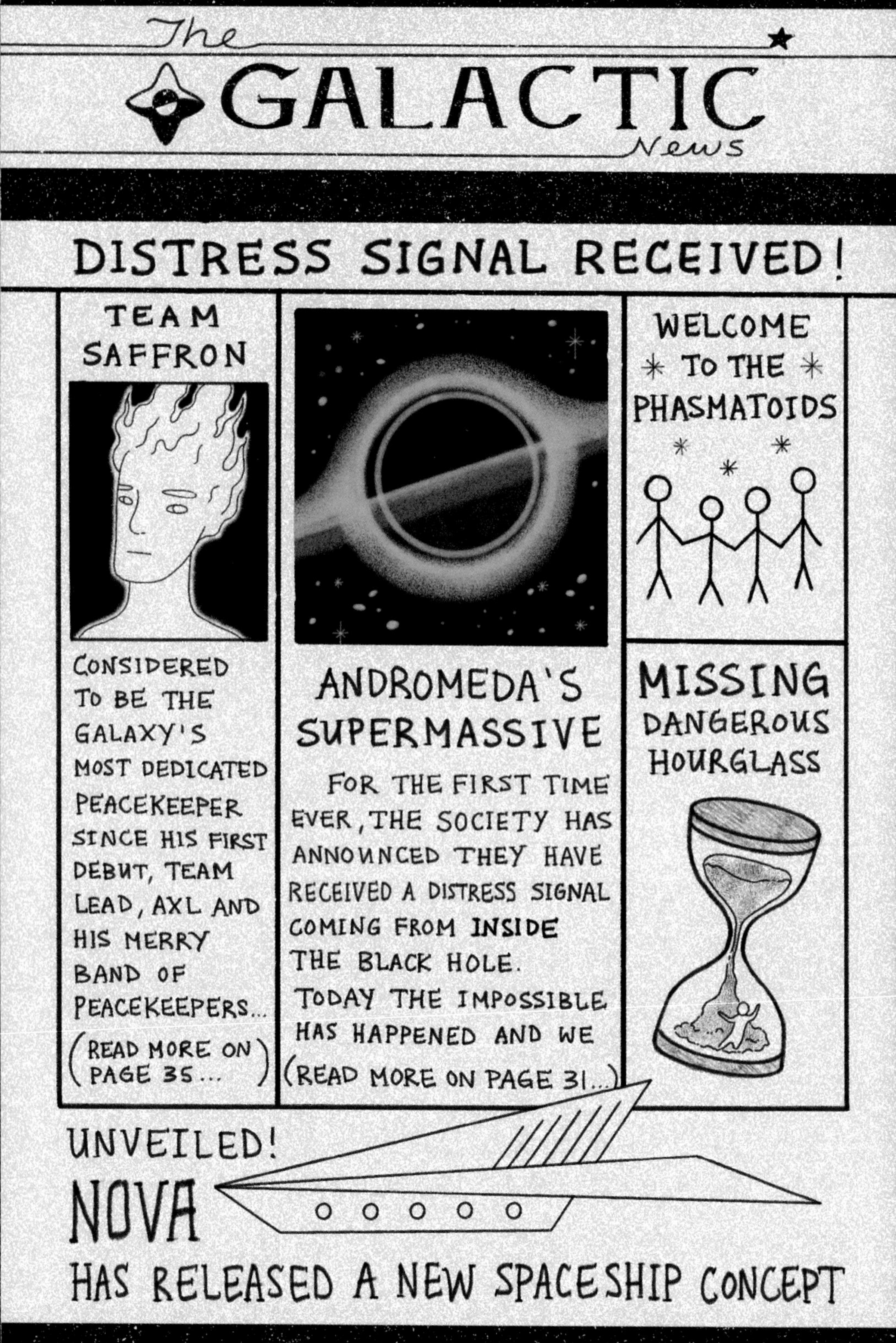
The GALACTIC News
DISTRESS SIGNAL RECEIVED!
TEAM SAFFRON
CONSIDERED TO BE THE GALAXY'S MOST DEDICATED PEACEKEEPER SINCE HIS FIRST DEBUT, TEAM LEAD, AXL AND HIS MERRY BAND OF PEACEKEEPERS...
(READ MORE ON PAGE 35...)
ANDROMEDA'S SUPERMASSIVE
FOR THE FIRST TIME EVER, THE SOCIETY HAS ANNOUNCED THEY HAVE RECEIVED A DISTRESS SIGNAL COMING FROM INSIDE THE BLACK HOLE. TODAY THE IMPOSSIBLE HAS HAPPENED AND WE
(READ MORE ON PAGE 31...)
WELCOME TO THE PHASMATOIDS
MISSING DANGEROUS HOURGLASS
UNVEILED!
NOVA
HAS RELEASED A NEW SPACESHIP CONCEPT